WEST PALM BEACH, FLORIDA 33406

The Tell-Tale Corpse

The Tell-Tale Corpse

An Edgar Allan Poe Mystery

HAROLD SCHECHTER

BALLANTINE BOOKS • NEW YORK

Copyright © 2006 by Harold Schechter

Published in the United States by Ballantine, an imprint of The Random House Publishing Group, a division of Random House, Inc., New York.

BALLANTINE and colophon are registered trademarks of Random House, Inc.

LIBRARY OF CONGRESS CATALOGING-IN-PUBLICATION DATA

Schechter, Harold.
The tell-tale corpse : an Edgar Allan Poe mystery / Harold Schechter.
p. cm.
ISBN 0-345-44842-1
1. Poe, Edgar Allan, 1809–1849—Fiction.   2. Boston (Mass.)—Fiction.
3. Authors—Fiction.   4. Elixirs—Fiction.   I. Title.

PS3569.C4776T45 2006
813'.54—dc22   2005053647

Printed in the United States of America on acid-free paper

www.ballantinebooks.com

2 4 6 8 9 7 5 3 1

First Edition

Book design by Susan Turner

For my daughters

LIZZIE *and* LAURA

PART ONE

~

Dark Days

Chapter One

I T HAS OFTEN been observed that the smallest, most trivial accident may, on occasion, produce momentous consequences. Who has not heard the story of the falling apple which—landing by chance upon the brow of the scientific genius reposing in the shade—led him to unlock the very secrets of the universe? However apocryphal this tale may be, it possesses a core (so to speak) of profound truth: namely, that matters of the utmost importance have, at times, been the direct result of the merest bits of happenstance.

These remarks may serve as a preface to the following adventures, which occurred in the latter months of 1845.

In New York City, on a gusty October evening, I was making my way through the bustling streets of the great metropolis, toward the rooms I shared with the two beings dearest to my soul. I refer, of course, to those angelic creatures I called by the fond soubriquets of "Sissy" and "Muddy"— i.e., my precious wife, Virginia, to whom I was bound by the double ties of cousin and spouse, and her mother, my darling Aunt Maria Clemm. I was returning from the office of my business partner, Mr. Charles Briggs, publisher of the *Broadway Journal,* a magazine which—thanks largely to my own editorial innovations—had enjoyed a steep rise in circulation in recent months.

The growing success of our enterprise was due in no small part to a highly popular series of articles I had been contributing to the past several issues. The title of this series was "The Secrets of Word-Mysteries." Each ar-

ticle was devoted to a different form of linguistic puzzle—acrostics, ana-
grams, ciphers, and codes of various kinds. After providing a concise history and explanation of each species of riddle, I would present an example
devised by myself and challenge the reader to solve it. Those who sent in the
correct answer would receive a free subscription to the *Broadway Journal*.
My cryptograms had proven so ingenious, however, that, to date, I had not
been obliged to hand out a single prize.

On the afternoon in question, I had applied myself to the composition
of the latest article in the series. The subject was the *rebus*. As always, I had
begun by explaining the origins of the term, tracing its etymology to the
Latin word for "things" and describing its relationship to such symbolical
forms of writing as Egyptian hieroglyphics and ancient Chinese pic-
tographs.

I had then defined the most commonly recognized modern meaning of
the term—i.e., a type of riddle which relies on the device of the visual or
linguistic *pun*. In its simplest form, I explained, the rebus employs graphic
representations of objects as a substitute for words or syllables. The word
"equal," for example, might be depicted in the following manner:

Because of the amusing ingenuity displayed in such a construction, this
elementary form of the rebus was highly popular among children, and it
was possible to find entire books of fairy legends and nursery rhymes composed in this charmingly pictorial form. There was also, however, a more
complex and sophisticated variety of rebus. This latter type depended not
on pictures but solely on letters and words, whose size, relative arrangement, and placement pointed to the answer to the puzzle. A comparatively
simple example would be:

MOMANON

Here, the word "man" appears inside the word "moon." Thus, the correct answer to this riddle is: "man in the moon."

After providing several more such examples, I had concluded my article
with a rebus of my own invention. It had required several minutes of inten-
sive concentration to contrive a suitably cryptic puzzle, but at length I had

constructed a riddle of such sheer—such *diabolical*—cleverness that it would, I felt certain, prove impossible for my readers to decipher.

By the time I had completed this article, the sun had set. Throwing on my coat, I had departed for home.

No sooner did I find myself out on the street, however, than a sense of insufferable gloom pervaded my spirit. For many months, I had been living under an almost unendurable emotional strain. Writing had been my only respite and nepenthe. Once freed of the distraction of work, however, my mind instantly reverted to the subject that filled my soul with despair.

As I strolled along Maiden Lane, my attention was suddenly drawn to the warm yellow light issuing from the window of a saloon called Hoffman's. I had passed by this establishment on many previous occasions as I wended my way home from work, though without ever having ventured inside. Contrary to the malicious rumors spread by my enemies, I had long maintained an unwavering abstemiousness in regard to the consumption of liquor. For many years—apart from those very rare occasions when the dictates of social etiquette required that I partake of small amounts of alcoholic drink—nothing stronger than coffee had passed my lips.

On this fateful autumn evening, however, the awful burden of worry I had been made to endure for so long became more than I could bear. My resolution wavered—my resistance collapsed—and, frantic for release, I succumbed to temptation. With a wild cry of abandonment, I plunged through the swinging doors of the saloon.

An hour later, I emerged once again onto the street, having imbibed several tumblers of brandy toddy. Far from improving my mood, however, the drink had only made me feel worse. In addition to my melancholia, I was now filled with an acute sense of shame, having managed to spend every coin in my purse—a meager enough sum, but far more than I could afford in view of my miserably straitened circumstances.

With a bowed head, I bent my steps (somewhat unsteadily) toward home. Though night had fallen, Broadway still teemed with people, and as I walked—or rather, staggered—along the sidewalk, I kept colliding with other pedestrians, a number of whom responded in the most uncivil way: with cries of "Watch where you go, you fool!"—"Filthy sot!"—and other, even more offensive comments.

Though I bristled at these insults, I could not pretend, even to myself, that they were unjustified. To be sure, I had not consumed an inordinate number of drinks. There could be no doubt, however, that—owing to my acute susceptibility to even small quantities of alcohol—I was thoroughly inebriated. Before long, I had completely lost track of precisely where I was. Pausing beneath a streetlamp, I lifted my head to get my bearings.

At that very instant, something crashed into me with such force that I was thrown onto the pavement. It was a relatively minor mishap of the sort that frequently occurs on the crowded thoroughfare. How could I know that it marked the beginning of an adventure replete with events of the most startling and unprecedented character?

Sprawled on my back, I had the peculiar sensation that I was lying prostrate on the deck of a storm-tossed frigate. At length I opened my eyes. The world was spinning madly. By slow degrees my dizziness subsided, and I became aware that someone was bending over me—a figure who appeared to be garbed in a hooded monk's habit. His visage being obscured by the shadows of his cowl, I could not, at first, discern his features. When I did, a gasp escaped my lips.

My initial thought was that the liquor had so wrought upon my senses as to derange my vision. How else explain the fellow's three eyes, two noses, and weirdly bifurcated mouth?

The answer came when he addressed me in a strange, gurgling manner, as though he were attempting to communicate while simultaneously retaining a mouthful of liquid: "Mr. Poe! That really you?"

"Otis?" I said, struggling to raise myself to an upright posture.

"Here. Let me help you," said the other. Reaching down, he clutched me by one arm and hauled me to my feet.

"Sorry for knocking you down," he continued. "Didn't see you. It's this damned hood."

"Perfectly all right," I said, my words sounding strangely slurred to my ears. "No need to apologize."

As I stood there on wobbly legs, I saw that we were standing before the garishly adorned façade of an all-too-familiar edifice: P. T. Barnum's world-renowned American Museum.

"You okay, Mr. Poe?" asked the hooded fellow.

Assuring him that I was fine, I bid him good-night and began to walk away. I had taken only a step, however, when my knees buckled. Had Otis not reached out instantly and caught me in his arms, I would have gone tumbling back onto the pavement.

"Oh, Otis," I cried. "What I said is untrue. I am not fine at all. On the contrary, I am in a most pitiable state."

"Then come with me," the other said gently. "Mr. Barnum will know what to do."

That my friend P. T. Barnum had few, if any, qualms about committing the most audacious frauds was a fact known to all the world. Indeed, he took positive pride in his reputation as the "Prince of Humbugs," filling his wildly popular showplace on the corner of Broadway and Ann Street with countless articles of highly dubious authenticity, from the beaded head-band allegedly worn by Pocahontas when she rescued Captain John Smith from her father's war club to the silver dagger purportedly used by Brutus when he delivered the *coup de grace* to Julius Caesar on the floor of the Roman Senate.

Still—in spite of the evident joy he took in playing the public for "suckers"—the showman was by no means a complete charlatan. A great many of his exhibits were bona fide wonders, among them his unparalleled assemblage of human curiosities—"freaks," in the common parlance.

The grotesquely disfigured being in whose company I now found myself—Mr. Otis Throgmorton, the Astonishing Split-Faced Man—was a spectacular case in point. There was nothing of the fraudulent about his bizarre congenital defect. This malformation—so inconceivably frightful that grown visitors to Barnum's museum, men as well as women, had been known to swoon at the sight of it—bore a physical kinship to a common harelip, albeit only in the sense that the Grand Canyon of the Far West re-sembles an ordinary riverbed. Beginning at the tip of his chin and extend-ing upward nearly to his hairline, a ghastly fissure bisected his countenance, dividing his mouth completely in half—separating his nose into two seem-ingly individual organs—and leaving his left eye at a level more than two inches above the right. His appearance was that of a man who had been struck squarely in the face with a woodchopper's axe or butcher's cleaver and whose sundered visage had subsequently fused itself together in the most shocking manner imaginable.

In addition, there existed in the very middle of his brow a small fleshy protrusion shaped uncannily like a third Cyclopean eye. Altogether, this singular being possessed a physiognomy that was difficult to view without feeling overcome by a sensation in which awe, terror, and revulsion were equally commingled.

Owing to the intense emotions he induced in observers, Otis—like most of his fellow freaks—rarely ventured out in public. The museum was not merely his place of employment but his home, Barnum having supplied his company of human curiosities with a spacious and comfortably appointed dormitory on the third floor of his establishment, where his Hall of Oddities was located. Even so, there were times when these physically anomalous performers felt the need to leave the shelter of the museum, whether to run an errand or merely to enjoy an invigorating stroll in the open air (if the noisome atmosphere of the metropolis can be described in such terms).

Now, having allowed Otis to lead me into the museum entrance, I followed him across the marble-floored lobby. Owing to the lateness of the hour, few visitors were to be seen. Making our way around a large wooden platform that supported an enormous scale-model tableau depicting the destruction of ancient Pompeii, we proceeded to a stairwell situated at the far end of the lobby, then descended to the basement where Barnum's office was located.

With Otis in the lead, we made our way along a narrow, labyrinthine corridor until, turning a corner, we came in sight of Barnum's office. The light from the open doorway cast a warm yellow glow in the gloom of the hallway, and I could clearly discern the showman's inimitable voice issuing from within as he addressed an unknown interlocutor.

"Got to hand it to Moses," he remarked with an appreciative chuckle. "The old scoundrel knows a good thing when he sees it. Imagine—getting his mitts on every last possession belonging to that young brute. The whole kit and caboodle, down to the fellow's skivvies! Of course, he'll keep the really prime stuff for himself—the bloody dress, the scalpel, and so forth. Well, who can blame him? Can't fault a man for putting his own interests first, eh, Fordyce? I'd do the very same in his position. Still, there's plenty to go around, especially if I make it worth the old rascal's while. Oh, it'll be a sensation, I tell you—one of the greatest things in the world! We'll have to keep the place open till midnight just to accommodate the crowds! It's a pity the poor woman's skin never turned up. Now, that—*that* would be something! Why, just a square inch or two would be worth—Good heavens, is that you, Otis? And who is that with you? Lord bless me, can that be you, Poe m'boy?"

We had by then arrived at the office and stood framed in the doorway. "It's us, all right," said my companion, drawing back his hood to reveal his remarkable countenance, while I stood mutely at his side.

"Well, come in, come in, no need to stand on ceremony," cried the showman as he rose from behind his desk, accompanying this invitation with an emphatic wave of the hand.

Stepping to one side, Otis allowed me to precede him into the room. As

I crossed the threshold, I saw that the person to whom the showman had been speaking was his old friend and trusted aide, "Parson" Fordyce Hitchcock, an exceedingly gaunt, bewhiskered fellow who—before entering Barnum's employ—had reputedly served for many years as a Universalist minister. He was standing beside the desk and turned to peer at us with a look of grave concern as the showman hurried across the room in our direction.

"My word, Poe, but you *do* look the worse for wear! Come, m'boy," he said, leading me to the claw-footed Chippendale divan that stood against the far wall of the office. "Rest yourself over here."

With a grateful moan, I lowered myself onto the embroidered cushion, while Barnum seated himself beside me.

"What the Dickens happened?" he said.

Briefly, Otis explained how—having waited for nightfall (when he was less likely to draw the notice of passersby)—he had gone out for a short walk and was hurrying back to the museum when he and I collided.

"And you, m'boy?" said Barnum, turning a critical gaze upon me. "Where the devil have *you* been?"

"A den of more than iniquity called Hoffman's," I said in a tremulous voice.

"I see," Barnum said grimly.

At this moment, Otis—after apologizing once more for having accidentally thrown me to the sidewalk—bid us good-night and took his leave. No sooner had he departed than Barnum glanced up at his associate and said:

"I've a favor to ask, Fordyce. Nothing difficult, just a little errand. As you can see, our friend Poe here is a tad, ah, under the weather. Needs a bit of bracing up before returning to the bosom of his family. A few strong cups of black coffee should do the trick. Be a good fellow, will you, and fetch a pot from Sweeney's. Have him charge it to my account."

Situated on Ann Street a short distance from the museum, Sweeney's was a popular neighborhood eatery and—as I knew from having dined there on one or two occasions with the showman—one of his favorite resorts.

"Happy to oblige," said the somewhat cadaverous-looking fellow. He then donned his tall beaver hat, threw on his cloak, picked up his walking stick, and strode from the office, shutting the door behind him.

No sooner had Hitchcock taken his leave than Barnum—his broad, somewhat coarse-featured visage wrought into an intensely sorrowful expression—addressed me thusly:

"No need to tell you, m'boy, just how sad—how profoundly *grieved*—I am to hear that you've been tippling again. Why, it defies comprehension! A genius like you! One the most stupendous minds of this or any other era! And here you are putting poison in your mouth to destroy that titanic brain of yours! Why, you might as well stick a gun to your head and have done with it all at once!"

"Do not imagine," I said miserably, "that the thought of self-destruction has not crossed my mind."

"But why, Poe, *why*? If you care nothing about your own well-being, then at least think of your loved ones—that wonderful aunt of yours, and your beautiful wife!"

"I think of little else," I said. "Indeed, it is the intense—the *unremitting*—contemplation of the awful fatality which has overtaken my darling Virginia that has driven me to this desperate state."

"Why, whatever do you mean?" Barnum said.

"She is dreadfully, perhaps hopelessly, ill!" I cried. "The woman whom I love as no man has ever loved before! And there is little, if anything, that can be done to save her!"

CHAPTER TWO

“G OOD LORD!” SAID Barnum, looking more stricken than I had ever before seen him. “I had no idea! But are you absolutely certain that her condition is as hopeless as you believe?”

“There can be no doubt,” I said. “Four years ago, the angelic creature ruptured a blood-vessel while singing. Her life was despaired of. I took leave of her forever and underwent all the agonies of anticipating her imminent demise. By God’s grace, she recovered partially, and I had reason to hope that all would be well. At the end of a year, however, the vessel broke again. I went through precisely the same torments. Again about a year afterward. Then again—and again—and even once again, at varying intervals. Each time I felt all the horrors of her death—and at each accession of the disorder I loved her more dearly and clung to her life with more desperate pertinacity.”

Here, my voice began to tremble so violently that I was forced to pause in my recitation. At length, having regained a measure of self-possession, I continued thusly:

“Two months ago—after a prolonged period during which the dread disease appeared to have loosened its grip upon her system and I allowed myself to believe that she might yet survive—my darling suffered another hemorrhage in her throat. The never-ending oscillation between hope and despair has driven me to the brink of insanity, and I now perceive that I must somehow find a way to accept, with all the fortitude that becomes a man, her inevitable dissolution."

"But have you tried every possible remedy for this terrible affliction?" the showman asked.

"Everything within my power," I said. "To the degree that my ever-straitened finances will allow, I have sought the advice of the most knowledgeable physicians. All of the most commonly prescribed medications—tincture of iodine, carbolic acid, opium, turpentine oil, and belladonna—have been administered. My darling Muddy, whose skills as a nurse far exceed those of the most experienced professionals, has devoted herself utterly to the care of her precious daughter. The recommended diets have all been tried, along with the various regimens which, according to the wisdom of the experts, are designed to ensure recovery. All to no avail!

"Ah, Phineas," I cried, "I pray that you and your own loved ones are spared the tortures that I have been made to endure—tortures infinitely worse than any of the diabolical cruelties represented in your waxwork display of medieval punishment devices."

And here—despite my efforts to maintain a stoical demeanor—I could not prevent my lachrymal glands from discharging a few tears that ran down my cheeks and dampened my mustache.

"There, there," said Barnum as he gave my shoulder a consoling pat. "All may yet be well. Here," he continued, extracting a handkerchief from his pocket. "Dry your eyes, dear boy."

As I obeyed the showman's bidding, a knock was heard on the door. This was followed by the entrance of the showman's associate, who carried a large mug and a tin coffeepot from whose spout there issued the delicious aroma of the invigorating beverage that Barnum had caused to be fetched. Immediately—without so much as removing his hat or cloak—Hitchcock filled the mug and passed it into my hands. Thanking him, I began to quaff the steaming liquid.

Barnum, whose handkerchief I had returned upon Hitchcock's arrival, was now looking at that article with a puzzled expression. "Why, Poe," he exclaimed, "there's blood here. Are you injured?"

"Not to my knowledge," I replied. Upon examining each of my hands in turn, however, I discovered a long and somewhat irregular laceration that extended across my right palm.

Emitting a grunt of surprise, I said: "I must have sustained this injury when knocked to the pavement by Otis." Perhaps because of the anesthetizing effects of the brandy I had consumed, I had been utterly insensible of the wound. Now that I had been made aware of it, however, it began to sting in an exceedingly unpleasant way.

"Well, that's a nasty-looking cut, m'boy, mighty nasty," said the showman. "But wait! I have just the thing for it!" Leaping to his feet, the showman crossed the floor to a large mahogany cabinet that stood behind his desk and began to rummage through the drawers.

"Let's see, it's in here somewhere—spotted it just the other day. Have old Fordyce here to thank for it, actually. Never would have known about it if it hadn't been for him—brought some back for me from his last trip to Boston. Why, it's the greatest medical marvel ever concocted by man! Can't tell you how often I've relied on it. Why, just last week I was in my Hall of Conchological Wonders, rearranging my world-renowned collection of rare South Pacific seashells, when I cut my little finger—cut? good heavens! *gashed* is more like it—on the edge of my giant Chambered Nautilus. Magnificent specimen, largest in existence, you wouldn't believe what I paid for it. Treacherous thing to handle, though—edges sharp as a razor. Well, I was bleeding so badly I thought it was the end of me—might as well make out my will and contract for the funeral. Then I smeared on a dollop of this amazing ointment. Began to work immediately—I could actually *feel* my finger start to mend! Two days later, it was as good as new! Most astonishing thing in the world! Not even the *trace* of a scar!

"Ah, here we are," he suddenly exclaimed. "Dr. Farragut's All-Natural Botanical Healing Balm!"

Holding up a small, octagonal-shaped, cobalt-blue bottle, the showman began to cross the floor in my direction. He had only reached the midpoint of the room, however, when he halted abruptly, his eyes widening as though he had been struck with a startling realization.

"Why, that's it!" he cried. "Of course! Lord bless me, why didn't I think of it before? Fordyce, didn't you tell me that your sister-in-law has actually consulted this Dr. Farragut?"

Having placed the coffeepot on a table beside the divan, Barnum's friend had divested himself of his hat and cloak and was now seated on a high-backed Dutch chair, one leg casually crossed over the knee of the other.

"That's right, P.T. Poor woman suffered dreadfully from the shingles. Finest physicians in Cambridge couldn't do a thing for her—worst case they'd ever seen. Then she heard about Farragut. Went out to see him in Concord. Next thing you know, she's completely cured. Evidently, the man's a sort of miracle-worker. Practices medicine based on Thomsonian principles, but with special improvements of his own. That balm is just one of his creations."

"Thomsonian, eh?" said Barnum, who had, by this time, completed his transit of the room and was now standing before me. "Well, I've heard of it, of course, though I don't pretend to know much about it. Here, Poe, rub some of this on that wound. Why, you'll be amazed, positively amazed, at the results."

In light of the showman's fondness for hyperbole, I greeted this claim with no small degree of skepticism. Nevertheless, I saw no reason to refuse the offer. Setting my empty coffee mug on the table beside me, I took the bottle from his extended hand and removed the cork. Immediately, a pungent, though by no means displeasing, aroma—among whose constituents I recognized spearmint, camphor, and balsam fir—wafted from the bottle. Inserting my left forefinger into the mouth of the receptacle, I extracted a small amount of the ointment and spread it upon my injury. Immediately, my palm was suffused with a delicious warmth, and the intense smarting sensation began to subside.

"Though it is too soon to gauge the ultimate efficacy of this substance," I said, "I am impressed by the speed with which it has already relieved my discomfort. It would seem as if there is real validity after all to the claims of the Thomsonians, about whose theories I have always harbored significant doubts."

"Ah, so you are familiar with the Thomsonians?" said Barnum. "Well, of course you are, what a foolish question. I tell you, Fordyce, there isn't a topic in the world that Poe here doesn't know something about. Why, the man's a veritable fount of information—a walking encyclopedia! Makes Signor Bertrelli, my Magnificent Mental Marvel, look like a simpleton!"

Ignoring this extravagant (if not wholly unwarranted) tribute to my erudition, I remarked: "My knowledge of the Thomsonian system derives from a biography of its founder, Dr. Samuel Thomson, written by one of his apostles and sent to me for review by its publisher. Following the death of his beloved mother—which he directly attributed to the mercurials, arsenicals, and other mineral-based drugs dispensed by her physician—young Thomson turned to the study of herbal medicine, which he viewed as a superior alternative to the established modes of treatment. His pursuits in this area eventually led him to formulate his method, which he denominated 'Botanical Science.' This approach is based on the premise that—heat being the source of all animal vitality—cold must therefore be the ultimate cause of all disease. The Thomsonian cure of illness, therefore, consists to a very large degree of the attempt to raise the body temperature of the sufferer through various means."

"Ah," said Fordyce, "so *that's* why my sister-in-law was always taking steam baths while undergoing Dr. Farragut's regimen!"

"That is, in fact, one of the key features of the Thomsonian regime. Equally important, if not more so, are the various medications, whose ingredients include such 'hot' botanicals as cayenne pepper and *lobelia inflata* or, as it more commonly known, Indian tobacco."

"Why, it makes perfect sense!" exclaimed Barnum, resuming his place on the divan. "Nothing mystifying about it! Keep warm, stay away from the poisonous concoctions of quacks, and rely on all-natural medications made from the blessings of Mother Earth!"

"According to his biographer," I said, "Dr. Thomson, who died several years ago, did in fact pride himself on the simplicity and common sense of his method and viewed the arcane language of professional medicine as nothing more than deliberate obfuscation, intended to endow its practitioners with a spurious air of learning. In recent years, his 'Botanical Science' has been perpetuated by various of his followers. Dr. Farragut is evidently one of the more prominent of these. As to the success of the Thomsonian treatment, there is no means by which to judge it beyond the enthusiastic testimonial of those who have undergone it. There can be little doubt that there are many people throughout New England who swear by the system and regard its inventor with a zeal that borders on the religious."

"Well, that settles it, then," said Barnum, delivering a hearty slap to my left thigh.

"Settles it?" I echoed. "What do you mean?"

"Why, you mustn't wait a minute longer! You must take your darling wife to see this Dr. Farragut without delay! Not only is he a famous practitioner of this amazing method, but—according to Fordyce here—he's actually found a way to improve upon it!"

Brought up short by this wholly unexpected statement, I stared mutely at the showman for a moment. "I do not see how that is possible," I said at length.

"Why on earth not?" asked Barnum, looking deeply perplexed.

"Among other reasons," I grimly replied, "the sheer expense of such an undertaking is utterly beyond my present means."

"Nonsense, m'boy!" cried Barnum. "Don't trouble your head about such matters for an instant. *I'll* foot the cost—every penny of it!"

As someone who had been known to charge his customers twenty-five cents each to view a supposedly genuine sea-serpent that turned out to be a stuffed South American boa constrictor equipped with a set of spiral horns and a row of spiny protrusions running down the length of its back, Barnum had a well-earned reputation as a man who would go to nearly any lengths to separate the public from its money. In my personal dealings with him, however, I had always found him to be exceedingly openhanded. Even so, the sheer generosity of his present offer took me entirely by surprise and touched me to the quick. I was not, however, prepared to agree to his proposition.

Conveying my heartfelt gratitude, I explained that I could not possibly accept his largess, as there was little hope that I could ever repay it, and my deeply ingrained sense of Southern propriety would not permit me to rely on his charity.

"Poe," he said, fixing me with a somber look, "this is no time for false pride. There's only one thing that's important right now, and that's doing everything possible to help your wife. Of course, there are no guarantees that this Farragut fellow, brilliant as he is, will be able to cure the dear girl. But it's certainly worth a try. 'Nothing ventured, nothing gained'—that's P. T. Barnum's motto."

For a moment, I considered this argument in silence. "You are right," I said at length. "I retract my refusal and accept your gracious offer with all my heart."

"Bravo!" cried Barnum. "You've made the right decision, m'boy! I'm very fond of your family, you know, terribly fond, and it breaks my heart to think of your poor wife suffering needlessly when help may be at hand."

As my right palm was still smeared with Dr. Farragut's ointment, I suppressed my impulse to grab Barnum's hand and give it a fervent shake. "If the occasion ever arises," I declared, "when I can repay you in any conceivable fashion—by rendering a service on your behalf, for example—I trust you will not hesitate to ask."

"Don't be silly, m'boy," said Barnum. "That's not why I'm doing this. Repayment's the last thing on my mind! Bless me, it does my heart good just to know that I'm able to help in any small way I can. Virtue is its own reward, you know—that's what I always say.

"Still," he continued, his visage assuming a pensive look as he reached up a hand to stroke his broad, dimpled chin. "If you really *insist* on returning the favor, there *is* a little task you can do for me—well, I shouldn't call it a task, actually. Makes it sound too much like work. This is something you'll enjoy, m'boy—right up your alley. Relates to that shocking murder up in Boston. You know the one I mean, Poe—that ghastly case involving the poor Bickford girl. Frightful stuff—perfectly horrifying. Just your cup of tea."

The crime to which the showman referred was indeed of a surpassingly hideous character. It had come to light two months earlier when a starving beggar, rummaging through the refuse barrels near a slaughterhouse by the Boston wharves, made an appalling discovery. Inside one of these receptacles, he had been startled to come upon a bloody carcass which, at first, he had assumed to be that of a small lamb or heifer. What was his amazement when, upon closer inspection, he recognized it to be the horribly mutilated corpse of a human being!

His terrified screams quickly attracted a crowd, including, before long, several police officers. The barrel was turned on its side—its fearful contents were removed. The body was unmistakably that of a woman, though further identification was impossible owing to the dreadful nature of the injuries that had been inflicted on the poor victim. To the inexpressible horror of everyone present, the corpse was completely denuded of its skin, from the peak of its brow to the soles of its feet. The chest had also been torn open and the heart and lungs removed. So revolting was the spectacle of the flayed and mutilated body—its exposed veins, sinews, and muscles glistening with clotted gore—that several of the policemen, accustomed though they were to the most shocking scenes of violence, were reported to have fainted at the sight of it.

In view of the place where the body was found, it was at first assumed that the perpetrator must be a slaughterhouse-worker who had committed the deed in a fit of madness. The victim, it was thought, was probably a denizen of one of the many houses of ill repute to be found in that noisome quarter of the city.

A closer look at the inside of the barrel, however, turned up an all-important clue: a small gold locket inscribed on the back with the initials *LB*. It was immediately deduced that the corpse was undoubtedly that of the missing shopgirl, Lydia Bickford. This poor but virtuous young woman had vanished from sight several days earlier after leaving her place of employment, and her mysterious disappearance had been a subject of much speculation in the newspapers.

It was not long before the savaged, skinless body was positively ascertained to be that of Miss Bickford. This was done with the help of a dentist who was able to identify the amalgam fillings he had recently used to repair the cavities in several of her molars. Interviewing the butchered girl's grief-stricken parents, the police soon discovered that a young medical student named Horace Rice had, for the past few months, been paying court to Lydia.

The officers immediately repaired to his rooms, where a thorough search uncovered incontrovertible proof of his guilt—to wit, the young woman's blood-soaked dress, bundled together with the implement he had evidently used to perform his unspeakable operation. These items were discovered beneath a loose floorboard in a far corner of the room. Confronted with this damning evidence, Rice professed his shock and amazement, insisting that he had no idea how these items came to be where they were found. He continued to maintain his innocence while locked up in jail awaiting trial. In the eyes of most observers, however, Rice's responsibility for the outrage was absolutely confirmed when he subsequently hanged himself in his cell—his suicidal act being widely interpreted as an expression of his overpowering remorse.

The combination of elements involved in this sensational crime—the youth and beauty of the victim—the horrible manner in which she had died—the shockingly double-faced nature of the perpetrator, whose respectable demeanor concealed a mind of monstrous depravity—conspired to produce intense excitement in the minds of the public, not only in Boston but throughout the Northeast. That the case had achieved such widespread notoriety was a fact of which I hastened to remind the showman.

"In referring to this appalling crime as 'just my cup of tea,'" I remarked, "you imply that my interest in such ghastly doings is somehow peculiar to myself. Nothing, however, could be further from the truth. While I do not deny that my soul thrills to accounts of extreme, even grotesque, acts of violence, I am by no means unique in this regard. On the contrary, the fascination with such morbid matters would appear to be a common, if not universal, feature of human nature."

"Exactly so, m'boy!" the showman exclaimed. "Couldn't have put it better myself! Why, everyone loves a good, juicy homicide! Well, not *everyone*, perhaps—there'll always be a handful of finicky souls who shy away from that sort of thing. But for the average man—and woman, too, when you come right down to it—there's nothing more stimulating than a spectacularly gruesome case of human butchery. Heavens, you've seen the mobs who come to gawk at my dioramic display of history's most infamous axe-murderers. Why, you can't get near that exhibit on weekends! Which is why it would be remiss of me, horribly remiss, if I let this opportunity slip through my hands."

"To what opportunity do you refer?" I inquired.

"You've heard me speak of Moses Kimball," said the showman. "Proprietor of the Boston Museum. Capital fellow, salt of the earth. Not without his faults, of course—a little gruff at times, not the easiest man to warm up to. Downright unpleasant, in fact—lots of folks can't stomach him at all. But then, which of us is perfect, eh, m'boy? Once you get to know him, he's not so bad as all that. The point is, Moses and I go a long way back. Do a lot of trading back and forth. Why, just last month, I shipped him a living three-horned goat—there are already two in my collection, didn't really see the need for another. Got a genuine Australian opossum in return—fascinating creature, a bit on the mangy side, but a marvelous addition to my world-renowned menagerie.

"Well," the showman continued, "it seems that Moses has managed to get his hands on the personal belongings of that fiendish Horace Rice. Don't ask me how, probably bought them from the landlady after that young devil did the world a favor and hanged himself. If I know Moses, he probably paid a pittance for them, too—the man's as shrewd as they come, I'll say that much for him. Anyway, m'boy, I just received a letter from the old rascal offering me the pick of the crop—well, not the pick, exactly, he'll hold on to the really prime stuff for himself, but the best of the leavings. Even that, though, is worth its weight in gold. You know how the public is, m'boy. Why, they'll travel miles for a glimpse of anything connected to a famous murder. Bless my soul, I once made a small fortune displaying a plank from the barn in which William Corder strangled poor Maria Marten!"

Though the showman had yet to come to the point, I had begun to perceive the nature of the task he wanted me to perform on his behalf. "Am I correct in assuming," I said, "that you wish me to take possession of the items that Mr. Kimball is offering you and bring them back with me when Sissy and I return to New York City?"

"Just so—you've hit the nail on the head! Since you'll be in Boston, anyway, I thought you could act as my agent. Visit Kimball at his museum, sift through the stuff he's willing to part with, pick out the articles you think are most interesting. You've got an eye for that sort of thing, m'boy. And while you're at it, you can also bring along the item I'll be sending him as my part of the trade."

"And precisely what is that item?" I inquired.

"Don't know yet. Have to see what Moses wants. I'll send him a letter first thing in the morning. By the time you're ready to leave, the matter will be settled. Don't worry, m'boy—I'll make sure it's something that won't cause you too much inconvenience. No three-horned goats, ha-ha!"

CHAPTER THREE

⁓

FOR THE PAST several weeks, my darling wife had enjoyed a remission
in the severity of her disease. Though I thanked God for this development, I knew from bitter experience that it was nothing more than an all-
too-fleeting respite. I could only pray that she would not be stricken with a
relapse before we had reached the dwelling of Dr. Farragut.

Despite my eagerness to embark on our journey, nearly a week elapsed
before we were ready to leave. At length—after bidding our darling Muddy
a tearful farewell—we set out for New England by steam railroad, arriving
in Boston on the evening of October 16.

At Barnum's prodding, his assistant, "Parson" Hitchcock, had commu-
nicated with his sister-in-law—the same woman whose affliction had been
so miraculously cured by Dr. Farragut. This individual, a widow named
Mrs. Randall, had kindly agreed to put us up during our brief stopover in
Boston. As we were total strangers to Mrs. Randall, I regarded this as an exceedingly hospitable gesture, and my gratitude was in no way lessened by
my awareness that—in engineering this arrangement—Barnum (who had
so generously offered to pay our expenses) would be saving money on our
lodging.

Arrived at Mrs. Randall's home on Pinckney Street, we found our hostess to be a handsomely attired woman of perhaps forty years of age. In no
conventional sense could she have been regarded as pretty. Her complexion
was coarse—her forehead low—her mouth inordinately large—her nose

unappealingly broad. Her mousy hair was finely frizzled and worn in a peculiarly braided fashion. When she smiled—which was often—her teeth revealed themselves to be wildly irregular. Her eyes, however, did not share in
the overall plainness of her other features. On the contrary. Gray in color—
sparkling with intelligence while radiating a singular warmth—these luminous orbs were charming in the extreme, and did much to redeem her
countenance from outright homeliness.

She could not have been more gracious. At the door, she greeted our arrival with the enthusiasm of one who suddenly finds herself reunited, after
a painfully protracted separation, with her oldest and dearest friends. The
sheer warmth of her welcome did much to allay our natural sense of awkwardness at thus imposing ourselves on her kindness.

The trip had proved intensely fatiguing—to Sissy primarily, but also to
myself. Politely declining Mrs. Randall's offer of food, my dear wife and I
promptly retired to our adjoining sleeping chambers. No sooner had I exchanged my traveling clothes for a nightshirt and thrown myself onto the
bed than I fell into a profound and dreamless slumber.

I awoke the following morning to an exceedingly dreary-looking day.
Outside my window, a drenching rain poured down from the sullen canopy
of clouds that seemed to press upon the rooftops of the city. As I gazed
through the water-streaked panes, I took the measure of my own feelings at
finding myself back, after so many years, in Boston.

In truth, my emotions were decidedly mixed. As the place of my nativ-
ity, I could hardly fail to view Boston with a certain fondness. I had also
resided there for a brief span of time during my early manhood, following
my abrupt departure from the University of Virginia. It was there that I had
published my first book of verse, *Tamerlane and Other Poems.*

In spite of these very happy associations, however, my affection for
Boston had cooled in recent years. Several factors had contributed to this
change. Not the least was the insufferable air of cultural superiority assumed by that city's leading literary figures, who behaved as though Boston
were the intellectual hub of the entire solar system and treated writers from
every other part of the country, myself included, with the utmost conde-
scension.

I also felt an intense disdain for the mystical maunderings of the so-
called "New England Transcendentalists." The most egregious member of
this supremely bombastic tribe was, by a very large measure, Mr. Bronson
Alcott. In various critical articles published in the *Broadway Journal* and
elsewhere, I had gone to considerable lengths to expose that gentleman's

pseudo-philosophical utterances for what they were—to wit, the most laughable kind of *gobbledygook*. My distaste for Alcott and his pontificating friends, most of whom were based in Boston and its environs, had further eroded the emotional bond I had once felt for that part of the world.

Putting these disagreeable thoughts from my mind, I quickly performed my ablutions, donned my clothes, and left my room. Stepping to the adjoining bedchamber, I carefully opened the door and peered inside. The window curtains were still drawn, and in the enveloping gloom I could discern the recumbent form of my darling wife beneath the bedclothes. The soft rhythmic sound of her respiration informed me that she was still fast asleep. Gently, I closed the door again, then tiptoed down the hallway to the stairwell.

As I made my descent, the delicious odor of coffee reached my nostrils. Following this enticing aroma, I proceeded to the dining room, where I was greeted by Mrs. Randall's servant, a grizzled, grandmotherly-looking woman who gave her name as Sally.

"Mrs. Randall likes to sleep in late," she informed me. "But she says I'm to give to you and your missus whatever you may wish if you come down early."

Explaining that my wife was still resting but that I myself would welcome breakfast, I took a place at the dining table, whereupon the good woman proceeded to serve me a meal of somewhat underdone eggs, cold veal slices, cheese, bread and butter, and strong hot coffee with cream. After consuming such a prodigious quantity of this repast that my trousers felt uncomfortably tight about my waist, I thanked Sally and rose from the table with a groan.

"Mrs. Randall says to make yourself at home," she declared as she began to clear the plates. "The library's back there. You are welcome to look around."

Following in the direction indicated by the elderly servant, I soon found myself in a spacious, lavishly appointed library. As was so often and lamentably the case in the homes of America's wealthier classes, the room possessed very little in the way of real decorative elegance. In contrast to England—where the true nobility of blood rather avoids than affects ostentation—our dollar-obsessed nation has made the sheer expense of an object the sole test of its merit. As a result, the dwellings of our parvenu rich tend to be crammed with inordinately expensive furnishings whose main purpose is not to please the eye but rather to trumpet their owner's wealth.

The library of the Randall home was a perfect epitome of this deplorable pattern, being decorated in a garish, *faux*-Elizabethan style complete with coffered ceiling, wainscoted oak wall-paneling, and a mantel carved with twisted columns and overly elaborate scrollwork. The furnishings themselves—the thronelike armchairs, rococo tables, pedimented bookcases—were sombre, massive, and ineffably ugly. Adding to the overall unpleasantness of the decor was the abominable floor-covering—an enormous blue carpet embellished with the figures of white unicorns, silver-clad knights upon prancing steeds, and kneeling maidens with flowing tresses of gold. Its presence alone was more than sufficient evidence of its owner's radical deficiencies in the realm of aesthetic taste.

It was all the more surprising to me, therefore, when—upon examining the contents of the bookcases that lined three of the four walls of the room—I found them to be filled with an impressive and exceedingly diverse assemblage of volumes. As I had learned from Barnum, the late Mr. Randall had earned his fortune as a merchant. Having been brought up by a member of this Philistine tribe, I knew only too well that the preponderance of gentlemen who made their living in this manner confined their reading to their ledger books. Mr. Randall, it appeared, was an admirable exception to this rule; for if the furnishings of his library bespoke a certain tendency toward vulgar display, the contents of his shelves revealed something very different—i.e., that he had been a man of discriminating sensibility and sophisticated, wide-ranging intelligence.

In addition to the works that a man of business might be expected to possess—Dr. Franklin's *The Way to Wealth,* for example, and Irving's *Astoria: Or, Anecdotes of an Enterprize Beyond the Rocky Mountains*—Randall's collection encompassed all the major fields of literature and art, history and geography, philosophy and science. To my great satisfaction, I also discovered a copy of my own *Tales of the Grotesque and Arabesque.* Its presence confirmed my impression of Mr. Randall's exceptional taste and acumen.

As I continued to inspect the library, one volume in particular caught my attention. It was all the more conspicuous as it protruded slightly from the surrounding books, as though it had been hastily reshelved by its owner following his perusal of it. This was a copy of *Ancient America: Or, An Inquiry into the Origins, Nature, and Destruction of the Antique Civilizations of the Western Hemisphere.* Its author was the eminent Professor Gottfried von Mueller. I had reviewed with admiration this gentleman's earlier volume, *History of the Tyrian Migration,* in which he sought to establish the identity of the aboriginal tribes of North America with the ancient Phoenicians and

Israelites. Though his argument had, in the end, failed to convince me, I was much impressed with his vast erudition, which was marred only slightly by his exceedingly ponderous prose. Curious as to the latest production of this highly original (if stylistically inept) scholar, I reached up and pulled the heavy book from the shelf.

Seating myself in one of the comfortless armchairs, I rested the volume on my lap and raised the cover; whereupon, as though guided by an invisible hand, the pages fell open to a spot approximately midway through the volume. Looking down, I was startled to find that the passage thus exposed to my view had an uncanny relevance to the mission I had agreed to perform for Barnum.

The passage had to do with the Aztecs of Mexico, whose society—to a degree perhaps unparalleled in the history of the world—combined the heights of civilized achievement with the unspeakable barbarities of pagan ritual. More particularly, the book had opened, seemingly of its own accord, to a discussion of one of the most hideous practices of that long-vanished race. This was the annual ceremony denominated in the Aztec tongue as *Tlacaxipehualiztli,* a term best translated, according to Professor Mueller, as the "Gentle Flaying."

Performed in honor of the fertility god Xipe-Totec, this ghastly rite involved the sacrifice of a highborn victim, sometimes a boy but more commonly a young female barely out of childhood, who—following a period during which she was encouraged to indulge in every variety of sensual excess—was led to the pinnacle of the temple and laid backward across the altar stone. Using obsidian knives, the priests then removed her still-beating heart, after which she was completely flayed. The smallest of the priests would then squeeze himself into the bloody skin of the victim and, thus arrayed, parade himself before the multitudes while his colleagues—playing flutes made of human bone—danced deliriously in his wake.

In relating this monstrous practice, Mueller had been inspired to unwonted heights of eloquence. Sparing the reader no grisly detail, he described—in a tone that bordered on the salacious—every stage of the process, from the peeling away of the victim's integument to the constricting sensation experienced by the high priest, whose movements were hampered by the tight and clammy skin in which he was enrobed. So sheerly gruesome was this account that, as I pored over the passage, I was overcome with a sensation of the purest horror. My flesh crawled—my heart quailed—my bosom heaved with the sudden onset of insufferable anxiety!

"Good morning, Mr. Poe."

Even under normal circumstances, this unexpected greeting—emanating from a spot directly to my rear—might have caused me to start in surprise. Mueller's inordinately graphic evocation of the hideous rite had so wrought upon my nerves, however, that my reaction was far more extreme. Emitting a terrified shriek, I leapt halfway out of my chair.

"Goodness!" cried the person behind me, whose voice—even in my agitated state—I recognized to be that of Mrs. Randall.

Springing to my feet, I turned to face my hostess, who regarded me with a look of astonishment.

"Are you all right, Mr. Poe?" she inquired.

"Perfectly," I declared, attempting, with only partial success, to adopt an insouciant tone. "I was merely caught unawares by your entrance."

"Well," she said, "I am sorry to have interrupted you."

"Not at all, not at all," I said. "My dear wife remaining asleep, I was beguiling the time with some reading—your maidservant, Sally, having indicated that I might freely avail myself of your late husband's library."

"And did Sally manage to provide you with breakfast, as I instructed her to?" she asked.

"Why, yes," I said, surprised by the acerbic tone of her question. "I was served a very satisfactory meal, for which—along with every other feature of your hospitality—I am exceedingly grateful."

"It is my pleasure," replied Mrs. Randall, as she lowered herself onto one of the armchairs. "I am just glad to hear that Sally actually did as she was told. I am afraid that she has grown increasingly remiss in her duties." Here, she exhaled a sigh before adding in a weary voice: "It is painful to think of, but after all these years, I may be forced to let her go.

"But that, of course, is no concern of yours," she continued, resuming a more normal tone. "Tell me, Mr. Poe, what book were you so engrossed in?"

"It is a chronicle of the ancient races of North America," I replied, holding out the volume so that its spine was visible to her gaze. "I was perusing a chapter about the religious rituals of the Aztecs."

"Very interesting," said my hostess as she examined the title. "I'm surprised that Mr. Randall never mentioned it to me. We often spoke about his reading at dinner. Books were his passion." As she uttered these words, her right hand stole—as if unconsciously—to the unusually large gold locket that depended from a heavy chain around her neck. "He was a great admirer of your own work, you know," she added.

"I am exceedingly gratified to hear it," I said. "Am I correct in inferring that the item of jewelry you are wearing contains a portrait of your late husband?"

Lowering her chin, she gazed down at herself. "Why, yes," she exclaimed, as though surprised to find herself clutching the locket. "You *are* observant. Would you care to see it?"

"Nothing would interest me more," I politely replied.

Undoing the tiny clasp, Mrs. Randall parted the oval locket and held it up for my inspection. Leaning closer, I saw that the right half consisted of a glass-enclosed compartment containing a small curl of dark brown hair. This tuft evidently belonged to the deceased Mr. Randall, whose image was mounted on the opposite half of the locket. Having assumed that the picture would be a painted miniature, I was very much surprised to find myself looking at a small daguerreotype. Far more startling, however, was the image itself; for the personage captured by the camera—an exceedingly gaunt, bearded fellow with his eyes closed, his hands folded over his chest, and his head resting on a pillow—was unmistakably a corpse!

For centuries, of course, people had preserved the features of their recently deceased loved ones by means of the visual arts, whether in sculpted death masks or mortuary paintings rendered prior to the subject's burial. That daguerreotype photography had been used for this purpose almost from the moment of its invention was a fact of which I was well aware. Until now, however, I had never seen such a picture, and as I gazed at the astonishingly realistic image of the hollow-cheeked cadaver, a shudder passed through my frame.

"It is remarkably lifelike," I observed. Even as this statement issued from my lips, I realized that—under the circumstances—my choice of adjective was singularly inapt.

Mrs. Randall, however, appeared not to notice. "It was made by Mr. Ballinger, a very excellent practitioner of the daguerreotype art," she said as she closed the locket and rested it upon her bosom. "Of course, Robert looked very different before he fell ill."

"Of what did he perish?" I inquired.

At this query, Mrs. Randall's expression underwent a pronounced change. Her eyes blazed—her mouth tightened—her nostrils flared. "The answer to that is quite simple. He was killed by his physician."

"Why, whatever do you mean?" I exclaimed.

"My poor husband suffered from an organic disease of the kidneys. We consulted one of the most eminent doctors in Boston. I will not mention his name, as it would stick in my throat. After examining Robert, this worthy offered a very learned diagnosis. Oh, you should have heard him, Mr. Poe, with his talk of *nephritis* and *albuminuria* and such. His knowledge of Latin was most impressive, most impressive indeed. He then prescribed a medication which, he assured us, would certainly impede the progress of the disease. He failed to mention that the main ingredient of this miraculous substance was arsenic bromide, and that its most marked effect would be to subject my poor husband to weeks of intestinal torment without producing any noticeable improvement of his condition."

By this point in her recitation, Mrs. Randall's voice had begun to tremble under the weight of her combined bitterness and grief. After pausing for a moment to regain control of her emotions, she continued thusly:

"When the end finally came, it was almost a mercy. The person you saw in this deathbed picture I wear close to my heart looks like an old man. And yet, my Robert was not yet forty-five when he died. Afterward, when I myself was afflicted with a debilitating illness, I began my search for a different sort of physician—a search which eventually led me to Dr. Farragut of Concord. My only regret is that I did not know about that wonderful man earlier, when he might have done my Robert some good."

"From everything I have heard about Dr. Farragut," I said, "as well as from my own experience in using his unguent—which promoted the very rapid healing of a small injury I myself had sustained—his method appears to be remarkably efficacious."

"It is little short of miraculous," affirmed Mrs. Randall. "And yet he himself is so modest, so thoroughly without the self-important airs of most physicians. I am sure he will do wonders for your wife."

"I pray that you are correct," I fervently replied.

"When do you plan on visiting him?" my hostess inquired.

"We are expected at his office three days hence, on Friday afternoon," I said. "I hope that our presence in your household for the next few days will not greatly inconvenience you."

"Why, you are welcome to remain here as long as you wish," said Mrs. Randall, rising from her chair. "And now if you will excuse me, Mr. Poe. I must go and see that Sally is attending to her chores."

Glancing out the nearest window at the rain which continued to fall with a torrential fury, she added: "I only hope that this dreadful weather improves so that you and Mrs. Poe can enjoy some of the attractions of our fair city before you depart."

———

As if in answer to Mrs. Randall's wish for a speedy improvement of the weather, the following day turned out to be singularly warm and brilliant— a perfect epitome of that strange *interregnum* of the seasons which in America is termed the Indian Summer. Following another ample breakfast served by Sally (who displayed no sign of the negligence of which her mistress had complained), Sissy and I bid farewell to Mrs. Randall and embarked on our tour.

Despite the debilitating effects of her illness, Sissy's exhilaration at finding herself afoot in the historic city was so great that she showed few outward symptoms of fatigue. For the next several hours, I acted as her tour guide, pointing out the many places of historical interest, while regaling her with anecdotes about the momentous events that occurred on the sites. We then strolled to the Commons, where—for the (somewhat exorbitant) sum of five cents—I obtained a large paper cone of roasted peanuts. We passed a pleasant hour in the park, nibbling on these delicacies.

By then, the afternoon was already well advanced and a marked chill had crept into the air. Sissy—who had begun to draw her shawl close to her body in an effort to ward off the cold—offered no very strong protest when I insisted that we return to our lodgings. Boarding a northbound omnibus at Charles Street, we disembarked at the corner of Pinckney, and, after a short walk, found ourselves back at Mrs. Randall's abode.

That evening, we supped on a meal of cold mutton and turnips. As we ate, our hostess inquired about our day and seemed to derive genuine pleasure from Sissy's excited account of our adventures.

"It *is* a wonderful city, isn't it?" said Mrs. Randall when my wife had finished her recitation. "And what are your plans for tomorrow?"

Though this question was addressed to Sissy, it was I who responded. "First and foremost, I must visit the Boston Museum in order to fulfill a personal obligation to Mr. Barnum," I said. Turning to Sissy, I then added: "I thought that I would undertake this errand on my own, Sissy dear, leaving you here to recuperate from today's exceedingly enjoyable but tiring outing."

"Oh, is *that* what you thought," said Sissy in a playfully chiding tone. "Well, I'll have you know, dearest Eddie, that I have no intention of missing out on Mr. Kimball's showplace."

"That *would* be a pity," said Mrs. Randall, directing her comments at me. "It's a marvelous place. And I don't think it would prove too fatiguing for your wife. There are benches in all the exhibition halls. And you can always rest for an hour or so in the theater. The shows are well worth seeing."

"Am I correct in assuming," I said, "that these shows, like those featured in Mr. Barnum's establishment, consist of a variety of performers—jugglers, comic singers, magicians, and the like?"

"Yes, for the most part," said Mrs. Randall, "though there are also dramatic sketches, as well as very informative lectures on literary, philosophical, and scientific subjects. I was there only last week and saw an absolutely fascinating demonstration of laughing gas conducted by a Mr. Marston. I think you would find him a most interesting character, Mr. Poe. He is a dentist by trade, but also a very accomplished poet. His talk is extremely entertaining—especially the part where he administers some of his gas to a volunteer from the audience."

"Oh, that *does* sound like fun," exclaimed Sissy.

It was not long after this conversation that—our meal being completed—Sissy and I excused ourselves and retired to our respective bedchambers. I did not go to sleep immediately, but spent an hour or so attempting to make my way through another chapter of Professor von Mueller's highly edifying tome. At length, my eyelids growing heavy, I betook myself to bed.

No sooner had I laid my head down on the pillow, however, than I became aware of a verbal commotion from directly below my bedroom, where the kitchen was located. Though I could not discern the words, the tone—as well as the volume—of the voices made it sufficiently clear that an argument was taking place, evidently between Mrs. Randall and her elderly maidservant. Very naturally, I felt extremely curious as to the nature of this altercation. My deeply ingrained sense of Southern propriety, however—coupled with the exceptionally solid construction of the hardwood floor—prevented me from eavesdropping. Before long, the angry sounds died out—the house fell silent—and, at length, I subsided into sleep.

CHAPTER FOUR

⌒

MRS. RANDALL HAVING a late-morning engagement in the vicinity of Mr. Kimball's museum, she invited us to ride along with her in her carriage, an offer we readily accepted. As the conveyance passed through the streets, she pointed out various places of interest, including the studio of Mr. Ballinger, the daguerreotypist who had made the postmortem photograph of her deceased husband that she wore about her neck.

"I have been thinking, Sissy," I remarked to my wife, "that we might have a daguerreotype picture made of ourselves as a gift for Muddy."

"What a lovely idea," my wife replied. "I wonder what the cost would be?"

"Oh, Mr. Ballinger charges a very reasonable fee," said Mrs. Randall. "Particularly since you are getting something priceless in return. Mr. Daguerre's invention really is one of the wonders of the age, wouldn't you say, Mr. Poe?"

"Indeed, there is something uncanny in its ability to capture and preserve the very image of life, a fact that accounts for the superstitious fear it elicits among many of our native aborigines, who view it a species of dark magic."

Very soon afterward, we came in sight of our destination. Disembarking at the corner of Tremont and Bromfield Streets, Sissy and I paused on the sidewalk to view the imposing edifice looming before us.

In contrast to Barnum's museum—whose surpassingly gaudy façade more nearly suggested a circus than a cultural institution—the structure that housed Mr. Kimball's collection had a tasteful, even stately, appearance, very much in keeping with the dignified residences surrounding it. Elegantly designed on the Grecian model—complete with a score of Corinthian columns supporting its roof—the building was blessedly free of the sort of brazen advertisements with which Barnum plastered the exterior of his own showplace. Indeed, there was nothing to identify it as Kimball's celebrated establishment beyond the words engraved beneath the pediment: "Boston Museum and Gallery of Fine Arts."

Mounting the front steps, we ascended to the main doorway, where—after explaining the nature of our visit to the ticket-seller—we were allowed to enter free of charge. We then passed into a spacious vestibule. Here, we were immediately confronted with the strange admixture of artifacts that, as I quickly discovered, was the distinguishing hallmark of Mr. Kimball's collection.

Dominating this gaslit, marble-floored lobby were a pair of stuffed African giraffes, which were exhibited alongside a case holding a half-dozen Etruscan vases. Nearby, a marble copy of the so-called "Saurocton" Apollo of Praxiteles stood beside a cabinet containing an extensive collection of tropical moths. The walls were characterized by the same heterogeneous mix of natural specimens and *objets d'art*, being hung with masterfully rendered oil paintings—including Thomas Sully's representation of *Washington Crossing the Delaware* and Rembrandt Peale's monumental *The Court of Death*—as well as with glass-fronted shelves displaying a vast assemblage of mounted insects, precious minerals, and rare South Pacific seashells.

Having obtained directions from the ticket-seller, we proceeded down the hallway toward Mr. Kimball's office, easily recognizable by the brass plate affixed to the door and engraved with the proprietor's name. I announced our presence with a staccato knock. There followed a silence so protracted that I assumed Mr. Kimball had stepped out. I was just about to convey this thought to Sissy when we were summoned inside by a brusque: "Enter!"

Obeying this command, we found Mr. Kimball seated behind his desk, making notations in a large volume that appeared to be a ledger. For several moments, he ignored our presence while continuing to write. At length, he set down his quill and looked up at us.

The visage that confronted us was one of the most unsettling I had ever seen. Its impact arose not from its features—which were in truth somewhat nondescript—but rather from its singularly *glowering* expression. A more ill-humored look I had rarely encountered. His appearance was rendered even more disquieting by the violent contrast between the absolute blackness of his hair and the sheer whiteness of the luxuriant whiskers which covered the entire lower half of his countenance and extended down to his chest.

"Who are you and what do you want?" he demanded by way of a greeting.

Having been forewarned by Barnum about his colleague's unusually gruff manner, I was not wholly unprepared for such rudeness. Sissy, however, reacted with silent dismay, tightly clutching my upper arm with both of her hands, as though for protection.

"I am Mr. Poe," I said. "And this is my wife, Virginia."

"Poe, eh?" growled Kimball. "About time. Been expecting you for several days."

"May we be seated?" I asked, less for my own sake than for that of my all-too-fragile wife.

"Seated?" he said, elevating his black, exceedingly bushy eyebrows in surprise, as though it had never occurred to him to offer this simple courtesy. "Why, I suppose so," he said, indicating a matching pair of chairs that stood before his desk.

"Now," he continued once Sissy and I were settled, "what have you brought for me?"

In truth, I was unsure of the precise nature of the object which Barnum had entrusted to me. The day before our departure for Boston, a messenger had arrived at our home. He bore a small, crudely carved wooden box, carefully tied with a string, along with a brief letter from the showman. "Dear Poe," this missive read, "this'll make Kimball happy, very happy indeed! Guard it well! It's a magnificent thing—absolutely dazzling! Worn by a genuine queen! You won't find another like it in the whole civilized world! I'd tell you what it's worth, but you wouldn't believe me. Godspeed, m'boy."

Despite my intense curiosity, I had resisted the impulse to untie the string and peek inside the box. Now, reaching inside my jacket, I removed the crudely made receptacle from my inner pocket and passed it across the desk to Kimball, who leaned forward and snatched it unceremoniously from my grasp.

Quickly tearing off the string, he pulled off the lid and plucked out the contents. What was my astonishment when I saw that the mysterious article was a sort of necklace—one, however, fashioned not of precious metals and gems but rather of small, irregularly shaped substances strung together on a cord like so many unsightly yellow beads.

Beside me, Sissy made a soft, startled noise. "Are those things what I think they are?" she whispered.

"I fear so," I replied. "The royal ornament that Mr. Barnum has asked me to transport appears to consist not of priceless jewels, but of several dozen very old—badly worn—and gruesomely discolored human teeth!"

"But what do you make of it?" asked Sissy, as Kimball scrutinized the grotesque object by the light of his Argand lamp.

"From my readings about the tribal practices of the savage inhabitants of the South Seas," I said, "I gather that it is a neckpiece worn by one of these islanders. I further deduce—based on Mr. Barnum's description of the object as having been 'worn by a queen'—that it was once belonged to a female of regal status among her people."

Without removing his eyes from the necklace, Kimball emitted a grunt and said: "That's a pretty fair guess. Barnum bought it from a whaling captain just back from the Marquesas. Belonged to one of the wives of a cannibal chief. I imagine these choppers came from some poor devil who ended up as Sunday dinner."

"Oh my," gasped Sissy.

"Well, Dr. Marston will be happy," said Kimball, referring to the dentist/poet/nitrous oxide performer mentioned by Mrs. Randall. "Guess I'll head upstairs and show it to him right now, before the show begins."

"But wait," I exclaimed. "In delivering this item to you, I have fulfilled only half of my obligation. The other, no less important, part relates to the hideous murder of Lydia Bickford by the medical student, Horace Rice. I have been instructed by Mr. Barnum to sort through the killer's personal belongings and select several items to bring back with me to New York."

"Be my guest," said Kimball, pushing himself away from his desk and getting to his feet. "I've kept what I want. Phineas is welcome to anything else. You'll have to come back next week, though. The stuff's in boxes in my warehouse. Can't get to it right now."

"Next week?" I cried. "But we are traveling to Concord the day after next."

"Do it on your way back, then," said Kimball with a shrug. "Come," he said, gesturing impatiently for us to rise. "I have to leave."

Ushering us from the room, he locked the door behind him, then—without a word of farewell—turned and strode off in the direction of the central staircase. Sissy and I watched him go, then turned to each other and exchanged an incredulous look.

"I can't believe it," Sissy said at length with a soft, astonished laugh. "Has there ever been a more unpleasant human being?"

"Few or none that I can recall having encountered," I concurred.

"And Mr. Barnum is so *nice*," said Sissy.

"Indeed, though not without his flaws—including, as he himself would cheerfully admit, a positive pride in *bamboozling* the public—Mr. Barnum is an exceedingly affable man. That he and the churlish Mr. Kimball have been friends for many years is a function, I suppose, of their mutually advantageous business relationship."

"And opposites *do* attract," said Sissy. "Just look at *us*—a person with my naturally sunny disposition in love with a man who writes about such morbid, horrible things."

"And here I have been laboring under the impression that your feelings for me were entirely the result of my dashing appearance."

"Oh, that, too, of course," said Sissy, giving my arm a squeeze.

Perceiving that we were alone and unobserved, I bent down and planted a soft osculation on the apex of my dear wife's widow's peak.

"At all events," I said, "we should not permit Mr. Kimball's uncivil behavior to interfere with our enjoyment of his museum. Shall we go see the show?"

"Oh yes," said Sissy. "I am especially curious about the laughing gas demonstration Mrs. Randall spoke of."

Proceeding to the main staircase, we ascended to the second floor and made our way toward the rear of the building, where the theatrical hall was situated. The strange incongruity I had already observed in the lobby prevailed throughout the museum. The exhibition salons were filled with a wildly eclectic collection of natural wonders, mechanical marvels, and historical relics—from the fossilized antlers of a giant Irish elk to a troupe of performing fleas trained by an Italian count—a diorama of the burning of Moscow to Daniel Boone's flintlock rifle—a life-sized automaton of a pirouetting ballerina to the ninety-foot skeleton of a creature identified as "The Great Zeuglodon," evidently a species of prehistoric whale. Coexisting with these curiosities were countless works of fine art, many of them of excellent quality, including paintings by Breughel, Copley, Guido, Kneller, Loutherbourg, Murillo, Poussin, Stuart, Vernet, and West.

As we passed through the galleries, I was struck by the air of sober decorum that suffused Kimball's establishment, so unlike the carnivalesque at-

mosphere that characterized Barnum's showplace. I attributed this difference to the staid demeanor of the typical Bostonian, as compared to the
crude vivacity of the average denizen of Manhattan.

It soon became clear to me, however, that in one respect at least—i.e.,
their interest in lurid and horrific crime—the patrons of Kimball's museum
were no different from their New York counterparts; for as we approached
the theater, I noticed an unusually large crowd of people gathered before a
tall glass cabinet. Curious, I guided Sissy toward this assemblage and saw—
by peering over their heads—that they were standing transfixed before a
display relating to the unspeakable butchery of the beautiful shopgirl Lydia
Bickford.

The objects in the case were, in themselves, not especially gruesome—a
tattered poplin dress, a scalpel crusted with a brownish substance, a wooden
barrel discolored with dark stains. What rendered these items so riveting, of
course, was their intimate connection to the monstrous crime, for—as the
accompanying placard explained—these articles were the actual garment
worn by the slaughtered victim on the day she vanished, the implement employed by her killer to perform his unspeakable deed, and the receptacle in
which the young woman's hideously violated remains were discovered.

Had the same display appeared in Barnum's museum, it would undoubtedly have been accompanied by a waxwork tableau, portraying—in
as much detail as propriety permitted—the excoriation of Miss Bickford's
body by her depraved lover. Kimball, however, had resorted to a different approach, one more in keeping with the aesthetic pretensions of his
establishment. To satisfy the public's morbid curiosity about the precise nature of the atrocity—while avoiding the too-blatant appearance of vulgar
sensationalism—he had mounted, on the wall beside the display cabinet, a
very creditable copy of the famous painting by Jusepe Ribera of Apollo in
the act of flaying alive the saytr Marsyas, who had dared to challenge the
god to a musical contest.

Those familiar with this picture know it to be one of the most sheerly
appalling images ever committed to canvas. Its overwhelming impact derives in part from the extreme realism with which the artist has portrayed
the slow peeling away of the skin from the victim's writhing body. Mostly,
however, it is the contrast between the expressions worn by the two figures
that renders the work so shocking: the agonized contortion of Marsyas's
face compared to the look of serene detachment on the countenance of the
deity, who displays no more emotion as he perpetrates his torture than a
hunter might while skinning a squirrel for supper.

So profoundly horrifying was this reproduction of Ribera's painting that—like the Gorgon's paralyzing gaze—its effect was to rivet me to the spot. How long I might have gone on standing there I cannot say, for I was suddenly roused from my awestruck contemplation of the fearful image by a sharp tug on my sleeve.

"Come away from here, Eddie," said Sissy, her own incomparably lovely visage wrought into a look of acute distress. "I can't bear to look at that horrid thing."

"Of course, Sissy dearest," I said, taking her by the arm and leading her hastily away. "I apologize for having exposed you to such an upsetting sight."

"Oh, Eddie," she said in a tremulous voice. "Do you really think the poor woman suffered as terribly as the man in that awful picture?"

"Not at all," I gently assured her. "My understanding, based on the newspaper accounts that I have read, is that the monstrous mutilations perpetrated on Miss Bickford's person occurred following her death. It is the only consolation to be derived from the dreadful affair."

"Yes, I suppose there is some comfort in that. But *why*, Eddie?" Sissy cried. "Why would anyone do such a thing—and to someone he *loved*?"

"That is a mystery all insoluble," I replied, while silently reflecting that at least two other, equally bewildering riddles would never be resolved now that the only person who could have provided the answers was dead by his own hand. What had the homicidal fiend done with the skin he had so painstakingly removed from the corpse of his beloved?

And where were the young woman's missing organs—her torn-out lungs and excised heart?

CHAPTER FIVE

⌒

Given the earliness of the hour—which had yet to reach noon—the theater was surprisingly crowded. For several minutes, we stood just inside the entrance, surveying the auditorium. At length, my eyes settled on a pair of vacant seats, centrally located at a distance not far from the stage. I led Sissy down the aisle, and we made our way along the row and settled into the plush, exceedingly comfortable chairs.

Occupying four of the places in the row before ours were a quartet of young girls. They were arranged, from left to right, in order of descending size, the smallest being situated directly in front of Sissy—a highly convenient circumstance that afforded my wife an unobstructed view of the stage. At first, I paid little attention to these children, my thoughts being preoccupied with the ghastly depiction of inhuman cruelty I had just viewed. Very gradually, however—as we waited for the show to begin—I became cognizant of the excited chatter passing among the four girls, whose bantering familiarity made it clear that they were sisters.

"Wasn't it *splendid* of Uncle Samuel to pay for our admission?" declared the tallest—and, I deduced, oldest—member of the foursome.

"Oh yes, Anna," replied the little one seated in front of Sissy. "He is the very pineapple of generosity!"

At this singular observation, the second biggest of the girls emitted a whoop of laughter. "Good heavens, May," she said. "If you mean *pinnacle*, I'd say so and not talk about pineapples, as if Uncle were a fruit!"

"Humph," replied the little girl denominated as May. "I know what I mean and you needn't be so sarcastic. I think it's proper to use big words and build up your vocabulary. At least I don't go about speaking in slang like you, Louy—it's so boyish."

"That's why I do it," retorted the girl with the peculiar cognomen of Louy.

"Well, I detest crude, unladylike girls," sniffed May.

"And I hate affected nimimy-piminy chits," countered Louy.

"Oh, children, please don't peck at each other," chided the eldest sister, Anna. "We were talking about Uncle, remember?"

Up until this point, the sister seated between the two bickering siblings had remained silent. Now, speaking in a very soft, almost diffident voice, she said: "Yes, I do believe he is the dearest old man in the world. I wish there was some way we could repay him."

"Oh, Lizzie," said Anna, "It is just like you to be so thoughtful."

"I'll tell you what we'll do," exclaimed Louy. "Let's each make him a special gift before we leave."

"What a capital idea," said May. "I know *just* what I will make. I will draw him a picture of those two giraffes in the lobby."

"And I will get up a nice pair of slippers for him," said Lizzie. "Do you think he will like that?"

"Oh yes, dear," said Anna. "I'm certain he will. I only wish that I had some special talent like the rest of you."

"What rubbish," said Louy. "Why, none of us can sew half so well as you. Tell you what. I shall write out several of my fairy stories and you can stitch them together in a nice binding."

"That's settled, then," exclaimed May, clapping her hands excitedly. "Don't you think Uncle will be pleased, Elsie?"

This query was addressed to another young woman, seated immediately to the right of the speaker. From my own vantage point, I could clearly perceive the profile of this individual. She was substantially older than the others—perhaps twenty-five years of age—and her thick, coarse hair, being of an inordinately coal-black hue, contrasted sharply with the much lighter tresses of her companions. From these facts, I inferred that she was not a member of the immediate family—a deduction confirmed when she replied:

"My, yes—tickled pink. I ought to join in with the rest of you gals and make him a little gift, too. It was awful good of him to include me in on the fun. Never worked for a nicer gentleman than your uncle."

"He is a trump, all right, and no mistake," the one called Louy chimed in.

At that moment, the gaslights dimmed—a hush fell over the auditorium—and the show got under way.

Like the performances staged at Barnum's establishment—a number of which I had attended during the past several years—Kimball's show consisted of what was commonly known as an "olio," a term signifying a medley or *potpourri* of entertainments. The program began with an appearance by the noted vocalist Miss Marion Manolta, who offered a heartfelt rendition of the well-known ballad "Beneath the Waves My True Love Lies"— one of those shamelessly sentimental lyrics which, much to my own chagrin, never failed to induce in me a very pronounced sensation of *globus hystericus*—or, as it is more vulgarly denominated, a lump in the throat.

Miss Manolta was followed onto the stage by the celebrated comical lecturer Napoleon Peabody, who performed his famous imitation of a Southern "darkie" debating on the philosophical question: "Ef a man have a pumkin' vine growin' close to de fence, an' dat vine run over de fence into his neighbor's yard an grows a pumkin' dar, who do dat pumkin' b'long to?" Needless to say, this priceless piece of mimicry soon had the entire audience reduced to a state of uncontrolled hilarity.

Next to appear was the famed juvenile delineator Little Mary Gannon, renowned for her performances of brief sketches in which she assumed the roles of the entire *dramatis personae.* Her enactment of the climactic scene from *Hamlet*—in which she impersonated no fewer than six separate characters, including both the Danish prince and Laertes—elicited an eruption of wild applause from every member of the audience, though none conveyed their appreciation more fervently than the four sisters seated ahead of us, who bounced up and down with such enthusiasm as to cause the whole row to quake.

Intermittently throughout the show, I glanced over at my wife, deriving extreme pleasure from the expression of rapt delight on her bewitching countenance as she thrilled to the dazzling musicianship of accordionist Jeffrey Jacobs, or marveled at the dexterity of the Oriental juggler Yan Zoo, or gaped at the dizzying gyrations of Miss Sophia Willard, an actual "Shaker" from the Society at Canterbury, New Hampshire, who made several hundred whirling rotations with the velocity of a top without displaying the least sign of vertigo.

Sissy's most enthusiastic response, however, was reserved for the well-known illusionist Professor Roscoe Powell, who astounded the audience with his celebrated feat, "The Incredible Coffin Escape." Professor Powell began his trick by summoning a volunteer onto the stage. This personage—a brawny young man, evidently chosen because of his superior strength—was first asked to secure the magician's wrists and ankles with two lengths of stout rope. Thus restrained, Professor Powell climbed into a black-painted coffin that lay on a long table at the center of the stage. Once the performer was settled inside, the volunteer was instructed to place the lid atop the casket and fasten it in place by driving a dozen tenpenny nails around its perimeter. A curtain was then drawn around the coffin, entirely obscuring it from view. No more than thirty seconds later—much to the amazement of the audience, who sent forth a peal of incredulous exclamations—the magician stepped from behind the curtain, inexplicably free both of his bonds and the tightly sealed casket.

As the audience rewarded Professor Powell with a prolonged ovation, Sissy turned to me and exclaimed: "Is it possible? I saw it with my own eyes and I *still* don't believe it!"

Chuckling fondly at my wife's endearing naiveté, I replied thusly: "Like all good illusionists, Professor Powell is highly skilled at creating the impression that he is possessed of preternatural powers. There is, however, nothing miraculous about his seemingly impossible feat. When the volunteer begins to tie his ankles and wrists, the magician tenses his limbs and exerts a subtle degree of pressure against his bonds. Once concealed inside the coffin, he relaxes his muscles to the utmost, causing the ropes to slacken. It is then a simple matter for him to work his hands and feet free of the restraints.

"The coffin itself," I continued, "is by no means as impenetrable as it has been made to appear. While the lid—as witnessed by the audience—is tightly secured with three-inch nails, the *end* of the casket nearest the performer's head is loosely affixed with much smaller fasteners. When the curtain is drawn, Professor Powell—who has already wriggled free of his bonds—simply pushes out this panel and crawls from the box."

I had scarcely completed this explanation when I became cognizant of a sharp *shushing* sound coming from the row ahead of me and slightly to my left. Glancing in this direction, I saw that the noise was being made by the girl named Louy, who—having swiveled in her seat—was vigorously tapping her right index finger against her lips while wearing a look of stern reproof.

Though piqued by the effrontery of the child, I had no opportunity to express my annoyance; for at that moment, Dr. Ludlow Marston himself took the stage, to thunderous applause.

From the gray hue of his long, thinning hair, I judged him to be in his sixties. He was of medium height and immoderate girth with a large, globular head that sat upon his shoulders without the apparent support of a neck. In physiognomy he was not prepossessing, with a low forehead—small, close-set eyes—inordinately pert, upturned nose—massive double chin—and a peculiarly feminine mouth whose fat, protruding underlip endowed him with a singularly petulant look. When he spoke, however, the voice that emerged from that orifice was one of the richest and most mellifluous I had ever heard.

He stood beside the table that had served as the platform for Professor Powell's black-painted coffin. The latter object having been removed, the table now held an assortment of items. All but one of these was too small to be identified from the distance at which I sat. The sole exception was an inordinately large, inflated leather bag, whose function I readily deduced.

As the applause that greeted his entrance subsided into silence, Dr. Marston struck an oratorical pose—one hand on hip, the other raised heavenward—and began to recite a poetical tribute to his chosen profession, whose opening verses went thusly:

> "If human teeth designed for various use
>   Decay and ache, 'tis only from abuse;
>   And lo, the dentist's art can well ensure,
>   At least a remedy, if not a cure.

> "When cavities come with stealthy pace to throw
>   Corrosive ink spots upon those banks of snow—
>   Do not delay, but seek out instant care
>   And fly for refuge to the dentist's chair!

> "With steady hand, obedient to his will
>   The practiced dental surgeon learns to fill
>   Each morbid cavity with consummate skill.

> "And thus, fair dental science, your magic wonders are combined
>   To prove a faithful friend to human kind!"

Had it not been for the very manifest sincerity with which Marston declaimed this doggerel, I might have taken it for a clever parody of literary pomposity and sheer poetical ineptitude. In my view of its utter absurdity, however, I appeared to be alone, for it was greeted with another hearty round of applause. Bowing to the audience, Marston explained that the verses formed a small portion of his work, *The Dentalogia: A Rhapsody on the Diseases of the Teeth and Their Proper Remedies,* consisting of twelve cantos along with a half-dozen appendices offering detailed advice on all matters pertaining to orthodontic health. This epical poem, he continued, would be available for sale following the show in a handsomely bound edition at a cost of a mere fifty cents.

By this point, I had already concluded that—in addition to being utterly devoid of anything resembling poetical skill—Dr. Marston was nothing more than an arrant huckster, one so shamelessly self-promoting as to make my friend P. T. Barnum seem positively self-effacing by comparison. I was just leaning over to share this opinion with Sissy when I was startled by his next words:

"Before I continue with my presentation," he declared, "I must make a confession. They say that envy is one of the Seven Deadly Sins. Well, my friends, if that is the case, then you are looking at a heinous sinner—for there is someone seated right here in our midst whose poetical genius I have envied for many years. During my long struggles over the composition of *The Dentalogia,* I often turned to his own poems for inspiration—and whatever of the sublime I have managed to achieve in my work I owe, in some measure, to him. Ladies and gentlemen, please join me in welcoming one of our country's most illustrious writers—Mr. Edgar Allan Poe."

Taken completely unawares by this surprising development, I remained frozen in place for a moment, while tumultuous applause—intermingled with chants of "Nevermore! Nevermore!" and "Hurrah for the Raven!"— filled the auditorium. At length, prodded by Sissy, I rose to my feet, turning this way and that as I waved one hand in acknowledgment of this unexpected, if well-deserved, tribute.

Even as I basked in this outpouring of admiration, however, I could not fail to notice that the four sisters seated in front of me were, very conspicuously, not participating in the general acclaim. They sat facing forward with their arms folded tightly against their bosoms—all, that is, except the one called Louy, who had swiveled in her seat and was staring up at me with an expression that I could not, in the dimness of the theater, read.

By degrees, the cheers and hand-clapping quieted. As I lowered myself back onto my chair, it occurred to me that I had, perhaps, been overly hasty in my judgment of Dr. Marston and his poem, the merits of which I had not fully acknowledged. Certainly it was one of the most highly *original* compositions I had ever encountered.

At that moment, Sissy reached over and gave my arm a squeeze. "Oh, Eddie," she whispered excitedly, "isn't it wonderful? So much for your belief that you are not appreciated by the people of Boston!"

"In truth, my surprise at this demonstration is no less extreme than my sense of gratification," I replied. "We must be sure to thank Dr. Marston following the show. He is clearly a man of highly discriminating sensibility, as well as rare—if not wholly unique—poetical talent. I am most eager to make his acquaintance."

We then turned our attention back to the stage, where Dr. Marston had resumed his presentation. He began with a talk, lasting approximately thirty minutes, on the history of dentistry, a subject that might easily have proved to be tedious in the extreme. Dr. Marston, however, had more than mastered the lecturer's art, which—as proverbial wisdom has it—is not merely to instruct but to delight as well. So adept was he at public speaking—and so well-versed in the arcane and often outlandish lore of his profession—that the audience's interest never wavered for an instant. Indeed, throughout his talk the crowd reacted with audible wonder as he described the many bizarre dental superstitions known throughout the world: the ancient belief that a toothache might be cured by spitting into a frog's mouth, or that a man might protect himself from the bite of a poisonous serpent by wearing a necklace strung with the incisor of a deer, or that a newly married wife might ensure her fertility by placing the pulverized molar of a dead man beneath her pillow.

Adding to the interest of this speech were the many fascinating dental artifacts he had collected over the years. These were the items I had noticed on the table. Periodically throughout his talk, he would hold one of these aloft and elucidate its significance. Among the items thus displayed were a fossilized twig employed as a toothbrush by a prehistoric cave-dweller—a fiercesome-looking set of tongs of the sort used by medieval barbers to perform extractions—a set of teeth taken from a Chinese courtesan which had been blackened with betel juice in keeping with that culture's singular ideal of female beauty—and a piece of bridgework fashioned by Paul Revere.

He concluded this portion of his presentation by exhibiting the grotesque tribal necklace I had delivered to Mr. Kimball just prior to the beginning of the show. Telling the audience that he had come into possession of this treasure that very morning, Marston described it as the ceremonial neckwear of the cannibal queen Anamoo-moo from the South Pacific island of Nukuheva, and explained that it served as a talisman to shield its wearer from the evil designs of enemy sorcerers.

By this point, the table held only one object that he had not as yet displayed. This was the enormous inflated bag, resembling an oversized bellows. Now, lifting it with both hands and cradling it in his arms, he stepped to the foot of the stage and declared:

"Ladies and gentlemen, if there is one thing the study of dental history teaches us, it is how far we have come from the barbaric customs of the past. Just think of the enormous strides we have made since the days when people tried curing their toothaches by spitting into frogs or rubbing their gums with ointments made from horse marrow and cobwebs. We should thank our lucky stars that we were born into a golden age of dentistry, an age of inventions our ancestors never even dreamed of. Reclining chairs. Fillings made of mercury amalgam. Mechanical drills operated by foot-treadle!

"Of all the blessings bestowed by modern science, however, the greatest of all is right here inside this bag. Nitrous oxide is its scientific name. You cannot see it or touch it. But its power to send the human soul soaring into indescribable realms of delight is nothing short of miraculous.

"The great Joseph Priestley was the first to discover it back in 1773. Twenty-five years passed before another famous chemist, Sir Humphrey Davy, fully explored its properties. For fourteen months, Sir Humphrey inhaled up to twelve quarts a week. Couldn't get enough of it. Made him feel like he was floating with the angels in heaven. No words could express the thrilling sensations it produced.

"It took one of our own countrymen, Dr. Horace Wells of Connecticut, to recognize its full potential as a boon to humanity. In one blinding flash of genius, he saw how it might be used to relieve the dreadful pangs of dental surgery. Just administer a dose to a patient before extracting a tooth and the person will suffer no pain—or if he *does,* he is feeling too happy to notice!

"And now, ladies and gentlemen, I am going to offer a few lucky members of the audience the opportunity to experience this wonderful gas for themselves. Rest assured that it is perfectly safe. No physical harm will come to you from taking it into your lungs. Of course, I cannot guarantee that your *dignity* won't suffer a little damage. People have been known to act in all kinds of peculiar ways under its influence.

"That," he concluded with an exaggerated wink and a sly, conspiratorial smile, "is where the fun comes in for the *rest* of us!"

As the audience chortled appreciatively, Marston called for a volunteer. Instantly several people elevated their hands. Peering out at the crowd, Marston selected a young gentleman who immediately leapt from his seat, strode to the front of the auditorium, and bounded onto the stage. After giving his name as Robert Gillray, he was instructed to seat himself in the armchair. Marston then came and stood directly over him, cradling the gas-bag under one arm. Young Gillray was then told to take hold of the long, hoselike nozzle that protruded from one end of the bag and place it in his mouth. No sooner had he done so than Marston reached out his free hand and pinched the young man's nostrils shut while simultaneously giving the bladder a protracted squeeze between his arm and body.

The spectacle that followed was every bit as amusing as Marston had suggested it would be. Within a few moments of inhaling the gas, the young man had torn off his jacket and thrown himself face-down on the stage, where he proceeded to pound the boards with his fists while emitting such wild, convulsive laughter as to reduce the entire audience—myself and Sissy included—to a state of utter hilarity. Three more volunteers, also male, fol-lowed Gillray onto the stage. Each responded to the gas in a different but equally uproarious way—one cavorting on his hands and knees while bray-ing like a mule—the second performing a series of pirouettes like a *prima ballerina*—the last leaping up and down on the chair while scratching be-neath his arms and making harsh, guttural noises in a perfect imitation of a Bornese *Ourang-Outang.*

"Well, my friends," said Marston, after the last of these fellows had been led (still scratching and grunting) from the stage by a friend, "I see that I have just enough exhilarating gas left for one more person."

"Me! Me!" came a shout from the row ahead of me. Looking to my left, I saw that this ejaculation had come from the young woman named Elsie, who—as I knew from her earlier comment—was employed by the uncle of her four younger companions. She had half-risen in her seat and was wav-ing one hand vigorously in the air.

"Bless me, Elsie!" exclaimed the eldest of the sisters. "What in heaven's name are you doing?"

"Having a lark!" she replied. "I so rarely get out that I am set on having all the fun I can!"

Having succeeded in attracting Dr. Marston's attention, the young woman was summoned to the stage. As she made her way down the aisle, the girl named Lizzie turned to her younger sister, May, and said, in a tone half of horror, half of awe: "I would sooner *die* than go up on that stage."

"Well," replied the latter, "I just hope she doesn't do something terribly mollifying."

"*Mortifying,* you silly goose," said the one called Louy. "And I for one think that what she's doing is perfectly splendid. Show the world that a girl can be as bold as any man!"

By this point, the intrepid young woman had climbed onto the stage and stood facing Dr. Marston. Up until that moment, I had gotten only a very partial view of her. She was, I now saw, a female of medium height, somewhat stockily built, but not at all wanting in personal attractiveness. Though her features lacked the exquisite delicacy that is the highest attribute of feminine beauty—and that my own dear wife possessed in such abundance—she radiated an aura of raw vitality that endowed her with a peculiar charm.

"And what is your name, child?" asked the dentist.

"Elsie Bolton," she replied. "I work as a servant in the home of Mr. Samuel May."

"Well, Miss Bolton, prepare yourself for a novel experience. You are about to be transported to new realms of delight!"

Having witnessed the preceding demonstrations, the young woman required no further instructions. She quickly lowered herself onto the chair, while Dr. Marston positioned himself in front of her, standing so close that his trousers brushed against the skirt of her plain muslin dress. As he extended the hose of his bladder, she took it gently in one hand and slipped it into her mouth, while staring up at him with bright, expectant eyes.

Though I had already seen this procedure done four times, watching it performed on a pretty young woman filled me with a vague sense of discomfort, whose origins I was at a loss to explain. My uneasiness was made even more intense by the reaction produced by the gas. Hardly had Dr. Marston removed the hose from her mouth than the young woman's head lolled back on the chair. A low, voluptuous sound—not unlike the purring of a cat—issued from her half-parted lips. Her right hand—which she had raised to her throat—began to slide down the front of her dress with a slow caressing motion and make its way toward her lap.

Looking greatly alarmed, Dr. Marston immediately dropped the empty air-bag onto the stage, leaned down, and—clutching the young woman by both shoulders—began to shake her gently, as though to rouse her from her trance.

"Miss Bolton, Miss Bolton," he said. "Are you all right, my dear?"

"Mmmmm," came the answer. "Just wonnerful."

At that moment there occurred something of such a startling nature as to elicit a gasp of amazement from the throat of every member of the audience. With the suddenness of a striking serpent of the species *Vipera,* the young woman threw both of her arms around the dentist's head—pulled him toward her with a violent *yank*—and kissed him directly on the mouth!

Grabbing her by the wrists, Marston wrestled himself free of her grasp. Standing erect, he turned toward the audience, his moon-shaped visage having assumed a deep crimson hue.

Forcing his lips into the approximation of a smile, he said: "Thank heavens Mrs. Marston is not present today, for she is of a most jealous temperament." Though attempting to make light of the situation, he sounded as flustered as he looked.

Miss Bolton, in the meanwhile, had risen from her seat and was now twirling slowly around the stage, as though waltzing to a melody audible only to herself.

Directly in front of me, the girl named Lizzie had scrunched down in her seat. "Oh, Anna, you must do something," she said.

Nodding, the eldest of the sisters got to her feet. Now that she was standing, I could see that she was a somewhat plump, exceedingly attractive young lady of approximately fifteen or sixteen years of age. Offering a polite "Pardon me" to the people occupying the intervening seats, she made her way to the end of the row, then marched down the aisle toward the stage.

"I see that one of Miss Bolton's friends has come to retrieve her," Marston said as he saw her approach, a distinct note of relief in his voice. "I thank you all for coming today, ladies and gentlemen, and trust that our program has provided you with a few hours of both profit and pleasure."

After acknowledging the audience's ovation with a deep bow, Marston stepped to the young servant girl—who was still dancing languidly to her private music—and, taking her by one hand, guided her to the small set of stairs at the far end of the stage, at the foot of which Anna awaited.

Buzzing excitedly over the spectacle they had just witnessed, the audience filed from the theater, Sissy and I in their midst. As we emerged into the spacious exhibition salon, I saw that a table, holding a large stack of Dr. Marston's volume, had been placed near the entrance of the theater. Behind it sat a hatchet-faced fellow with inordinately bushy eyebrows and a luxuriant mustache, who called out: "Get your copy of the greatest poetic epic of modern times! Dr. Ludlow Marston's *The Dentalogia*! More than one hundred pages! Fully illustrated with engravings depicting the anatomy of the teeth, diseases of the gums, and objects from Dr. Marston's personal collection of rare dental artifacts! Only fifty cents!"

"What fun that was," exclaimed Sissy as we paused near the table. "Did you see Dr. Marston's face when that young woman kissed him? It looked just like an overripe tomato."

"Indeed, his embarrassment seemed no less acute than his surprise. It must be assumed that Miss Bolton was the first of his subjects to respond in that manner."

"It *did* seem awfully unusual," said Sissy. "I thought that laughing gas just made you act silly."

"That is a common misconception," I replied. "Its effect, so it is said, is to make those who inhale it behave according to the leading traits of their character. Many do become exceedingly jovial under its influence. Others, however, have been known to grow torpid—bombastic—or even bellicose to the point of violent rage. From her own actions, it would appear that Miss Bolton is of an unusually amorous disposition."

"Hmmm," Sissy said in a musing tone. "I wonder what would happen to *me* if I tried it."

"In view of your seraphic nature," I replied, "I am certain that you would instantly sprout wings and begin to glide around the auditorium."

"Oh, Eddie, you silly thing," Sissy said with an enchanting laugh.

At that moment, someone tapped me on the shoulder. Turning, I found myself face-to-face with the elderly dentist himself, who—having recovered his composure—wore an expression of unrestrained delight.

"Mr. Poe! What a pleasure to meet you, sir," he cried, grabbing my right hand and shaking it with excessive vigor. "When Mr. Kimball informed me that you were in the museum, I hoped that you would attend the show. And may I assume that this charming young lady is Mrs. Poe?"

Acknowledging the accuracy of his surmise, I introduced him to my ever-gracious wife, who complimented him on his excellent performance and expressed her gratitude for the handsome tribute he had paid me.

"Meant every word of it," avouched Marston, his inordinately pendulous double chin wobbling as he spoke. "I am not, by nature, a humble man, Mrs. Poe. And yet, the sheer genius of your husband's verse has made me painfully aware of my own poetic shortcomings. Still, I flatter myself that I have achieved something quite extraordinary with *The Dentalogia*. Would you do me the honor of accepting a copy, Mr. Poe?"

Before I could respond to this offer, he had stepped to the nearby table and snatched the topmost volume from the stack.

"With my compliments," he said, placing the book in my hands.

"I am very grateful," I said. "Not having any of my own works with me at present, I am sadly unable to reciprocate."

"No need for that," said Marston. "I already own every poem you have written. Carry them with me at all times. Up here," he said, tapping the side of his head. " 'The Raven'—well, *everyone* knows that one by heart, of course. 'Annabel Lee'—absolutely magnificent! 'Ulalume'—sublimity itself! 'The Conqueror Worm,' 'Israfel,' 'The City in the Sea'—each one more thrilling than the last! And, of course, my favorite—'The Bells.' Do you know, Mr. Poe, there is a section of *The Dentalogia* modeled directly on that immortal lyric:

> "Oh, the gums, how they swell,
>   Causing pains straight out of hell.
>   What a world of agony does *pyorrhea* foretell!"

"That's just a sample," the dentist added. "It goes on like that for several pages."

For a moment, I merely stared wordlessly at Marston, uncertain how to respond. From the evidence of these lines, it was clear that—in the guise of paying *homage* to my work—he was not merely guilty of shameless literary theft but had produced a poem so egregiously awful as to border on parody. At the same time, I could hardly doubt that his actions were motivated by sincere admiration.

I was saved from the awkwardness of the moment by Marston himself, who—peering over my shoulder—suddenly exclaimed: "And what have we here?"

I turned to glance behind me. The reader will readily conceive of my surprise at the sight that greeted me. There, looking up at us, was none other than the little tomboy called by the masculine-sounding cognomen, Louy.

I now had an opportunity to observe her more closely. Though her age was difficult to gauge with absolute precision, I estimated that she was twelve or, at most, thirteen years old. She was tall and thin, with long arms and large boyish hands. Her complexion was brown, as though she spent a goodly portion of time engaged in outdoor pursuits. Her features were pleasant, though by no means conventionally pretty, being marred by an oversized mouth, unusually sharp cheekbones, and a prominent nose. By far her most becoming attribute was her thick—dark—lustrous hair, tresses of which were visible beneath her carelessly tied bonnet.

"Sorry to interrupt," she declared. "I musn't linger, everyone's waiting downstairs for me. I told them I forgot one of my gloves in the theater and had to run back for it. We had a jolly time at your show, Dr. Marston, even if your exhilarating gas *did* make Elsie act rather queer."

"Why, thank you, my child," said the dentist, sounding somewhat amused at the brash little woman.

She then turned to me and said:

"I couldn't go away without speaking to you, Mr. Poe. I just wish to say that I think you are a splendid writer, even if it does seem dreadfully disloyal to Poppa to say so. I have read everything of yours that I can get hold of. Of course, I must do it in secret. Anna would be dreadfully cross if she caught me with one of your tales. Even Lizzie would scold me, and she's a regular angel!"

"I hardly know what to say," I replied to this remarkable declaration. "I am, of course, gratified by your appreciation of my tales. *Why* you must conceal your reading from your family, however, remains a mystery to me—as does your identity. I know that your given name is Louisa and that your uncle is Mr. May. Am I correct in assuming, then, that you are Miss Louisa May?"

"Almost," she replied. "May is the name of my mother's family; Uncle Samuel is Marmee's brother. Alcott is my name. Louisa May Alcott."

CHAPTER SIX

S O GREAT WAS my astonishment over this revelation that the following morning I was still marveling at it.

"Imagine—a child of the insufferable Bronson Alcott so enamored of my work!" I remarked to Sissy as our omnibus rattled and jounced along the cobblestoned thoroughfare.

We were on our way to the studio of Mr. Ballinger. As it was our last day in Boston prior to our departure for Concord, I had suggested over breakfast that we use the morning to have our daguerreotype made for Muddy. My proposal was motivated by another consideration as well. Though the activities of the preceding days had not, so far as I could tell, been in any way detrimental to my dear wife's health, I did not wish to risk overtaxing her strength. Sitting for our portrait, I reasoned, would be an enjoyably novel—but not inordinately strenuous—experience for her.

"As you well know, Sissy dearest," I continued, "I am not the sort of person to indulge in the odious act of *gloating*. Nevertheless," I said with a low-throated chortle, "I find it deliciously ironic that the otherworldly Mr. Alcott—whose writings are so rarefied as to be positively *gaseous*—has produced a daughter with such a keen appreciation for imaginative fiction as wildly exciting as my own."

Before taking leave of us the previous day, the young Miss Alcott had, in fact, not merely attested to her admiration of what she described as my "wonderfully thrilling blood-and-thunder stories" but announced her determination to become a writer of just such fiction herself when she grew up.

"Maybe it's not as strange as it seems," said Sissy. "I know that many people laugh at Mr. Alcott's ideas about education. But perhaps there's some validity to his philosophy after all. He certainly appears to have raised at least one very independent-minded daughter."

"Yes, I suppose we must give the devil his due," I conceded, "if one may employ such a metaphor in relation to a man whose admirers describe him as nothing less than saintly."

"Besides," Sissy observed, "children often develop interests and tastes that are very different from their parents'."

"No one is more cognizant of that truth than I," I replied, thinking of the extreme—the *radical*—disparity between my own poetic inclinations and the sheerly prosaic concerns of the small-minded merchant who had raised me.

Our ride on the omnibus lasted only another few minutes. Disembarking at the corner of the street upon which Mr. Ballinger's studio was situated, we strolled to the entrance. A little bell affixed to the interior of the frame jangled as we pushed open the door.

We found ourselves in a handsomely appointed salon, furnished with a settee of rosewood and crimson silk, several Hepplewhite chairs, and a pedestal table whose octagonal top was formed of gold-threaded marble. Affixed to the walls were a series of shelves, each of which held an array of daguerreotype portraits, displayed in their embossed leather cases. These were very obviously samples of Mr. Ballinger's work.

At first, no one appeared to have noted our entrance. I was on the verge of announcing our presence with a loud "Hello," when a door at the rear of the chamber opened and a gentleman emerged. As he approached— walking with a pronounced limp—I perceived that he was about five feet eight or nine inches in height, and fairly proportioned—neither stout nor thin. I judged his age to be thirty-five or -six. His eyes were round and dark—hair deep brown and curling—nose ill-formed—complexion pale— mouth unremarkable and, at the moment, arranged in a frown.

"Mr. Ballinger, I presume," I said as he halted before us.

Shaking his head, the fellow replied: "I am his assistant, Benjamin Bowden. Mr. Ballinger is not here at present."

"Ah," I said. I then introduced myself and Sissy, explaining that we had come by to see about having our portraits made.

Gesturing toward the chairs, Mr. Bowden invited us to seat ourselves. The daguerreotypist, he explained, was expected momentarily. He then excused himself and, limping back to the rear of the salon, disappeared behind the door from which he had emerged.

Placing my hat upon the marble tabletop, I crossed my legs and glanced about me.

"On the whole, the appointments of the room evince a high degree of taste on the part of the proprietor," I said, casting an appreciative glance at the Argand lamp with a plain, crimson-tinted shade that depended from a chain in the center of the ceiling.

"But where is his equipment?" asked Sissy.

"As the making of daguerreotype pictures requires an abundance of natural illumination," I replied, "Mr. Ballinger's studio is undoubtedly located on a higher floor, where the sunlight can enter through the windows without any obstruction from the surrounding buildings. This is merely a waiting area."

At that moment, my gaze was arrested by one shelf in particular. In addition to a dozen or so pictures, it held a large card supported by a small wooden easel and printed in a flowing hand. The text read as follows:

> Mr. Ballinger is prepared to take memorial pictures of DECEASED persons, children or adults, on one hour's notice. Our arrangements are such that these photographs can be made either in our studio or at private residences. Mr. Ballinger takes great pains to make his posthumous portraits agreeable and satisfactory, photographing the subjects in so natural a manner as they seem to be in a deep sleep.

Looking more narrowly at the photographs surrounding this notice, I saw that—like the image in Mrs. Randall's locket—they were pictures of corpses lying peacefully on their deathbeds and ranging in age from mere infancy to advanced old age.

"Ugh," said Sissy with an exaggerated shudder, "I can't look at those things. I find them dreadfully morbid."

"To see death captured with such uncanny realism cannot help but be unsettling," I conceded, "even to someone like myself, who has always been captivated by the ghoulish and macabre."

As we continued to sit there, awaiting Mr. Ballinger's arrival, I sensed that the proximity of the melancholy photographs was having an oppressive effect on my wife. Extracting my watch, I saw that the time was fifteen minutes past the hour of eleven. I was about to propose to Sissy that we take our leave and return later in the day, when I heard the tinkle of the bell over the door.

Turning in that direction, I saw that the signal had been produced by the entrance of a gentleman whom I took to be the daguerreotypist.

"Mr. Ballinger?" I said, rising from my chair.

"Yes, that's right," he said, removing his hat and striding forward to greet me.

As he drew nearer, I saw that, in age, stature, and general physiognomy, he bore a surprising resemblance to his assistant—so much so that the two men might have been brothers. Unlike Mr. Bowden, however, the daguerreotypist did not walk with a limp. His complexion, moreover, was somewhat mottled, as though flushed from exertion.

"A great privilege to meet you, Mr. Poe," he exclaimed when I had introduced myself and Sissy, and explained the reason for our visit. "I would be honored to do your portraits. I pride myself, you know, on having made daguerreotypes of many of our most eminent literary men, among them Mr. Longfellow, Mr. Emerson, and Mr. Lowell."

Though not entirely pleased to be lumped with these highly overrated individuals, I smiled politely and asked if this was a convenient time for a sitting.

"Unfortunately," he said, consulting his watch, "I have an appointment at eleven o'clock, which, I see, is only fifteen minutes from now."

"Why, it is already a quarter past the hour," I exclaimed. "I checked my own watch only moments ago."

"Really?" he said. "Huh! I suppose my watch has run down."

As he made this remark, he ran his fingers over his watch-chain—glanced down at it with a frown—then, emitting a small grunt of annoyance, hastily snapped the timepiece shut and replaced it in his vest pocket.

At that instant, the entrance bell sounded again and a portly middle-aged man came rushing through the door.

"Forgive me for being late, Mr. Ballinger," he said breathlessly. "I was held up by a business matter."

"That is perfectly all right, Mr. Prescott," said Ballinger. "I only just arrived myself."

Perceiving that this was the individual whose portrait the daguerreotypist was already scheduled to make, I inquired as to when we might return.

"Why don't you come back in an hour," said Ballinger. "That will give me plenty of time to complete Mr. Prescott's picture and ready my equipment again."

"Very well," I said. Then, bidding the daguerreotypist and his client farewell, Sissy and I took our leave.

"How are you feeling, dear wife?" I asked as we stood on the sidewalk just outside the studio.

"Perfectly fine, dear husband," she playfully replied. "What shall we do for an hour?"

"Anything your heart desires."

"I know!" she exclaimed. "Let's go visit the Hancock mansion. We never got to see it the other day."

"Very well," I said. "Come, let us proceed to the omnibus."

"No, let's walk," said Sissy. "It's such a beautiful day."

"The Hancock house is at least a half-mile away, Sissy dearest," I said. "Though that is by no means an inordinately great distance from here, I had hoped that you would not exert yourself today even to that extent."

"Oh, Eddie, don't make such a fuss," she said in a half-pleading, half-chiding tone. "I hate it when you treat me like an invalid. I'll tell you what. If I feel tired when we get there, we can take the omnibus back."

Acceding—albeit somewhat reluctantly—to this compromise, I gave her my arm and off we set at an unhurried pace. As we strolled along the bright, busy streets, Sissy chatted gaily about a variety of charmingly inconsequential matters. Though concerned, as always, about the state of her health, I was reassured to see her in so buoyant a mood.

As it happened, however, her desire to view the landmark was fated to go unsatisfied.

We had been walking for no more than fifteen minutes when we saw, just ahead of us, a sizable crowd of people congregated before a handsome residence. At my first glimpse of this assemblage, I was seized with a sense of foreboding. As surely as a wheeling flock of vultures signifies that carrion is close by, such gatherings, I knew, could only mean that something calamitous had just occurred in the vicinity.

"I wonder what's happening over there," said Sissy.

"Nothing good, I am sure," I gravely replied.

My assessment of the situation proved accurate. As we drew closer to the scene, I could hear a few anxiously muttered words emanating from the assemblage: "Terrible tragedy!" "Poor girl!" "How awful!" Pausing at the periphery of the crowd, I gazed over their heads at the broad-fronted brick house. Three men were standing on the front stoop, engaged in an animated discussion. What was my astonishment when—peering more closely at this trio—I perceived that one of them was the dentist-performer, Dr. Ludlow Marston, while another was his employer, the exceedingly gruff museum proprietor, Mr. Moses Kimball!

Sissy recognized them, too. "Look, Eddie!" she exclaimed. "Isn't that—?"

Before the final words of this query could issue from her lips, Marston—as though possessed of a supersensory faculty that allowed him to intuit our presence—suddenly glanced in our direction. His little eyes widening to their fullest extent, he grabbed the museum-owner by the arm—turned him around so that he was facing us—and pointed excitedly to where we were standing. No sooner had Kimball's eyes lit on my face than he spoke some words to Marston, who raised one hand and made an urgent beckoning gesture.

"It appears that we are being summoned," I remarked in a puzzled tone. "Come, Sissy."

Placing a hand on the small of her back, I guided my wife through the crowd of onlookers, who made way for us without protest. As we drew nearer to the house, I saw that the dentist wore an excessively stricken expression, while Kimball looked even more forbiddingly grim than he had during our previous meeting. The third gentleman—whose identity was unknown to me—was a man of perhaps thirty years of age, powerfully built, and exuding a palpable air of authority. His not unhandsome visage was wrought into a stern, appraising look as he scrutinized me through narrowed eyes.

In another instant, Sissy and I reached the front of the house. Hardly had we mounted the stoop than Marston clutched my right hand in both of his own as though greeting a long-lost brother.

"Oh, Mr. Poe!" he cried. "Something awful has happened! She's dead!"

"Dead?" I exclaimed. "Why, to whom do you refer?"

"The Bolton girl," answered the dentist. "The one who caused such embarrassment at yesterday's performance."

At this intelligence, I gave a little start, while a gasp of dismay escaped Sissy's lips.

"She was found in the bathtub this morning," Marston continued. "Drowned. Oh, God, I am ruined!" And here, he emitted a tremulous moan and buried his face in his hands.

"Take hold of yourself, man," Kimball said gruffly, gazing at Marston with a look of distaste as though repelled by the dentist's despairing outburst.

"That's easy for you to say," Marston cried, gazing up at his employer with a frantic expression. "You aren't the one being blamed!"

"But why should *you* be held responsible for the young woman's death?" I asked.

"Because of the nitrous oxide I administered," he said. "The coroner says she must still have been woozy when she got into the tub this morning. But that cannot be so!"

"Of course it's not," Kimball said. "Why, thousands of people have tried Marston's gas with no ill effects at all. Besides, the girl had a dose yesterday noon. The effects would have worn off long ago."

Turning toward the third gentleman—to whom I had not yet been introduced—Kimball added: "I tell you, Lynch, there's something else at work here. Perhaps even foul play."

"Well, I ain't seen no evidence of it," said the latter.

"Maybe we need a keener pair of eyes," said Kimball, gazing meaningfully at me.

Perceiving this exceedingly pointed look, the fellow denominated as Lynch said: "Afraid I ain't had the pleasure."

"Sorry," said Kimball. "Poe, this is Constable Lynch. Lynch, this is Mr. Edgar Allan Poe."

"Oh yeah, I've heard of you," said Lynch, reaching out to shake my hand. The constable, I immediately discovered, was of that species of gentleman who view this gesture less as greeting than as demonstration of muscular strength. Extracting my now-aching extremity from his grip, I said to Kimball: "Am I correct in assuming that you wish me to view the scene of this tragic occurrence in the hope that I might discover evidence overlooked by the authorities?"

"That's right. Just like you did for Phineas," said Kimball, alluding to two earlier cases in which I had put my ratiocinative skills to highly effective use in the service of P. T. Barnum.

"I am happy to assist in any way that I can," I said. "Assuming that Constable Lynch has no objection."

"It's all right with me," said the latter with a shrug. "It's a waste of time, though."

"God bless you, Mr. Poe," cried Marston, his visage now suffused with hope. "I'll never forget this."

"Before proceeding inside, however," I said, "I must see that my wife, Virginia, is returned to our place of lodging."

"I'll take her home," offered Kimball.

The thought of finding herself in the care of the singularly disagreeable museum-owner evidently filled my dear wife with alarm; for at Kimball's words she cast me an entreating look.

Kimball, however, proved to be more sympathetic to the feelings of others than he appeared. Perceiving the look of distress that flashed across Sissy's countenance, he emitted a soft chuckle and said: "Don't worry, my dear. My bark is worse than my bite. Come, my coach is just around the corner."

A moment later, my dear wife had departed, Kimball escorting her on his arm through the milling crowd.

Then—with Constable Lynch preceding me and Marston to my rear—I crossed the threshold into the house where the grim phantasm DEATH had visited that morning.

CHAPTER SEVEN

W E ASCENDED TO the second floor and made our way down a long, narrow corridor, passing a number of closed doors, behind one of which I thought I detected the sound of someone weeping. At the far end of the hallway, one door stood open. Without breaking his stride, Constable Lynch crossed directly into this room. I was about to follow, when, behind me, Dr. Marston grabbed me by the shoulder.

Turning, I saw that his visage had once again assumed a look of extreme agitation. His voice quivering with emotion, he explained that he had already been inside the death-chamber once that morning, when he had been interviewed by the coroner. He did not think that his nerves could tolerate a second exposure to the site of the tragedy.

"If you don't mind, I will wait out here," he said. Then, speaking in an excessively fervent tone, he added: "Bless you, my friend. I'll never forget this."

Assuring him that I would do everything in my power to help, I turned and stepped into the room.

I found myself inside a very spacious bedchamber. Two elderly gentlemen stood in the middle of the floor, conferring in low, earnest tones with Constable Lynch. So engrossed were these three in their talk that, for a moment, they seemed unaware of my entrance, affording me a brief opportunity to survey my surroundings.

The furnishings were of the sort one would expect to find in such a domicile—a six-legged highboy chest veneered with walnut burl, a matching dressing table with accompanying stool, a Chippendale easy-chair, and several other equally handsome and finely crafted pieces. These appurtenances I took in at a glance. What arrested my attention was the low-post mahogany bedstead arranged against one wall—or rather, the melancholy object that occupied the center of the mattress.

It was a shrouded human form—clearly that of the high-spirited young woman who had impressed me, less than twenty hours earlier, as the very epitome of youthful vitality. An embroidered sheet had been thrown over the corpse, concealing all but the feet, which protruded from the covering. The sight of these bare, somewhat calloused—but surprisingly dainty—extremities sent a pang of ineffable sadness through my bosom, while serving as a very palpable reminder that the poor victim had met her death in a state of utter and helpless nakedness.

The tub in which the drowning had occurred stood in a distant corner of the room. The folding screen that, under ordinary circumstances, would have hidden it from sight had been set to one side, affording me an unobstructed view of this object. It was manufactured of iron, with an enameled interior. The bathwater, which had been suffered to remain undisturbed, rose more than halfway to the top, and a slender oblong of soap floated forlornly on the surface.

I was roused from my observations by Constable Lynch, who now invited me to join him and the other two gentlemen. These, as I had already surmised, proved to be Coroner Tilden and Mr. Samuel May—proprietor of the house, uncle of the Alcott girls, and employer of the deceased.

"Yes, my niece Louisa mentioned that she had seen you at the museum yesterday," said the latter after we had been introduced. He was a gentleman of perhaps sixty-five years of age, very short, with a benevolent, somewhat ruddy, countenance—inordinately blue eyes—and a tuft of frizzled white hair sprouting from either side of his head. His most remarkable feature was a curious purple birthmark that covered much of his left cheek and resembled nothing so much as the silhouette of a beetle of the genus *Scarabæus*.

"And how *are* your nieces?" I inquired.

"How would you expect? They are dreadfully broken up. All of us are. Especially my poor wife, who discovered the body."

"It is not entirely clear to me, Mr. Poe, what you hope to accomplish here." This remark was addressed to me by Coroner Tilden, an inordinately thin, stoop-shouldered man whose gray, somewhat greasy-looking hair fell in matted locks down to his shoulders, and who peered at me with watery eyes through octagonal-shaped spectacles.

"I am well aware of your interest in mysteries," he continued. "Indeed, I have very much enjoyed reading your tales of detection. But there is nothing mysterious about the present case. Miss Bolton drowned after dozing off in the bathtub. It is an all-too-common accident, I'm afraid, one which I have seen many times over the years."

"It is entirely possible that you are correct, Coroner Tilden," I replied. "Still, there are certain aspects of the case that, at first blush, strike me as being somewhat odd."

"Like what?" demanded Constable Lynch, who had been listening intently to the conversation.

"To begin with," I said, "I am curious both as to why Miss Bolton was bathing at such an unconventional hour—midmorning, as I understand it— and what she was doing in this bedchamber, which, judging from its commodious size and handsome appointments, I cannot believe to be that of a mere maidservant."

"You are right about that," said Mr. May. "This is the room shared by Mrs. May and myself. As to why Elsie was using our tub this morning, the answer, Mr. Poe, is quite simple: She shouldn't have been. She is"—here he caught himself and emitted a heavyhearted sigh—"she *was* supposed to confine her bathing to the kitchen, where she kept a small tub. Evidently, she took the opportunity to sneak in here and enjoy a more luxurious bath while the rest of us were away."

"I see. So there was no one at home at the time of the occurrence?"

Mr. May shook his head. "My nieces had gone out, apparently to purchase materials for something they wished to make for me. Some sort of thank-you gift for yesterday's treat. As for Mrs. May and myself, we left early to bring a basket of food to her sister in Roxbury, who is bedridden with a nasty catarrh. When we left, Elsie was in the kitchen, polishing the silverware."

"So you see, Mr. Poe," said the coroner, "there is nothing strange about the situation after all."

"I cannot *wholly* agree with you," I said. "I confess that I saw Miss Bolton on only one occasion. Nevertheless, she struck me very forcibly as a person of singular vivacity. Even allowing for the soporific effects of a warm bath, it seems peculiar to me that someone who was positively overbrimming with the energy of youth would fall asleep at such an early hour in a room suffused with morning sunlight."

"I don't deny that most accidents of this kind occur in the evening, often after the victim has consumed a large meal," said Tilden. "Or drunk one too many glasses of port. That's exactly why I hold Marston to blame. The poor girl was obviously still suffering from the aftereffects of his gas."

"And yet," I said, "from everything that I have read on the subject, those who take nitrous oxide recover from its intoxicating influences within a matter of hours. Miss Bolton's death, by contrast, occurred nearly twenty-four hours following her inhalation of the gas."

"Different people react differently to these things, Mr. Poe," said the coroner with a shrug.

In view of my own extreme susceptibility to even small amounts of alcohol, I could hardly gainsay the coroner's observation.

For a moment, I stood there mutely, stroking my chin with thumb and forefinger while contemplating the mournful object laid out upon the mattress. All at once, my gaze was riveted by something I had not previously noted.

From my present position in the center of the room, I was in much closer proximity to the bedstead than I had been upon entering. I now perceived that the sheet which had been placed over Miss Bolton's corpse had left not only her feet exposed but her ankles as well. The latter were unusually slender for a young woman who, as I had observed the previous day, possessed a distinctly sturdy frame.

It was not, however, their delicate construction which now caused me to step to the bedside and examine them more narrowly.

"What are you doing, Poe?" asked Constable Lynch.

Ignoring this query, I bent more closely to the body. There were peculiar marks visible on the tapering portion of the lower legs, just above the area where the *tali,* or anklebones, protruded. Overcoming my natural aversion to touching the dead, I reached down with both hands and gently lifted her feet, turning them outward so as to gain a better view of the entirety of the ankles. I then lowered them back onto the mattress and, turning to the coroner, declared:

"I fear that your opinion as to the cause of Miss Bolton's death does not correspond to the facts, Coroner Tilden. Mr. Kimball and Dr. Marston appear to be right after all. Her drowning was no mere accident."

The effect of this pronouncement on all three men was dramatic. Coroner Tilden's mouth fell open—Mr. May looked positively thunderstricken—while Constable Lynch growled, "What the hell are you talking about?"

"Allow me to draw your attention to these discolorations on the sides of the young woman's ankles," I said as the three men gathered around me.

Holding his spectacles by one of the sidepieces, Tilden bent low to scrutinize the indicated markings. "What of them?" he said.

"Had you noticed them before?"

"Well, yes, I suppose I did. Didn't make anything of them. She probably laced her boots too tight."

"They are finger marks," I said. "Someone gripped her legs with such force as to bruise the flesh. This contusion here was caused by the thumbnail digging into the skin."

"Hogwash," said Constable Lynch.

"A simple experiment will verify my conclusion," I said to the police officer. "If you will stand at the foot of the bed, facing the body, and wrap your hands around the ankles, you will find that these markings correspond to the placement of your fingers."

Exchanging a look with Coroner Tilden—who nodded as if giving Lynch permission to proceed—the constable did as I suggested, emitting a grunt of surprise when my prediction proved correct.

"All right, so they're finger marks," he said, letting go of the corpse's feet, which fell back onto the bed with a soft thud. "That don't mean she was murdered. You don't drown someone by grabbing their ankles. You shove down on their heads and shoulders and hold them underwater until they're dead."

"Were the average man to attempt to drown someone in a tub, that is indeed the method he would employ," I said. "It is not, however, an especially efficient one. On the contrary. Unless the attacker is inordinately strong—and the victim especially weak or disabled—it is exceedingly difficult to kill a person in that way. Thrown into a frenzy, the victim of such an assault will struggle with every fibre of his being. With his arms and hands free, he will instinctively flail, grip, and claw, perhaps inflicting severe injury on his attacker.

"Miss Bolton, as we know, was by no means a frail person. Had she been set upon in the manner you suggest, she would undoubtedly have put up an energetic, even ferocious, resistance. There is, however, no evidence of such an occurrence. Allowing for the displacement caused by Miss Bolton's body, the water level in the tub remains at its maximum level. None, in short, has spilled onto the floor, as would have been the case had she engaged in a violent battle for her life. The bar of soap, moreover—which almost certainly would have been cast from the tub during any sort of commotion—is still floating on the surface of the water.

"On the other hand, to drown a person in the manner that I have suggested—i.e., by grabbing his ankles and raising his legs in the air—affords the victim no opportunity to struggle. Caught unawares, he simply slides under the surface, water rushing into his mouth and nose. Lying on his back, with his head and trunk submerged, he is helpless to elevate himself, even with his hands free to grasp the sides of the tub. He may attempt to kick his feet in order to liberate them from the killer's grasp. The latter, however, has merely to retain his hold on the victim's legs for several minutes to accomplish his homicidal intent."

"I don't buy it," muttered Constable Lynch.

"It can be easily demonstrated," I said, "though we must have a volunteer willing to immerse himself in Mr. May's bathtub."

"I'll do it," cried a voice from the doorway.

Turning in that direction, we saw that Dr. Marston had stepped into the room. He explained that, from his vantage point in the hallway, he had heard everything that had been said and was more than willing to lend himself to the test I had proposed if it would help determine the true cause of Miss Bolton's death and thus exonerate him from blame.

Receiving no objection from Mr. May, Coroner Tilden, or Constable Lynch, the dentist began to doff his clothing, carefully placing each article on the armchair as it was removed. He had stripped down to his undergarment and was beginning to unbutton the collar when Tilden hastily informed him that it would not be necessary to disrobe completely. Looking greatly relieved at having been spared the embarrassment of entirely exposing his body, Marston stepped to the tub, took hold of either side, and began to climb in.

Under other, less solemn circumstances, the sight of the elderly, distinctly *roly-poly* dentist stepping into the tub in his "long-johns" would have struck me as exceedingly comical. As it was, the spectacle seemed merely grotesque.

Shivering slightly in the bathwater—whose heat had long since dissipated—Marston lay back as far as he could, until only his head and knees remained above the surface.

Constable Lynch, in the meanwhile, had removed his frock coat and laid it atop the chiffonier. Now, rolling up his shirtsleeves, he stepped to the foot of the tub.

"The moment you go under," I said to Marston, "do all you can to lift your head above the surface."

The dentist, looking somewhat apprehensive, nodded.

No sooner had he done so than, without warning, Lynch plunged his hands into the water, grabbed Marston's ankles, and lifted his legs in the air.

The results were precisely as I had anticipated. Before he could so much as let out a yelp, the dentist's head vanished beneath the water. His hands convulsively clutched at the sides of the tub, while his legs kicked feebly in Lynch's grasp. With no leverage to raise the upper part of his body, however, he was utterly powerless. There could be no doubt that, held in that position for another few minutes, the dentist would drown. Peering over the side of the tub, I saw that his face had taken on a look of utmost panic. His eyes bulged and his cheeks were inflated to their fullest extent.

Coroner Tilden had also been observing Marston's submerged countenance. "Release him," he said to Constable Lynch, who quickly let go his hold.

Coughing and gasping for breath, Marston immediately popped to the surface. With the coroner's assistance, he struggled to his feet, while Mr. May snatched the towel from the nearby wooden stand and draped it over his shoulders. He was then helped from the tub and guided across the room, where he perched on the dressing-table stool, a small puddle of water quickly forming at his feet.

"Damned if you wasn't right," said Constable Lynch, regarding me for the first time with a look of real, if somewhat grudging, respect. He then turned to the coroner and said: "Looks like we got a murder on our hands, Tilden."

CHAPTER EIGHT

⌒

MURDER!" GASPED Mr. May, his face having gone perfectly ashen. "In my own home! How could such a thing happen?"

While Constable Lynch removed a small notepad and pencil from the inner pocket of his frock coat, preparatory to questioning the elderly householder, I approached Dr. Marston. He was hunched on his stool, tightly clutching the towel to his shoulders, his lank gray hair plastered to his skull.

"Are you all right?" I inquired.

"I scarcely know *how* I feel," he replied somewhat hoarsely as he looked up at me with bloodshot eyes. "Relieved, I suppose, to have my name cleared—thanks entirely to you, my dear fellow. It is hard to rejoice, however, knowing what's happened here. Why, just being held underwater like that for one minute was the most terrifying experience of my life. Imagine the torment that poor girl must have gone through!" And here he gave a violent shudder—though whether from the thought of Miss Bolton's suffering or from his own damp and chilled condition, it was impossible to say.

In the meantime, Lynch had begun to interrogate Mr. May, who assured him that the victim did not have "an enemy in the world."

"Any sweethearts?" asked the police officer.

Again, Mr. May replied in the negative.

"You said that no one else was at home this morning?" said Lynch.

"That's right. My nieces went out at around, oh, I should say nine o'clock. Mrs. May and I left a short while later."

After inscribing some notes in his pad, Lynch asked: "You lock the front door when you left?"

"Why, no. There was no need to with Elsie here."

"So anyone could've just walked in and done it," said Lynch.

"If I may interject a word," I said. "It seems highly unlikely that a person harboring murderous designs would risk exposing himself to possible identification by entering through the front door, particularly at the height of an exceedingly pleasant morning when he might easily be seen by one of the many pedestrians passing along the street. A rear entrance would make a far more logical point of ingress for such a malefactor."

"There's a back door leading into the kitchen," said Mr. May. "We only lock it at night."

"Kitchen, eh?" said Lynch. "Guess I'll have a look down there." Replacing his pad and writing implement in his pocket, he then added: "You coming, Poe?"

That the constable—who had formerly viewed me with such undisguised skepticism—was now openly soliciting my help further attested to his revised and greatly elevated opinion of my unique analytical abilities.

"I shall be happy to lend whatever assistance I can."

"My poor wife," said Mr. May, shaking his head sadly. "This news will come as an even greater shock to her. I had better go break it to her as tenderly as possible."

Leaving Coroner Tilden and the dentist in the bedchamber, the elderly gentleman then stepped from the room, followed closely by Lynch and myself.

While Mr. May paused before a door halfway down the corridor (the same one, I observed, behind which I had previously heard the sound of weeping), Lynch and I headed for the stairway—made our descent—then proceeded to the kitchen.

Checking the back door, we found that it was indeed unlocked, as Mr. May had intimated it would be. The door opened onto a small wooden platform. A little staircase, consisting of a half-dozen weatherworn steps, led down to a backyard surrounded on three sides by a shoulder-high slatted fence. A swinging door in this enclosure offered access to a narrow passageway between the Mays' residence and the neighboring house.

It was immediately clear that an intruder could easily step from the street, slip down the alleyway, pass through the door in the fence, and enter the rear of the house without notice.

The kitchen itself appeared, at a glance, to offer no clues that might point to the culprit's identity. It was spotlessly clean, albeit suffused with a very distinct aroma of fish—the lingering evidence (so I at first assumed) of the previous night's dinner. All of the pots, pans, kettles, and other cooking implements were neatly arrayed on shelves or hanging from large iron hooks in the ceiling.

The single exception to the prevailing orderliness was a set of silverware somewhat haphazardly dispersed across a countertop, along with a crumpled rag and a jar of cleaning agent. I knew from Mr. May's testimony that Miss Bolton had been engaged in polishing the cutlery that morning, and it seemed evident that—seizing the opportunity afforded by the departure of her employers—she had interrupted her labors to sneak upstairs and use their bathtub.

My view of one portion of the kitchen was obstructed by Constable Lynch, who had situated himself in a corner and was slowly surveying the room, arms folded across his chest, his right index finger tapping his opposite biceps with metronomical regularity. All at once, he stirred from his position and crossed to the other side of the room. As he did, the source of the fishy odor I had detected upon entering suddenly revealed itself. Occupying the center of a small corner table was a paper-wrapped parcel from one end of which there protruded the tail of a member of the class *Pisces*.

Stepping to this table, I parted the wrapping. A half-dozen mackerel of the Atlantic variety lay inside.

"Find something?" asked Lynch, coming to stand beside me.

"Do you observe anything peculiar about these fish?" I inquired.

After studying them for a moment, Lynch shook his head. "Nothing I can see."

"When pulled from the ocean with its scales soaking wet," I said, "the Atlantic mackerel possesses a very distinctive coloring. A line of intensely black bars runs across the top half of the body, which is tinted an iridescent blue-green. The underbelly is silvery white. Very naturally, these vivid hues begin to grow more muted the longer the fish remains out of water. The faded appearance of these creatures suggests that they have been sitting on this table for several hours at least."

"So?" said Lynch.

"We must assume that these fish were intended for today's dinner. Why were they not immediately placed in the icebox upon being brought into the house? Miss Bolton, after all, was singularly efficient in her duties, as the excessive tidiness of this kitchen attests."

"Maybe she got caught up in something else, like shining this silverware, and she just forgot about them."

"Perhaps. Two arguments, however, militate against that conclusion. First, polishing the cutlery was neither so urgent nor so all-absorbing a task that she did not immediately put it aside in order to use Mr. and Mrs. May's bathtub. Second, it would be difficult to ignore the presence of so odoriferous an object as this bundle of mackerel."

"What exactly you getting at, Poe?" said Lynch.

"Perhaps Miss Bolton did not place the mackerel in the icebox because she did not know that they were here," I said. "Perhaps they were not brought into the house until she had already gone upstairs to bathe."

For a moment, Lynch said nothing, though I perceived from his expression that his mind was working furiously to grasp the implications of my remark. All at once, his eyes widened with awareness. "You saying someone left them here while she was upstairs?"

"I believe it to be entirely likely. Let us hypothesize as follows. Assume that Mrs. May had placed an order for a half-dozen mackerel, to be delivered this morning. Such deliveries are invariably made to the kitchen entrance. Arrived at the rear of the house, the person charged with this errand knocks repeatedly but receives no reply. Rather than return to the market with the order, he tries the door and, finding it open, steps inside and places the package on the nearest table. He now finds himself alone in a house with an exceedingly attractive—utterly vulnerable—and fully unclothed young woman."

"But if she was upstairs in the tub, how would he even know she was there?"

"Perhaps Miss Bolton made a sound that alerted him to her presence," I ventured. "It is not at all uncommon, for example, for people to sing while they bathe. I myself often—"

I did not complete this statement, for at that moment I became aware of a rapid footfall on the staircase, as of someone dashing downstairs at a breakneck speed. An instant later, who should come bursting into the kitchen but my unlikely admirer, Miss Louisa Alcott.

"Is it true, Mr. Poe?" she cried. "Was Elsie really murdered, as Uncle says?"

"I am afraid so," I gravely replied. "The evidence leaves little doubt as to the cause of her death."

"It's too dreadful for words," she exclaimed. "I've read of such things in books, of course—bloodthirsty villains skulking about and killing people in their own homes. I never dreamed it could happen in real life, though—and to someone as dear and sweet as Elsie!"

"Regrettably, 'real life,' as you designate it, is replete with instances of savage and unmotivated violence," I said. "And the good—the pure—the innocent are its all-too-common victims."

"Oh, I shan't *ever* get over it, not as long as I live!" exclaimed the girl.

"Mind me asking you something, miss?" said Constable Lynch, removing his pad and pencil from his jacket. "When was the last time you saw Miss Bolton?"

"Just this morning," answered the child in a mournful voice. "I came down for a bite to eat before going out with my sisters and found her in here working on the silverware. We started chatting and laughing about yesterday's trip to Mr. Kimball's museum. She had a perfectly splendid time, though she couldn't remember much of what happened after she swallowed Dr. Marston's gas. I was describing how silly she behaved, and she thought it was the most comical thing in the world. That was just like dear Elsie. She loved to have fun and didn't give a fig for what other people thought of her."

"Notice anything different about the kitchen since you was in here?" inquired Lynch after inscribing some notes in his pad.

"Different?" echoed the little girl, casting her gaze about the room. "Not really, no," she declared. "Unless you mean those fish. They weren't here this morning."

Shooting a glance in my direction as if to acknowledge the acuity of my own earlier observation, Lynch then turned back to the little girl and said: "You sure about that?"

"Oh yes, perfectly. In fact, we were wondering why they hadn't arrived yet. I was with Auntie when she ordered them yesterday afternoon. She's a dear old soul and likes having me along for company. I always have jolly times with her, even when we are doing nothing more exciting than going to the market."

"What market was that?" asked Lynch.

"Musgrave's," she replied. "On Water Street."

"Yeah, I know the place," said Lynch. Then looking at me, he added: "It's for sure old Musgrave don't handle the deliveries himself."

"The identity of the person who *does* must be ascertained without delay," I remarked.

"I can tell you that," said the girl.

This announcement brought ejaculations of surprise from both Lynch and myself.

"There's a boy who works there," continued the girl. "His name's Jesse. When Auntie and I arrived yesterday Mr. Musgrave was giving him a big package of fish to take to someone's house on Congress Street."

"Jesse, eh?" Lynch said with a frown. "What's he look like?"

"He's a very queer-looking boy, I should say maybe eighteen or nineteen years old, not tall but terribly strong with very wide shoulders and muscular arms. It's his one bad eye, though, that you notice most of all. It's very pale blue, almost white, as though it's covered with a film. It was very shocking to see, both ugly and fascinating at the same time, if you know what I mean. I had to try very hard not to stare at it—Papa says we musn't treat people with infirmities any different from the rest of us, you know."

As the girl spoke, Lynch's countenance assumed an increasingly ruminative look.

"Am I correct in inferring," I said, "that Miss Alcott's exceedingly detailed description has struck a chord of recognition with you?"

Nodding, Lynch replied: "There was a lad named Jesse McMahon lived in that neighborhood. Had one bad eye—other kids used to tease him, call him 'Vulture Eye.' Got into a bad scrape a few years back. Must've been about thirteen, fourteen years old. Him and another boy robbed a cigar store and was sent to the reformatory at Westborough. He'd be out by now. Could be he's the one."

"Do you seriously mean to say," asked Miss Alcott, regarding me with a look of horror, "that poor Elsie was murdered by that boy?"

"Though his guilt has by no means been established," I replied, "circumstances suggest that he well may be the responsible party. Ah, Coroner Tilden!"

This latter remark was addressed to the elderly coroner, who had suddenly materialized in the kitchen.

"Have you gentlemen managed to discover anything?" he asked.

In reply to this query, I proceeded to summarize our findings, explaining in the most concise manner possible the character of those inductions that had led to the identification of a possible suspect in the person of the young man denominated as "Jesse."

"I'm heading over to Musgrave's right now to talk to the boy," Lynch said to the coroner.

"I'd better inform Chief Fallon," said Tilden. "The sooner he hears about all this the better."

The two men then strode from the kitchen, Miss Alcott and I following close behind. While the coroner paused to remove his cloak and hat from the tree stand in the foyer, Lynch threw open the front door. Gazing out at the sidewalk, I perceived that the crowd of curiosity-seekers had thinned considerably. I had little doubt, however, that it would quickly redouble in size once the news began to circulate that the death of the Mays' vibrant young servant-girl was no mere accident but the result of a shockingly cold-blooded murder.

After thanking the girl for her assistance and giving my hand another pulverizing shake, Lynch hurried down the stoop to the curb, where he un-hitched and mounted his horse and trotted off down the street. Tilden departed a moment later. Standing at the threshold of the open front door, we watched the coroner's buggy disappear around the corner. I then walked outside onto the stoop and, turning to the gangly young female, said:

"I, too, must take my leave, Miss Alcott. In order to assist Dr. Marston, I was compelled to send my wife, Virginia, back to our lodgings in the excessively stern and forbidding company of Mr. Kimball. I have little doubt that she is now anxiously awaiting my return. Please believe me when I say that I am deeply sorry that such a terrible fate has befallen your friend Miss Bolton, who impressed me as a very admirable young woman."

"She was a regular good one, she was," said the girl as her lachrymal glands discharged a flow of tears. "Oh dear," she continued, extracting a handkerchief from the pocket of her apron and dabbing at her eyes. "If life is as hard as this, I don't know how I shall *ever* get through it."

Reaching down, I placed a comforting hand on her shoulder. "It cannot be denied that life is fraught with adversity. Misery is manifold. The wretchedness of existence is multiform. Death—disease—suffering—and loss are the inescapable calamities that each of us must endure on our torturous journey to the grave. This is not to say, however, that the world—however rife with horror—is wholly devoid of solace. There is, for instance—"

I did not get a chance to complete my consoling remarks; for at that moment, my young auditor—who had shifted her gaze away from my face and was staring at something behind me—suddenly exclaimed:

"Christopher Columbus! It's *him*!"

"Him?" I said, greatly perplexed. "To whom are you referring?"

"That boy, Jesse!" cried the little girl. "He's standing right there!"

"What!" I exclaimed, turning to see.

From my elevated vantage point at the head of the stoop, I had an un-obstructed view of the opposite side of the street. I now perceived a figure who appeared to be lurking beside a lamppost directly across from the Mays' residence. He was a stockily built young man, short in stature but with an upper body of remarkably muscular, if not Herculean, mould. His closely cropped hair—low, sloping forehead—flattened nose—and thick, protuberant lips endowed him with a distinctly simian appearance. His most unsettling feature, however, was his opalescent left eye. Even from the distance at which I viewed him, my blood ran cold at the sight of this ghostly ocular organ.

At that moment, a tug on my sleeve drew my attention back to my juvenile companion. "What do you make of it, Mr. Poe?" she asked, keeping her voice low, as though afraid that the bizarre-looking youth might overhear her. "Isn't it strange that he's here just now?"

"It is far from uncommon for a murderer to return to the scene of his atrocity shortly after its commission," I replied. "The reasons for this behavior are unclear. Some attribute it to the proddings of a guilty conscience. Others ascribe it to a far more insidious motive—to wit, the pleasure derived by the perpetrator from viewing the general consternation produced by his crime. In any case, the presence of Mr. Musgrave's delivery boy at this moment would appear to be further confirmation of his culpability."

By this time, I had resumed my observation of the young man, who was behaving in a singular manner. He appeared to be in a state of extreme ir-resolution. At one moment, he would step to the curb, as though intending to cross the street and join the crowd in front of the house. In the next, he would suddenly retreat to his post by the streetlamp and half-conceal him-self behind this object.

So far, he did not seem to be aware that he was under my scrutiny. All at once, however, he turned his unnerving gaze directly at me. I quickly averted my eyes, pretending that I had not been staring at him—but to no avail. Thrusting his hands deep in his trouser pockets, he spun on his heels and hurried off down the street.

"Oh my! He's getting away!" exclaimed Miss Alcott.

"There is not a moment to lose," I cried. "He is proceeding in the direc-tion of the harbor. Perhaps he is attempting to abscond. How far is it to Mr. Musgrave's fish market?"

"No more than fifteen minutes away from here," said the girl.

"You must run there at once and tell Constable Lynch what has transpired here," I said. "I will follow the boy and keep him in sight."

"I will go like the wind!" exclaimed the little girl. In the next instant, she had dashed down the stoop—made her way through the diminished but still numerous crowd of bystanders—and disappeared around a corner.

By then, I, too, had descended to the level of the street. My progress was momentarily impeded by several of the onlookers, who clutched at my coat and demanded to know what was taking place inside the house. Ignoring these queries, I freed myself from their grasp and elbowed my way to the curb. Hurriedly crossing the street, I bent my steps in the direction taken by the boy.

For an instant, I was seized with anxiety, for he had already disappeared. With some little difficulty I at length came within sight of him, approached, and followed him closely, yet cautiously, so as not to attract his attention.

During the span of the next six or seven minutes, we proceeded in this fashion, walking swiftly in tandem along a busy thoroughfare with an unbroken line of lofty houses on either side. By and by he passed into a cross street which, although densely filled with people, was not so much thronged as the one he had quitted.

Thus far, he had remained unaware of my presence. As we hurried along the pavement, however, a shopkeeper emerging from the door of his establishment inadvertently jostled the youth in such a manner as to cause him to glance to his rear. A startled expression passed over the young man's countenance as he recognized my face. Rudely pushing the shop owner aside, he dashed to the end of the street, turned the corner, and vanished.

Abandoning all effort at concealment, I bolted after the lad. As I rounded the corner, I saw him duck into an alley halfway down the street.

The sidewalk was deserted. Striding boldly to the spot where I had last seen my quarry, I paused at the entrance to the alley. It was bounded on one side by an abandoned livery stable and on the other by a small dark edifice of two stories, the second of which projected over the lower floor. An exceedingly rank smell, as of decomposing offal, emanated from the dark, narrow lane between these two ramshackle structures.

Peering into the gloom, I could perceive nothing beyond several ancient barrels that appeared to be overflowing with refuse. The reader may readily conceive my feelings at that moment. The prospect of venturing into the exceedingly dismal and foetid passageway where the hulking juvenile now lay in hiding suffused my bosom with the darkest forebodings. Perhaps, I ruminated, I could merely stand guard at the entrance until the police—

alerted by little Louisa Alcott—arrived on the scene. Even as this thought passed through my mind, however, I realized that such an expedient was not feasible. There might well be a means of egress at the opposite end of the alley, and I could not take the chance of allowing the young suspect to escape.

There was no point in hesitating a moment longer. Girding myself, I stepped into the alley.

Almost immediately, I drew to a halt. Squinting into the gloom and straining my auditory faculties to the utmost, I attempted to detect any sign of the young man's presence. Except for several rodents, however—recognizable by the tell-tale scrabbling of their claws—I could perceive no sign of life. Barely daring to breathe, I moved another few steps into the depths of the alley.

With a piercing yell, the young brute named Jesse sprang from behind the nearest barrel. My blood froze—my heart ceased to beat—I felt my eyes starting from their sockets.

It was not merely the extreme suddenness of his movement—nor the hair-raising shriek that issued from his throat—that caused me to respond in this manner. It was the object clutched in his meaty right hand. Though the poor illumination made it difficult to distinguish this item with ab-solute clarity, I saw that it was unmistakably a metallic implement of some sort, evidently a knife or dagger.

His visage wrought into a look of extreme malice, the young man took a step toward me, his right hand thrust outward in a menacing gesture.

Though possessed of considerable pugilistic skills—which, in my boy-hood, had rendered me a figure of awe among my schoolmates—I quickly recognized the folly of attempting to disarm the muscular young brute with my bare hands. Desperately, I cast my gaze about for an object with which to defend myself. But, though the alleyway was littered with rubbish, I saw nothing that might serve such a purpose. My only recourse, I perceived, was to employ the most potent weapon at my disposal—my powers of persua-sion.

Accordingly, I drew myself up to my full height—cleared my throat—and addressed the boy thusly:

"Jesse—for such, I have been told, is your cognomen—permit me, as a gentleman of mature age and superior experience, to tender a word of ad-vice. You have evidently committed an outrage. Nevertheless, your youth—combined with whatever mitigating circumstances you may be able to adduce in your own defense—may yet save you from the ultimate penalty of the law. If, on the other hand, you persist in your rash and hopeless course, you will almost certainly end by forfeiting your own life. I urge you, for your own good, to lay down your weapon at once and surrender to the police who, even now, are on their way here."

My speech seemed to have the desired effect. The burly youth halted in his tracks, his apelike countenance wearing a look of intense confusion, as though the sheer forcefulness of my words had filled him with doubt as to the wisdom of his actions.

At length—speaking in a high-pitched, even feminine, voice that seemed bizarrely at odds with his appearance—he exclaimed: "I ain't going back to that place!"

Assuming that he was referring to the Mays' residence, I said: "As you were there only a few moments ago, I am somewhat puzzled over your reluctance to revisit the scene of your crime. Nevertheless, I am certain that once you turn yourself over to the police, they will be happy to transport you directly to jail, without compelling you to view the site of your grim handiwork. And now," I continued, slowly holding out my open right hand, "may I ask you to relinquish your weapon until the officers arrive?"

Again, my words left the boy somewhat slack-jawed with wonderment. For a moment, he merely gaped at me mutely.

All at once, his visage contorted into a look of fury. "You want it so bad?" he screamed. "Here, damn you! Take it!"

Then—raising his right hand high over his head—he hurled his shining weapon directly at me!

A shriek of terror burst from my lips as the implement came hurtling toward me. Reflexively, I raised my arms crossways over my face—only to feel the hard metallic object strike me directly in the center of my chest!

With a horrified cry, I staggered backward against the wall of the derelict stable and sank to the ground with a moan. As I did, the murderous young villain emitted a shrill, triumphant shout and, with a bound, leapt over my prostrate body and fled into the street.

My back propped against the wall of the stable, I lay there for a moment, blood pounding in my ears, my brain spinning with the terrible knowledge that I had been impaled through the breastbone, and that my life, even then, was draining away. True, I experienced no pain. That fact, however, was of little comfort to me, as I knew that even deep and mortal knife wounds do not make themselves felt immediately.

At that instant, I became dimly cognizant of a wild commotion issuing from the direction of the street: a clattering of wheels and pounding of hooves—the frantic *neighing* of horses—an agonized yell—followed almost immediately by shrill exclamations of horror and distress.

These bizarre and unaccountable noises are the last sounds that I will ever hear, I said to myself. With trembling hands, I reached up and groped at my chest, expecting to feel the handle of the boy's weapon protruding from my body. To my surprise, nothing was there. Quickly, I patted the bosom of my shirt, which—I assumed—would be saturated with my blood. It felt perfectly dry. Opening my eyes, I stared at my palms. Not a drop of sanguinary fluid was to be seen on them.

Quickly glancing down at myself, I saw that I was completely unharmed. Evidently, the boy had misthrown his weapon, so that I had been struck by its handle and not the point of its blade. An inexpressible sense of gratitude and relief flooded my unscathed bosom.

As I struggled to my feet, I could still hear the tumult on the street—the pounding of many feet, shouted cries of "Help!" and "Fetch a doctor!" Though deeply curious as to the nature of this disturbance, I remained where I was, scanning the area at my feet for the weapon that had been aimed at my heart. In the disorder of the garbage-strewn alleyway, it took a moment for my gaze to alight on the object of my search. When I saw it, my eyes widened with confusion.

It was not a knife after all.

It was a spoon.

PART TWO

Little Women

CHAPTER NINE

～

THE DRIVER OF the conveyance that killed eighteen-year-old Jesse McMahon was scarcely older than the victim himself. His name was Peter Heffernan. The twenty-year-old son of Mr. and Mrs. James Heffernan of Water Street, young Peter was at the reins of his family's runabout when a mongrel dog, in pursuit of an alley cat, dashed into the gutter and startled the horses, causing them to bolt. Despite his most strenuous efforts, the galloping beasts could not be restrained. As the runaway vehicle plunged down the avenue, a hansom rounded the corner. Marshaling every particle of his strength, young Heffernan yanked on the left rein in a desperate effort to avoid a collision with the cab.

It was at that moment that Jesse McMahon came bounding out of the alleyway and into the street. Whether he perceived the danger bearing down on him will never be known. Heffernan, according to his own later testimony, never saw McMahon. Even *had* he noticed the burly young man, he would have been powerless to avoid the ensuing tragedy.

As Heffernan's vehicle swerved to one side, its right wheel hit the boy a glancing blow, causing his baggy jacket to become entangled in the spokes. Jesse was dragged along the street for a full forty feet before Heffernan finally succeeded in bringing the team to a halt.

By the time I arrived, only moments after this mishap occurred, at least two dozen people were already gathered at the scene, while others had hurried off in search of medical assistance. Announcing—not without a degree of truth—that I was there in a semi-official capacity, I pushed my way through the crowd until I stood beside the desperately injured boy.

He presented an exceedingly doleful sight. He lay flat on his back, eyes closed, his arms and legs outflung in a "spread-eagle" position. Most of his clothing had been torn off. He still clung to life, though only barely. The tortured heavings of his chest—no less than the stream of blood issuing from the back of his head and pooling in the declivities between the cobblestones—made it painfully clear that he could not possibly survive for very long.

Despite the vicious and depraved nature of the crime he had evidently committed, it was impossible to look upon the dying young man without pity, and as I stared down at him my bosom was suffused with a sense of the purest melancholy. All at once, his eyes fluttered open and his dull gaze fixed on me. His lips began to move, though no audible sound emerged. Quickly, I knelt at his side. As I did, he reached up and grabbed my forearm with his left hand, applying such force that, even through the fabric of my garments, I could feel his fingernails digging into my flesh.

The sheer intensity of his grip suggested that he was making an urgent attempt at communication. I bent my ear to his mouth—only to hear a ghastly liquid gurgle that seemed to emanate from the very core of his being, followed by a slow hissing noise that signified the exhalation of his last breath.

"He's gone," I heard someone say behind me.

Even then, his lifeless hand continued to exert its powerful grip. Reaching down, I began to pry away his fingers one by one. It was only then that I noticed something which caused my brain to spin with confusion—my heart to beat at a wildly accelerated pace—and a violent shudder to course through my frame.

"Four fingers! Do you mean that one of them had been severed?"

The source of this query was our hostess, Mrs. Randall. She was seated across the dining room table from Sissy and myself. The time was approximately seven o'clock in the evening.

In the hours that had elapsed since the events described above, news of the shocking murder of the lovely young servant girl Elsie Bolton—and of the gruesome vehicular accident that claimed the life of her alleged slayer—had already spread throughout the city, the earliest accounts having appeared in the evening newspapers. For readily apparent reasons—the youth and beauty of the victim, the shocking manner of her death, the hideous end met by the adolescent brute presumed to be her killer—the story could hardly fail to generate intense excitement among the populace. That a key figure in the drama was none other than "the renowned author of 'The Raven' " (as I was invariably characterized by the press) only added to the interest of the case.

Constable Lynch—who had been alerted by little Louisa Alcott—was the first official to arrive, galloping up on horseback shortly after the young man expired. He was followed in short order by several other officers, along with a neighborhood physician and a handful of reporters from the city's various daily gazettes. For nearly an hour, I remained on the scene, answering questions as to what had transpired during my pursuit of the suspect, and describing in detail my final confrontation with the menacing youth which had reached its climax when he flung the silver utensil at my breast. Just prior to emerging from the alleyway, I had taken a moment to retrieve this object, and I now turned it over to Constable Lynch, who examined it curiously for several moments before inserting it into the side pocket of his jacket. About the unsettling observation I had made while removing the dead boy's hand from my arm I said nothing, as I was still deeply uncertain as to what, if any, significance it might possess.

At length, I was permitted to leave. Making my way back to Mrs. Randall's home, I received a joyous welcome from my darling wife, who—having last set eyes on me as I was about to enter the Mays' residence—had been awaiting my return in an agony of suspense. The day's events, however, had left me so exhausted—both physically and emotionally—that I begged to be permitted to enjoy a brief rest before embarking on another account of my adventures. I then proceeded upstairs to my room, where I quickly divested myself of my jacket and boots—flung myself onto the bed—and fell instantly asleep.

When I awoke, dusk had already fallen. Feeling much refreshed—and perfectly famished—I quickly made myself ready and descended to the ground floor, where I was gratified to find supper already set out on the dining room table and my wife and hostess awaiting my appearance.

The meal, prepared by Mrs. Randall's much-deprecated housemaid, Sally, consisted of fricasseed chicken, baked beans, and asparagus. I lost no time in tucking into the food, recounting the momentous events of the day between mouthfuls. Now—having consumed the last remnants of my meal (which, in truth, was so poorly prepared that only my inordinate hunger rendered it at all palatable)—I had reached the point in my narrative where

I had looked down at the dead boy's left hand and been startled by what I had seen—i.e., that it possessed only four fingers.

Responding to Mrs. Randall's very logical suggestion that the young man had, perhaps, suffered an accidental amputation, I said: "That, of course, was my first assumption. Indeed—in view of the exceedingly savage battering he had sustained—I thought it entirely possible that one of his fingers had been torn off as his body was dragged over the cobblestones. A closer look at his hand, however, assured me that the disfigurement was not caused by the accident, but was rather a congenital defect."

"And how did you arrive at *that* conclusion?" inquired Mrs. Randall, who had barely touched her food, having laid down her utensils with an expression of intense distaste after sampling a few bites of the mucilaginous gravy in which the chicken was drenched.

"The thumb, index, and little fingers," I replied, "were perfectly normal. In place of the middle and ring fingers, however, McMahon possessed a single, monstrously enlarged digit. This condition is caused when the bones of the two fingers fuse inside the womb and are covered over by a single sheathing of skin. Such anomalies have been extensively documented by physicians and, indeed, are among the most common of what are termed the minor *terata,* or grotesque physical malformations."

"Now that you mention it, Eddie," Sissy remarked, "I remember seeing a man with a hand like that years ago. I couldn't have been older than five or six. It was very disturbing to me at the time. I must have kept Muddy awake for a month with my nightmares. I'd forgotten all about it until now."

"Yes, I can imagine how upsetting something like that would be to a small child," said Mrs. Randall. "I'm surprised to hear you say, however, that *you* were so troubled by it, Mr. Poe."

"Please do not misunderstand," I replied. "No one who has spent as much time as I in the company of Mr. Barnum's curiosities—whose ranks include some of the most spectacularly deformed human beings in existence—would find such a relatively trivial abnormality unsettling *in itself*. It was what young McMahon's disfigurement implied about his guilt that affected me so adversely."

"Why, what do you mean, Eddie?" asked Sissy, while Mrs. Randall raised her eyebrows in surprise.

"You will recall that, upon examining the exposed legs of Miss Bolton, I noticed nail-marks on each of her ankles," I said. "Indeed, it was this observation which led me to conclude that a murder had occurred. To test this deduction—and persuade Constable Lynch of its validity—I invited him to grasp the dead girl's ankles. As I anticipated, his fingers perfectly matched the imprints on her skin. In short, it would appear that Miss Bolton was drowned by someone with two normal hands."

"But surely," said Mrs. Randall, "there must be some uncertainty on that point. The markings on her legs couldn't have been so absolutely distinct as to leave no room for doubt."

"It is possible," I conceded, "that in her struggles to free herself of her killer's grasp, Miss Bolton kicked her legs in such a way as to produce a set of scratch-marks that were somewhat distorted in appearance. But then there is the matter of the spoon."

"What about it?" asked Mrs. Randall. "Surely it's further evidence of his guilt."

"It certainly seems that way to me," Sissy agreed. "After all, it proves that he was inside the house at the time of the murder."

"That the utensil was in his possession," I replied, "merely proves that he was guilty of theft. From young McMahon's ignominious history, we know that he had larcenous tendencies. We also know that Miss Bolton interrupted her cleaning of the silverware to take advantage of her employers' absence by sneaking upstairs for a bath. There can be little doubt that, while she was gone, McMahon arrived with his delivery, entered the kitchen, and noticed the utensils laid out on the counter. Let us suppose that—seized by temptation at the sight of the unguarded silver—he snatched the spoon and absconded.

"Later," I continued, "overcome with guilt—or fearing that he would inevitably be identified as the thief and arrested—he returned to the house, perhaps intending to replace the utensil before its disappearance was noted. Seeing a crowd gathered in front of the residence, however, he changed his mind and hurried away. When he saw that he was being chased, he may have reasonably assumed that I was a member of the family—or perhaps even an officer of the law—attempting to apprehend him. That would account for the strange remark he made to me after I trapped him in the alley: 'I ain't going back to that place.' I now believe that he may have been referring to the penal institution to which he was sent following his earlier act of juvenile larceny. If this theory is correct, then it is entirely possible that in hurling the spoon at my chest, he was not attempting to distract me while effecting his escape, as I originally thought. Rather, he was throwing me the stolen object in the hope that I would abandon my pursuit.

"In short," I concluded, drawing a deep breath and exhaling it slowly, "it now strikes me as possible that young McMahon was not merely innocent of the homicide but *never even knew that one had been committed!*"

For a moment, my two auditors regarded me mutely. From their expressions, it was plain that they viewed my hypothesis with the greatest skepticism.

It was Mrs. Randall who broke the silence. "But really, Mr. Poe," she said in an incredulous tone, "is it likely that someone *else* showed up and killed the poor girl while she was bathing? Isn't it far more logical to assume that the young wretch simply grabbed the silver as he fled the house after committing the horrid deed?"

"It can hardly be denied that—in postulating the existence of another, still unknown perpetrator—my conjecture appears unnecessarily complex," I replied. "Indeed, it is a manifest violation of the principle articulated by the medieval philosopher William of Occam, who famously stated, *'Entia non sunt multiplicanda praeter necessitatem'*—a precept which may be translated thusly: 'Of two competing theories or explanations, all other things being equal, the simpler one is to be preferred.'

"Nevertheless," I continued, "though pure deductive reasoning clearly points to Jesse McMahon as the obvious culprit, I cannot seem to free myself of the troubling sense that someone else was involved."

"Can it be, Mr. Poe," Mrs. Randall asked gently, "that you are simply letting your emotions color your judgment in this matter? You said yourself that you were overcome with pity when you saw the boy lying there in the street."

"It's true," Sissy said, reaching out to squeeze my right hand tenderly. "You know how sensitive you are, Eddie dear. Maybe you've begun to think that he was innocent because you ended up feeling so sorry for him."

"That possibility has occurred to me," I said with a sigh. "There can be little doubt that the mere sight of his dreadfully mangled body was productive of the most intense feelings of distress."

"Poor Eddie," said Sissy. "It's been a perfectly dreadful day for you, hasn't it? Beginning with Miss Bolton. Viewing her dead body must have been terribly upsetting, especially after seeing her so happy and full of life just yesterday."

"It has indeed been a day replete with occurrences of a most unsettling nature," I concurred.

"Well, if you want *my* opinion," said Mrs. Randall, "I think you should banish any doubts from your mind, Mr. Poe. The fact is that you've been absolutely marvelous. Why, you singlehandedly solved the entire case. The whole city regards you as a hero. Just look at the newspapers. To say nothing of the debt that Dr. Marston owes you. Heavens, the poor man's entire career would have been destroyed. Who knows—he may even have ended up in prison!

"And incidentally," she added, "I'm not sure I thanked you properly for your gift. It was very kind of you."

This latter statement referred to the copy of *The Dentalogia* which Dr. Marston had presented to me and which—knowing her admiration for the author—I had subsequently bestowed upon our hostess as a small token of gratitude for her hospitality. In truth, in offering her the volume, I was making an exceedingly negligible sacrifice, as I had no intention of ever so much as glancing at that preposterous work.

"It was nothing," I now truthfully replied.

At that moment, the rapping of the brass knocker affixed to the front door resounded through the house.

"Sally!" called Mrs. Randall. "Someone's at the door."

For a moment, the three of us sat wordlessly, listening for the expected sounds—the maid's footsteps proceeding down the main hallway, the opening of the door, the exchange of voices. Nothing beyond silence, however, greeted our ears. At length, the rapping noise occurred again, this time more emphatically.

"Can you believe it?" said Mrs. Randall, regarding Sissy and me with a look of astonishment. "That woman—impossible!"

Her visage flushed with annoyance, our hostess pushed her chair away from the table, rose to her feet, and hurried from the dining room.

"Did you see her face?" Sissy whispered to me when she had gone. "She looked absolutely *furious*."

"She can hardly be blamed," I replied, *sotto voce*. "I have rarely encountered a domestic servant so seemingly indifferent to her duties."

A few moments later, Mrs. Randall returned, her anger—to judge from her expression—having in no wise abated during her brief absence. In one hand, she carried an envelope.

"It's for you," she said, extending it to me across the table.

Somewhat surprised, I took it from her hand, tore open the sealed flap, and removed the letter, which I unfolded and proceeded to peruse.

"What does it say, Eddie?" Sissy inquired after a moment.

"It is a note from Mr. May," I replied, "thanking me for my part in resolving the tragedy. 'Though I take no joy in contemplating the terrible death met by poor Elsie's killer,' he writes, 'I cannot help but feel that he was struck down by the just hand of God.' "

"You see, Mr. Poe?" said Mrs. Randall, who had resumed her seat across the table. "What did I tell you? No one doubts that the young scoundrel was guilty."

"So it seems," I replied, my eyes still on the letter. "He goes on to say this: 'It is my understanding that you and your wife will be traveling to Concord tomorrow morning. As it happens, my nieces will also be aboard the stage. I would have escorted them home myself, but the condition of my wife—who remains prostrated with shock over the horrid event—forbids me from doing so. I must also remain in Boston to make funeral arrangements for Elsie, who, being an orphan, has no family to see to the matter. I am comforted in knowing, however, that my nieces will be journeying homeward in the company of so laudable a gentleman as yourself. I have taken the liberty of composing a letter to their mother, my sister, urging her to extend the greatest hospitality to you and your wife. I am aware, of course, of your literary differences with my brother-in-law, Mr. Alcott. (To be perfectly frank, I, too, have always found Bronson's pontificatings somewhat difficult to swallow.) In any event, there should be little problem in that regard, as he is away from home on one of his frequent lecture tours.' "

Here, I looked up from the letter and remarked to Sissy: "This is a most unexpected turn. It appears that we are being invited to reside in the Alcott abode during our sojourn in Concord."

"Have you made any other arrangements?" Mrs. Randall inquired.

"Not at all," I replied. "I assumed that we would find lodging at a local inn."

"It might be nice to stay in a more homey place," said Sissy in a somewhat wistful tone. Then—as if realizing that her comment might be interpreted as a criticism of our present lodgings—she hastily added: "Not that it could ever be as pleasant as your own house, Mrs. Randall."

"Well, my dear," said the latter, "you're more than welcome to visit again on your way back. And I can assure you," she added, casting a dark look in the direction of the kitchen, "that the next time you are here, you'll at least dine on better fare. There are going to be some changes made in this household. I've let things go on this way for far, *far* too long."

In view of the shocking and sorrowful events that had blighted the final day of their vacation, it was hardly to be wondered at that the mood of the Al-

cott girls was greatly subdued at the start of our journey. Even the excessively high-spirited Louisa—after an initial burst of *chattiness*—soon subsided into silence, gazing pensively out the window as the stage rumbled
along the road leading out of the city toward the village of Concord.

Louisa had taken the place to my left when we first climbed into the
coach; Sissy was settled on my right. Across from us sat the three remaining
girls: Anna, the oldest and prettiest, whom I had observed two days earlier
when she had marched to the front of Kimball's theater to rescue the intox-
icated Miss Bolton; her younger sister, Lizzie, a rosy-cheeked girl of perhaps
eleven years of age who huddled shyly against her older sibling, resting her
head on the shoulder of the latter; and the littlest one of all, May, an unusually pretty and self-possessed child of seven or eight, with eyes of a startlingly intense shade of blue and long, curling yellow hair.

As I have previously noted, these three girls, like their sister, Louisa, had
fallen into a profoundly uncommunicative state almost immediately upon
our departure. Their silence, I felt, reflected the melancholy frame of mind
into which the murder of their friend had very naturally cast them. Added
to this was the sense of constraint they undoubtedly felt at finding themselves in the company of two more-or-less complete strangers. Indeed, it is
conceivable that we might have made the entire trip without exchanging
more than a few polite words had it not been for an involuntary physio-
logical reaction on the part of little May.

We had been traveling for slightly more than an hour when the distinctive noise of *borborygmi,* or growling of the stomach, was to be heard, so
loud as to be audible even above the rattling of the vehicle. This very common symptom of hunger—caused, as the reader is no doubt aware, when
the walls of the empty alimentary organ grind against each other—is a universal source of keen personal embarrassment when it occurs in a social
situation. As there were six of us inside the coach, it would have been impossible to identify the source of this disturbance had not the little girl
(who, as I had already observed, was much given to those comical verbal
blunders known as *malapropisms*) immediately exclaimed:

"Oh, dear! I must be even more ravishing than I thought!"

"The word is '*ravenous,*'" said Louisa. "And your stomach wouldn't be
making those ridiculous noises if you weren't such a little fussbudget. We
told you to finish your breakfast this morning."

"But you know how much I detest porridge," responded the little girl
with a pout.

"Heavens, what did you expect?" said the oldest sister, Anna, in a chiding tone. "A farewell feast? You are altogether too particular, May. Your thoughts shouldn't be on your own selfish desires, anyway, but on our poor departed friend, Elsie."

"Well, you needn't be so snippy," protested the little girl. "As a matter of fact, I was thinking about Elsie only a moment ago."

"And what were thinking, May dear?" inquired Lizzie with a gentle smile.

"How dreadful it is that she will never cook for us again," replied the child with a tragic sigh. "Remember that lovely nut loaf she made for us last week? Why, it makes my mouth water just picturing it."

"I still can't believe she's gone," said Lizzie.

"Do you think it was wrong of us to leave before the funeral?" asked Louisa. "Perhaps we should have stayed another day."

"How could we?" said Anna. "Marmee made us promise that we'd come home today, and she'd be worried sick if the stage arrived without us being on it. Besides, you and I can't afford to miss any more school, Louisa. We've already fallen horridly behind on our lessons."

"Yes, I suppose you're right," said Louisa with a sigh. "It does seem a shame, though, that we won't be there to pay our last respects."

"I haven't mentioned it till now," said the bashful sister, Lizzie, "but I picked some flowers from Aunt Lucretia's garden and placed them beside the bathtub as a remembrance. I was frightened to go into the bedroom at first because of the dreadful thing that happened there, but then I remembered how good Elsie always was to us, so I forced myself to do it."

"That was sweet of you, dear," said Anna, placing her arm around her sister's shoulders and giving her a hug.

"I left something by the tub, too!" exclaimed little May. "A picture of Elsie with angel wings, flying up to heaven. I drew it this morning."

"I don't suppose Elsie was an angel, but a regular down-to-earth girl, full of fun and mischief," said Louisa. "But her heart was pure and true. She was a good 'little pilgrim,' as Marmee would say, and if anyone deserves to be let into the Celestial City, she does."

"Your mother must miss having her children around," said Sissy, addressing the four girls as one. "How long have you been away?"

"Since Tuesday last," answered Anna. "It *shall* be nice to be back home again and see Marmee."

"Do you think she'll like the gift we are bringing her?" said Amy.

"Like it?" exclaimed Louisa. "Why, she'll be tickled pink."

"What gift is that?" inquired Sissy.

"Let me show you," said Anna, pulling open the drawstring of her purse and removing a rectangular object that I recognized at once as the type of small, morocco case used to house daguerreotype pictures. She then passed this item to Sissy, who undid the little hook and parted the two halves of the case.

Peering down, I saw that the portrait was of the four sisters. They were posed in the most charming manner imaginable, with Anna seated in the center—Louisa and Lizzie standing on either side of her, clinging fondly to her arms—and little May seated in front, resting her head on her older sister's lap. While perfectly capturing the individual likenesses—and even something of the personalities—of the four girls, the daguerreotypist had also, in his arrangement of his subjects, managed to portray them as a single—intensely loving—indivisibly bound—entity.

"I'm sure she'll treasure it," said Sissy, returning the picture to Anna. "You all look so lovely."

"It was taken by Mr. Ballinger," remarked May. "They say he's the finest daguerreotypist in Boston."

"How funny," said Sissy. "Eddie and I planned to have our picture taken by him, too—for *our* Muddy. We went to his studio yesterday morning and were told to come back in an hour. But of course, with everything that happened, we never returned."

Reaching over, I took my wife's hand and gave it a gentle squeeze. "There will still be ample time to have our portraits made, Sissy dear," I said. "Following our stay in Concord, we will return to Boston and remain at Mrs. Randall's for at least a day or two prior to our departure for New York."

"Don't mean to be a nosy Parker," remarked Louisa, "but if you don't mind my asking, Mr. Poe, what brings you to Concord, anyway?"

"Your curiosity is perfectly natural, Miss Alcott," I replied.

"I ain't 'Miss Alcott'—just Louy," she declared.

"Well, then, Louy," I said, "we are traveling to your village in order to consult with Dr. Samuel Farragut about my wife's health."

"Oh, I'm very sorry to hear that you aren't feeling well, Mrs. Poe," said Louy. "But whatever's wrong, I'm sure Dr. Farragut will cure it. People come from all over to see him. They say he's a regular miracle-worker."

"I hope that is true," said Sissy.

Something in my dear wife's voice caused me to peer at her more narrowly. From the excessive pallor of her complexion, I saw that my efforts to shield her from any undue strain during our brief stay in Boston had been in vain. The trying events of the preceding day, I noted with dismay, had clearly taken a toll on her all-too-fragile constitution.

"Are you all right, Sissy dearest?" I inquired.

"I'm fine, Eddie," she responded, mustering a smile that—in its brave attempt at reassurance—only caused my heart to ache more deeply.

A somber atmosphere now descended on the coach, as the four sisters relapsed into a profound and gloomy silence. As for myself, my mind was wholly occupied with concern over Sissy's health. Indeed—though I was still not fully convinced of the McMahon boy's guilt—I had ceased to give the question any thought. In the end, it was none of my affair, but a matter for the police to resolve. I had come to Boston not to solve a crime, but to do everything in my power to save my darling's life.

For the next twenty or thirty minutes, the six of us rode along without exchanging so much as a word. This dreary situation persisted until Louy—as though rousing herself from a stupor—suddenly exclaimed:

"My patience, how blue we are! Elsie would never approve of the four of us moping about in this way. You know how much she loved to laugh and joke and have fun!"

"What do you propose, Louy?" said Anna. "You can hardly expect us to be carefree and gay at such a time."

"Well, at least we can do something to while away the time. How about a game of Rigmarole?"

"Oooh yes," exclaimed May, clapping her hands.

"And what precisely is the nature of this pastime?" I inquired.

"It's very very amusing, Mr. Poe," replied Louy. "I'm sure you'll enjoy it. One person begins a story, any nonsense they like, and tells as long as they please, only taking care to stop short at some exciting point. Then the next person takes it up and does the same. It makes a perfect jumble of tragical-comical stuff to laugh over. Who wants to go first?"

"I will," said Anna. After a brief pause, during which the rest of us gazed at her expectantly, she launched into her narration:

"Once upon a time, there was a beautiful but very poor young girl named Margaret who was always envying her richer friends, for they had such beautiful jewelry and clothing to wear, while all she owned were a few tattered frocks, hardly better than rags. One day, while she was out walking in the woods, she met a little old woman who had a big, heavy sack slung over her shoulder. The woman, who was partially crippled, seemed to be having a terrible time of it. 'May I offer you some help?' asked Margaret.

'That is very kind of you, my dear,' said the old woman, 'but, like all of us, I must carry my burden by myself. Since you have shown yourself to be a very good-hearted young lady, however, I wish to offer you a reward. If you look into those waters there,' she said, pointing a gnarled finger at a nearby pond, 'you will see something very wonderful.' Filled with curiosity, Margaret walked to the edge of the pond and peered into the surface. Much to her surprise, she saw—"

"A beautiful mermaid!" little May broke in excitedly. "She had lovely curling yellow hair and big blue eyes, very much like mine. Reaching out of the water with her slender white arms, she grabbed Margaret by the shoulders and pulled her to the bottom of the pond, where she sat Margaret down on a chair made of coral and then disappeared into a little cave. A few minutes later she came out again, carrying a handsome box made of seashells. 'What is that?' asked Margaret, who was very surprised to find that she could breathe underwater. 'It is my magical paint box,' said the mermaid. 'I am a wonderful artist, and you are so pretty that I would like to make your portrait.' Margaret was very pleased. The mermaid then set to work, using a large sheet of seaweed as a canvas. It took her just a few minutes to finish. 'Come see the beautiful picture I've made,' she said. Margaret swam over to look. Just then, however—"

"A fishing line came down, caught Margaret around the throat, and yanked her to the surface," cut in Louy. "Before she knew what was happening, she was dragged into a rowboat, where a handsome young man sat holding a fishing pole and looking perfectly amazed. 'Christopher Columbus!' he cried. 'I thought you were a sunfish. Who *are* you and what were you doing at the bottom of this pond?' Margaret tried to answer but found that her voice was gone. Spotting a pencil and notebook that the young man happened to have brought along with him, she snatched it up and wrote the story of everything that had happened to her that day. When the young man read it, he marveled at how splendid it was. 'Why, you are a regular Shakespeare!' he cried. 'And pretty, to boot! Please allow me to introduce myself. I am Prince Theodore, but you may call me Teddy. I have been searching high and low for a wife, and I wonder if you would do me the honor of marrying me?' Margaret didn't give a fig about love and such nonsense. Still, since Prince Teddy was so handsome—and had such excellent taste in literature—she saw no good reason to refuse. So he carried her off to his castle, where—"

Interrupting herself, Louy smiled encouragingly at her sister Lizzie, who had been watching each of her siblings in turn with an expression of rapt fascination. Now, however—as she realized that she was being invited to continue the narration—a horrified expression suffused her gentle countenance. "Oh, gracious!" she cried. "I can never think of what to say. I much prefer just listening to the rest of you, if you don't mind."

"That's all right, dear," said Louy, reaching across the cabin to pat her sister on the knee. "I'm sure Mrs. Poe will be happy to take over."

All eyes now fastened on my dear wife, who, after collecting her thoughts for a few moments, spoke thusly:

"Now that she was a princess, Margaret had riches beyond her wildest dreams. No other girl in the entire kingdom had such magnificent jewelry and clothing. She was very surprised to find, however, that she *still* wasn't completely satisfied. For a long time, she could not imagine what was missing from her life. Then it occurred to her—a baby! How wonderful it would be, she thought, to have a child to cherish and care for. But when she mentioned this to her husband, he said: 'Why do we need children when we have each other? Aren't I your own little Teddy? And you my dearest little Maggie? But if you really feel the need of something to take care of, I will see what I can do.' Well, Margaret waited and waited, wondering what her husband had in mind. A few weeks later, as she sat reading in the garden, she looked up from her book to find the prince standing before her, holding a basket. 'This is for you,' he said with a smile. Margaret took the basket from his hand, opened the lid, and gave a gasp of surprise. Inside was the most remarkable kitty anyone had ever seen. Its fur was white as snow, with bright red stripes that went all around its body. Even its eyes were red-and-white striped. 'Oh, thank you, Teddy,' she said, lifting out the puss and hugging it to her cheek. 'I will call it Peppermint.' "

Here, my darling wife turned in my direction and indicated, with a gesture of her hand, that she was now passing the narration over to me. Being the last of our little party to contribute to the tale, I paused for a moment to formulate a suitable conclusion. I then cleared my throat and said:

"For years, Prince Theodore and his bride enjoyed a love that was more than a love—a love so singular in its intensity as to be envied by the seraphs in heaven. By slow degrees, however—through the instrumentality of the Fiend Intemperance—the general temperament and character of the prince underwent a radical alteration for the worse. He grew, day by day, more moody—more irritable—more regardless of the feelings of others. He suffered himself to use intemperate language to his wife. At length, he even offered her personal violence. The cat, Peppermint—upon whom Prince

Theodore had previously lavished all the tenderness of a doting parent—was not exempt from the deplorable effects of its master's ill temper.

"One day, after imbibing more than his wonted share of Amontillado wine, Prince Theodore was staggering down the central corridor of his castle when he encountered the feline. Imagining, in his stupefied condition, that the creature was staring at him in an insolent manner, the prince roughly seized Peppermint; whereupon the frightened animal inflicted a slight wound upon its master's hand with his teeth. Instantly, the fury of a demon possessed the inebriated man. He began to throttle the helpless feline, who emitted an inhuman screech of terror. Alerted by the noise, Princess Margaret quickly materialized upon the scene and, crying for her husband to desist, attempted to wrestle the animal from his grasp. Goaded by her interference into a rage more than demoniacal, the prince released his hold on the cat—wrapped his hands around the throat of his wife—and strangled her until her body slumped limply to the floor.

"The dreadful deed accomplished, Prince Theodore set himself forthwith, and with entire deliberation, to the task of concealing the body. Lifting it in his arms, he bore it down to the deepest reaches of the castle's dungeon, where he placed it in a small damp vault behind a massive door of iron. As he paused to take a final look at the face of his once-beloved wife, he was startled to see her eyelids quiver and her slightly parted lips begin to move. His wife was not dead after all! All at once, her eyes opened wide. As they focused on her husband, a look of inexpressible sorrow passed over her countenance. Hardly knowing what he was doing, the maddened prince bolted from the vault and secured the iron door behind him, entombing Princess Margaret alive! As he fled from that region of horror, he could hear her anguished voice echoing through the dungeon: 'For the love of God, Teddy! For the love of—' "

Though I had yet to reach the climax of my narrative, I was prevented from continuing by the intervention of my wife, who—administering a sharp poke to my right side with one of her elbows—leaned close to my ear and whispered, "Eddie! What in the world . . . ?"

"Why, what is the matter?" I inquired, looking at Sissy, who, with a sharp movement of her head, directed my attention to the opposite side of the cabin. So engrossed had I been in my story—so vividly had I conjured up its images and events before my own mind's eye—that I had become oblivious of my auditors. I now perceived that my tale had produced a very marked effect upon the three girls seated across from me. Anna's countenance wore a look of thunderstricken horror—Lizzie's face had grown ab-normally pale—while little May sat whimpering audibly and seemed to be on the brink of tears.

Only Louy appeared to have enjoyed my contribution to the tale. "What happens next, Mr. Poe?" she eagerly inquired. "Aren't you going to finish?"

I cast another glance at my wife, who gave me an uncharacteristically stern, if not admonitory, look, as if to say: *You had better come up with some-thing more suitable for juvenile sensibilities, Eddie.*

Chastened by this tacit warning, I hastily contrived a new conclusion for my story, far sunnier than the one I had originally intended. In this revised version, Prince Teddy, after being overcome with remorse, frees his wife from her prison, renounces drink, and returns to his earlier, happier state, enjoying a long and blissful life with Princess Margaret and Peppermint the cat.

As the three sisters across from me expelled sighs of relief, my dear wife remarked: "You'll have to forgive my husband, girls. He means well, but he lets his imagination run away with him sometimes."

Though this observation was intended for Anna, Lizzie, and May, it was Louy who responded.

"No need for apologies," she said. "The very last bit was a trifle senti-mental for my taste, but otherwise I thought it was first rate. I don't see how you can think up such deliciously creepy stories, Mr. Poe. I'm *so* glad you accepted Uncle Samuel's invitation to stay with us at Hillside. What jolly times we're sure to have!"

CHAPTER TEN

⌒

SITUATED APPROXIMATELY ONE-HALF mile from the center of the village, Hillside—as the Alcott home was denominated—was one of the
oldest dwellings in Concord. Its distinctive architectural features—peaked
gables, gambrel roof, massive stone chimney—attested to its antiquity,
the central portion of the wooden edifice having been constructed in
the latter years of the seventeenth century. Subsequent improvements had
transformed the original four-room farmhouse into a substantially larger,
though by no means ostentatious, residence. Sheltered by magnificent elms
whose branches blazed with the glorious effulgence of the New England autumn, the house—painted a muted olive hue—presented a most pleasing
appearance. An air of enchantment seemed to hang about the place—a
placid, intensely *homey* atmosphere that, upon my first glimpse of it, immediately infused my soul with a sense of the greatest calm.

The spirit of tranquility that pervaded the picturesque homestead was
personified by Mrs. Alcott herself. Marmee—to employ the endearingly
childish soubriquet by which her daughters called her—was a stout, somewhat plain-looking woman of middle years. Though she bore little physical
resemblance to my own dearest Muddy, she shared with the latter a quality
of sheer maternal benevolence that endowed her with a singular charm.

From the worshipful tones in which her daughters invariably spoke of
her, I had already deduced that an unusual bond of intimacy—even greater
than that which one normally obtains in such relationships—existed be-

tween the four girls and their mother. Now, upon our arrival at Hillside, I witnessed this firsthand. Although Louy and her sisters had been away from home for only one week, they flew into their Marmee's arms as though they had endured a much longer separation. Tears were shed—cries of joy emitted. The fervor with which Mrs. Alcott embraced her little ones was undoubtedly made all the more intense by the circumstances of their reunion. News of the tragic events in Boston had already reached her ears, and it was with the greatest imaginable relief that she welcomed her babies back into the sanctuary of the maternal bosom.

Her behavior toward Sissy and me was far more restrained. This was hardly to be wondered at. The invitation that had brought us to her door had not, after all, been extended by herself. We had never set eyes on each other before. She knew me, of course—but only as a writer who had been openly and repeatedly critical of the literary effusions of her absent husband.

Once she had perused the letter from her brother, however (transmitted by Anna into whose care it had been entrusted), Mrs. Alcott's manner underwent a material alteration from mere politeness to genuine amiability, and we were welcomed into the household with all the warmth and hospitality for which we could have hoped.

The four girls sharing two bedchambers, Sissy and I were given the use of the room belonging to Louy and Lizzie, who moved in temporarily with their sisters. After unpacking our bags, we joined the family for a simple but savory meal of cold chicken, biscuits, and boiled potatoes. Then—my dear wife feeling excessively fatigued from our journey—we retired to our chamber, leaving Mrs. Alcott seated in an easy chair by the hearth, with Louy at her feet, Lizzie and May perched on either arm, and Anna leaning against the back. As we mounted the staircase, I could hear Louy say in an imploring tone: "Tell us a story, Mother, before we go to bed. The one about traveling to the Celestial City and fighting Apollyon and passing through the valley where the hobgoblins are!"

I awoke to sunlight filtering through muslin-curtained windows. For several moments, I lay in bed, uncertain as to my whereabouts. It was not until I glanced about and perceived the unmistakable signs of girlish habitation—the engraved prints of puppy dogs and pussycats torn from popular magazines and affixed to the walls—the shelves holding an array of playthings, including a half-dozen rag dolls (some in a state of extreme disrepair)—the wooden pegs upon which were hung small bonnets and shawls and other items of female apparel—that an awareness of my surroundings came flooding back to me.

Leaping from my bed, I quickly performed my ablutions and donned my clothing. I then crossed to the opposite side of the room, where Sissy lay sleeping. After gently awakening her, I stepped into the hallway and closed the door behind me. As I waited for her to make ready, I could hear the muffled sound of voices emanating from belowstairs.

Five minutes later, my angel emerged from the room, appearing much refreshed, though still—to my eyes—worrisomely gaunt, her face having lost so much of its usual plumpness that her cheekbones were visible. I gave no indication of my concern, however, but rather complimented her on her radiant loveliness, then offered my arm and ushered her downstairs.

Descending to the dining area, we found the four girls and their mother already at their breakfast, the table being set with large platters of savory foodstuffs: buckwheat pancakes, fried eggs, biscuits, sausages, and ham. This feast, I was to discover, represented a radical departure from the usual fare consumed by the family, who—adhering to an exceedingly Spartan diet based on Mr. Alcott's vegetarian principles—rarely ate more than apples, cold water, and coarse bread in the mornings. With her husband away on his lecture tour, however, Mrs. Alcott had prepared a special welcome-home treat for her daughters, who had nearly completed their meal by the time Sissy and I made our appearance.

After being warmly greeted by Louy and her sisters, we took our places at the table; whereupon Mrs. Alcott immediately loaded two plates with large helpings of the delicacies and set them before us.

"Sorry I can't stay to keep you company, Mr. Poe," said Louy as I tucked my napkin into the collar of my shirt, took hold of my fork, and fell to, "but Anna and I must be off."

"I simply can't wait until next year when I am old enough to go to school and wear nice clothes every day and play with other girls at recess," remarked little May.

"Was there ever a child in such haste to grow up?" said Louy. "You should be grateful, May, that you don't have to peg away at schoolwork all the live-long day. Mr. Hosmer's lessons can be dull as the desert in the Sahara. And some of the girls are dreadful snobs who plague you if you don't know your lessons, or tease you if your family isn't rich, or laugh at you if your clothes aren't just the fashion."

"That's the reason I stay here and get my lessons from Papa," offered

Lizzie, whose inordinate timidity evidently prevented her from venturing out into the world.

"Lucky girl," said Louy. "I'd much rather be at home working on my new play, *The Witch's Curse: An Operatic Tragedy.* It's rather a nice thing, quite the best I've ever written, though I'm having a bit of trouble figuring out a suitably exciting climax."

"I don't mean to act in any more plays after this time," said Anna, laying down her utensils. "I'm getting too old for such things."

"Fiddlesticks," cried Louy. "You are the best actress we've got, and there'll be an end to everything if you quit the boards."

"Did you know that Mr. Poe's mother was a famous actress?" interposed Sissy, who—I could not fail to note—had barely sampled her food, while I had already emptied my plate of a considerable portion of its contents.

"Really?" cried Louy, gazing at me with excited eyes.

"Indeed," I said, washing down a mouthful of pancake and sausage with a swig of strong coffee. "My sainted mother, Elizabeth Arnold Poe, was one of the ornaments of the American stage. Her performance in the ingenue *rôle* of Biddy Blair in David Garrick's *Miss in Her Teens* won plaudits from the most eminent theatrical critics of the day, while her portrayal of the doomed Cordelia in *King Lear* was hailed as a marvel of the thespian's art."

"Oh, how splendid," Louy exclaimed. "I'd love to try my hand at Shakespeare one day. *Macbeth* is my very favorite. I've always wanted to do the killing part. 'Is that a dagger I see before me?' " And here, the young girl rolled her eyes and clutched at the air in the manner of a classical tragedian. Though performed with perfect sincerity, the effect was so comical that it was only with the greatest effort that I managed to repress a smile.

"Well, dearies," said Mrs. Alcott, "you mustn't tarry any longer. You will have plenty of time to chat with Mr. Poe and compose your masterpiece and do whatever else your heart desires when tomorrow comes around, Louy."

"Hurrah for Saturdays," cried Louy, rising from her chair. "The perfect time for lounging and larking!"

"Once you have finished your chores, of course," added Mrs. Alcott. "Which reminds me, dear. Will you bring in some more firewood when you come home from school? Our supply is running low."

"Happy to oblige, Marmee," said Louy, giving her mother a kiss on the cheek. "That's Poppa's job, and since I'm the man of the house when he is away, it's only right that I take over."

Anna, too, had gotten to her feet. All at once, the serenity of our meal was broken by a startling occurrence. As the pretty young woman stepped toward her mother, she gave a sudden, violent lurch, as if thrown off her balance, while emitting a sharp cry of distress. Only the quick, reflexive motion of her hands, which immediately clutched at the edge of the table, prevented her from crashing to the floor.

As the rest of us cried out in surprise, Mrs. Alcott leapt from her chair and hurried to her daughter's side.

"Goodness, dear, are you all right?" she cried. "What on earth happened?"

Her face flushed with anger and embarrassment, Anna quickly bent to the floor. When she stood erect again, one hand was clutching a small red object which I immediately identified as a brightly colored rubber ball.

Waving it in an accusatory fashion in the direction of her younger sister Lizzie, the young woman exclaimed: "It's this stupid cat toy. I've asked you a hundred times, Lizzie, to keep it in your bedroom."

Then, in an access of irritation, she drew back her hand and flung the ball into the parlor. It bounced several times on the floorboards before rolling to a rest on the hearth rug, where it was immediately pounced upon by a handsome calico cat that had been curled on the cushion of Mrs. Alcott's easy chair.

"Really, Anna," said Louy, "you needn't be such a crosspatch. There's no harm done."

"That's all well and good for *you* to say," replied her sister. "You didn't give your foot a dreadful wrench."

"Come, you poor wounded soul," said Louy, stepping to her sister's side and taking her by the arm. "You can lean on me as we go. Good-bye, everyone. We are a pair of regular grouches this morning, but we will come home perfect angels."

No sooner had the two girls departed than Mrs. Alcott came over to Lizzie, whose normally placid expression had been replaced by a look of acute distress, evidently brought on by the scolding she had just received from her older sister. Even with her head bent low, I could see the tears welling up in her eyes.

"There, there, dear," said Mrs. Alcott, reaching down to give the little girl a hug. "You mustn't take Anna's sharp words to heart. All of us get impatient at times."

"But *you* never do, Mother," said the child with a tremulous voice.

"Oh, but I do, my child. It's just that I have learned to control it by checking the hasty words that rise to my lips. Your sister loves you very much, as we all do. Now, dry your eyes, dear. It is making poor Portia dreadfully sad to see you so upset. Why, just look at her—I do believe she is still hungry and would like another taste of sausage."

This latter remark was in reference to an exceedingly shabby-looking doll that sat upon the little girl's lap. Throughout the meal, Lizzie, between bites of food, had held her fork to the stitched mouth of the tattered manikin, as though offering it sustenance.

"*Portia,*" said Sissy as Lizzie patted her eyes with her napkin. "What an interesting name for a doll."

"She belonged to Louy," chimed in little May. "She was named after the heroine in one of Shakespeare's plays. *The Merchant of Vengeance,* I believe."

"*Venice,* dear," said Mrs. Alcott, who had resumed her seat and was sipping from a cup of tea.

"Louy can be frightfully hard on her toys," Lizzie said softly. To illustrate this observation, she peeled away the little plaid blanket that was wrapped around the doll's body, exposing a pair of ragged stumps where its arms should have been.

"They came off one day when Louy was swinging her around and around in circles," explained Lizzie. "After that, Louy lost interest in her, so I adopted her. I have a whole collection of injured dollies in my room. I take them in and nurse them when no one else wants them."

"Yes, your infirmary was the first sight that greeted me when I awoke this morning," I declared. "I do not hesitate to say, Miss Alcott, that it is exceedingly kind of you to lavish such tenderness upon these poor orphaned playthings. Speaking as someone who was bereft of parental care at a painfully early age, I can attest to—"

I progressed no further with my remarks; for at that moment, my attention—as well as that of my auditors—was diverted by a very loud and insistent *rapping* emanating from the rear of the house.

"Who can that be at such an early hour?" asked Mrs. Alcott, placing her teacup down on the table.

"I'll go see, Mother," cried little May, springing from the chair and dashing toward the kitchen.

A moment later, as the rest of us listened in silence, I heard the back door open and a low-pitched voice—obviously that of a man—speak a few words, too muffled for me to distinguish. In another instant, May came running back into the dining area, looking exceedingly agitated.

"Good heavens, child!" cried Mrs. Alcott at the sight of her daughter. "What's the matter?"

"Oh, Mother, there's a man at the door," said the little girl. "He's awfully strange-looking and gave me quite a start when I first set eyes on him. He asked for some food."

"Just a poor homeless fellow, I am sure," said Mrs. Alcott, getting to her feet. "I will go speak to him."

As our hostess repaired to the kitchen, Lizzie—whose complexion had paled at her sister's words—turned to the latter and, in a quivering voice, asked: "What does he look like, May? Is he really so horrid?"

"He's like nobody I've ever seen," said the little girl, who had resumed her place at the table and whose words came spilling out in an excited rush. "He wears his hat pulled very low, almost down to his eyes, which are very small and strange—awfully. You can just see his eyebrows. They are very dark, especially compared to his face, which is pasty-white, even whiter than yours is right now, Lizzie. It's his beard, though, that makes him look so peculiar. It is very long and bushy, growing halfway down his chest, and the queerest color you ever saw—so bright red it's practically orange.

"Brrr," she added, giving her shoulders an exaggerated shake. "Just thinking of him gives me the shivers."

"Gracious me," gasped her older sister, clutching her mutilated dollie, Portia, tightly to her body.

In another moment, Mrs. Alcott reappeared.

"Has he gone away, Mother?" asked Lizzie.

"Yes, dear," said our hostess, reseating herself. "There's no need to be worried. He was only a beggar, as I supposed. Poor man. I gave him the rest of last night's chicken and he went off very happily."

"Oh, Mother, you didn't," said May. "I was so looking forward to eating that for lunch."

"Now, now, my child," said the mother gently. "We may not be wealthy, but we have more than enough to eat and drink and a good many comforts and pleasures compared to others. It is a blessing to be able to lend a help-ing hand to those less fortunate than ourselves."

"Yes, Marmee," said the little girl, looking somewhat chastened. "Thank you for reminding me. I'll try not to be so selfish in the future."

"If you are still hungry, May," Sissy interposed, "you are welcome to the rest of my breakfast." Then, casting an apologetic look at our hostess, she added: "The food is very delicious, Mrs. Alcott, but I'm afraid I'm not terri-bly hungry."

"That's all right, dear," the latter responded. "I'm just sorry to see that your appetite is off. It's good that you are visiting Dr. Farragut today. Have you arranged to see him at any particular time?"

It was I who replied to this query. "In point of fact, we should be on our way right now."

After receiving directions to the doctor's home from Mrs. Alcott, Sissy and I rose from the table—bid our hostess and her two daughters farewell—then donned our outer garments and took our leave.

According to the instructions imparted to us by Mrs. Alcott, the doctor's house could be reached by one of two means. Had we been traveling on horseback, the quickest way would have been been via the Lexington Road. As we were proceeding on foot, however, we chose the alternate route, a narrow path through the woods that served as a shortcut to our destination.

It was a morning of singular beauty, the dazzling sun and limpid sky imparting to the atmosphere a quality of crystalline purity. As we entered the footpath arm-in-arm, I glanced at my darling wife, who already seemed greatly invigorated by the crisp autumn air. An unwonted sense of hopefulness suffused my bosom. If the mere atmosphere of Concord could serve as such an elixir, perhaps the natural medicaments of the celebrated Dr. Farragut would indeed prove as efficacious as they were reputed to be.

We spoke little as we proceeded along the charming woodland path, which was bordered by birch trees and carpeted with golden leaves. Very gradually, an odd conception took hold of me. I began to imagine that Sissy and I were characters from a tale in one of her beloved collections of European wonder-stories—brother and sister, cast out of their home by an unnatural stepparent, who find themselves wandering through a strange forest until they come upon a magical dwelling constructed of various confections.

"I sincerely hope that you are wrong, Eddie," Sissy remarked with a smile when I mentioned this phantasy to her. "Especially for your sake. If you recall, the nice person who lives in the gingerbread house turns out to be a cannibal who plans to devour the little boy after fattening him up."

"Indeed, I had forgotten how that particular story ends," I said. "How gruesome! For sheer unmitigated horror, few imaginative works can equal the seemingly artless narratives of the European peasantry."

"Oh, I can think of some," said Sissy with a mischievous expression. "Written by a certain American author—my favorite in the world."

At these endearing words, a sensation of the purest love coursed through every fibre of my being. Only the impediment of Sissy's bonnet prevented me from placing an impassioned kiss upon her cheek. As no mere words could convey the intensity of my emotion at that instant, I merely gave her gloved right hand a fervent squeeze. Silently, we continued on our way.

At length the trail led us to a clearing, at the center of which stood not a dwelling composed of pastry, gumdrops, and peppermint canes, but a large square house built of wood and painted a somewhat faded shade of gray. Behind it lay a spacious garden whose luxuriant shrubs and neatly disposed plants seemed to bask in the abundant sunlight. Loosely tethered to a hitching post at the side of the house stood a roan chestnut mare, lazily nibbling on the grass.

As Sissy and I approached this handsome abode, the front door creaked open. Out stepped a man who, after pausing for an instant on the porch, descended the stairs and strolled around the side of the house toward the masticating equine. Becoming aware of our presence, he tipped his hat, revealing his countenance, which had been shaded by the brim.

Beside me, I felt Sissy stiffen and heard a soft involuntary gasp issue from her lips. Her reaction was perfectly understandable; for the visage thus exposed was one of the most unsettling I had ever witnessed outside the precincts of P. T. Barnum's Hall of Human Oddities. It was not the features of the man (whose age was impossible to determine) that made him so disquieting. The dimensions of his nose were unexceptional—his mouth was well formed—he possessed the normal complement of eyes. What rendered him remarkable was his complexion—every inch of which was covered with pustules of an angry crimson hue. In terms of sheer unsightliness, his condition was surpassed only by the grotesque dermatological abnormality that endowed Barnum's "Alligator Boy" with his presumed resemblance to a member of the crocodilian species.

Despite the disfiguring effects of his affliction—which might have been supposed to make him somewhat diffident around strangers—the man seemed perfectly at ease. Indeed, after introducing himself as Mr. Ezra Winslow, he appeared positively eager to draw attention to his diseased countenance.

"Blasted eczema," he said, pointing to his face, as though we might somehow have failed to perceive that it was entirely overspread with flaming red sores. "Itches like the devil. Tried every quack in Boston. Then I heard about old Doc Farragut. Gave me this here cream."

Reaching into his coat pocket, he extracted a small cylindrical container.

"Farragut's Vegetable Balm for Morbid Eruptions of the Skin," he continued, reading from the label. "Made of balsam fir and gum myrrh and bitterroot and heaven knows what. The doc swears it'll fix me right up."

"If my own experience with Dr. Farragut's botanical ointments is any guide," I said, "I am sure that it will prove highly efficacious."

"Hope you're right, mister. It's getting so my own wife don't enjoy my company at the dinner table. Well, good luck to you both."

Untying the reins from the hitching post, he then mounted his steed and, with another tip of the hat, trotted off toward the Lexington Road.

No sooner had he vanished from sight than we were startled by a booming voice, emanating from nearby:

"You know, the very first medications I ever concocted were meant for insect bites and rashes. You might say I started from scratch."

Turning our eyes toward the house, we saw, framed in an open window, a figure whom I took to be Dr. Farragut himself. Seated beside the wide-flung casement—through which he had evidently overheard our conversation with Mr. Winslow—he was visible only from the shoulders up.

"Come on in, friends," he said, rising from his chair. "Meet you at the door."

Taking Sissy by the arm, I guided her to the front of the house. As we ascended the porch steps, the green-painted door swung open and there stood the personage upon whom all my hopes for my dear wife's recovery were now fastened.

At my first glimpse of him, I felt greatly encouraged. From all that I had heard about Dr. Farragut, I knew him to be a man approaching seventy. And yet, so sheerly robust was the figure now standing before me that he might have been twenty—nay, thirty!—years younger. He was about five feet ten inches in height, with broad shoulders—erect carriage—and exceedingly well-proportioned frame. His snow-white hair was thick and glossy and fell in a leonine mane to the level of his shoulders. His forehead was capacious—his chin massive and projecting, indicative of exceptional mental energy. His complexion positively glowed with health, while his clear blue eyes beamed with intelligence and warmth. Altogether, he presented a picture of such youthful good health as to be a walking advertisement for the benefits of his botanical cures.

"Mr. and Mrs. Poe, I presume," he said with a smile that caused the corners of his eyes to crinkle. "What a pleasure. Come in, come in."

Leading us to the parlor, Dr. Farragut invited us to seat ourselves on a horsehair sofa, while he lowered himself onto a facing armchair. The room was neat—simply furnished—and exceedingly bright, sunlight flooding in through the unobstructed windows, whose sills were lined with an array of small clay pots containing a variety of flowering plants. Framed engravings—a few depicting scriptural scenes but most of botanical subjects—hung upon three of the walls. The fourth wall was entirely occupied by a mahogany bookcase. Its shelves were packed with volumes, a number of them—to judge by their time-darkened bindings—of an excessive antiquity.

"Well, well, well, how delightful to meet you both," said Dr. Farragut, bringing his hands together with a loud slap. "I was expecting you yesterday—but of course, when I heard about that nasty business in Boston, I assumed you'd be delayed. What a horror! Thank God you were there to solve the case, Mr. Poe. Why, your own Monsieur Dupin couldn't have done any better."

"Though gratified by your obvious familiarity with my tales of ratiocination," I replied, "I do not wish to claim more credit for the resolution of that tragic affair than is warranted." This statement was no mere declaration of false modesty but rather a genuine reflection of the nagging qualms I continued to feel about the culpability of the McMahon boy.

"Pish!" cried the doctor. "Why, that poor girl's killer would be out there yet if it weren't for you. I know what you did, Mr. Poe—read all about it in the paper. Masterful piece of detection. And I speak as a man who knows something about the subject. A doctor's got to be a bit of a detective himself, you know—observing the smallest details of a case, searching for clues, drawing the proper deductions."

Here, he turned his clear blue eyes on Sissy and, after studying her countenance for a moment, spoke to her thusly: "Take your own case, my dear. To the practiced eye, the signs of your condition are unmistakable."

"Oh, Dr. Farragut," cried my darling wife, "is it really so bad as all that?"

"Not at all, my child, not at all. On the contrary. I'm very heartened by what I see. Of course, I'll be able to tell a great deal more once I've examined you. I can say this much, however—you've done the right thing by seeking out my help. Now, come," he continued, getting to his feet.

Taking his proffered right hand, Sissy rose from the sofa while I stood up beside her.

"No need to get up, Mr. Poe," said the doctor. "It's better for you to stay here. The examination should take no more than, oh, twenty or twenty-five minutes. A half-hour at the most. You can read a book, if you like. You'll find plenty to interest you."

As he ushered Sissy from the room, the doctor's eye was caught by one of the houseplants crowding the window ledges. Pausing, he raised the pot and, after examining its contents, said: "Poor fellow—looks a mite wilted. Afraid I've been somewhat neglectful of late. Must remember to give him some water as soon as I've finished with your wife. Wouldn't do for a doctor of botanical science to get caught with his plants down, eh, Mr. Poe?"

I had already surmised—from his earlier punning remark about "starting from scratch"—that Dr. Farragut belonged to that species of wit who regards such painfully labored wordplay as the height of hilarity. Now he looked at me expectantly, awaiting my reaction. Not wishing to disappoint him, I managed to produce what I hoped was a convincing chuckle.

Favoring me with a good-natured wink—as if to say, "I know my puns aren't very funny, but I enjoy making them and appreciate your efforts to indulge me"—the doctor then disappeared down the main hallway of the house with Sissy.

As they vanished from sight, I took stock of my feelings about the doctor. All in all, he had made a highly favorable impression upon me. Apart from his obvious physical vigor—so unusual for a man of his age—he exuded a palpable aura of fatherly concern, intellectual acuity, and professional competence. Even his puns—though far more likely to induce a wince than a smile—betokened an unusual degree of mental agility. I was heartened, too, by his optimistic assessment of Sissy's condition.

I realized, however, that that assessment was based on an exceedingly cursory inspection of my darling wife, and that a more definitive diagnosis would depend on the examination she was about to undergo. Now I could do nothing but wait—a circumstance guaranteed to place me in a state of the greatest imaginable anxiety, similar to what a defendant must feel while the jury deliberates on the verdict that will determine his fate.

To distract myself during this agonizing interval, I decided to follow the doctor's advice and peruse one of his books. Stepping to the massive case, I surveyed his library. Most of the volumes, as might be supposed, were on medical and anatomical topics, with titles like Gunn's *Anglo-Saxon Leech-Craft*, Ewall's *Domestic Physician*, Hahnemann's *Organon of Rational Healing*, and Drake's *Systematic Treatise on the Diseases of North America*. A large number dealt specifically with the subject of botanical medicine. These included, of course, the various volumes penned by Dr. Samuel Thomson himself—upon whose theories Dr. Farragut's own practice was founded—as well as a number of rare and curious works. Among the latter were a small octavo edition of the *Herbarium* of Apuleius Platonicus and a quarto copy of the *Causae et Curae* of the medieval visionary Hildegard von Bingen.

Of all the books, however, the one that seemed to promise the greatest diversion was a slender volume titled *Medical Delusions of Olden Times* by a writer, unknown to me, named Palmer. Pulling this work from the shelf, I resettled myself on the sofa and, within minutes, was thoroughly engrossed in its pages.

Palmer's writing left much to be desired in regard to grace, clarity, and, at times, simple coherence. He had managed, however, to cull, from a wide variety of sources, examples of ancient beliefs and practices so strange—so bizarre—so sheerly incredible—that even his flagrant deficiencies as a stylist could not diminish the fascination exerted by his book.

As I leafed through its pages, I found myself marveling at the remedies employed by medieval physicians, who prescribed drinks made of hound's blood and honey for indigestion—eyedrops compounded of hare's brain and melted fox loin to help restore dimming sight—and a salve produced by blending goat dung with vinegar to remove unsightly blemishes from the face. During Shakespeare's time, amulets containing a mixture of dried toad, arsenic, and coral were recommended as protection against heart disease; while the renowned seventeenth-century physician John Grosse averred that a noose taken from the neck of a hanged man and tied around the head would relieve the suffering from a migraine. As late as the mid-1700s, certain village doctors in Britain believed that epilepsy could be cured by digging up a coffin from a churchyard—removing the nails from its lid—fashioning three of these into a ring—and wearing this macabre item of jewelry around the middle finger of the right hand.

To read these and dozens of other, similar examples uncovered by Palmer was to be forcibly reminded that, throughout most of human history, the so-called "healing arts" were little more than a branch of primitive magic. Nowhere in his book was this more apparent than in the author's discussion of so-called "cadaveric" medicines—i.e., treatments prepared (incredible as it may seem) from the anatomical parts of human corpses! Not only in the ancient Orient—where such barbarous practices might be expected to exist—but in Europe as well, patients were routinely given these unspeakable remedies for a variety of ills: liquefied brains for dizziness—powdered thighbones for rheumatism—distilled body fat for contusions—ground gallstones for hiccoughs—and other such concoctions too loathsome to repeat.

Though the chapter was written in Mr. Palmer's characteristically ponderous style, the mere description of these odious elixirs evoked a powerful mix of emotions in my breast: awe—disbelief—intense queasiness. Above all, I felt inordinately grateful to be living in an age when science had at last begun to liberate medicine from the superstitious ignorance to which it had been shackled for millennia.

So engrossed was I in the book that I had lost all track of the time. All at once, I became cognizant of the sound of footsteps approaching from the rear of the house. Quickly setting down the volume on a side table, I rose to my feet just as Sissy and Dr. Farragut made their appearance.

I perceived at a glance that all had gone well. Sissy—who had, very naturally, seemed somewhat anxious when she went off with the elderly physician—now appeared markedly relieved, while the latter wore a look of quiet satisfaction, as though the examination had confirmed his first, optimistic impression of my darling wife's health.

Reaching out toward Sissy, I took her by the hand and gave it a welcoming squeeze. The two of us then seated ourselves side by side on the sofa, while Dr. Farragut took his place in the armchair.

"Well, my friend," he said to me, "it is just as I thought. Your wife, as you know, is suffering from pulmonary consumption. Is her condition serious? Yes, of course. There's a reason that this ailment has been called the King of Diseases. But even kings are sometimes forced to haul down their colors and concede defeat on the battlefield. There are ways to fight this enemy, halt its advances, even vanquish it altogether. I can supply the right weapons. It will be up to you, my dear," he said, shifting his gaze to Sissy, "to be strong and steadfast in wielding them."

"I will be a regular Joan of Arc," Sissy said with a smile.

"That's the spirit," said Dr. Farragut. "There's no doubt in my mind that a cure is possible, assuming that my prescribed course is strictly pursued."

"I need hardly observe, Dr. Farragut, that I am greatly encouraged by your words," I declared. "But tell me, of what, precisely, does your treatment consist?"

"Warm baths to raise the body temperature are a vital element of the Thomsonian method, along with massages using a special stimulating liniment. A proper regard for diet, exercise, and air is also essential. I will write out the exact regimen in detail. Most important are the special pills that I will make up for Mrs. Poe. They must be taken with absolute regularity, every four hours for three consecutive weeks."

"May I inquire as to the composition of these medications?" I said.

"Tamarack bark, dandelion root, thoroughwort, and several other ingredients—all natural, of course. I will need some time to prepare them. Why don't you come by tomorrow morning, Mr. Poe, and I will have them ready for you?"

"Shall I come, too, Dr. Farragut?" asked Sissy.

"No need to, my dear, though of course I am happy to see your pretty face at any time."

Offering profuse and heartfelt expressions of gratitude, Sissy and I then rose from the sofa and made ready to depart.

"I see you were were looking at Palmer," said Dr. Farragut, who—upon getting to his feet—had evidently noticed the volume I had placed on the side table. "Fascinating stuff, eh?"

"Despite its many stylistic shortcomings, it is indeed a most illuminating book," I replied. "At the very least, it should be recommended to all those who deplore the coarseness and vulgarity of the present age and long for a presumably more idyllic past. I myself have been prone to such yearnings. After reading, however, that the prescribed treatment for anemia was to imbibe a cup of warm blood drawn from the neck of a newly slain gladiator, I no longer feel quite so nostalgic for the glory that was Greece and the grandeur that was Rome."

"Yes, I suppose we should all be glad to be living in modern times," said Dr. Farragut. "Still, there is *some* medical wisdom to be gleaned from the ancients. They knew a thing or two about the healing properties of plants and other natural substances."

"I do not doubt the truth of that assertion," I said. "The herbal remedies employed by the medicine men of our own aboriginal tribes, for example, are known to be highly efficacious in regard to certain disorders."

"That's exactly right, Mr. Poe," said the doctor. "You can learn from the old ways. Of course, not everyone around here thinks so. Take my young friend Henry. Claims he's never heard a single syllable of useful advice from his elders. Ah well, he's a cantankerous sort of chap, is Henry."

Sissy and I having donned our outer garments, Dr. Farragut conducted us to the front door. As we stepped onto the porch, I turned back to the physician and asked: "What time shall I return tomorrow?"

"As early as you like," he said, regarding me with a sly expression. "Most of my neighbors rely on their roosters to awaken them in the mornings. I, however, own a pair of ducks I use for that purpose."

So peculiar was this remark that, for a moment, I merely stared blankly at the doctor. All at once, I was struck with a realization.

"I must assume, then," I remarked, "that it is normal for you to arise at the quack of dawn."

A delighted smile spread across Dr. Farragut's ruddy countenance. "Well done, Mr. Poe! You *are* a clever man. I look forward to seeing you again tomorrow."

After giving my hand a farewell shake, he stood at the door while Sissy and I descended the porch steps and proceeded toward the path in the woods.

As we entered the pretty, leaf-blanketed way, my heart swelled with a hopeful feeling, stronger than any I could recall having experienced in recent years. I was only too keenly aware, of course, that the affliction from which my poor wife suffered had proved immune to all previous attempts at a cure. Nevertheless, there was something about the elderly physician that inspired me with confidence, not only in himself but in the unconventional brand of natural medicine he practiced.

I conveyed these feelings to Sissy, who declared that she, too, had formed an exceptionally high opinion of Dr. Farragut.

"He certainly tells awful jokes, though," she added.

"His evident addiction to a particularly debased form of *paronomasia* is indeed a regrettable feature of his otherwise agreeable personality," I replied.

"Paronomasia?" echoed Sissy. "Is that the technical word for a horrible pun?"

"It does indeed signify a pun, though not necessarily a bad one," I said. "While the inordinately strained quips of practitioners like the good Dr. Farragut have made the term synonymous with leaden humor, there is in fact a long and venerable history to punning. The legendary orator Cicero was a devotee of such linguistic play, as was Aristotle, who applied himself to a classification of puns. In later centuries, both Dr. Johnson and the great satirist Jonathan Swift defended the pun. Indeed, the latter published a work entitled *Ars Punica,* or the *Art of Punning,* in which he offered seventy-nine rules for the aspiring punster. The works of Shakespeare are likewise rife with this type of verbal wit. For example . . ."

Walking arm-in-arm with my darling, I proceeded to treat her to a brief disquisition on the subject of Shakespearean wordplay. I was just completing my detailed enumeration of the thirty-nine separate puns that scholars had identified in *The Merry Wives of Windsor* when we came in sight of our destination.

As we drew near to the Alcott abode, I glanced at my wife and saw, to my great consternation, that a somewhat glazed look had come over her eyes. Attributing this to the physical strain she had undergone in walking to and from Dr. Farragut's residence, I suggested that she lie down for an hour or so as soon as we went indoors.

"Yes, I do feel a little weary," she said.

Stepping into the house, we heard a sweet girlish voice, trilling in the parlor:

> "Mid pleasures and palaces though we may roam,
>   Be it ever so humble, there's no place like home.
>   A charm from the skies seems to hallow us there,
>   Which, seek through the world, is ne'er met with elsewhere."

The singer, as we quickly discovered, was young Lizzie. Featherduster in hand, she was engaged in tidying up the room. Upon our entrance, she blushed furiously, as though inordinately embarrassed to have been over-heard.

Perceiving her discomfiture, Sissy exclaimed: "Why, that is my favorite tune, Lizzie. And you sing it so beautifully. I would dearly love to hear the rest of it sometime."

Though her cheeks remained flushed, the little girl looked exceedingly pleased. "If you'd really like me to, I guess I wouldn't mind," she said softly. She went on to explain that she was alone in the house, her mother and younger sister having gone to the village on an errand.

"How was your visit to the doctor, Mrs. Poe?" the sweet-tempered child then inquired.

"Very successful, thank you, dear," answered Sissy. "He feels I'll be cured in no time. But you must call me Virginia." Then, turning to me, she said: "I guess I'll go upstairs now and rest for a bit, Eddie."

After asking if she wished me to bring her a nice cup of tea or other refreshment—an offer she refused—I stood at the foot of the stairs and watched her ascend to the second floor.

Lizzie in the meanwhile had returned to her dusting. I now found my-self with nothing to do. Wishing to find some useful way to occupy myself, I suddenly recalled the request that Mrs. Alcott had made to Louy prior to the latter's departure for school that morning—i.e., that the girl bring in some firewood for the stove.

Deciding to repay the hospitality of my hostess by performing this chore, I announced my intention to Lizzie. I then stripped off my coat, went back outside, and walked around to the rear of the house, where the wood-pile was located.

Rolling up my shirtsleeves, I went to work. Though the morning sky had been clear, the weather had changed, the day having grown overcast and windy. Behind me, I could hear the rustle of the dry autumn leaves in the woods that bordered the extensive backyard.

All at once, a peculiar sensation stole over me. Science has yet to account for the phenomenon commonly referred to as the "sixth sense." This seemingly preternatural faculty—which all human beings have experienced at one time or another—functions as a sort of innate warning mechanism. Through its operations, we become aware that we are being closely watched, if not spied upon, by a silent, unseen presence.

It was just this feeling that took hold of me as I stood with my back to the trees and my arms cradling a dozen pieces of split and seasoned firewood. Someone, I felt sure, was staring at me from behind. I had only to look to my rear and I would come face-to-face with this unknown observer. The absolute conviction that I was being made the object of such scrutiny sent a chill down my spine and caused each separate hair on the nape of my neck to bristle.

At length, the tension became unbearable. Drawing a deep breath, I slowly turned around.

Though I had braced myself for a shock, the sight that greeted me was still startling in the extreme—for the figure that stood at the edge of the woods was every bit as unnerving in appearance as little May had described him that morning. If anything, the child's description of the beggar with the penetrating eyes—hueless complexion—and flaming beard—had failed to convey the surpassingly bizarre look of the man. *Why* he had come back to the Alcott premises was a mystery, though I could not help but feel that there was something distinctly sinister about his reappearance.

For several moments, we stood facing each other while he studied me with a look of peculiar intensity. At length, I resolved to call out to him and demand to know why he had returned. Gathering a sufficient quantity of moisture on my tongue to facilitate speech (for my mouth had gone dry at my first glimpse of him), I opened my lips to speak.

Before I could say a word, however, he spun on his heels and vanished into the gloom of the woods.

CHAPTER ELEVEN

⌒

H AS ANYONE SEEN my gloves?"
The source of this query—uttered in the most urgent tone—was the oldest of the Alcott sisters, Anna. For the past ten or fifteen minutes, she had been rushing about the house, frantically searching for the articles in question. Now she stood in the center of the parlor, arms akimbo, a look of acute exasperation on her plump, pretty countenance.

"No, dear," said her mother, who—attired in her hooded cloak and clasping a wicker basket—was preparing to bring the remnants of the morning's breakfast to a poor German widow who dwelled in a shanty a short distance away with a brood of six malnourished children. "Not since yesterday evening. Keep searching, though, my child. I'm sure they will turn up."

Then, bidding us all farewell, the good woman left to deliver her alms.

"I simply don't understand it," cried the girl, venting her frustration by stamping one foot on the floor. "I was sure that I left them on top of my workbasket last night after sewing on the new buttons. Oh, whatever shall I do? I can't go to Annie Moffat's party tonight without them. Gloves are more important than anything else—you can't dance without them."

"I'm happy to lend you mine, though one of them is a little soiled with lemonade," said Louy, who—lying on her stomach on the parlor rug—was busily scribbling in her notebook. "I know!" she continued, without looking up from her writing, "you can wear the good one and keep the other one scrunched in your hand, and nobody will be the wiser."

"Thank you, Louy, but I can't possibly go around all evening carrying a stained glove," said her sister. "Besides, your hands are bigger than mine and the good one will never fit properly."

Nearly twenty-four hours had elapsed since the events recounted in the preceding chapter. At no point during that interval had I mentioned—either to Sissy or to any of the Alcott females—my encounter with the disquieting red-bearded vagrant. To do so, I felt, would only alarm them needlessly. I had taken the precaution, however, of remaining downstairs the previous night until the rest of the household had retired to their rooms. I had then gone around the first floor, checking to make sure that the windows were tightly closed and both the front and back doors latched from inside. Only then had I proceeded to bed.

I was now seated at a little writing table that stood in one corner of the parlor, composing a letter to Muddy about our visit to Dr. Farragut. Pausing to consider Anna's quandary, I recalled having seen a pair of cream-colored kidskin gloves—their backs embroidered with a delicate floral pattern—in the very place she had mentioned: to wit, resting atop the workbasket she had left beside her chair the previous evening when she went upstairs to sleep.

"I knew it!" she cried when I apprised her of this fact. "But they're certainly not there now—nor anyplace else that I can see. Heavens—I can't remember *when* I've felt so vexed!"

"If you'd like, Anna, you are welcome to borrow *my* gloves. They're a little worn, but still quite presentable, and I'm sure they'd fit your hands." This generous offer was tendered by my own dear wife, who was seated on the sofa beside Lizzie, helping the latter to sew clothing for her collection of derelict dolls.

"That's ever so kind of you, Virginia," said Anna, who, like the other members of her family, had been instructed by my wife to call her by her Christian name. "I noticed your gloves when we were riding together in the coach. They are spandy nice, and I would be happy to wear them, if you really don't mind. Still, I would very much like to know where my own have disappeared to."

"Maybe Barnaby took them," said May, referring to the family cat. Seated primly in her mother's easy chair—her feet barely reaching to the floor—the little girl was sketching in a large drawing tablet that rested upon her lap.

"Barnaby would never do such a naughty thing," cried Lizzie, who, as I had gathered, regarded the feline as her special pet. "He is far too gentle and well behaved to go stealing other people's belongings."

At that moment—as though waiting to hear his name invoked before putting in an appearance—the creature in question came trotting into the room. Clutched in his mouth was a dead member of the genus *Apodemus sylvaticus*, or common field mouse, which he proceeded to deposit at the foot of the sofa, eliciting a chorus of shrieks from all of the females except Louy.

"Heavens, what a squeamish bunch," said the latter. Rising from her re-cumbent position, she stepped to where the deceased rodent lay, and—after shooing away the feline—lifted the mouse by its long tail, carried it to the front door, and flung it outside.

"What a wicked beast!" said May, who had instinctively drawn her feet up onto the chair cushion. "I don't see how you can call him well behaved, Lizzie," she continued as she assumed her former position. "Why, he is al-ways bringing in some poor helpless creature he's killed—birds and baby rabbits and such."

"But he only means them as gifts," said Lizzie, sounding deeply pained by her little sister's harsh denunciation of the feline. "It's his way of showing us how much he loves us. Doesn't your cat do the same, Virginia?"

"Not so much anymore, now that she's an indoor puss," said my wife, who, over breakfast, had regaled her new companions with various anec-dotes about our own pet—including an amusing description of Cattarina's remarkable efforts to operate the latch of the door separating her from the kitchen. "She did when we lived in the country. She was a good deal wilder then. We had a little hatch in our back door, just the same as you do, and she would come and go as she pleased."

"I suppose Barnaby *might* have carried off your gloves, Anna," said Lizzie, albeit in a distinctly doubtful tone. "Have you checked under my bed? It's his favorite hiding place."

"I'll go look there now," said Anna with a disheartened sigh, "though I can't believe I'll find them there. Oh dear, why *will* life be so trying?"

And so saying, she turned and left the parlor.

Following her departure, the rest of us returned to our respective labors, which we pursued in a companionable silence. At length, the atmosphere of quiet concentration was broken by May, who exclaimed:

"There! Dead mice and baby bunnies might be a cat's idea of a nice gift, but I'm sure mine will suit Poppa much better."

"What have you drawn, May dear?" asked Lizzie.

"Yes," said Louy, looking up from the floor, her chin resting on one hand, "let's see the latest masterpiece."

"It's me!" the little girl exclaimed, turning the pad so that the picture was visible to her sisters, as well as to Sissy and myself.

Gazing at the crayoned self-portrait, I was obliged to confess that the child possessed a certain measure of talent. Though bearing only the most distant resemblance to herself, the drawing had been rendered with decided flair. It seemed entirely possible that—with proper training, assiduous practice, and unflagging discipline—little May might someday develop into a more-than-competent artist.

"Why, it looks just like you," cried Lizzie with the utmost sincerity. "I don't see how you can draw such splendid things, May."

"I am just a very creational person, I suppose," said the child with a look of perfect self-satisfaction.

"Creational in your speech, too," said Louy with a laugh. "Still, it is a very handsome piece of work, and I daresay Father will be very pleased to have it when he comes home next month. It surprises me, though, that you chose to make a picture of yourself when we've just brought home that por-trait."

The item to which Louy referred—i.e., the daguerreotype image of the four sisters which they had exhibited to Sissy and me during our trip from Boston—now occupied a central place on the mantel. Mrs. Alcott had placed it there the previous day, after receiving it from her daughters with heartfelt exclamations of surprise and delight.

"I thought Father might like a separate picture of me," said May. "Be-sides, I don't much care for the way I look in that silly old daguerreotype. My nose is too flat and my hair doesn't seem nearly as curly as it is in real life. And we all look so grim—except for you, Louy. You're the only one of us who's smiling."

"I do look like the cat that ate the canary, don't I?" said Louy. "Can't re-member why, exactly. Wait—now I recall. It was that splendid daguerreo-type of Dickens—I had just noticed it among the other portraits in Mr. Ballinger's gallery. Did you know, Mr. Poe, that when Charles Dickens came to Boston a few years ago, Mr. Ballinger took his picture?"

"During our brief visit to his studio," I replied, "that gentleman did in-deed inform me that he had made daguerreotypes of various literary figures, though he did not mention the esteemed author of *The Pickwick Papers*."

"That's my favorite of all Mr. Dickens's novels," exclaimed Louy. "I kept rattling on about it and asking Mr. Ballinger a million questions about meeting Mr. Dickens. I'm afraid I made a terrible pest of myself, though Mr. Ballinger didn't seem to mind."

"Not in the least," said Lizzie. "He seemed tickled by your interest. He took a real shine to you, Louy."

"Impressed with my brains, no doubt," said the girl with a laugh. "Certainly not my beauty."

Having completed my letter to Muddy, I laid down my quill and consulted my pocket watch. The time was just a few minutes short of ten A.M. Though Dr. Farragut had indicated that I might come and fetch Sissy's medication as early as daybreak, I had decided to wait until a more respectable hour. To begin with, I could not be certain that his remark was meant to be taken seriously, as it had been couched in one of his excessively labored puns. Moreover, a steady rain had been falling all morning, and I was hoping that it might abate somewhat before I ventured outdoors.

Now, peering through the window, I saw that—though the sky was of a leaden hue—the precipitation had, in fact, all but ceased. Rising from the desk, I announced my attention to perform the errand.

"I think I'll stay here, Eddie, if you don't mind," said Sissy, looking up from the miniature garment she was mending.

"Of course, Sissy dearest," I said. "Much as I cherish your company, there is no need for you to expose yourself to the inclement weather, as I am merely picking up the pills Dr. Farragut has prepared for you."

"Maybe I'll come along," said Louy. "I've been pegging away at this play for hours, and my mind feels all rumpled up. A little exercise will do me good." And so saying, she sprang to her feet and raced upstairs.

A few moments later, we heard the pounding of her footsteps as she dashed back down the staircase and burst into the parlor. She was wearing rubber boots, a tartan sacque, and, upon her head, an old-fashioned, broad-brimmed, leghorn hat that she had tied round her chin with a red ribbon.

"Oh, Louy, you aren't going to wear that silly thing, are you?" said May. "It's too absurd. Why will you insist on making a guy of yourself?"

"This is Father's old hat, and it is just the thing for nasty weather," Louy replied as she made for the front door. "I don't mind being a guy if I'm comfortable."

"Has your sister found her gloves?" asked Sissy.

"No," said Louy. "She's given up searching for now. Heaven knows where they are. Probably somewhere right out in the open, just like in your splendid 'Purloined Letter' story, Mr. Poe. Well, good-bye, girls. Good-bye, Virginia. We'll be back with Dr. Farragut's miracle potion in no time."

The shortcut Sissy and I had followed the previous day held little attraction at present, the woods being exceedingly wet. I therefore proposed that we take the main road, a suggestion to which Louy readily assented. It was not a day for a leisurely stroll, and we proceeded at a brisk pace, the hoyden-ish girl sometimes skipping at my side to keep up with my more extensive stride.

For several minutes, my little companion remained uncharacteristically silent. Though I could not see her face beneath the brim of her hat, I inferred that she was absorbed in thought. At length, she burst out impatiently: "Fiddlesticks!"

"Why, what is the matter, Louy?" I inquired.

"It's my play, *The Witch's Curse.* I've reached the very last act, but I've run into a problem, and no matter how hard I wrack my brain, I can't seem to come up with a solution."

"Perhaps I may be of help," I volunteered. "What precisely is the nature of your difficulty?"

"It's the message that my hero, Roderigo, smuggles from his dungeon cell, warning his sweetheart, Princess Zara, to be on the lookout for the evil witch Irene, who is coming after her. It must be written in a secret code, but nothing too complicated—something that will seem very clever to my audience, which is composed mainly of May's friends and other little boys and girls from the neighborhood."

"Perhaps you can employ a rebus," I suggested.

Louy never having heard of this species of cryptogram, I proceeded to offer a concise definition before offering a practical example that might serve her purpose.

"The warning 'Watch for Irene,' " I explained, "might be represented by a combination of the following objects and characters: a timepiece—the numeral four—and an eye added to the letters *rene.*"

"What a capital idea!" exclaimed Louy. "That's *just* what I shall do! Many thanks, Mr. Poe. Now that I have my secret message, it will take me no time at all to finish my play."

"And is this your first attempt at dramatic composition?" I asked.

"Heavens no," said the girl. "I've written several others—*The Captive of Castile, The Moorish Maiden's Vow, Fatal Follies,* and *Dr. Dorn's Revenge.* Nothing quite as fine as *The Witch's Curse,* though."

"I am impressed that you have already succeeded in producing so sub-stantial an oeuvre," I remarked with a smile.

"Oh, I dearly love to write. Why, if I didn't have to peg away at my schoolwork, I'd happily spend all my mornings scribbling in my room. I mean to do something splendid with my life—something that won't be for-gotten after I'm dead."

"That is a commendable goal," I said. "Are your sisters possessed of simi-larly lofty aspirations?"

"Not Lizzie," said the girl. "She is a perfect angel and would be content to stay at home safe with Father and Mother and help take care of the fam-ily. Anna's dearest dream is to have a lovely house, full of all sorts of luxuri-ous things—nice food, pretty clothes, handsome furniture, and heaps of money. May wants to go to Rome and study painting and become the best artist in the world. As for me, I want to astonish everyone—to write won-derful books and get rich and famous and make life easier for Father and Mother and the girls."

Being all too familiar with the harsh realities of the literary life in America—where even a writer of genius may find himself in a perpetual struggle to fend off poverty—I was momentarily tempted to inform the lit-tle girl that her chances of achieving great wealth and renown as an author were all but hopeless. Such tidings, however unwelcome, might end up spar-ing her years of unavailing effort—repeated disappointment—and intensi-fying bitterness. So sheerly artless was her enthusiasm, however, that I could not bring myself to destroy her childish illusions. Instead, I merely praised her for her laudable ambitions and redirected our conversation to the sub-ject of Mr. Dickens's *The Pickwick Papers,* a book of which the little girl was so wildly enamored that she could recite entire passages of it by heart.

In another few minutes, we arrived at Dr. Farragut's abode. Mounting the porch with Louy at my side, I rapped on the door. When this signal elicited no response from within, I tried again, but with similarly fruitless results.

"I guess he's not home," said Louy.

"So it would seem," I answered. Glancing across the lawn to the barn, whose great door stood open, I pointed to the conveyance clearly visible in-side. "As he did not take his carriage, however," I said, "we can assume that he has gone no very great distance and is likely to be back within a reason-able time."

Trying the doorknob, I found that it was unlocked.

"Let us remain here for twenty minutes or so and see if he returns,"

I said. "I do not think that Dr. Farragut will object if we wait inside his parlor."

Pushing open the door, I ushered Louy inside. I was immediately struck by the intensely gloomy atmosphere that pervaded the interior. No lamps appeared to be burning in any portion of the house, and though the curtains were pulled back on all of the windows, the day was so gloomy that little light was admitted through the panes.

Proceeding to the parlor, I quickly lit a table lamp. No sooner had I done so, however, than I heard a sound which froze the current of my blood: a low—ghastly—tremulous moan, as of a person in the extremes of distress.

"Dear me, what was *that*?" said Louy, her eyes wide beneath the oversized brim of her hat.

"Perhaps Dr. Farragut is at home after all, and is even now treating some poor individual who is suffering from an acute and intensely painful ailment," I suggested. "If so, it is conceivable that the physician is so deeply engrossed in his task that he failed to hear us when we knocked."

"Yes, I suppose that makes sense," said Louy, without sounding entirely convinced.

Seated beside the little girl on the same sofa I had occupied the previous day, I strained my auditory faculties to the utmost. When the sound came again a moment later, I felt every fibre in my frame thrill as if I had touched the wire of a galvanic battery. This time there was no mistaking the source.

The voice was that of Dr. Farragut himself. And the agonized utterance that issued from his throat was not merely a groan but a plea:

"Hel—help me."

Chapter Twelve

⌒⁀

W E FOUND HIM in a room that, to judge by its appurtenances—beakers, flasks, mortar-and-pestle, shelves lined with medicine bottles—very obviously served as his laboratory. He was perched on a three-legged stool, elbows propped on his thighs, his head bent low and resting on his hands. From the large puddle of what appeared to be coagulated blood in the center of the uncarpeted floor, I deduced that he had just dragged himself onto his seat after having lain unconscious for a considerable time.

As I hurried to his side with Louy at my heels, the elderly gentleman gazed up at me. Even in the obscurity of the unilluminated room, I could see that his countenance was wrought into a look of intense confusion.

"Wh—who?" he stammered. "Please, no, I beg you! Don't hit me again!"

"Have no fear, Dr. Farragut," I said gently. "You are safe. It is I, Mr. Poe."

"Poe?" he echoed in the tone of a man attempting to recall a long-forgotten name. "But what . . . how?"

At that moment, the room suddenly grew brighter. Glancing over my shoulder, I saw that my juvenile companion had enkindled an oil lamp standing on a cluttered worktable.

"Oh Lord," moaned Dr. Farragut, gingerly touching the back of his skull. "My poor head."

"Allow me to have a look," I said, stepping behind him.

Though the floorboards were excessively stained with gore, I knew that even minor wounds to the head often produced a shocking quantity of blood, the scalp being unusually rich in sanguinary vessels. Now, as I carefully parted the matted hair surrounding the injury, I saw that it was, in fact, far less severe than it might have been, consisting of a long and ragged but superficial flesh wound. The surrounding area was also exceedingly swollen, having formed itself into what is commonly known as a "goose-egg."

"Though your injury is somewhat grisly in appearance and undoubtedly a source of intense discomfort, it does not look to be in the least dangerous," I said. "After being cleansed, treated with one of your own marvelous unguents, and bandaged, it will, I feel sure, heal swiftly. But tell me, Dr. Farragut, what on earth happened here?"

"I'm not sure," said the doctor. "My mind is so cloudy. Let me think for a minute.

"I can recall being here in my lab," he continued after a brief pause, "standing at my table. I was preparing some pills."

"Were they, perhaps, the ones you had promised to make for my wife, Virginia?" I suggested.

"Why, yes," said Dr. Farragut. "That's right. It's all coming back to me now. It was shortly after dinner—seven o'clock or thereabouts. I had just come in here and set to work. Suddenly, I thought I heard a sound. Before I could turn around, something struck me on the back of the head. That's the last thing I remember."

"Would you like me to bring you something to drink, Dr. Farragut?" interposed Louy, who had come to stand before the injured gentleman. "A glass of water, perhaps?"

"No, thank you, my dear," said Farragut, studying the child closely. "Do I know you?"

"I am Louisa May Alcott," said the little girl. "I came along with Mr. Poe."

"Yes, of course, one of the Alcott sisters. I thought you looked familiar."

"Tell me, Dr. Farragut," I said, "had you secured the doors to the house prior to retreating to your laboratory?"

The physician began to shake his head, then winced and said: "No. I never lock up until just before bedtime."

"Anyone, then, could have entered freely while you were absorbed in your work," I said.

"I suppose so. But who? Who would want to do such a thing?"

"Two possibilities immediately suggest themselves," I said. "The assault might have been perpetrated by an unknown enemy who—bearing a grudge against you for a real or perceived injury—wanted to strike back at you, without going so far as to commit murder. Alternatively, you may have been attacked by a robber who wished to render you unconscious before plundering your home."

"Unknown enemy?" said Farragut, frowning deeply. "I certainly can't think of anyone who'd want to harm me. I suppose robbery makes better sense, though there's nothing of any real value that I can—"

All at once, the doctor's countenance underwent a striking change. His jaw fell open and his face—already drained of color from the effects of his ordeal—turned an even ghastlier hue.

"It's gone!" he exclaimed, staring in shock at his worktable.

Upon my inquiring as to what object he meant, the physician cried: "My case! My special case! It was right there on the table!"

"Calm yourself, my friend," I said to the elderly gentleman, who had grown so violently agitated that I feared he might relapse into a swoon. "Can you be absolutely certain that this item is missing?"

"Of course I'm sure," Farragut exclaimed. "It's always kept right there."

"But what exactly is this case?" I asked.

"A very rare and wonderful thing. Presented to me many years ago by a wealthy Boston merchant after I had cured his only son of a dreadful case of the scrofula. It's made of burled walnut, inlaid with ivory in delicate floral designs. Lock, hinges, and carrying handle all beautifully crafted of bronze and held in place with hand-chased fittings. Oh Lord," he cried, burying his face in hands. "I can't believe it's gone."

"Dear me," said Louy, "it does sound regularly splendid."

"I fear that it may not be your only loss," I grimly remarked. "Once you have sufficiently recovered your strength, it will be necessary for you to take stock of your belongings, to see what else, if anything, was taken by the thief."

"Nothing else matters to me," groaned Dr. Farragut.

Feeling slightly bewildered by the sheer depth of his misery, I merely studied him for a moment before addressing him thusly: "Though the receptacle you have described does indeed sound unusually lovely, Dr. Farragut, I confess to being somewhat perplexed by the feelings which its loss has occasioned. However exquisite its craftsmanship—however costly the material from which it was fashioned—surely it cannot be quite so priceless as your anguished reaction suggests."

"But you don't understand," said the physician, who had removed a handkerchief from his pocket and was now holding it to the wound on his head. "It's not just the case. It's what's *inside.* My most precious ingredients are stored there—the whole essence of my cures."

This statement greatly puzzled me. "But how can that be?" I asked. "According to my understanding, the Thomsonian system of botanical medicine—upon which your own practice is based—relies on plants that are commonly found in the wild."

"Very true," said Dr. Farragut. "But I have improved on Dr. Thomson's methods by using special ingredients whose virtues he failed to recognize. Without them, my medications lose one-half of their efficacy—at the very least."

"But cannot these ingredients be replaced?"

"Who knows? Possibly. But not easily. And in the meantime," he said, glancing up at me with a pregnant look, "I have no way of helping my patients."

It took but a moment for the full—the *ominous*—import of this statement to strike home. "Including my own wife?" I said with a gasp.

"I am afraid so, Mr. Poe," was the reply. "I had just begun to prepare her medication when I was set upon. I never got a chance to add the most important ingredient."

"But what *are* these mysterious, wonder-working substances?" I cried.

For a moment, Farragut considered my question in silence. "Forgive me, Mr. Poe," he said at length. "It is not that I don't trust you. Or you, my dear," he added, glancing at Louy. "But as I'm sure you understand, there are some secrets I must keep. The discoveries I've made—based on long years of practical experience and constant experimentation—are the very heart and soul of my practice. Should they become widely known, they would instantly be appropriated by the entire medical profession. One day, when I grow too old to carry on, I will publish them to the world. For now, I'm afraid they must be jealously guarded."

"But what, then, is to be done?" I cried. "Apart from the terrible loss to yourself, it would appear that the health—perhaps the very survival—of my darling wife depends upon the recovery of these ingredients."

"I will make every effort to obtain a fresh supply as quickly as possible," said Dr. Farragut. "In the meantime, the greatest effort must be made to find my case. And we must pray that whoever stole it does not simply dispose of the contents, since they will undoubtedly seem utterly worthless to him."

"We'd better tell Sheriff Driscoll right away," said Louy. "Shall I run to the village and let him know what's happened?"

So touching was the little girl's faith in the capacities of the local con-
stabulary that I hesitated a moment before replying thusly:

"Though unacquainted with the personage in question, I am sure that
he is exceedingly competent in regard to his primary duties: to wit, main-
taining peace in the community and ensuring the safety of its members.
Unfortunately, the urgent situation which now confronts us requires investigative skills which few mere law officers possess."

"Yes, I see what you mean," said Louy. "Just like in Boston. It was *you*
who solved the mystery of poor Elsie's murder, not the police. So now it will
be up to you again, won't it, Mr. Poe—to play detective, I mean, and find
out who stole Dr. Farragu—"

Before the girl could complete this statement, I hushed her by raising a
finger to my lips. In the stillness that ensued, I cocked an ear in the direction
of the front parlor. I *thought* I had heard an unexpected sound. An instant
later, all uncertainty vanished.

Someone was inside the house!

Bending over the seated physician, I cupped a hand to his ear. "Are you
expecting any other visitors this morning?" I whispered.

His features wrought into a look of intense anxiety, the elderly doctor
mouthed the word "No."

This response confirmed a belief I had already formed: namely, that the
person who had entered the house unannounced and was now moving
through it in so seemingly stealthy a manner was the perpetrator of the assault upon Dr. Farragut. *Why* he had returned I could not venture to say,
though his motive was undoubtedly sinister. It is true I could not know all
this for a certainty. Instinct, however, assured me that my assumption was
correct.

In view of the ruffian's proven capacity for violence, it seemed urgent
that I find some way to arm myself without delay. Signaling to my companions to remain silent, I cast my gaze about the room. Almost at once, my
eyes lit on a small cast-iron heating stove that occupied one corner. Beside
it lay a small pile of firewood.

Hurriedly crossing the room, I took hold of a stick several inches thick
and perhaps a foot and a half in length. I then positioned myself by the door
and—by means of hand gestures—directed Louy to douse the light, an
order she instantly obeyed.

The seconds that followed were fraught with the greatest imaginable
tension. With my back pressed against the wall and my makeshift weapon
poised to strike, I listened in an agony of suspense to the approaching foot-

steps of the unknown intruder. All at once, he came to a halt just outside the threshold of the room. I held my breath, my heart beating at such an accelerated rate that I feared its violent pounding might actually be audible in the absolute stillness of the house.

The stranger did not hesitate for long. In another instant, he stepped into the room.

Though the lamp had been extinguished, sufficient light filtered in through the windows to permit me to form a general impression of the man. He appeared to be of medium height and sturdy physique. He wore a black slouch hat and coarse woolen coat, both of which were thoroughly soaked from the rain. In one hand he carried a large staff or walking stick, roughly fashioned (so it appeared) from a sapling stripped of its branches.

I saw at a glance that, in a direct confrontation with the fellow, my own little club, though possessed of a certain heft, would be no match for his much heavier and more sizable implement. There was no time for vacillation. With a savage cry, I raised my cudgel and brought it down upon the top of his head.

Dropping his staff, he fell to his knees with a groan. As I raised my club high over my head—prepared to strike again should the fellow offer any resistance—I shouted for Louy to rekindled the lamp. An instant later, the room was suffused with light.

His hat having been dislodged by the force of my blow, it was now possible to see the features of the intruder, who remained in a kneeling position, uttering soft whimpers of pain. He was a distinctly homely-looking individual, with a horsey countenance—exceedingly prominent nose—wide, thick-lipped mouth—protuberant brow—and a ragged fringe of beard sprouting from his jawline. His inordinately deep-set blue eyes, though open, seemed slightly unfocused. Altogether, his physiognomy suggested that he belonged to a singularly dangerous and depraved class of criminal.

What was my astonishment, therefore, when—upon glimpsing his visage—my two companions emitted simultaneous ejaculations of dismay:

"Henry!" cried Dr. Farragut.

"Mr. Thoreau!" cried Louy.

"Henry Thoreau?" I exclaimed, addressing the girl. There was, I knew, a personage of that name who, like Louy's own father, was one of the principal adherents of Mr. Emerson's so-called "Transcendental" philosophy. "Do you mean the writer?"

"Yes," said Louy as she hurried to the fellow's side. "Oh me, how dreadful! Are you all right, Mr. Thoreau?"

"What hit me?" said the latter as, with the help of the little girl, he struggled to his feet.

"I am afraid that I am the person responsible for that unfortunate act," I somewhat sheepishly confessed.

"And who in heaven's name are you?" said Thoreau, gingerly feeling the spot on his head where I had struck him.

"My name is Poe," I replied. "Edgar Allan Poe."

"Poe the writer?" said Thoreau. "No wonder they call you the 'Tomahawk Man.' "

This epithet had been coined by one of my literary foes who, smarting from my scathing review of his woefully deficient poetry, had accused me of performing my critical duties with the viciousness of a bloodthirsty savage—an almost laughably unmerited charge in view of the absolute impartiality and fair-mindedness with which I rendered my aesthetic judgments. Under ordinary circumstances, I would have taken the strongest possible exception to Thoreau's use of this inordinately offensive phrase. As it was, I thought it best to let the matter pass without comment.

"Oh, my head," moaned Thoreau, who seemed somewhat wobbly on his feet. "Something told me that I shouldn't leave my cabin this morning. I suppose this is what comes of ignoring the deepest promptings of your soul. 'Obey thy instincts'—that's what Emerson always says."

"On the contrary," I remarked. "This unhappy turn of events only proves the opposite; for it was instinct, not reason, that led me to commit my somewhat precipitate assault. I deeply regret having hit you with such force."

"Make the most of your regrets," Thoreau replied rather cryptically. "To regret deeply is to live afresh. After all, in the long run, men hit only what they aim at."

"But what are you doing here, Henry?" asked Dr. Farragut.

"I gathered a nice bunch of thoroughwort while I was sauntering around Walden Pond yesterday, and I thought I'd bring it by."

"Henry often collects plants for me when he's traipsing around the woods," explained Dr. Farragut.

"It was splendid of you to walk all the way here in this downpour just to bring Dr. Farragut his herbs, Mr. Thoreau, when you could have stayed all snug and cozy in your cabin by the pond," said Louy.

"An early-morning walk is a blessing for the whole day," replied Thoreau. "Besides, I am soothed by the raindrops. Every globule that wets me is my life-insurance. Disease and a raindrop cannot coexist."

Thinking of my boyhood friend Thomas Cadwalleder—who had perished of pneumonia at the tender age of fourteen after being caught in a severe thunderstorm—I stared in mute amazement at the fellow. Had I not been familiar with the quasi-mystical pronouncements that routinely issued from the pens of Thoreau's fellow Transcendentalists, I might have attributed this and his other muddleheaded observations to the effects of his being struck so forcibly on the cranium.

Indeed, my blow did appear to have reduced him to a somewhat stupefied state, for it was only now that he seemed to grow aware that Dr. Farragut had suffered an injury even greater than his own.

"What on earth happened to *you,* Erasmus?" he asked, employing the physician's given appellation. "Did Poe clobber you, too?"

"No, no, nothing like that," said Dr. Farragut, who proceeded to apprise him of the crime that had occurred on his premises.

"Robbery, eh?" said Thoreau when the doctor had completed his tale. "This just goes to prove what I've been saying all along. If all men lived as simply as I do, thieving and robbery would be unknown. A bed, a table, a couple of chairs, a kettle, some knives, forks, and plates, maybe a lamp to read by after dark—what more does an honest man need? I once had a piece of limestone on my desk to use as a paperweight, but I was terrified to find that it required to be dusted weekly when the furniture of my mind was all undusted still, so I threw it out the window in disgust."

"Yes, yes, Henry," said Dr. Farragut in a somewhat impatient tone. "We all know what a paragon you are. But this isn't the time for your philosophizing. What we really need is some help identifying the thief. You are as well-acquainted with this area as any man. Have you noticed any suspicious characters around here of late?"

"It's true that I have traveled a good deal in Concord and have closely observed the lives of its inhabitants," said Thoreau. "Still, I don't recall seeing anything peculiar lately—just the usual quiet desperation."

"Wait!" I cried, having been struck by a sudden realization. "There *is* a man of exceedingly shabby, if not unsavory, mien who has been skulking about the vicinity. Do you recall, Louy, the beggar who came to the back door of your home yesterday morning and gave your little sister May such a severe shock? Though I deliberately withheld this information for fear of alarming you and your family unnecessarily, that same individual made a second appearance later in the day. I encountered him in the backyard when I went to fetch firewood." I then proceeded to describe the vagrant's physical appearance in minute detail.

"Now that you mention it," said Thoreau, "I *did* spot a fellow like that a few days ago. I was seated by the shore of Walden Pond, tossing pebbles into the water and thinking about how the ripples symbolized the eternal flux of Time, when I heard a noise behind me. I looked around and saw a strange-looking fellow with a bushy red beard making his way along a path in the woods. From the direction he was following, he seemed to be heading toward the farm of—"

At that instant, something occurred of so anomalous a nature that I could make no sense of it. Before completing his sentence, Thoreau closed his eyes—lowered his chin to his chest—and began to snore! Though still standing, he appeared to be fast asleep!

"Good heavens! What has happened?" I cried, feeling a sharp pang of guilt. "Could this be the result of the blow that I so impetuously administered to Mr. Thoreau's head?"

"No, no, not at all," said Dr. Farragut. "It's an old affliction of Henry's. Happens at the oddest times. He's awake one moment, then all of a sudden—bam!—he's sound asleep. I gather it runs in the family. One of his uncles used to doze off while shaving. Just give him a little shake—he'll snap right out of it."

I did as I was instructed; whereupon, Thoreau's eyes sprang open—he blinked several times in rapid succession—then regarded me with a confused look.

"My mind seems to have wandered," he said. "What was I saying?"

"You were talking about the red-bearded stranger you saw in the woods," I replied. "You said that he was proceeding in the direction of someone's farm."

"Ah yes," said Thoreau, his countenance darkening.

Then—speaking in a tone so inordinately bitter that the mere pronunciation of the name seemed to be wormwood on his tongue—he declared:

"Peter Vatty—that devil."

CHAPTER THIRTEEN

L ESS THAN TWENTY minutes later, Louy and I were on our way to Peter
Vatty's farm, following the same sinuous path through the woods
that—according to the testimony of Henry Thoreau—the red-bearded vagrant had taken several days before. By then, the rain had ceased, and scattered patches of blue were visible in the heavens. Even so, the woods were so
excessively wet that the merest puff of wind would cause a small deluge of
droplets to descend upon us from the overhanging boughs.

As she cheerfully confessed, my little companion was an unabashed
"chatterbox" ("I'll rattle on all day if you'll only set me going," she once remarked. "Anna says I never know when to stop."). Now, as we bent our steps
toward Vatty's place, she confirmed this self-characterization by talking
away about the individual we were preparing to visit. Her tale did much to
explain the inordinately acrimonious look that had crossed Thoreau's face
at the mere mention of Vatty's name.

"It's a terribly tragic and romantic story," she began. "It happened quite
some time ago, perhaps six or seven years. I was quite young then, of course,
so I hardly remember it at all, but I've heard whispers and gossip about it
for ever so long.

"To see him now you wouldn't think it possible," she continued, "but
they say Mr. Vatty was a very handsome youth back then, quite as dashing
as any hero from one of Mr. Scott's novels. He was wildly in love with a girl

named Priscilla Robinson, the daughter of a poor farmer who lived just down the road. People who knew her say she looked very much like Anna, and you would have to search far and wide to find a prettier girl than my sister, as I'm sure you would agree, Mr. Poe."

"She is indeed an exceedingly attractive young woman," I concurred, even while thinking that—however considerable the physical charms of Louy's eldest sibling—her beauty paled beside that of my own angelic wife.

"Of course," said Louy, "too much prettiness can be a bad thing for a girl, as Marmee often says, leading her to behave in all sorts of foolish and unmaidenly ways. But that wasn't true of Priscilla Robinson. She hadn't a smidgen of immodesty about her. Everyone says she was as good as gold—as beautiful inside as out. I'm sure that's what attracted Mr. Thoreau to her."

"Thoreau!" I exclaimed.

"Yes, he was madly in love with Priscilla Robinson, too. Poppa has told me that he never saw Mr. Thoreau behave in such a sentimental way. He would bring Priscilla all sorts of pretty little gifts—bunches of wildflowers he picked on his strolls, or songbirds in cages he'd weave from reeds and twigs, or little hand-sewn booklets of poems with pressed leaves or butterfly wings on the covers. He'd walk about all day, mooning over her in that silly way people do when they're in love. I dearly hope it never happens to me. I am bound and determined to avoid such foolishness and mean to stay a bachelor all my days!"

"Your feelings, while appropriate for your age, may well undergo a significant alteration as you mature," I said with a smile. "I must confess that, from my brief encounter with Mr. Thoreau—as well as from my familiarity with his writings in *The Dial* magazine—it is difficult to imagine him in the *rôle* of ardent suitor."

"People can be very mean about Mr. Thoreau, claiming that he cares nothing for other human beings and would sooner spend his days communing with squirrels or talking to trees," said Louy. "It vexes me no end to hear such rubbish. I've known him for as long as I can remember. He's a dear friend of the family—father helped him build his cabin at Walden Pond, you know. All of us children think he's a capital fellow—as kind and gentle as can be. He is always taking us on hikes through the woods and teaching us loads of wonderful things about nature—how hummingbirds fly backwards, or the way to follow a honeybee to its hive, or where to find the sweetest huckleberries. It's true that he can be a little gruff at times, but at bottom he is the dearest, sweetest soul in the world, even if he doesn't always show it. Mercy me—I'd hide my feelings, too, if they'd been hurt so badly the one time I tried to share them with somebody!"

"I take it, then, that, in the rivalry between Mr. Vatty and Mr. Thoreau for Miss Robinson's affections, the former was the victor," I said.

"Yes, in the end she chose to marry Peter Vatty. You couldn't really blame her, for he *was* terribly handsome and he loved her every bit as much as Mr. Thoreau did. Besides, he was known to be an excellent carpenter who made splendid cabinets and tables and other furnishings that he sold to the people in town. So he could afford to buy her heaps of nice things, which she'd never have gotten if she'd picked Mr. Thoreau. He doesn't give a fig for owning things, you know—he's happy as a cricket living in his little cabin and eating beans and wearing old clothes. Of course, Mr. Thoreau was perfectly heartbroken and, to this day, he has never so much as looked at another woman. Even so, I don't think he truly hated Peter Vatty for taking Priscilla away from him—not until she died."

"Died!" I gasped.

"She took sick with the cholera and went just a few months after their wedding," said Louy. "Mr. Thoreau was horribly upset and blamed Mr. Vatty for not taking better care of her, which I daresay was a trifle unfair, for I am sure he did everything humanly possible to save her. Her death was a terrible blow to poor Mr. Vatty. He gave up his business and retreated to his farm and became a hermit—even more so than Mr. Thoreau, who often leaves Walden Pond to visit friends or have dinner with his parents."

"Do I understand you to say," I inquired, "that Vatty has isolated himself to such an extent that he never ventures from his home?"

"Almost," replied Louy. "I've heard it said that he comes to town every six months or so to get drunk in Osborne's tavern. The last time I myself set eyes on him was more than a year ago. I shan't ever forget it. It was Sunday morning, and we were coming home from church when we saw a queer-looking man with a terribly pale face and filthy unkempt clothing and long stringy hair lounging by the front fence. At first I didn't recognize him, he had changed so immensely. Poppa knew who it was, though. He gave Mr. Vatty a very kind and friendly greeting, but Mr. Vatty said nothing, just kept staring at Anna in such a peculiar way that she began to tremble. Poppa finally had to ask Mr. Vatty to leave the premises and never come back. Afterward, Marmee said that he'd gone crazy from grief."

"I can well believe that to be the case, for of all the calamities that may befall a man, the loss of a beautiful and beloved young wife is the one most likely to induce a total loss of reason," I grimly replied. "We must hope that, in the interim since you last encountered Mr. Vatty, his madness has in some measure abated. If not, our efforts to derive any useful information from him will almost certainly prove to be futile."

By this time, we had come in sight of Vatty's residence. The dwelling-house itself was—or rather, *had* been—a handsome cottage, constructed of gray-painted shingles and distinguished by an excessively steep roof that swept down from the ridge beam and extended at least four feet beyond the front wall, forming the roof of an open porch or veranda. At the west end of the building rose a very tall and rather slender chimney of Dutch bricks, alternately black and red, with a slight cornice of projecting bricks on top.

This harmoniously proportioned and well-constructed abode must have been, at one time, picturesque in the extreme. Sadly, it had been permitted to fall into an excessive state of disrepair. Though traces of its former charm were still perceptible, the house presented a woeful picture of neglect, with missing shingles, mouldy paint, shattered windowpanes, sagging roof, and splintered porch. The front yard had relapsed into a hayfield, and a little garden that stood to one side was wildly overgrown with weeds. An air of utter hopelessness—desolation—and decay—pervaded the premises, mirroring the extreme mental deterioration that its owner had evidently undergone since the loss of his beloved.

"Christopher Columbus!" said Louy, employing her pet exclamation. "I'm no fraidy-cat, like some children I know who think that every broken-down old house is haunted by ghosts and goblins. But there's something about this place that gives me the shivers."

"It is indeed a singularly dreary—dismal—sight," I said. "I marvel that any human soul could call such a sorrowful dwelling his home."

"I wonder if Mr. Vatty's inside," said Louy, surveying the building. "It's awfully dark in there."

To climb the porch and knock on the door would have been the most logical way of resolving this mystery. So rickety did the veranda appear, however, that I was reluctant to mount it for fear that the boards would give way under my feet. Instead, I cupped my hands to my mouth and called out a loud "Hello!"

An instant later, this greeting was answered by a sound emanating from the rear of the house—the sharp slamming of a wooden door. Exchanging an inquisitive look, Louy and I proceeded in the direction of the noise. As we rounded the corner of the cottage, we perceived a bedraggled figure hastily locking the door of a ramshackle shed. Completing this operation, he shoved his key into the pocket of his ragged trousers, then spun around to face us.

The appearance of Vatty (for there could be no doubt of his identity) was singular in every respect. He was excessively tall and stoop-shouldered. His limbs were thin to the point of emaciation. His arms were the longest I had ever seen on a human being, his large gnarled hands reaching down nearly to the level of his knees. His forehead was broad and low. His graying hair had been suffered to grow unheeded and hung about his face in a greasy tangled webwork. His complexion was nearly bloodless. His mouth was large and somewhat slack, the underlip hanging down in an imbecilic manner, revealing a set of hideously discolored teeth. His bloodshot eyes were abnormally large and glinted with an unnatural lustre.

That this entirely repulsive-looking being had once possessed even a modicum of physical beauty was nearly impossible to credit. A shudder—compounded of equal measures of horror and sympathy—coursed through my frame as I contemplated him. *Here,* I thought, *is living proof of the awful ravages—to both body* and *soul—that the loss of a dearly beloved wife can inflict on a man.*

"Who the hell are you?" snarled Vatty, regarding me with a look of intense wariness.

Before I could reply to this loutish query, his gaze shifted to the little girl at my side. All at once, he gave a little start of surprise.

"I damn well know who *you* are, missy," he said. "One of them Alcott girls. Not the pretty one, though."

Though the sheer incivility of Vatty's remark—to say nothing of his inordinately unnerving appearance—might have been expected to rattle the child's composure, her voice remained steady as she boldly replied:

"That's Anna. I'm Louisa, and I'm not in the least insulted by your comment, Mr. Vatty, since you mean it as a compliment to my sister."

For another moment, Vatty continued to study the little girl while chewing nervously on his flaccid lower lip. Then—turning his attention back to me—he said:

"You ain't answered my question yet, mister. Who are you and what're doing here? It don't make me happy when strangers come snooping around."

"Though we have come in the hope that you will answer some questions, we are not here to 'snoop,' as you put it," I coolly replied. "As for my name, it is Poe. Edgar Allan Poe."

The effect of this pronouncement upon the unsavory fellow was nothing less than remarkable. His eyes seemed to start from their sockets—his lips began to tremble uncontrollably—he reached both hands to his bosom of his frayed, filthy shirt and clutched convulsively at the fabric.

"Poe!" he cried. "You ain't shittin' me?"

So coarse—so vile—so utterly unfit for the ears of my juvenile companion—was this exclamation that I felt a hot flush of indignation suffuse my countenance, even as I was filled with wonder at his evident familiarity with my name.

Though my impulse was to offer the strongest possible rebuke to the foul-mouthed fellow, I held my tongue, as I could not risk antagonizing him. Subduing my feelings, I therefore calmly replied:

"I would not, under any circumstances, mislead you about my identity. I am indeed Edgar Allan Poe."

Hardly had I spoken these words than the hideously bedraggled fellow came rushing up to me and grabbed me by the shoulders.

"Do you really believe it, Poe?" he asked, thrusting his face so close to mine that his unspeakably rank breath infused my nostrils. "What you wrote in that story? About the man whose wife comes back from the dead?"

So dizzying was the villainous stench of the man—and so dumbfounding his question—that it took me a moment to grasp his meaning. At length, I understood that he was referring to my story "Ligeia," which had been published to great acclaim several years earlier and had obviously made a profound impression upon the wild-eyed being now confronting me. As all literate people know, this tale concerns a man whose beloved wife, after perishing of a wasting disease, appears, in the end, to return to life—though whether the resurrection observed by the narrator is real or merely a product of his inflamed imagination is left for the reader to determine.

Had I chosen to be entirely honest with Vatty, I would have replied to his question in the negative. My story, I would have explained, was meant to convey not a belief in the possibility of actual physical rebirth, but rather an emotion common to all human beings—i.e., the desperate longing to be reunited with our departed loved ones.

From all that Louy had told me of Vatty, however, I knew that such an answer would only deepen his sense of despair. Even now—many years after the death of his adored bride—he was evidently clinging to the mad hope that she might one day miraculously return to him. Should I express my honest belief—that the deceased are lost to us forever—his regard for me would vanish in an instant. He would feel angry—resentful—betrayed. It was clear that if I hoped to secure his cooperation, I would have to equivocate.

"My belief," I accordingly replied, "is that all things are *theoretically* possible. To paraphrase the Bard, there are more things in heaven and earth than are dreamed of in our philosophy."

This response seemed to satisfy the madman.

"Damned right," he said, nodding enthusiastically. "Oh, it'll happen one day, sure as fate. They'll find a way to bring corpses back to life. With electrical currents, maybe. Why, that Italian fellow could make dead frogs dance. Just touched 'em with a wire and they were alive and kicking! Why not human beings?"

Though this allusion to the great Luigi Galvani entirely misrepresented his famous experiments—in which he produced involuntary contractions in the limbs of dissected amphibians by attaching electrical wires to their exposed muscles—I said nothing to correct Vatty.

" 'Course, they'll have to be nicely preserved," observed Vatty. "Wouldn't do to bring back rotting flesh—eh, Poe?"

"That would be exceedingly ill-advised," I replied, feeling my heart sink. It was all too apparent that Vatty's hold on reality was tenuous in the extreme. That he might assist in my efforts to recover Dr. Farragut's stolen medicine chest seemed more unlikely with each passing moment.

A brief interlude of silence ensued, during which Vatty appeared to be engaged in an intense inner debate. Sticking a filthy thumb into his mouth, he chewed meditatively on the fingernail while regarding me with a look of peculiar intensity. At length, having evidently arrived at a decision, he removed the grimy digit from between his teeth and said:

"How'd you like to see something, Poe?"

Needless to say, this question left me somewhat nonplussed. Though my curiosity was naturally aroused, it was accompanied by an acute sense of uneasiness, even foreboding. What, exactly, did he wish me to view? In light of his manifest mental instability, I could not begin to imagine. I therefore replied in the following way:

"Your question is difficult to answer, as I am completely in the dark about the nature of this unnamed 'something.' Can you be more precise?"

"It ain't something I care to talk about out here," said Vatty, casting a pointed look at my companion. "You know what they say about little pitchers."

"Plain looks, and big ears, too!" said Louy with a laugh. "My goodness, I can see that you have an awfully low opinion of me, Mr. Vatty. Well, I won't be offended, for you don't know me at all, and though some 'little pitchers' may have big mouths to go along with their ears, that isn't true of *me*. Secrets don't agree with me, anyway; they make me feel all rumpled in my mind."

Glancing up at me from beneath the broad brim of her floppy hat, she continued thusly:

"You go ahead, Mr. Poe—you needn't worry about me. I shall find ways to amuse myself. Now that the sun has peeked out from the clouds, I don't feel the least bit scared of the old house. I noticed some lovely asters growing around front. They are Marmee's favorite kind of wildflower, and I'm sure she would be very pleased to have a bouquet."

And so saying, the spirited little girl went skipping away.

No sooner had she vanished around the corner of the dwelling than Vatty fixed me with a look of eager expectation. "How about it, Poe?" he demanded. "You interested?"

Still clinging to the hope that I might yet glean some useful information from him regarding the red-bearded vagrant, I suppressed my qualms and nodded in the affirmative.

Emitting a satisfied grunt, Vatty extracted a large iron key from the pocket of his threadbare trousers—turned toward the shed—and undid the lock. The hinges creaked loudly as he pushed open the door.

"In here," he said, indicating with a wave of the hand that I should precede him into the ramshackle little building.

A shudder of superstitious dread coursed through my frame as I stepped over the threshold. Vatty followed at my heels, slamming the door behind him and throwing the bolt.

Though there were several windows (whose panes, unlike those of the main dwelling-house, were fully intact), the interior was excessively gloomy—so much so that at first I could discern nothing at all. An instant later, a match flared in the darkness as Vatty lit a candle. By the feeble glow of the taper I now saw that I was inside a carpenter's workshop.

What impressed me at once was the surpassing *tidiness* of the place. The workbenches were neat and uncluttered. The tools—some standing on shelves, others depending from wall-pegs—were meticulously arranged according to type and size: hammers, handsaws, chisels, augers, files, planes, and more. The contrast between the great care that Vatty evidently devoted to the maintenance of his workplace and the wild disorder into which he had allowed the rest of his property to lapse could not have been more striking.

I had little time to dwell on this paradox, however, for as I glanced about the room, my attention was riveted by the object that Vatty was so eager to display. I easily recognized it as such, for it was the only product of his craftsmanship to be seen. It rested on a pair of wooden supports, or "sawhorses," and at my first glimpse of it, I felt my nape hairs bristle and the skin of my arms erupt into that dermatological condition commonly known as "gooseflesh."

The object was a coffin.

That Vatty was experienced in the construction of such somber artifacts was not in itself surprising. In small towns and villages, the building of containers for the dead was a service often performed by local furniture-makers, and—as Louy had informed me—Vatty had been a skilled and respected artisan prior to the tragedy that had reduced him to his present pitiable circumstances.

Even so, it was intensely disconcerting to find myself shut up in such dismal confines with an apparent lunatic who had brought me there for the purpose of proudly exhibiting a coffin. Adding to my sense of unease was the peculiar appearance of the latter object. To begin with, it was inordinately bulky, having the approximate dimensions and general contour of an Egyptian sarcophagus. It also possessed several curious features—the sides, as well as its lid, being equipped with small hinged panels whose function I was at a loss to explain.

Crossing the floor, Vatty lowered the candle toward the casket. Illuminated from below, his countenance assumed the lurid appearance of a Hallowe'en jack-o'-lantern.

"She's a beaut, ain't she, Poe?" he asked in a strange, dreamy voice. "Know what it is?"

"Why, yes," I replied, somewhat surprised at so obvious a question. "It is a coffin of unusual construction, fashioned, it would appear, of highly polished walnut."

This response elicited a dismissive snort from Vatty. "A coffin ain't nothin' but a corpse-holder," he said. "This here is something else entirely. Step closer, Poe, and I'll show you."

As I obeyed this command, Vatty proceeded to raise the square wooden panel that was built into the center of the coffin-lid.

"Look here," he said.

Peering into the space thus exposed, I saw that the panel concealed a little compartment, lined with perforated tin and measuring approximately two feet square and six inches in depth.

"Got the same arrangement down here," he continued, reaching down to the side-panels and undoing the latches that held them in place.

"Ice goes in there," indicating, with a motion of the hand, all three of the metal-lined compartments.

Passing me the candleholder so that both his hands were free, he then took hold of the entire lid and—with a slight grunt of effort—removed it from the main portion of the casket. Carrying it several paces, he carefully set one end down on the floor and leaned the top against the wall.

As he returned to my side, I held the candle aloft and examined the interior of the casket. It, too, was lined with tin into which dozens of small holes had been drilled. Across the bottom lay a kind of platform made of narrow wooden slats.

"Body rests on there," said Vatty. "The cold air comes through the holes in these pans, moves all around. There's another pan underneath that you can pull out and dump any water that drips down."

By that point, I had, of course, unriddled the mystery of the oddly designed casket. "It is a sort of icebox for the dead!" I exclaimed.

"The Corpse Cooler—that's what I call it," Vatty said with a distinct note of pride in his voice. "Body'll stay fresh a good long time. Just have to keep replacin' the ice as it melts."

As I continued to scrutinize Vatty's handiwork, I found myself modifying my initial opinion of the fellow. To be sure, I still viewed him as someone whose mind had become severely unhinged by grief. At the same time, I no longer believed that he was quite so deranged as I had previously feared. However macabre his "corpse refrigerator" might appear, it was by no means a preposterous invention. On the contrary, it possessed very real and practical applications.

How often did it happen in the modern world that a person died far from home—while traveling, working, or living in a distant place? At present, such unfortunates were generally subjected to the most drastic forms of embalming before being shipped back home—their internal organs removed and their cavities stuffed with sawdust, their veins injected with oil of turpentine, their corpses packed in salt. By the time they arrived at their destination, they were scarcely recognizable—a circumstance bound to magnify the distress of their loved ones. Vatty's "corpse refrigerator" would obviate the need for such measures. Though it would not preserve a dead body for an indefinite time, it would surely keep one in a reasonably lifelike condition for the period required to transport it even over a considerable distance.

"It is a very ingenious creation," I earnestly observed.

"Knew you'd like it," said Vatty, eyeing me narrowly. "I've read more than one of your stories, Poe. You and me, we got a lot in common."

As I gazed into his excessively haggard visage—made even more unsettling by the lurid glow of the candle—my brain reeled with a multitude of conflicting thoughts. Could there be any truth to his observation? Surely there was nothing that I shared with this debased—this wholly unsavory— creature! And yet, as we stood there face-to-face, a strange fancy crept into my mind. I felt as though I were peering into one of the weirdly distorting mirrors found in Barnum's museum and seeing myself not as I *was*, but as I might *become;* for who could say to what despairing—to what *degraded*— depths I, too, might sink upon the loss of my beloved?

This thought aroused in me a renewed sense of urgency. To stave off the dread eventuality of Sissy's death I must bend all my efforts to a single purpose: the speedy recovery of Dr. Farragut's stolen medicine chest and the precious ingredients contained therein.

Accordingly, I cleared my throat and said:

"Like you, Mr. Vatty, I have sensed that we are, in some degree, kindred spirits. It is therefore my hope that you will be able to assist me with a matter of the greatest importance."

"What might that be?" he asked, instantly assuming the same look of extreme wariness with which he had first greeted me.

"I am in search of a man—an apparent beggar, very shabbily attired," I said. "His most conspicuous feature is a bushy red beard of an unusually vibrant hue. I have reason to believe that he was in the vicinity of your home several days ago. My first question is: Have you seen such an individual?"

This query produced a very striking reaction in Vatty, who began to blink his eyes nervously while biting on his lower lip.

"Yeah, I seen him," he answered at length. "Couple of days ago. I was right here in my shop, working on my Corpse Cooler. Thought I heard someone walkin' around outside. Looked up and there he was, standing right there, outside that window."

Glancing up at the casement indicated by Vatty, I studied it for a moment before asking: "At what time did this occur?"

"Can't say for sure. After dark sometime. Eight, maybe nine o'clock."

"I see. And what happened after you became aware of him?"

"Nothin' much," replied Vatty. "He just turned and walked away."

"Do you know where he may have been going?"

"No idea," he answered with a shrug. "Headin' north, seemed like."

It need hardly be said that I was gravely disappointed by this exceptionally meager information. There was no reason to prolong my visit. By that point, moreover, the dismal atmosphere of the workshop had begun to weigh heavily upon my spirits. The oppressive nearness of the coffin—to say nothing of the corpselike *foetor* of Vatty himself—were sufficiently intense to make my brain swim and my knees grow weak.

"I thank you for your help," I muttered. "Now I must take my leave."

In another instant, I had made my way to the front of the shed—thrown open the door—and hurried outside. As I stood before the little structure, gratefully drawing in deep breaths of the crisp autumn air, I became aware that my little companion, Louy Alcott, had returned from her flower-gathering expedition. I could hardly have failed to notice her presence, in view of the exceedingly energetic activity in which she was currently engaged.

Wielding a three-foot wooden lath as though it were a rapier, she was engaged in a duel with an invisible opponent: parrying—thrusting—and capering about the backyard in a wholly unself-conscious manner while crying out:

"What ho, Hugo! Take *that*—and *that*! Aha! A hit—a very palpable hit!"

As she delivered a wound to the imaginary Hugo, her shining eyes lit upon me.

"Mercy me, are you all right, Mr. Poe?" she said as she lowered her weapon. "You look dreadfully pale."

"I am fine," I said, mustering a smile. "Though made slightly light-headed by the inordinately close air of the shed, I feel much reinvigorated now that I am once again out in the open. I see that, in my absence, you have armed yourself against an unseen foe whom, I gather, you have just dispatched with a lethal stroke of your blade."

"I found it in the grass while I was gathering Marmee's bouquet," she said, indicating with a tilt of her chin a small bunch of purple flowers resting atop a nearby tree stump. "It makes a capital sword—just what I need for Roderigo. He's the hero of my play. I hope Mr. Vatty won't mind if—oh, there you are, Mr. Vatty."

"What's that you was saying about me?" growled the ill-mannered fellow as he stepped from the shed and slammed the door behind him.

"I was just telling Mr. Poe about this old stick of wood that was lying around your yard," answered Louy, seemingly unfazed by the fellow's sour tone. "I don't suppose you'd care if I kept it?"

For a long moment, Vatty studied the narrow length of scrap-wood.

"Guess that'd be all right," he said at length, in a tone so begrudging that he might have been allowing the little girl to retain one of his most cherished possessions instead of a piece of refuse.

"Come, Louy. We have taken up enough of Mr. Vatty's time," I said. I then turned to the latter and, after thanking him again for his assistance, bid him a polite farewell.

"Nice meeting you, Poe," he said. "I'll keep my eyes peeled for that red-bearded fellow."

Moments later, my little companion and I were on the path leading back to the Alcott residence, Louy walking beside me with her wildflowers clutched in one hand and her make-believe sword in the other. We proceeded in silence until we were well out of earshot of Vatty.

"Poor Mr. Vatty," Louy said at length. "I can't say I care for his manners—or his dreadful language. But it's hard not to feel sorry for him. Heavens, he looks even worse than when I saw him last. Were you able to learn anything useful from him, Mr. Poe?"

"Sadly, no," I replied. I then told her of Vatty's ostensible glimpse of the red-bearded vagrant several nights earlier.

"Why, that's a big fat fib if ever I heard one," Louy said.

"What makes you think so?" I inquired.

"I tried peeking through the window of the shed," she replied. "Couldn't help myself—curiosity got the best of me. But I could hardly see anything, the glass was so thick with dirt. Most of it seemed to be on the outside, and I thought about wiping some away, but I was afraid of being seen, so I gave up."

"My own observations, made within the shed, were entirely in keeping with yours," I said. "The exteriors of the windows were so excessively begrimed as to be nearly opaque. At night, from inside, Mr. Vatty would have been incapable of observing someone on the opposite side of the panes. Indeed, with his candle burning, he would have seen only one thing had he glanced into the darkened glass of the window."

"What's that, Mr. Poe?" asked Louy.

"Himself," I replied.

CHAPTER FOURTEEN

THE INCIDENTS THAT had occurred since Louy and I set out for Dr.
Farragut's home had been distressing in the extreme. Now, as we approached the Alcott residence, my heart was filled with trepidation. Sissy, I knew, must be awaiting my return in a state of the keenest anticipation, believing that I would be bringing her the precious botanical elixir. Instead, I had only grim tidings to deliver. How, I wondered, would she react when she learned that Dr. Farragut's medicine chest had been stolen and, with it, the rare and mysterious ingredients upon which her hopes for a cure depended? I trembled to think of the pernicious effect upon her fragile constitution that this shocking news might produce.

It was characteristic of my tender-hearted wife that—after I informed her of the dismaying turn of events—her first concern was not for her own well-being but for that of Dr. Farragut. I explained that his injury had proven to be far less severe than its gruesome appearance initially suggested and that, though still somewhat dazed from the blow he had sustained, the elderly physician already seemed greatly recovered when Louy and I had taken our leave of him. It was only after receiving this assurance that Sissy permitted herself to display a degree of disappointment on her own behalf, exclaiming in a tremulous voice: "Oh, Eddie, it is just too upsetting for words. To have traveled all this way—for *this*!"

"Don't give up hope, Virginia," said Louy. "I know Mr. Poe won't rest until he finds the rascal who made off with Dr. Farragut's special box, and you can count on us to help out any way we can."

We were seated by then in the parlor, along with the rest of the Alcott females, who had gathered to hear our account of the morning's events. As Louy and I related the tale of our visit first to Dr. Farragut's plundered house and then to Peter Vatty's decaying farm, her mother and sisters listened intently, occasionally emitting soft, incredulous gasps or little cries of dismay.

"Did you really talk to Mr. Vatty, Louy?" asked Lizzie in an awestruck tone. "How brave you are! I know it is wicked to think badly of someone who has suffered so much, but I still have bad dreams about him sometimes. He looked so frightful when he showed up here last year!"

"Yes, it was quite a shock to see what has become of him, poor fellow," said Mrs. Alcott with a sigh. "I don't believe I've ever known a man so terribly altered by misfortune."

"And to think how handsome he once was," said Anna, "even with those funny long arms."

"I do remember that he looked awfully strange," said little May. "But not half so scary as that red-bearded beggar who came to the door yesterday. Goodness, he was a regular beetle-bub! Just the sort who would go around breaking into people's homes and stealing their nicest things."

"We do not, of course, know for a certainty that the crime was committed by that individual," I observed, not bothering to correct the child's comical mispronunciation of the devil's ancient appellation. "Still, both his appearance and behavior were sufficiently sinister to make him a likely suspect."

"But what will you do now, Mr. Poe?" asked Anna.

"Yes, Mr. Poe," said Louy in an eager tone. "Where do we go from here?"

In truth, I was at a loss as to *how* to proceed. The excessively trying events of the day—combined with my intense anxiety over Sissy—had so wrought upon my nerves as to leave me in a sadly debilitated state, both mentally and physically. For the present at least, I was incapable of concentrated thought.

Perceiving my fatigue, Mrs. Alcott—whose motherly intuitions were nearly as acute as my own blessed Muddy's—declared: "I think what Mr. Poe needs right now is a nice cup of hot tea and some toast."

"What a capital idea!" cried Louy.

"You sit right there, Marmee. I will fix the tea," said Anna, rising from her seat.

"And I will toast the bread," said Lizzie, making for the hearth, beside which the toasting fork rested.

"I'll go fetch the strawberry jam from the cupboard," said May, skipping toward the kitchen.

"Thank you, my darlings," said Mrs. Alcott. Then, leaning forward in her seat, she reached out and gave Sissy's hand a comforting squeeze.

"Everything will turn out all right, my dear," she said in a tone so reassuring that it was impossible to doubt her. "Just you wait and see."

By the following morning, I had settled on a course of action. Having promised Louy that I would apprise her of my plans once they were decided, I sought out the little girl. After a fruitless search of the parlor, dining room, and kitchen, I made inquiries of Mrs. Alcott, who had just returned from her daily visit to the poor German widow, and who suggested that I look in the garret.

Mounting the stairs, I found Louy snugly ensconced in the cramped but congenial space, which evidently served as her personal library and work area. She was seated on a battered three-legged sofa beneath a sunny window, bending over an old steamer trunk that she had made into her desk. She was busily writing in a book with gray-marbled covers, evidently a journal. So absorbed was she in her task that she did not become aware of my presence until I announced it with a loud *"Ahem."*

"Oh, hello, Mr. Poe," she said, looking up from her book. "How are you feeling this morning?"

"Somewhat more clearheaded than when we returned from our adventures yesterday afternoon," I replied. "I must say, Louy, you have made a very charming refuge for yourself up here."

"Yes, it makes me happy as a lark to retreat up here for a few hours, where the world don't bother me and I can scribble away at my leisure, or settle down with a nice book and a half-dozen russets. Have a chair, Mr. Poe," she continued, motioning toward a battered tin washtub that had been turned upside down. "Sorry for the accommodations; don't get many visitors up here."

As I could not stand upright in the low-ceilinged attic, I accepted her invitation, despite the intensely unappealing aspect of the overturned tub.

"Have you figured out your next step yet?" asked the little girl after I had lowered myself onto the makeshift—and supremely uncomfortable—seat.

"Yes," I replied. "You will recall that—following our conversation with Mr. Thoreau—I hastened with you to Peter Vatty's farm, without pausing to conduct even a cursory examination of Dr. Farragut's premises. Having failed to learn anything of use from Vatty, I now plan to return at once to the physician's home and conduct a thorough search."

"And just what will you be looking for?" asked the girl.

"Anything that might assist in locating the thief," I said. "Though Dr. Farragut seemed certain that only his medicine chest had been taken, it is possible that a more minute investigation will turn up other stolen objects. A knowledge of such missing items might prove vitally important in resolving the case. There may also be small but significant clues to the identity of the perpetrator: a bootprint, for example, that indicates his approximate size, or a coat button torn from his garment with, perhaps, a scrap of distinctive fabric still attached. It is not inconceivable that I might even discover a few strands of his hair, which would confirm—or disprove—my hypothesis that the red-bearded fellow is indeed the person responsible for the crime."

"I trust you'll let me come along and help, Mr. Poe," said Louy. "I have a sharp eye for little things and can play detective with the best of them. Why, just look at this," she continued, holding up her journal so that its open pages faced me.

For a moment, I was uncertain as to what, precisely, I was meant to observe, until Louy indicated the upper corner of the right-hand page, which was slightly defaced with a tiny scarlet stain or smudge.

"Strawberry jam from a very small thumb," said Louy. "I spotted it this morning and saw right away that May has been sneaking looks at my diary again. For all her ladylike airs—always prinking over her plate and quirking her little finger when she drinks from a teacup—she rarely manages to finish a piece of toast without getting jam on her hands. Oooh, it makes me so mad I could burst! Just wait until I get hold of her, that wicked, wicked child!"

"Why, Louy, I do not hesitate to say that I am surprised by this outburst," I said. "From the composure you maintained yesterday in the face of Mr. Vatty's extreme incivility, I assumed that you were a person who rarely permitted her anger to get the better of her."

"Heavens no!" she exclaimed. "I have a perfectly dreadful temper. It sometimes seems as if I could do anything when I'm in a passion. I get so savage that the sharp words fly out of my mouth before I know what I'm about. With Mother's help, though, I am learning to control it."

At that moment, a rich, sweet-toned voice came echoing up the stairwell.

"There's Marmee now," said Louy. "It sounds as if she's calling your name, Mr. Poe."

"So it does," I said, rising carefully so as not to smash my head on the low-hanging roof beam directly above my perch.

"I'll be down shortly," said Louy. "I just want to finish what I'm writing. You'd be very proud of me, Mr. Poe. I'm doing it as a rebus, to make it harder for May to spy on me."

As I descended the stairs, Mrs. Alcott called to me again. Following her voice to the front hallway, I saw that she was standing by the door, talking to someone whom she had evidently just admitted into the house. What was my astonishment when, upon my nearer approach, I saw that the visitor was none other than Dr. Farragut!

He was standing with his hat in one gloved hand while clutching a small leather case with the other. "Ah, there you are, Poe," he said as I came over to greet him.

"Good day, Dr. Farragut," I said. "I confess that I am greatly surprised to see you here. How are you feeling this morning?"

"A tad worse for wear," he replied, tilting his head to reveal a strip of adhesive plaster covering the area of his wound. "Getting hammered on the skull isn't all it's cracked up to be, ha-ha. Fortunately, this old noggin of mine is made of solid stuff."

"May I offer you a cup of tea, Dr. Farragut?" asked Mrs. Alcott.

"Very kind of you, Mrs. Alcott, but thank you, no. I can only stay a few minutes. There's something I must speak to you about, Poe, but first I'd like to see your wife."

"I will go fetch her," I said. "I believe she is upstairs in our bedroom."

"Oh, no," corrected Mrs. Alcott. "She came down a short time ago. She's in the parlor right now with Lizzie."

Proceeding to the parlor, we found my wife and the shy little girl seated side by side on the bench before the old upright piano that stood against one wall. They were poring over some sheet music. As we drew near, they glanced up together, Sissy's eyes widening at the unexpected sight of the elderly physician.

"Dr. Farragut!" she exclaimed, swiveling on the bench as though preparing to arise.

"Don't get up, my dear," said the doctor. "Just came by to see how you're feeling."

"Very well, thank you," said Sissy, though—to my own eyes—her complexion had assumed a worrisome, somewhat waxen hue. "But how are *you*, Dr. Farragut? I was so terribly sorry to hear about what happened."

"Yes, it was most unfortunate for any number of reasons. But here," he said. Setting his case down on a side table, he opened the latch, reached inside, and extracted a small brown bottle that he handed to Sissy.

"Is—is it your special medication?" Sissy asked, gazing with wonder at the small amber receptacle.

"I'm afraid not, my child," said Dr. Farragut. "Without the substances in my stolen case, there's only so much I can do. These pills won't cure you, but they should arrest the course of your disease for now. They are made of very excellent ingredients—lobelia, horehound, hemlock bark, snakeroot, one or two others. You must be sure to take them twice a day, one pill in the morning, another before retiring at night."

"Thank you for bringing them, Dr. Farragut," said Sissy, attempting to conceal her disappointment behind a brave smile.

"You're very welcome, my dear. And now, Poe, if you don't mind," he said, turning to me, "I'd like to have a word with you in private."

"You may use the kitchen if you wish," said Mrs. Alcott. "No one will bother you in there."

"Lead the way, Poe," said Dr. Farragut.

As the physician and I left the parlor, I could hear Lizzie say: "Shall we try this one, Virginia? I'll play the melody if you sing the words. It's one of my favorites."

"Mine, too," answered Sissy.

A moment later, as Dr. Farragut and I reached the kitchen, the melodious sound of the charming old tune "Good-bye, Sweetheart, Good-bye"— entrancingly vocalized by my darling wife to the accompaniment of the little girl's surprisingly skillful playing—reached our ears:

"The bright stars fade, the morn is breaking,
The dew-drops pearl each bud and leaf,
And I from thee my leave am taking
With bliss too brief, with bliss too brief. . . ."

"Pretty voice your wife has, Poe," said Dr. Farragut. "She—"

At that moment, the air was split by a radically different kind of noise: a harsh infernal screech that might have issued from the throat of a demon. Almost simultaneously, a dark form sprang from beneath Dr. Farragut's feet—darted across the floor—and disappeared through the little flap affixed by leather hinges to the bottom of the rear door.

"Good Lord," cried Dr. Farragut, so startled by this occurrence that he grabbed his chest and staggered backward several paces, coming to a halt beside the massive fireplace within which stood a heavy iron crane holding several kettles.

"Are you all right, Dr. Farragut?" I cried, hurrying to his side.

"Yes, yes, fine," he said, though he held on to the fireplace with one hand while, with the other, he continued to clutch at his bosom, as though to subdue the wild beating of his heart. "Just a bit shaken up, is all."

"It was the Alcott's pet feline," I said. "You must have inadvertently stepped on its tail while it was napping."

"What an unholy noise," said the doctor. "I suppose that's why they call it a *cat*erwaul."

"Ha-ha, very good," I said. "I take it as a sign of your recovery that you have regained your fondness for amusing wordplay."

"Yes, well, what I have to say is no laughing matter," he grimly remarked. "I believe I know who stole my case—and *why*."

"What!" I exclaimed. "Come, sit here, and tell me at once."

Taking him by the arm, I guided him to a stool that stood beside an old maple-topped worktable upon whose scarred surface there lay a variety of implements, including several wooden spoons, a flour sifter, and a rolling pin. Perching himself on the seat, Dr. Farragut addressed me thusly:

"It came to me this morning. Would have occurred to me sooner if I'd been thinking more clearly. I'd been assuming, you see, that someone snuck into my house with larceny on his mind and made off with the most valuable thing he could find—my priceless, handmade medicine case. The contents wouldn't matter to him. More likely than not, he'd just toss them away—that was my fear, at any rate.

"Then it struck me," he continued. "I'd got things completely backward."

"Backward?" I echoed. "In what way?"

"The ingredients—that's what he was after!" exclaimed Dr. Farragut. "He doesn't care about the case at all."

"Do you mean to say that the perpetrator of this deed entered your home with the deliberate intent of stealing the rare natural substances that constitute the secret to your cures?"

"That's what I believe, yes," said Dr. Farragut.

For a moment, I pondered this theory in silence.

"If your supposition is correct," I said at length, "then the thief must be someone familiar enough with your habits to know precisely where you kept the treasure he was seeking."

"Not necessarily," said Dr. Farragut. "All he'd have to know—or *assume*—is that they were stored in a special place. And what could be more special than my medicine case? Heavens, it's the first place *I'd* look if I were searching for something precious."

"But as I understand it, your ingredients are not *in themselves* precious," I observed. "Their value, that is to say, resides entirely in the use to which they can be put by a practitioner of botanical medicine."

"Or by some supposedly learned member of the established medical profession who wishes to possess the key to my treatments," said Dr. Farragut in a pregnant tone.

"I take it from the tenor of your remark that you have a suspect in mind," I said.

"I do," answered the elderly physician. "His name is MacKenzie. Dr. Alistair MacKenzie."

"And on what basis do you believe this individual responsible for the crime?"

"Very simple. He's one of my bitterest enemies," said Dr. Farragut. "The medical establishment despises me, you know. And why not? We Thomsonians threaten its very existence. MacKenzie has done everything he can to discredit the botanical system in general and me in particular. Oh, you should hear the things he's said about me. Claims I'm the worst kind of quack, the sort whose cures do more harm than good. But that's all a smoke screen. Do you want to know the real reason he hates me? Because I'm *right*, and he knows it—knows that my methods really work. *That's* what eats away at him. And that's why he'll go to any lengths to get his hands on my secrets."

"But is it likely that such a personage—a reputable member, as I gather, of the medical profession—would commit such a crime?" I asked.

"Oh, I don't suppose he did it *personally*," said Dr. Farragut. "Sent a hireling to do the job, no doubt. That's probably who that red-bearded fellow was—some scoundrel paid to steal my special remedies. From what I hear, it wouldn't be the first time that the good Dr. MacKenzie was involved in criminal activities. He's dirtied his hands before—very literally."

"Why, whatever do you mean?" I said.

"MacKenzie runs an anatomy school in Boston," said Dr. Farragut. "On Lewis Street. Quite a profitable little venture, as I understand it. How much do you know about anatomy schools, Poe?"

"I confess to having a fairly extensive knowledge of the subject," I replied, "having recently perused a fascinating, if somewhat carelessly translated, edition of Giacomo Berengarius's classic text, *Anatomia Humani Corporis*. I know that, for centuries, the scientific study of the human body was greatly hindered by the extreme abhorrence with which the public viewed the act of medical dissection. In most places, only the corpses of recently executed murderers were authorized for this purpose. Faced with a severe shortage of legally approved cadavers, professors of anatomy, along with their students, frequently resorted to the odious act of grave-robbing to obtain subjects for their study. In response to the spread of this ghastly practice—and, more particularly, to hideous crimes of the infamous 'resurrectionists' Burke and Hare, who progressed from grave-robbing to murder to provide their medical clients with a steady supply of fresh corpses—more liberal legislation was enacted both here and abroad. These news laws permitted the dissection, not merely of hanged criminals, but of deceased inmates of various public institutions—hospitals, infirmaries, workhouses, poorhouses, foundling-houses, and so forth—assuming that such corpses went unclaimed by relatives. So great is the current vogue for anatomical dissection, however, that—even with these additional sources—there has been a constant scarcity of human bodies for study."

"Exactly right," said Dr. Farragut. "Cadavers are still devilishly hard to come by. Can't teach anatomy without them, though. No cadavers, no students—no students, no income. So a man like MacKenzie will go to great lengths to procure the raw material for his business."

"Are you suggesting," I said, "that he traffics in bodies plundered from the grave?"

"Those are the rumors," said Dr. Farragut.

"But if his involvement in this repugnant activity has been so widely bruited about, why has he not been arrested?"

Regarding me with a look that seemed to say, *Really, Poe, I am surprised that I must explain this to a man of your remarkable intelligence,* Dr. Farragut extended one hand, palm upward, and—with a rubbing motion of his thumb and fingers—made a gesture whose meaning could not be mistaken.

"Ah," I said, "so the authorities have been bribed to turn a blind eye to his malfeasance."

"Which is why there's no point in notifying the Boston police about my stolen case," said Dr. Farragut. "Even if they bothered to question MacKenzie, their investigation would be nothing but a sham."

As I considered the information that had just been imparted to me,

Dr. Farragut, with a grimace, reached up and tenderly touched the bandage on the back of his head.

"Are you not feeling well, Dr. Farragut?" I asked.

"Throbs a bit from time to time," he said. "The wound should have been stitched, I suppose, but I was the only doctor around. Would've been a case of 'suture self,' so to speak.

"But Poe," he continued after pausing briefly, apparently to afford me the chance to appreciate this ostensible witticism. "Are *you* all right? You've suddenly gone as white as a ghost. What is it?"

"I thought I heard something," I said, listening intently.

All during my conversation with Dr. Farragut, I had been aware, however dimly, of the surpassingly melodious sounds emanating from the parlor. Sissy and Lizzie had performed a succession of popular songs for the benefit of Mrs. Alcott, whose enthusiastic clapping could be heard following the conclusion of each number.

The music, however, had come to an abrupt halt—and in its place, I thought I had detected a noise so alarming as to send a shiver of dread coursing through my frame.

"What is it, Poe?" Dr. Farragut repeated.

Before I could respond, the fearful sound reached my ears again. This time, there could be no doubt as to its origin. Looking at Dr. Farragut, I could see by his startled expression that he had heard it, too.

In another moment, we had dashed into the parlor. The sight that smote my eyes caused the marrow to freeze in my bones.

Sissy, still seated on the piano bench, was coughing convulsively into a white handkerchief that was clutched in one hand; while Mrs. Alcott, Lizzie, and Louy (who had evidently just descended from her aerie) stood nearby, looking on helplessly.

Springing to the side of my stricken wife, who was bent nearly double from the violence of the paroxysm, I laid a comforting hand upon her shoulder.

"Oh, Eddie," she managed to gasp, lowering her handkerchief and gazing up at me with pleading eyes.

I tried to reply but my powers of speech had totally failed. A numbness— an iciness of spirit—pervaded my frame. For as I gazed down at Sissy, I saw—to my inexpressible horror—that her lips and chin were smeared with red, and her handkerchief glistened with blood!

With an air of cool command that I had not previously witnessed in him, the elderly physician immediately took charge of the crisis, directing

Mrs. Alcott to bring him a number of items—i.e., a bowl of water, heated almost to boiling; one of the wooden spoons he had seen on the worktable in the kitchen; a sieve; a drinking glass; several clean strips of cotton cloth; and two of the warmest blankets in the house.

As the good-hearted woman hurried off to assemble these articles with the help of her daughters, Dr. Farragut ordered me to fetch his case. He then helped Sissy to her feet, and, placing one arm around her waist, led her from the parlor and upstairs to our bedchamber, while I followed directly behind them, the physician's black leather bag clutched in one hand.

Within a very short time, my wife—whose coughing had mercifully subsided—was settled comfortably beneath the blankets with her head propped up on pillows, while Dr. Farragut—who had stripped off his coat and rolled up his shirtsleeves—stood at the dresser by the window, concocting a medicinal drink from the heated water and several powdered substances he had removed from his bag. I remained at the bedside, holding one of Sissy's hands and telling her—with more assurance than I felt—that all would be well.

When Dr. Farragut had completed his preparations, he took me aside and suggested that I wait downstairs. It was important, he explained, to treat my wife in the most tranquil possible atmosphere.

While loath to be separated from Sissy, even for a few minutes, I saw the wisdom of this request. Though I had tried my best to subdue the terror that had gripped my soul, my agitation was too great to conceal. Despite my comforting words, my presence, I saw, could only serve to upset my angel, who—in her typically selfless way—would worry less about her own dire condition than about the anguish I was suffering as a result of it.

Accordingly, I lifted Sissy's right hand to my lips, placed a fervent kiss upon its dampened palm, then left the room and hurried downstairs to the parlor.

I spent the next twenty minutes in a state of agonized suspense, striding wildly back and forth across the floor, while Louy and her mother endeavored to calm me.

"Keep hoping for the best, Mr. Poe, that will help you lots," said the little girl. "Dr. Farragut won't let anything bad happen to Virginia. She's sure to pull through this, just you wait and see."

"May I bring you a nice cup of tea?" asked Mrs. Alcott. "It will help soothe your nerves."

In making this kindly offer, Mrs. Alcott once again put me in mind of my own, ever-solicitous Muddy. The thought of that saintly woman waiting faithfully at home, oblivious of the crisis now unfolding here in Concord, was almost too agonizing to bear. Should the worst occur, it would fall to me to inform her that instead of receiving the hoped-for cure, her only child had died! How would Muddy survive such a calamity? And how would I?

Feeling too overwrought to speak, I declined Mrs. Alcott's offer with a shake of the head, then returned to my frantic pacing. An eternity seemed to pass before I heard Dr. Farragut's footsteps on the stairs. The instant he set foot in the parlor I hurried to stand before him. With my first glimpse of his visage, I felt an iciness—a sinking—a sickening of the heart.

"I won't lie to you, Poe," he said in a tone as grim as his facial expression. "It's worse than I first thought. But," he quickly added as a strangled cry of despair issued from my lips, "the situation isn't hopeless. Your wife is resting comfortably right now. She's in no imminent peril. But she's at a critical juncture. Blast it all! If only my medicine chest hadn't been stolen!"

All at once, a remarkable transformation occurred within me. I was possessed with a sense of preternatural calm. My agitation fell away as at the dropping of a mantle.

Taking a step back from the elderly physician, I drew myself up to my full height, placed my right hand upon my heart, and, in a voice made firm with resolve, declared: "You shall have your case back, Dr. Farragut. I solemnly swear it."

The following morning, I was on the stagecoach back to Boston.

PART THREE

The Mysterious Key

CHAPTER FIFTEEN

THE ANXIETY I felt at parting from Sissy was mitigated by my knowledge that she would receive the most attentive care, not only from Dr.
Farragut (who promised to visit each day), but from the members of the Alcott household. All four of the sisters had assured me that they would do
everything in their power to cheer and comfort her during my absence.
Louy, moreover, offered to send me letters on a regular basis, keeping me informed of my dear wife's progress. As for Mrs. Alcott, I had the utmost faith
in her capacities as a nurse. Apart from Muddy, I had never known a
woman who so fully embodied the essence—the very *soul*—of maternal de-
votion.

Though I fervently hoped to complete my mission in the shortest possible time, I had no way of telling how long I would be away. Even under the
best of circumstances, my stay in Boston would certainly extend for a period of several days. Upon reaching the city, therefore, I proceeded directly
to Mrs. Randall's home on Pinckney Street, intending to avail myself once
again of her hospitality.

Not having been forewarned of my arrival, she was, of course, greatly
surprised to see me on her doorstep, carpetbag in hand. Her wonder, however, was quickly replaced by her usual graciousness. Inviting me inside, she
led me to the parlor and motioned for me to have a seat.

As she settled into an armchair across from me, I could not fail to notice how pale and drawn she looked, as though she had recently been subjected to an experience fraught with emotional strain.

"Forgive me," I said, "if I have come at an inopportune time."

"You're always welcome, Mr. Poe," she said with a wan smile. "If I seem a bit frazzled, it's just that the last few hours haven't been very pleasant. You remember my difficulties with my housemaid, Sally. Well, after putting it off forever, I finally informed her this morning that I was letting her go."

"I assume that she did not accept her dismissal in a docile fashion," I said.

"Quite the contrary," said Mrs. Randall. "Surprising, really, how badly she took it. She could hardly have been unprepared for it.

"But what about you, my dear Mr. Poe?" she continued, her brow furrowing with concern. "It's delightful to see you, of course, but I didn't expect to enjoy that pleasure quite so soon. And without your darling wife. Is everything all right?"

"I am afraid," I answered with a sigh, "that events have taken a most unfortunate turn."

I then proceeded to apprise her of the dismaying incidents of the past several days. As I described the assault upon Dr. Farragut—the theft of the chest containing his rare *materia medica*—and the repercussions of that loss as regards Sissy's condition—Mrs. Randall's expression grew increasingly horrified.

"Oh, how awful," she exclaimed when I was done. "Poor Virginia. And Dr. Farragut—why, he must be frantic. I remember that inlaid box of his quite clearly from my own visit to his home. Beautiful thing—absolutely exquisite. I was quite surprised, frankly, that he used it as a storage chest. I told him that it was like using the *Venus de Milo* as a tailor's dummy. He answered with one of his terrible puns, of course."

"Having to do, no doubt, with how *fitting* your comparison was," I remarked.

"Something like that, yes," Mrs. Randall acknowledged. "But Mr. Poe, what exactly is your plan, if I may know?"

During my trip from Concord, I had, in fact, resolved on a course of action. I now briefly explained it to Mrs. Randall.

"I see," she said. "Well, of course you're welcome to stay here as long as necessary. I wish I could offer you more pleasant accommodations, but I've agreed to let Sally keep her room until she finds a new position, so I expect that things will be rather tense around here. But you'll let me know if I can be of any help."

For moment, I made no reply.

"As a matter of fact," I said at length, "there is something—or rather, several things—that would be most useful to me at present."

The steeple bells had just announced the hour of ten when I set out from Mrs. Randall's home.

Muffled in my heavy cloak (for the night air was exceedingly cold), I bent my steps in the direction of the harbor. The city thoroughfares, so thronged with life during the daylight hours, were almost entirely deserted. The few pedestrians I encountered were, like myself, proceeding at a rapid pace—some, no doubt, hurrying homeward to the comfort of their hearths; others—to judge by their furtive air—on their way to assignations of a dubious, if not dissolute, nature.

In the silence of the empty streets my footsteps echoed loudly. Apart from the occasional barking of a dog—the distant clatter of a coach—and the strident laughter of some debauched female creature prowling the darkened byways for her prey—no other noises were to be heard.

For half an hour, I held my course. At length, my senses informed me that I was at no very great distance from the wharves. I could smell the tar— hear the lapping of the water against the massive piles—see the masts of vessels piercing the moonlight above the tops of the buildings.

Turning a corner, I found myself on a street of mean appearance, on either side of which a row of dilapidated buildings straggled toward the harbor. Some of these edifices appeared to be trading warehouses. Others were small, shabby dwellings. Lights were visible in the second-story windows of a few of these abodes. The only other illumination was the spectral glow emanating from the bright three-quarter moon.

I cautiously made my way down one side of the street, then up along the other, peering closely at each darkened doorway. In short order, I found the object of my search, easily recognizable by a small wooden sign affixed to the right of the front door. "MacKenzie Academy," it read.

That the gentleman in charge of this establishment had chosen this unsavory neighborhood as its home is not at all to be wondered at. Even in the enlightened city of Boston, the practice of human dissection was viewed with extreme distaste—if not active revulsion—by many. Certain influential ministers condemned it outright. Evidently, Dr. MacKenzie felt it prudent to conduct his business away from the censorious gaze of his critics.

If, moreover, it was true that MacKenzie obtained the raw material for his classes from graveyard sources, it would be to his advantage to operate his school in such a sparsely inhabited quarter as this—a section of the city where he could carry on his unhallowed dealings unobserved.

Gazing about me to make sure that I was indeed alone on the street, I swiftly ascended the stoop. Reaching into my pocket, I removed one of the articles supplied to me by Mrs. Randall. This was a handsome, mother-of-pearl–handled penknife belonging to her late husband. Opening the slender blade, I inserted it into the keyhole and, within a very few moments, managed to undo the lock (a trick taught to me by a former acquaintance, the brave young journalist George Townsend, whose appalling murder at the hands of the notorious "Liver-Eating" Johnson still intermittently haunted my dreams).

I quickly slipped inside the building and closed the door behind me. Instantly my sense of olfaction was assaulted by a smell so intensely disagreeable as to cause my gorge to rise. I had, of course, assumed that the atmosphere of MacKenzie's establishment would be unwholesome in the extreme. Nothing, however, could have prepared me for the heavy—the *overpowering*—stench that suffused the premises: a noxious effluvium compounded of the acrid aroma of chemical preservative and the sickly sweet redolence of rotting flesh.

With trembling fingers, I pulled out my oversized handkerchief and—like a highwayman concealing his identity behind a bandanna—tied it about the lower half of my face. Shielded somewhat from the ghastly odor, I then removed from the inner pocket of my cloak two additional items I had gotten from Mrs. Randall: a phosphorous match and a candle. Using the first to enkindle the second, I crept down the long, narrow corridor, accompanied by a monstrous shadow that slid along the blank, unadorned wall at my side.

A heavy door of dark mahogany stood at the opposite end of the hallway. I turned the knob—pushed—and the door creaked open.

In another moment, I was standing inside the dissection room.

By the glow of my candle, I perceived that the room was approximately thirty feet long and twenty wide. A pair of tables—each large enough to accommodate a human body—stood in the center of the bare wooden floor. Thankfully, there were no corpses visible at the moment. I understood from this fact that the rank odor of mortality which I had found so revolting was an intrinsic feature of the place: that, over the years of its existence, its very walls had become steeped in the foetor of death.

Holding my candle aloft, I gazed around and saw that there were several high windows which, during the day, would provide abundant illumination for the students and their teacher. At present, however, these were tightly shuttered. I was in no danger of being detected from the street. I therefore stepped to a small table that stood in one corner of the room and, with the flame of my candle, lit the oil lamp it held.

I was now able to make a more complete inspection of my surroundings. In addition to the two dissecting tables, the principal furnishings consisted of a small heating stove—a pair of workbenches holding various surgical instruments (tenacula, scissors, forceps, scalpels, needles, etc.)—a case of shelves on which were displayed assorted anatomical specimens (including an entire human head!) floating in jars—and a tall wooden storage cabinet, or closet, measuring approximately six feet high by two and a half in breadth. The walls were hung with medical charts depicting the vascular, muscular, alimentary, and reproductive systems of the human organism; while a dozen frocks of india-rubber cloth depended from hooks.

Whether the object of my search could be found on these premises I had no way of knowing. MacKenzie's establishment had simply struck me as the most logical spot to commence my quest. At a glance, however, I saw no sign of the stolen medicine chest. In the entire room, there appeared to be only one place in which it might conceivably be hidden: the tall wooden cabinet. I therefore stepped to this piece and swung open the door.

Hovering several inches above the floor of the cabinet—as though afloat in the gloomy interior—was a human skeleton.

A shriek of delirious horror rose to my lips, and it was only by clamping a hand over my mouth that I managed to stifle my scream. With my opposite hand, I immediately slammed the door shut, then staggered backward several steps and leaned against a wall, my brain reeling from the stupefying sight.

By slow degrees, my dizziness subsided. I could reason more clearly. The ghastly apparition I had seen was, very obviously, nothing more than a mounted anatomical specimen, dangling by a wire from the ceiling of the cabinet. The inordinate nature of my response could be traced to several sources. So tightly wound were my nerves at the present moment that the sheer *unexpectedness* of the sight had produced an excessively violent reaction.

Added to this was my long-standing aversion to any glimpse of human bones. This feeling stemmed from an incident that occurred in my early childhood, when—during a visit to a local physician—I had been terrified by the bleached skull of an adult male that he kept on his desk as a paperweight. The realization that this leering monstrosity lurked within the flesh of every living being had impressed me with a species of horrified awe that I had never fully overcome.

Now—shaking off from my spirit the lingering effects of the shock I had just suffered—I considered how best to proceed. Even from my fleeting glance into the cabinet, I could see that it did not contain the object I was seeking. There was no point in remaining any longer in the dissection room. Undoubtedly, there were other places in the school where the stolen chest might be hidden. It seemed probable, for example, that Dr. MacKenzie kept an office elsewhere in the building.

Crossing the floor, I extinguished the lamp after reigniting my candle. I then cautiously stepped to the door.

I had just placed my hand on the knob, when I heard a sound that froze the current of my blood.

The front door of the building had opened, admitting several people who were conversing in urgent tones. The words were too muffled for me to understand, though I thought I could discern three separate male voices. In another instant, they began to make their way slowly down the hallway toward the dissection room!

Never shall I forget the overwhelming sensation of alarm that seized me at that moment. I was hopelessly trapped! Desperately, I cast my gaze around the darkened room. There was no place to hide—with one, fearful exception.

Every fibre of my being rebelled at the thought of resorting to such a dreadful expedient. But what alternative did I have? Subduing my qualms as best I could, I hurried to the cabinet that housed the mounted remains. I then extinguished my candle—threw open the door—stepped inside—and shut myself in just as the trio entered the room.

The stifling darkness that now enveloped me was made even more intolerable by the proximity of the skeleton, which pressed so close upon me that I could feel its hollow ribs rubbing against my back—its dangling femural bones scraping against my legs—its hinged jaw resting upon my shoulder. An indescribable feeling of dread stole over me. Perspiration burst from every pore, and my heart began to race wildly. I could not, however, permit myself to tremble, for the slightest movement would cause the bones to rattle and thus betray my presence.

Summoning every particle of self-control that I possessed, I attempted to ignore the ghastly thing beside me, and focused my attention on the activity now occurring in the room. By straining my auditory faculties to the utmost, I could hear the scraping of several pairs of feet—the panting of men undergoing extreme physical exertion—then a breathless voice say:

"Almost there, Jackie boy, almost there. Come on. Up we go."

This remark was followed by a loud grunt—then a thump as of a heavy burden being laid upon one of the tables.

"Gently, William, gently," said another, deeper voice. "The dead must be treated with respect."

"Yessir," said the first.

Someone struck a phosphorous match. An instant later, dim rays of light filtered through the cracks around the door of my hiding place as a lamp was ignited.

"Shall we remove her from the sack?" asked one of the younger men.

"Yes, Jack, let's have a look at her," replied the deep-voiced fellow, whom—to judge by his authoritative manner, as well as the deferential way in which the others addressed him—I took to be Dr. MacKenzie himself.

There was a sound as of the rustling of burlap fabric, accompanied by the shifting of a heavy object upon the table.

"Nice, very nice indeed," said Dr. MacKenzie in an appraising tone of voice, "considering how long she's been in the ground. She won't keep much longer, though. The internal organs have already begun to putrefy—see this greenish tint on the lower abdomen? The dissection must be performed no later than tomorrow."

"He always finds us prime specimens, don't he?" said the youth denominated as William.

"Yes, he's proven to be a very useful fellow," said Dr. MacKenzie. "In more ways than one."

"How do you mean, Dr. MacKenzie?" asked the one named Jack.

"I can't say more about it at present," replied the physician. "Only that he is bringing me something I have desired for a very long time. Something that will prove to be a great boon to my practice. I expect to have it any day, now that he has returned from Concord."

It is hardly possible to describe the sensations I felt at that moment. Horror and revulsion thrilled through every particle of my frame at the realization that—as rumor held—Dr. Alexander MacKenzie was a desecrator of graves. For it was unmistakably clear from his comments that the corpse now lying on the dissection table had just been removed from the cemetery.

At the same time, my heart beat wildly with excitement. That MacKenzie expected to receive a long-coveted object from Concord—conveyed to him by an accomplice—appeared to confirm every point of Dr. Farragut's suspicions. At present, the precious item was evidently still in the possession of MacKenzie's confederate—a man who also assisted somehow in supplying bodies for the anatomy school. Who was this mysterious individual? I listened intently, praying that his identity would be revealed.

In this hope, however, I was destined to be disappointed; for—after exchanging a few more words with the younger men—MacKenzie exclaimed:

"Heavens—look at the time! I really must be off. Many thanks, lads. You've done yeomen's work tonight."

"Shall we stay here and clean her up?" asked Jack, a peculiarly eager note in his voice.

After a moment's hesitation, MacKenzie replied: "Why, yes, I suppose that makes sense. Save us time in the morning. Well, gentlemen, I must fly. I shall see you and your fellow students on the morrow."

No sooner had he departed than I heard one of the younger men cross the room and transfer water from a pitcher into a basin. He then returned to his partner.

"Hand me that cloth, will you, Bill?" said Jack.

"Awfully keen to get your hands on her," said the other with an insinuating laugh.

"Nothing of the kind!" his companion indignantly replied. "Here, *you* do it if that's what you think!"

"Not me," said William. "Wouldn't deprive you of the pleasure. Besides, my arms are so weary I can barely move them. Why the devil does MacKenzie always order *us* to do the digging?"

"Who else would he ask?" answered Jack, who—from the sound of it— had begun to lave the body. "Thornton? Lippard? Weymouth? Why, there's not a stout arm among them."

"Yes, I reckon we're the men for the job, all right. Still, it's a nasty business. Risky, too. I was certain we'd been spotted by that watchman as we were loading the sack into MacKenzie's coach."

"No need to worry about the law," said Jack. "MacKenzie's seen to that."

"Yes, I suppose you're right. Say, Jackie, ain't those bubbies clean yet? You've been washing them long enough."

"Damn you, Bill," came the angry response. "Watch what you say, or I swear I'll—"

"Now, now, Jackie boy, I meant no offense. Nothing wrong with having a little feel. Not when they're still as nice and round and plump as that handsome pair." Here, he heaved an exaggerated sigh. "Pity she died so young. What a waste."

"At least she'll be put to a worthy use and not simply moulder in the grave," said Jack.

"Yes, she's much too fine a piece to end up as worm food," William said. "Strange how that fellow always knows where the nicest ones are buried."

"Nothing strange about it. It goes with his job," observed Jack.

I could hear him dip his cloth into the basin, squeeze out the excess water, then return to his task. For the next few minutes, the two young men were silent.

"There," said Jack at length. "Done. Shall we take care of the teeth?"

"Leave that till tomorrow," said William, yawning loudly. "No sense in ruining that pretty face just yet."

"She is a lovely girl, all right," said Jack. "*Was,* I mean. Reminds me of Horace's woman."

"Poor Rice," said William. "Never dreamed he had it in him."

"When it comes right down to it," said Jack, "I suppose we have Horace to thank for these splendid cadavers we've been getting. He was the one, you know, who introduced Dr. MacKenzie to— What was *that*?"

"What?"

"That noise. From the cabinet. Didn't you hear it?"

At these words, my hair stood erect on my head and my heart ceased utterly to beat. Despite my efforts to remain perfectly still, a combination of factors—the insufferable closeness of the box in which I was concealed, the ghoulish activities going on just beyond my hiding place, the skeleton squeezed so tightly against me that I was virtually within its embrace—had sent an involuntary shudder coursing through my limbs, causing the dry bones to rattle. My greatest fear had come to pass. I had been discovered!

"The cabinet?" William said with a laugh. "Bless me, Jack, do you fancy the old rackabones has suddenly sprung to life?"

"I tell you, I heard something, Bill."

Cold sweat burst from my brow and stung my eyes. My mind raced. What was I to do? Only one course of action suggested itself. I would wait until one or both of the young men came to investigate the noise. I would then throw open the cabinet and make a dash for the door, trusting that, out of sheer surprise, they would remain immobilized long enough for me to effect my escape.

As it happened, I was spared the necessity of resorting to this desperate plan; for—even as I was steeling myself to act on it—I heard William say:

"Go ahead and look inside, if you wish. I'm sure it's just a rat."

For a long, agonizing moment during which I barely dared to breathe, Jack made no reply. "Yes, I expect you're right," he said at length. "This building is swarming with the filthy things. I wish MacKenzie hadn't opened his school so close to the wharves."

"Well, there's one good thing about the neighborhood," said William. "Plenty of groggeries. Come on, Jackie boy—I could use a dram about now."

"All right. Let me just cover her up."

"Sure you wouldn't care for a little taste of her charms? I could leave you two alone for a bit."

"Didn't I tell you to shut that filthy yap of yours, Bill?"

"Ha-ha. Calm yourself, Jack. Only having fun with you."

In another moment, I heard the rustling of cloth—then the rapid tread of footsteps. The lamp was extinguished—the door was opened—and the two men departed, leaving me in utter darkness with no other company but the dead.

Exerting all the willpower at my disposal, I forced myself to wait another few moments until I was certain that the two men had left the building. Then, with a tremulous cry of relief, I flung open the cabinet door and stumbled outside.

Tearing the handkerchief away from my face, I drew deep, grateful breaths of air. However noisome the atmosphere of the dissection room, it seemed positively bracing in comparison to the suffocating closeness of the coffinlike box in which I had been immured. Gradually, my respiration assumed a more normal rhythm and I recovered some degree of presence of mind.

However fraught with anxiety and even terror, my mission had not been wholly fruitless. It was time for me to go. In the utter darkness that enveloped me, however, I was uncertain as to the location of the door. Extracting my candle and the last of my matches, I enkindled the wick and glanced around.

As I did, my gaze fell on the shrouded form stretched out on the table. All at once, I was seized with an overpowering curiosity. Advancing to the table, I reached out with trembling fingers and slowly drew down the topmost portion of the sheet. The rays of my candle fell vividly upon the countenance thus exposed. I looked—and a numbness, an iciness of feeling instantly pervaded my frame. My knees tottered—my brain reeled with confusion—the blood congealed in my veins.

With a strangled cry of horror, I staggered backward from the table, then spun on my heels. From that chamber and from that building, I fled, aghast.

The corpse I had seen was that of the Mays' murdered servant girl, Elsie Bolton.

CHAPTER SIXTEEN

Y DREAMS THAT night were of the most fearful description. Among other incidents of a supremely disquieting nature, I found myself in the company of a mysterious figure, tall and gaunt and shrouded in the habiliments of the grave, who led me down an extensive corridor toward a massive door of polished ebony. Swinging open this portal, he ushered me into a cavernous hall with a lofty ceiling and white, featureless walls. The sole source of illumination was a single tall and narrow Gothic window, situated at so vast a distance from the oaken floor as to be altogether inaccessible from within. Feeble gleams of encrimsoned light made their way through the trellised panes, bathing the chamber in a lurid glow.

Occupying the center of the hall was an enormous oblong table, laden with silver platters that bore a profusion of what appeared to be odd, multi-hued delicacies. A dozen men dressed in servants' garb stood in attendance, their unblinking eyes fixed on the feast that overspread the table. At first, I could not determine the precise nature of the peculiar comestibles upon which their attention was so intensely riveted. At length, reaching out a bony hand to clutch me by the arm, my guide led me closer, until—to my inexpressible horror—I saw a bloodcurdling sight.

The platters held the grisly remains of a butchered female body!

Here lay an arm, whose soft and beautiful outlines were terminated by a small and graceful hand—and over that alabaster arm and snowy hand, the blue taint of decay spread like a foul curse, turning loveliness into loathing.

There lay a reeking trunk, lopped short below the waist. The head had been severed, and below the purple neck, two white globes—the bosom of what had once been a woman—were perceptible.

"Have you ever seen so many different colors?" whispered the shrouded figure at my side. "It's like a rainbow."

Though sickened to the core of my being, I could not turn my eyes away from the hideous spectacle. Peering more closely, I perceived that my companion was correct. A rainbow of corruption suffused that once-milky flesh; and blue and red and purple and gray and pink and orange were mingled there together in one repulsive mass of decay.

A terrible nausea overcame me. "Take me away from here," I pleaded to the skeletal thing beside me.

"But you have yet to see the *pièce de résistance*," he said in a tone that contained a distinct trace of mockery.

Glancing back at the table, I saw that it was now completely empty except for a large serving dish covered with a silver dome. At a nod from my companion, one of the servitors stepped forward and slowly raised the lid.

Standing upright on the platter was the head of a surpassingly beautiful young woman. As I gazed in an agony of horror at her exquisite, all-too-familiar features, the eyes fluttered open, two tears rolled down the cheeks, and her lips formed my name.

My teeth began to chatter—a shudder resembling a fit of the ague agitated every nerve and muscle of my frame—I felt my eyes starting from their sockets—I gasped convulsively for breath.

At that instant, I found myself seated bolt upright in bed, sweating profusely and panting as heavily as if I had just run a great distance. For several moments, my conceptions were in a state of the wildest disorder. By slow degrees, my head cleared and I became aware of my actual circumstances.

I was in the guest room of Mrs. Randall's abode. The horrors I had just witnessed had been merely a nightmare. This realization brought with it an acute sense of relief, which proved, however, to be excessively short-lived. For as my thinking faculties returned, I recalled my adventures of the previous night and instantly felt profoundly unsettled. What I had heard and witnessed in Dr. MacKenzie's academy had been nearly as disturbing as the contents of my dream.

It had been well after midnight by the time I had gotten back to Mrs. Randall's home and flung myself into bed. From the intensity of the sunlight filtering through the muslin curtains, it now appeared that the morning was well advanced. Feeling exceedingly *shaky*—for my slumber, though lengthy, had been not at all restful—I dragged myself from bed, performed my ablutions, threw on my clothing, and left the room.

As I made my way toward the stairwell, I thought I heard a doleful noise emanating from the chamber that (as I knew from my earlier visit) belonged to Mrs. Randall's now-disemployed maidservant, Sally. Pausing outside the closed door, I listened intently. Sure enough, I could discern the muffled sound of sobbing, interspersed with bitter cries of "How could she?" and "What will become of me now?" Though her dismissal was evidently well-deserved, it was impossible not to feel sorry for the poor creature. As I could offer her no relief, however, I merely turned away and hurried downstairs.

Many hours had elapsed since I had last eaten a meal. My hunger was extreme and added in no little measure to the unsteadiness I had felt upon arising. Proceeding directly to the dining room, I saw that the table held several dishes of food, along with a setting for one. Mrs. Randall was nowhere to be seen. As I stepped closer to the table, I perceived a folded sheet of paper leaning against the flower vase that served as a centerpiece. This proved to be a note from my hostess, informing me that she had been called away on an errand. She would return in several hours. In the meantime, I was to help myself to the breakfast she had left for me, which—as I saw to my deep satisfaction—consisted of thick slices of cold ham, several varieties of cheese, hard-boiled eggs, rye bread, and strawberry jam.

Seating myself at once, I shoved my napkin in my collar and fell to with gusto, focusing all my attention on the food. At length, feeling greatly refreshed, I sat back in my chair and pondered upon the events of the previous night.

Though I had failed in my primary mission—i.e., to retrieve Dr. Farragut's stolen case—my quest had not been wholly futile. I had learned several significant facts. Most importantly, I now knew that Dr. MacKenzie was still waiting to receive the precious object, which had not yet been delivered by the thief. It was this unknown person, therefore, that I must now try to identify.

What did I know about him? From the comments I had overheard, it seemed clear that—among other services he performed for MacKenzie—he was somehow able to direct the anatomist to particularly desirable corpses that could then be exhumed, under cover of night, for the purpose of dissection. This ability "went with his job," in the words of the student named Jack. It was reasonable to assume, therefore, that the person I sought was engaged in some occupation related to mortuary matters—an undertaker, say, or coffin-maker.

No sooner had I reached this conclusion than I thought of the Alcotts' eccentric neighbor, Peter Vatty, inventor of the refrigerator casket he had so proudly displayed. That Vatty might be engaged in illicit activities seemed perfectly plausible. Certainly he was a man who did not inspire confidence in his honesty. As the reader will recall, I had come away from our interview feeling sure that I had been lied to. Death, moreover, appeared to be not merely a topic of interest but a veritable *obsession* with him.

On the other hand, there were compelling reasons to doubt that he was MacKenzie's mysterious confederate. Foremost among these was his extreme reclusiveness. Clearly, the man involved with the anatomist must be someone with an intimate knowledge of recently deceased Bostonians—including poor Elsie Bolton, whose desecrated corpse I had been so horrified to discover on the dissection table. It seemed exceedingly unlikely that this man could be Peter Vatty—a veritable hermit who, by all accounts, ventured from his farm no more than once or twice a year.

To be sure, from my experiences as a detective, I knew that the least obvious person often turns out to be the perpetrator of the crime. I could not, therefore, absolutely dismiss Vatty as a suspect. For the present, however, I resolved to focus my attention on other possibilities.

It was a great source of frustration to me that I had inadvertently caused the skeleton to rattle at such an inopportune moment; for it seemed clear that I had interrupted the young man named Jack just as he was about to reveal the identity of Dr. MacKenzie's accomplice. Even so, I had gathered an important piece of intelligence—namely that the person I was seeking had apparently been an acquaintance, if not a close friend, of Horace Rice, the viciously depraved medical student who had flayed and butchered his female friend, the shop girl Lydia Bickford. This fact now constituted my best and most hopeful lead. I could not, of course, question Rice directly, as he had hanged himself in his jail cell while awaiting execution. Still, there was another potential source of information regarding Rice's life.

Checking my watch, I saw that it was already past eleven o'clock. Pulling my napkin from my collar, I rose from the table and proceeded to the entranceway, where I donned my cloak and hat and hurried out onto the street.

Then—walking at a rapid clip—I bent my steps toward the Boston Museum.

Upon entering the museum, I proceeded directly to the office of its proprietor, Moses Kimball, and rapped on the door. No one responded from
within. Recalling my earlier visit, when Sissy and I had been forced to "cool
our heels" in the corridor before we were admitted, I tried again, but with
the same disappointing result. Evidently, Kimball was not inside.

As I stood there wondering how I might locate him, I spotted, striding
down the gallery a short distance away, Professor Roscoe Powell—the magician who had so impressed my darling Sissy with his seemingly miraculous (though, in fact, perfectly mundane) "coffin escape." He was easily
recognizable not only by his squat, powerful frame and luxuriant "mutton-
chop" whiskers but from his red-lined cape and the inordinately tall opera
hat out of which he had produced a veritable menagerie of small creatures
during his performance.

Hurrying to intercept him, I planted myself in his path and, with a tip of
my own hat, introduced myself.

For a moment, he merely studied me through narrowed eyes. "So you're
Poe, eh?" he said at length. "Well, what do you want?"

I was so taken aback by the unaccountable gruffness of his manner that
I was briefly rendered speechless. At length, having somewhat recovered my
composure, I asked if he knew where I might find Mr. Kimball.

"In the statuary hall," he replied, continuing to regard me with an expression of undisguised distaste. "And now, if you don't mind." He then
stepped around me and proceeded on his way, without offering so much as
a perfunctory farewell.

As I stood there, watching his receding back, I felt utterly bewildered.
What could have possibly prompted such ill-mannered behavior on the
part of the magician, an utter stranger with whom I had had no previous
contact whatsoever? Only one answer suggested itself. Having already been
subjected to the inordinate rudeness of Moses Kimball himself, I could only
assume that an attitude of extreme incivility now prevailed in his establishment, as though his subordinates had become infected with their employer's churlish style of behavior.

At all events, there was no point in lingering over the riddle. Putting it
from my mind, I made my way down the main hallway, peering into each of
the salons in turn.

It did not take me long to find the one I was seeking. Peering through an
arched doorway, I saw a cavernous chamber filled with marble sculptures

displayed on pedestals. As I approached this exhibition room, I could discern the tall, somewhat stoop-shouldered figure of Kimball himself, easily identifiable by the startling contrast between his coal-black hair and excessively bushy, snow-white beard. He was standing in a corner of the room beside a full-sized, plaster reproduction of Michelangelo's *Dying Gladiator* (which had been augmented with a tactfully positioned fig leaf), gazing down at a small, curly-haired girl, who appeared to be inordinately upset.

Face flushed, features contorted, she stood with her fists tightly clenched at her side, angrily addressing the museum-owner, who said nothing in reply. As I drew nearer, the little girl—who, from her stature, appeared to be no older than five or six—stamped one foot violently on the floor, then spun on her heels and stormed away. As she passed me on her way out of the hall, I could hear her muttering, in her slightly lisping, high-pitched voice: "Lousy goddamned son of a bitch."

The sound of this imprecation issuing from the lips of a mere child—whom I recognized to be none other than Little Mary Gannon, the celebrated juvenile thespian whose Shakespearean performance had so thrilled the Alcott sisters—was so thoroughly dismaying that my mouth fell open and my cheeks began to burn. My consternation must have been clearly etched upon my visage, for as I came up to Kimball, he raised his thick black eyebrows and exclaimed:

"Poe! Something wrong?"

"I—I am shocked almost to the point of speechlessness," I stammered. "Unless my ears deceived me, I thought I heard language of the vilest sort uttered by the little girl with whom you were just conversing."

Kimball's reaction to my statement was surprising in the extreme. He emitted a loud guffaw and declared:

"Oh, I wouldn't be as shocked as all that. Minnie's not as little as you think. Not as far as her age is concerned, anyway."

"Why, whatever do you mean? And why do you refer to her by the appellation 'Minnie.' Is she not the renowned juvenile actress Little Mary Gannon?"

"She is when she's in Boston," said Kimball. "Other times, she goes by her real name. Minnie Warren, the Midget Queen of Beauty."

A moment passed before I grasped the full import of Kimball's statement. "I see," I remarked at length, feeling exceedingly abashed at having falling victim to what I now realized was a classic piece of *humbuggery.* The ostensible five-year-old phenomenon was not, in fact, a child at all, but rather a fully grown midget! "And precisely how old *is* Miss Warren?"

"Middle twenties, I'd guess," Kimball answered with a shrug. "I believe Phineas advertised her as twenty-three last time she performed at his museum."

"Ah—so she alternates between your establishments?"

"Yes, lots of traffic between our museums," Kimball replied. "Always shared our attractions, Phineas and I. Have to tailor them to the audience, though. Here in Boston, folks don't seem to go for freaks the way New Yorkers do. They're mad for child prodigies, though."

"Well," I observed, after taking a moment to absorb this information, "while I cannot condone the use of such uncouth language in anyone— least of all a female—I suppose I should be grateful to learn that the speaker was not, at least, a minor. But tell me: Why was Miss Gannon—or rather, Miss Warren—so extremely upset?"

"Prima donnas come in all shapes and sizes," said Kimball with a snort. "Don't have to be females, either. Roscoe Powell was just in here griping about the same thing."

"Yes, I encountered that gentleman only moments ago," I said. "I cannot say much for his manners. Rarely, if ever, have I received such discourteous treatment from a stranger."

Kimball made a dismissive motion with one hand. "Oh, pay no attention to that. It's envy, plain and simple. You aren't to blame."

"Aren't to blame?" I echoed in bewilderment. "For what?"

"For what's happened with Ludlow Marston. Ever since you helped him out of that pickle, the public can't get enough of him," said Kimball. "Couldn't care less about the other performers—Roscoe, Minnie, and the rest. That's what's eating them."

"But Dr. Marston was already the star of the show," I observed. "Hasn't his popularity always exceeded that of his colleagues?"

"Not like this," said Kimball. "You know how it is, Poe. Anything to do with a good juicy murder brings the crowds flocking in droves. Ludlow's become a bona fide sensation. Everyone wants to have a look at him. Why, you can hardly get near his office these days, there are so many patients waiting to see him."

"Do you mean to say that in addition to his public performances, Dr. Marston continues to maintain a private practice?"

"Why, yes," Kimball said, as though surprised that I was ignorant of this fact. "On Tremont Street, not far from King's Chapel. Mighty fine dentist, too. Have a look at these."

Here, Kimball—whose most characteristic expression was an impatient scowl—arranged his features into a look I had never before seen him wear. He stretched his mouth into a broad smile, revealing a set of exceedingly authentic-looking dentures embedded in what appeared to be gums of a singularly unnatural brown hue.

"Ludlow just put them in yesterday," said Kimball. "Cost a small fortune but worth every penny. Real human teeth. Base is some newfangled material, Vulcanite. Can't tell you how good it feels. Hardly know it's in my mouth. Nothing like my last set of choppers. Hellish things. Felt liked they'd been designed by Torquemada."

Gazing at Kimball as he proudly displayed his handsome new dental appliance, I wondered if his notoriously brusque demeanor had been caused, to some extent, by the extreme discomfort he had evidently suffered from his earlier set of false teeth. Certainly, he appeared to have undergone a material change for the better. Indeed, in marked contrast to his former surliness, he now appeared not merely friendly, but positively *chatty*.

"But Poe," he said, his visage taking on a quizzical look, "what are you doing here? You and your wife back from Concord so soon?"

Even before arriving at the museum, I had decided that there was no point in sharing with Kimball the true reason for my unexpected return. Accordingly, I shook my head and said:

"The medical treatment which Mrs. Poe is receiving will require her presence in Concord for at least another week. Finding myself with little to do while she undergoes her *regime,* I resolved to put my time to profitable use by fulfilling my deferred obligation to Mr. Barnum. I have therefore returned to Boston in order to sort through the effects of the degenerate medical student Horace Rice, and select the most suitable articles to take back to New York."

"You're in luck," said Kimball. "Just had them brought from the warehouse this morning. Come along, I'll show you."

As we proceeded along the central hallway, Kimball proudly pointed out a few of his newest acquisitions: a wheel from the royal chariot belonging to the great pharaoh Ozymandias—the pelt of an adult grizzly bear slain by the legendary frontiersman Daniel Boone—the world's largest oyster—a steam-powered knitting machine—a bust of Marie Antoinette made entirely of matchsticks—and a copy of Jacques-Louis David's incomparable portrait of Jean-Paul Marat, who sits slumped in his bathtub, having just been mortally stabbed by the Royalist Charlotte Corday.

"Tried to buy the tub where the Bolton girl was killed," said Kimball, as we walked past a group of perhaps a dozen spectators gathered before this painting. "Figured I'd display it alongside the picture. Sort of a theme, you see—famous bathtub murders. Couldn't persuade Mr. May to sell it to me, though."

In short order—after turning a corner and proceeding down a dimly illuminated passageway—we arrived at a door that my companion quickly unlocked with a key from a massive ring worn on his belt. He then threw open the door and disappeared into the darkness of the room. An instant later, he struck a match—lit a lamp—and beckoned me inside.

Stepping over the threshold, I found myself in a spacious custodial storeroom furnished with every species of workman's tool, hardware, and cleaning implement necessary for the maintenance of so complex an enterprise as Kimball's museum. The proprietor himself stood near the center of the floor, beside a wooden crate whose lid he was in the process of removing with a small pry bar. In another instant, the job was done.

"Help yourself. I'll be in my office should you need me," said Kimball, who, it seemed, had suddenly reverted to his former *curtness*. Then—without another word—he stepped around me and strode from the room.

For several moments, I merely stood there, gazing down at the receptacle containing Horace Rice's belongings. This box measured approximately three feet in each of its dimensions. How long it might take me to sift through its contents I could not say. Wishing to make myself as comfortable as possible while I worked, I glanced around the storeroom. All at once, my eyes lit on a small oil cask resting on its side a short distance away. Rolling this to the center of the floor, I stood it on one end and seated myself on the other. Thus perched beside the open crate, I reached a hand inside and began to remove the contents, item by item.

My emotions, as I performed this task, were varied in the extreme. Horace Rice himself, of course, meant nothing to me. I viewed him as a young madman whose crime was of such a surpassingly hideous nature as to defy comprehension. My feelings for him—insofar as they existed at all—were ones of pure horror and revulsion.

Now, however, as I scrutinized each of his belongings, a distinct sensation of pity arose in my bosom. Apart from the items on display in Kimball's gallery, the box contained the entirety of Rice's earthly possessions. These were so meagre in number—and so shabby in condition—as to bespeak a life led in the direst poverty. Indeed, in comparison to the penury he had evidently endured while pursuing his studies, my own perpetually straitened circumstances seemed positively luxurious. There were several threadbare shirts—woolen trousers with patched knees and tattered cuffs—

some chipped dinner plates and tarnished utensils—a pair of reading spectacles with one cracked lens—a hairbrush with a splintered tortoiseshell handle—a badly nicked razor and excessively worn strop—a broken clay pipe—a rust-stained candleholder—and other equally worn and worthless objects the mere sight of which could not fail to inspire a sensitive observer with feelings of the deepest melancholy.

At the same time, I was possessed by a sense of the greatest urgency; for it was somewhere among these inordinately paltry effects that I hoped to find a clue to the identity of the man who had purloined Dr. Farragut's medicine case. As I carefully examined each individual item before setting it on the floor beside the crate, however, my mood became increasingly disheartened. I could find nothing that shed light on the mystery. That I might discover a cache of personal letters or perhaps even a diary had seemed like a distinct possibility. Other than a half-dozen volumes on medical subjects, however, and a small notebook in which Rice had made rather crudely rendered sketches of the anatomical specimens he had studied, I uncovered no written matter whatsoever.

As the contents continued to dwindle, so did my hopes. At length, the crate was empty. A terrible feeling of defeat oppressed me. My shoulders slumped—I heaved a dejected sigh. As I began to rise from my perch, however, my gaze fell upon something lying in a darkened corner of the box. Leaning down, I took hold of this object and raised it to the light.

It was an old, exceedingly battered carpetbag, thoroughly crushed by the weight of the items that had been piled on top of it. From its flattened condition, it appeared to be empty. As I tilted it toward the lamp for a better view, however, something moved inside it.

Resting the bag on my lap, I pulled it open and thrust my hand inside. Instantly, my fingers closed around a small, hard, rectangular object. Even before I removed it from the bag, I knew—both from its shape and from the feel of its embossed leather surface—precisely what it was.

It was a daguerreotype case.

Undoing its latch, I opened it and held it to the light.

The case held two facing images. One was of a handsome young couple, the man standing beside the seated female. The other was a portrait of the woman by herself.

As I peered more closely at the pictures, a startled gasp escaped my lips. The woman was Elsie Bolton!

Or so, at least, I initially believed. As I continued to study the daguerreotypes, however, I perceived that—despite a distinct resemblance to the murdered servant girl—the young woman in the pictures was someone else en-tirely. Her chin was more pointed—her eyes more widely spaced—her nose more aquiline in contour.

Her companion was a young man with a sensitive mouth—well-formed nose—deep-set eyes—dark, curling hair—and a forehead of unusual breadth.

Gazing at this attractive pair, I knew that I was looking at the maniac Horace Rice and the woman who eventually would meet such an appalling death at his hands, Lydia Bickford.

How the daguerreotype had ended up in the worn-out article of luggage I could not say. Perhaps, I speculated, it had been carelessly thrown into the old carpetbag by the person responsible for gathering up Rice's belongings and then overlooked by Kimball when the latter had gone through the mur-derer's effects.

At all events, Barnum would be delighted to have it. As for myself, I felt keenly disappointed; for my last hope of finding a clue that might lead me to the stolen medicine case had now been dashed.

As I continued to study the faces of Horace Rice and his doomed lady friend, however, it occurred to me that there was something peculiar about the mere existence of their portraits. Though not prohibitively so, da-guerreotypes, I knew, were a relatively expensive luxury. In view of his ex-treme indigence, I could not understand how Rice had been able to afford not one but two of these items.

Curiosity took hold of me. Digging into my pocket, I removed the penknife I had borrowed from Mrs. Randall—opened the blade—and used the point to pry up the filigreed metal frame surrounding the portrait of Lydia Bickford. Holding the picture up to my eyes, I examined it closely.

Scratched into the corner of the glass plate was the name of the da-guerreotypist in whose studio the pictures had been made:

"H. Ballinger."

CHAPTER SEVENTEEN

IN ADDITION TO the little case containing the two daguerreotype portraits, I selected several items to take back to Barnum: one of Rice's
soiled shirts—the nicked and rust-stained razor—an old leather belt—and
a book entitled *An Illustrated Treatise on Human Anatomy for Colleges and
Academies,* written by a physician with the peculiarly apt cognomen of
"Cutter." While there was nothing at all exceptional about these articles, I felt
confident that the showman—with his genius for shameless hyperbole—
would easily find a way to transform them into the sort of lurid curiosities
sure to attract large numbers of paying customers to his museum.

After packing the items in the carpetbag for transport, I replaced the remainder of Rice's belongings in the crate—extinguished the lamp—and left
the storeroom. On my way out of the museum, I stopped at Kimball's office.
Seated at his desk—where he was busily inscribing entries in an oversized
ledger—he glanced up just long enough to offer a perfunctory farewell. For
once, I was grateful for his brusqueness, as I had no desire to engage in a
lengthy conversation that might compel me to reveal my discovery of the
double-sided daguerreotype—an object that Kimball, if he knew of its existence, might very well wish to keep for his own collection.

As I bent my steps toward Mrs. Randall's home, I revolved in my mind
the significance of what I had found. In themselves, there was nothing re-
motely sinister about the two daguerreotypes. That Horace Rice had owned
these pictures at all, however, suggested the *possibility* that he was on friendly

terms with their maker, who had provided them to the destitute medical student at a greatly reduced cost—perhaps even *gratis*. Could Ballinger, then, be the acquaintance whom Rice had introduced to Dr. MacKenzie and who now performed various illicit services for the latter? Could he be the man who—in addition to stealing Dr. Farragut's secret ingredients—also helped procure corpses for dissection? But what connection could the daguerreotypist possibly have to mortuary matters?

No sooner had I posed this question to myself than the answer struck me so forcibly that I halted abruptly in my tracks, nearly causing a collision with the pedestrian behind me. I remembered the portrait that Mrs. Randall wore in a locket around her neck. I recalled the pictures that had so unsettled Sissy during our brief visit to the daguerreotypist's studio.

Ballinger specialized in making memorial photographs of the dead!

This realization struck me with the shock of a galvanic battery, for it showed conclusively that Ballinger shared one all-important characteristic with the man I was seeking: a job that brought him into contact with newly dead corpses, thus allowing him to evaluate their condition and identify suitable subjects for exhumation and dissection.

Even this, however, hardly constituted proof of Ballinger's guilt. While the facts I had uncovered were certainly suggestive, they were, I realized, circumstantial in the extreme. Before I was justified in regarding the daguerreotypist as a serious suspect, I would require far stronger evidence of his culpability.

As I continued on my way, I did not imagine, of course, that just such evidence was even then awaiting me at Mrs. Randall's residence.

Immediately upon entering the house, I became aware of a noise that—however commonplace in itself—occurred so rarely upon those premises as to be positively startling. Owing to the state of tension that existed between Mrs. Randall and her servant, Sally, I was accustomed to overhearing the most disagreeable sounds: bitter complaints, violent altercations, piteous weeping. What I had never before heard within those walls—but which now fell upon my ears—was hearty female laughter.

Following this pleasant noise to its source, I found myself in the library, where my hostess was seated in an easy-chair, a cup of tea resting on the table beside her, and in her hands a slender volume from which she was deriving such enjoyment.

Glancing up from its pages, she bid me welcome, then—noticing the carpetbag clutched in my hand—asked, with a note of surprise, if I was going somewhere. I explained that I had just come from the Boston Museum, where I had gathered up some articles to bring back to Mr. Barnum.

"I see," said Mrs. Randall. "And did you happen to attend Dr. Marston's performance while you were there?"

"Why, no, not at all," I replied. "Why do you ask?"

"I've been sitting here reading his book, *The Dentalogia*, which you were kind enough to give me," said Mrs. Randall. "I must say, I find it perfectly delightful."

"I am glad that it affords you such pleasure," I said.

"Imagine composing an entire epic poem about dental hygiene," said Mrs. Randall. "Quite an accomplishment when you think about it. And parts are actually quite skillfully done, though others are rather comical—unintentionally so, I'm afraid."

"I assume that you were enjoying one of the latter passages just now," I observed.

"Yes, a stanza about the importance of cleaning your teeth each morning. Here, listen," said Mrs. Randall, lowering her eyes to the page and declaiming thusly:

> "If sloth or negligence the task forbear
> Of making cleanliness a daily care;
> If fresh ablution, with the morning sun,
> Be quite forborne or negligently done;
> In dark disguise insidious tartar comes
> Encrusts the teeth and irritates the gums!"

"Though one can hardly fault the advice," I dryly remarked as she looked up at me with a merry sparkle in her exceptionally attractive eyes, "it would appear that certain topics are simply unsuited for poetical treatment—regular tooth-brushing being foremost among them."

"You must give him credit for sincerity, though," said Mrs. Randall, closing the slender volume and placing it on the table beside her teacup. "He's obviously quite passionate on the subject. And it's passion, perhaps even more than technical skill, that makes a poet. At least that's what my Robert always argued."

As one who believed firmly in the supreme importance of craftsmanship, I could not have agreed *less* with the opinion of Mrs. Randall's late husband. Indeed, my own masterwork, "The Raven," had been composed with the precision and rigid consequence of a mathematical puzzle. Still, there was little to be gained from arguing the point. Instead, I merely made a noncommittal noise before saying:

"I am sincerely sorry that I did not have the opportunity to make the acquaintance of your late husband."

"He would have liked that very much," said Mrs. Randall, her right hand rising unconsciously to the locket that rested upon her bosom.

"May I ask a question about the memento you wear about your neck?"

"Why, yes, of course," said Mrs. Randall, looking somewhat surprised.

"As there are undoubtedly a number of daguerreotypists in the city," I said, "why did you choose Mr. Ballinger to make the picture?"

"As a matter of fact," Mrs. Randall replied, a shadow of sadness passing over her countenance, "I learned about him from Robert. It was shortly after Mr. Ballinger opened his studio. Robert happened to pass by the window and was quite taken with the pictures on display. He went inside—my husband told me this over dinner that evening—and spoke to Mr. Ballinger about having our portraits done. They were to be our anniversary gifts to each other."

Here, Mrs. Randall's lower lip began to tremble and her eyes grew moist. Reaching down for her handkerchief, she wiped a tear from her cheek, then cleared her throat and continued thusly: "It was not to be. Robert went into a decline soon afterward and passed away before we could have our pictures made for each other."

"I am very sorry," I said. "Am I correct in assuming, then," I continued after pausing briefly to permit her to regain her composure, "that you contacted Mr. Ballinger following your husband's death and arranged for him to make the posthumous portrait?"

Mrs. Randall shook her head. "No. He came by the house quite unexpectedly the morning after Robert passed. Somehow he had heard about it and wished to offer his condolences. He was the one who proposed taking the picture. I was reluctant at first, but then agreed. And I am very glad I did, for it is the only daguerreotype image I have of my dear husband."

"And what, on the whole, was your impression of Mr. Ballinger?" I asked.

"Why, he was a perfect gentleman. Very considerate. In most cases, as I understand it, the daguerreotypist himself prefers to prepare the subject before making a memorial picture—to comb the hair just so, to arrange the body in a particular position, and so forth. Mr. Ballinger sensed that I wished to perform those rites myself and allowed me the privacy to do so while he waited down here."

"I see. I take it, then, that—beyond the facts gleaned from your personal dealings with Mr. Ballinger—you know nothing more about him."

"I believe that he formerly operated a studio in Philadelphia before moving to Boston," said Mrs. Randall. "And that he counts among his clients a number of very prominent figures from our city's literary and artistic community. Including our epic poet of dental hygiene."

"How is that?" I said.

Plucking the slender volume from the side table, Mrs. Randall opened the cover—leafed through several pages—then reached the book to me.

Taking it from her hand, I saw that she had opened it to the frontispiece illustration. This was an engraved portrait of the author in three-quarters profile, looking appropriately solemn. Beneath the picture were the words: "Dr. Ludlow Marston, from a daguerreotype by Mr. Herbert Ballinger."

"Interesting," I said.

"But why are you so curious about Mr. Ballinger?" asked Mrs. Randall.

"Only because I still intend to avail myself of his services," I prevaricated. "Owing to the unfortunate events that transpired here, my wife and I were prevented from having a daguerreotype made of ourselves. I am still hoping that Mr. Ballinger will be able to do our portrait when I bring Virginia back from Concord."

This remark elicited a most peculiar response from Mrs. Randall. Her eyes grew wide and—raising one hand—she delivered a little slap to the center of her brow. "I'd almost forgotten," she exclaimed. "You received a letter from Concord."

"A letter?" I said in surprise.

"It was delivered by a very nice gentleman," said Mrs. Randall. "A neighbor of the Alcott family. He arrived in Boston by the morning stage. He was asked to deliver it to you at this address. I placed it on the bureau in your room."

"I had better go look at it right away," I said, feeling a sharp pang of apprehension within my bosom. I then excused myself and hurried upstairs to my chamber.

Tossing the carpetbag onto the bed as I entered the room, I strode to the dresser and snatched up the envelope. No sooner had my fingers closed around it than I felt a small, oddly shaped bulge in one corner. I quickly tore open the envelope and inverted it; whereupon a little gold watch key slid from its interior and fell into my palm. Deeply puzzled, I set the key upon the top of the dresser, then reached into the envelope and removed a piece of paper that—upon being unfolded—turned out to be a communication from Louy Alcott. Hastily scribbled on what was evidently a page she had ripped from her notebook, it was ornamented with all manner of smudges and blots. The message read as follows:

Dear Mr. Poe—

Here is a letter, as I promised. Forgive the spatters and spots, but I never *can* seem to write without making a dreadful mess. I don't know how Anna does it. You should see her letters—they are perfectly elegant, without a jot of stray ink on the page. But then, she is so proper and ladylike, while I—well, I'm Louy and never shall be anything else!

Virginia is feeling heaps better. She is coughing much less than before, and her appetite is improving nicely. Yesterday, Marmee was called away on an errand, so I decided to fix a nice dinner for us all. I slaved away the whole afternoon, and it turned out regularly splendid, though the asparagus *did* come out rather overcooked. Next time, I shan't boil them for a whole hour. The blancmange was a bit lumpy, too. Still, it was very sweet and soothing, and Virginia ate nearly a whole bowl of it, which shows how well she is recuperating.

When I haven't been pegging away at my schoolbooks or grubbing at my chores, I have been spending my shining hours finishing *The Witch's Curse*. We had our first full rehearsal yesterday. We held it in Virginia's bedroom so that she could watch. On the whole, things went quite well, though May is stiff as a poker in her fainting scene. She is afraid of making herself black and blue, you see, so instead of falling down, she carefully lowers herself to the floor as if she is performing a curtsy. Still, I have high hopes for my "Operatic Tragedy." I ended up using a rebus for my secret code, just as you suggested, and have become quite an expert in composing messages in picture form.

Dr. Farragut has been a trump. He visits every day, and he and Virginia get on capitally. When she told him that she had grown up in Baltimore, he became very excited. It seems that Dr. Farragut studied medicine there. May thinks he's the jolliest fellow who ever lived, for he is always amusing her with his silly little jokes, like the one about the man who went outside while it was raining cats and dogs and stepped in a poodle. May was drinking from a glass of water when he told that one, and she laughed so hard that the water squirted out of her nose, which made *me* burst out laughing. The silly child got dreadfully cross at me and went stomping off to her room.

Lizzie, who is a perfect angel and the family "peacemaker," urged me to go upstairs and beg May's pardon for laughing at her. I declared that I wouldn't. When the evening came, though, I resolved not to let the sun set on our anger, so I went to her room to make up with her. I found her seated on the floor with her "treasure box," playing with the little gold key you have already, I'm sure, found inside the envelope. Naturally, I was burning with curiosity to know where she'd gotten it. At first, she refused to tell, for she was afraid that I would take it away from her. But I finally coaxed the story from the little goose.

Do you remember during our trip back home from Boston when May said she'd left a drawing of an angel at the foot of the bathtub where poor Elsie was drowned? Well, it seems that, while she was placing the picture there, she spotted the little gold key lying on the floor just underneath the tub and decided to take it with her as a keepsake. It never occurred to the silly child that it was undoubtedly from Uncle Samuel's watch. It must have fallen off the chain in all the confusion.

I finally got it away from her by bribing her with a few pennies to buy pickled limes, which are all the fashion now among the little girls in our neighborhood. I know you are dreadfully busy, but if you have a moment to spare, it would be splendid if you could return the key to Uncle Samuel. He has probably been searching far and wide for it.

I hope you are having success in your search for Dr. Farragut's medicine chest.

Your friend,
Louy Alcott

As the reader will readily conceive, I felt greatly relieved upon perusing this missive. My initial fear—upon learning from Mrs. Randall that a letter had arrived for me from Concord—was that a crisis had occurred. I now saw that the opposite was the case. My darling wife's health was evidently much improved and the entire Alcott household appeared to have returned to a state approximating the normal.

Still, I was painfully aware that—in view of Sissy's underlying condition—the situation could reverse itself at any moment and my wife be seized with another and perhaps more deadly paroxysm. The urgency of my quest remained acute.

As I set the letter down upon the dresser, my eyes fell upon the gold watch key. At that instant, there floated through my brain a vague, half-formed thought of—what? After several fruitless moments of attempting to bring the elusive idea to the forefront of my mind, I abandoned the effort.

Consulting my own watch, I saw that the hour was nearing four. There was still ample time to perform the errand Louy had requested of me. Besides, I had another motive for wishing to visit her uncle, Mr. May—one directly related to my own mission.

Plucking the little key from the dresser, I carefully inserted it into my vest pocket and left my room.

Twenty minutes later, I was seated on a sofa in the parlor of Mr. Samuel May. Among other indications of refined taste, there were many books, drawings, pots of flowers, and a handsome pianoforte. A cheerful fire blazed in the hearth. Altogether, the room exuded an intensely hospitable atmosphere, perfectly in keeping with the welcoming personality of the elderly proprietor himself, who—seated across from me in a Dutch roundabout chair—was now regarding me intensely with his startlingly blue eyes.

I had arrived at his doorstep only minutes before. After recovering from his initial surprise at seeing me, he had ushered me into the parlor and questioned me eagerly about his sister and nieces. After assuring him that all was well at Hillside, I explained—with a certain deliberate vagueness—that I had returned to Boston on an errand relating to my wife's medical condition. I then politely inquired after his own wife, who had been so adversely affected by the tragedy that had occurred on their premises.

"Poor Sophia," he said with a sigh. "She's been a nervous wreck since it happened. Won't set foot in the bedroom anymore—thinks it's haunted. She was quite attached to the girl, you know. And the funeral, of course, only made things worse. Quite an upsetting scene—especially after that young fiend's mother appeared."

"What do you mean?" I said.

"Haven't you heard?" he said. "That McMahon boy—the one who committed the foul deed. His mother showed up at the cemetery just as we were lowering poor Elsie into the ground. Started ranting like a madwoman—about what an innocent little lamb her Jesse was, how he'd never hurt a fly. How *we* were the killers because we'd caused her son's death. Can you imagine?"

With one hand on the arm of his chair, the portly old man rose partway to his feet—dug the opposite hand into the pocket of his trousers—and removed a voluminous handkerchief. He then lowered himself back into his seat—blew his nose with a loud *honking* sound—and inspected the interior of the handkerchief before returning it to his pocket and continuing thusly:

"Well, I suppose it's not so surprising after all. I've seen it before. Some brute commits a horrid crime and his mama insists that he couldn't possibly be guilty, not her dear little sonny boy. Doesn't matter how monstrous a man is. Why, I'll wager even Nero's *mater* thought he was the gentlest soul in creation."

Though Mr. May might have a chosen a more persuasive example (the mad emperor Nero having reputedly disemboweled his own mother, Agrippina, out of a depraved desire to view the womb from which he had sprung), his *general* point could hardly be disputed. Still, I could not help but be troubled by his story; for—as the reader will recall—I myself had been afflicted with certain doubts as to the culpability of the McMahon youth.

"I am sorry to hear about your wife," I remarked.

"Poor thing is inconsolable," said Mr. May. "Thank God for the laudanum—only thing that gives her some relief. Nothing I say helps. I tell her that Elsie is at rest, but it doesn't seem to make a jot of difference. Why, Poe—is something the matter?"

At the old man's reference to Miss Bolton's ostensible state of repose, I had felt myself blanch; for—unlike him—I knew the dreadful truth about the final disposition of her remains. Far from being at rest, the young woman had been subjected to a hideous postmortem violation. Indeed, at that very moment, her corpse was undoubtedly undergoing the ghastly process of medical dissection.

"Can I bring you a glass of water?" asked Mr. May.

"Thank you, no. I'm fine."

For a moment he continued to study me with an anxious expression. "Well, all right, if you say so," he said at length, sounding distinctly unconvinced. "But tell me, Poe, what brings you here today?"

Inserting the thumb and index finger of my right hand into the pocket of my vest, I extracted the little gold key and held it out for the old man's inspection. I then explained that the item had arrived that morning with a letter from his niece Louisa, who wished it to be returned to Mr. May without delay.

"But it isn't mine," said the latter.

"I beg your pardon?"

"I haven't lost my watch key," he said. "Here—see?" Removing his pocket watch from his vest, he displayed the fob, from which—as I clearly perceived—a little key was dangling.

"But it was found in your bedchamber beneath the bathtub in which Miss Bolton was drowned."

"Well, that's mighty strange," said Mr. May, puckering his mouth. "I suppose it might belong to Constable Lynch or Coroner Tilden. They were poking around there quite a bit."

"Yes, that's possible," I said, returning the key to my pocket. "In any event, your niece will be relieved to hear that the key isn't yours. She was concerned that you had been engaged in a futile—and excessively frustrating— search for it."

"She's a good one, that Louy," said Mr. May. "A bit rough at the edges, but kindhearted as they come. Sorry that you made the trip here for nothing, Poe."

"Not at all," I answered. "It was in no way a bother. And I confess to having another motive for my visit."

"Yes?"

"I have question about Miss Bolton. It may seem peculiar. I can assure you, however, that—though circumstances do not permit me to reveal the reason for my query—it does not derive from mere idle curiosity."

"Well, you've made *me* very curious, my boy," said Mr. May, looking at me through narrowed eyes. "Go ahead and ask this strange question."

"Do you know whether Miss Bolton was acquainted with a daguerreotypist named Ballinger?"

Mr. May's reaction was surprising in the extreme. He started visibly and gazed at me with a look of unconcealed astonishment.

"How on earth did you know?" he exclaimed.

"Know what?" I replied in a tone nearly as surprised as his own.

By way of answer, the elderly gentleman got to his feet and stepped to the fireplace. Arrayed upon the mantel were several pieces of bric-a-brac, including a small bronze statue of an Indian maiden—a little marble head of George Washington—a porcelain bowl adorned with the Great Seal of the United States—and, I now saw, a daguerreotype case. Removing the latter from its place, Mr. May carried it back to the sofa and handed it to me.

Even before I accepted it from him, I felt certain as to what I would see. A single glance confirmed my expectation.

The picture showed Elsie Bolton in death. She was garbed in a white linen gown, her head supported by a pillow, her hands folded over her bosom, a look of serenity on her handsome countenance.

"It was Mr. Ballinger who made that," said Mr. May.

An irrepressible tremor pervaded my frame. Here was tangible evidence of a link between Ballinger and Dr. MacKenzie: a daguerreotype made by the former of a corpse that, within days of its burial, would end up in the dissection lab of the latter!

"Was this portrait done at your request?" I asked.

"Heavens no," said Mr. May. "It was his idea."

"Then you yourself are an acquaintance of Mr. Ballinger's?"

"Not in the slightest," replied Mr. May. "He appeared here one afternoon out of the blue. First time I ever laid eyes on the man. Said he'd read about the murder in the newspapers and wished to do something for the family. Offered to take a memorial picture of Elsie free of charge. I couldn't see the harm in it—thought it might bring Sophia a bit of comfort to have a memento of the girl."

"When, precisely, did this occur?"

"Just a day or two after the murder. Right after you and the girls left for Concord, in fact."

"I see," I said, continuing to study the daguerreotype. "May I ask where the image was taken?"

"Up in the bedroom. That's where Elsie was laid out. But really, Poe, what is this all about?"

"I must beg your indulgence, Mr. May," I said. "At present, I am not at liberty to divulge the reason for these inquiries. Suffice it to say that my interest in the daguerreotypist relates to a matter of extreme urgency involving the medical treatment of my wife."

"Another of your mysteries, eh, Poe?" said the elderly gentleman with a sigh.

Returning the daguerreotype case to Mr. May, I rose from the sofa, preparatory to taking my leave.

"If you're so curious about this Ballinger fellow, why don't you visit his studio?" said Mr. May. "I believe it's not very far from here."

"Yes, I know," I said. "My wife and I were there, albeit very briefly, on the very morning of Miss Bolton's mur—"

At that instant, the elusive thought of which I have previously spoken suddenly flashed upon my mind, startling me into silence. I should not, in fact, call it a *thought*. Rather, it was an image—one of such vivid intensity that I could picture it as clearly as if it were taking place in front of me at that very moment.

I saw Sissy and myself, waiting patiently in Mr. Ballinger's studio for his return. I saw him arrive and introduce himself. I saw him consult his pocket watch, only to discover that his timepiece had run down some minutes earlier. I saw him run his fingers over the chain—glance down at it with a frown—then, after making a disgruntled sound, return the watch to his vest pocket, *without having rewound it.*

At the time, I had thought nothing of his actions. Now their significance was startlingly clear to me. He had not wound his watch for a very simple reason.

The key was missing from the chain!

CHAPTER EIGHTEEN

A S I MADE my way back to Mrs. Randall's abode, my mind was in a
perfect tumult. So confused, so *chaotic* were my thoughts—and so
intense my efforts to arrange them into a coherent form—that I was utterly
oblivious of my surroundings. As I proceeded along the busy streets, I was
only dimly aware of the dense and continuous tide of humanity through
which I moved. It was not until I inadvertently jostled an elderly woman—
knocking her cane from her hand and nearly throwing her to the ground—
that I was momentarily shaken from my reveries by the outraged cries of
several passersby who shouted: "Watch where you go!" and "Clumsy fool!"

Muttering an apology, I stooped to retrieve the old woman's walking
stick and, after returning it to her with an apology, continued on my way,
instantly becoming absorbed again in my conjectures.

Nothing I had thus far discovered about Herbert Ballinger could be
construed as definitive proof of any criminal conduct on his part. Taken together, however, the meagre yet certain results of my investigation pointed
strongly to the daguerreotypist as the man whom I was seeking.

The latter, I knew, was a confederate of Dr. MacKenzie, to whom he had
been introduced by the homicidal medical student Horace Rice. In addition
to other services performed for the anatomist, the suspect was someone
whose profession gave him access to newly dead bodies, allowing him to
gauge their suitability as potential subjects for dissection. One of these

corpses, as I had so shockingly discovered, was that of the Mays' murdered servant girl, Elsie Bolton.

The daguerreotypist fit all of these requirements perfectly. I knew from the dual portraits I had uncovered among Horace Rice's belongings that Ballinger was acquainted—and perhaps even on intimate terms of friendship—with the former. As a maker of mortuary images, he was in an ideal position to identify the most desirable anatomical specimens. And from my interview with Mr. May, I had learned that Ballinger had taken a portrait of Elsie Bolton's corpse just prior to her burial.

For what reason would the daguerreotypist assist Dr. MacKenzie in this unhallowed enterprise? The obvious explanation—pecuniary gain—did not seem to apply in this case. For centuries, money had been the fuel that drove the traffick in human corpses. Dr. Robert Knox of Edinburgh, for example, had paid a bounty of £7.10s for every cadaver provided to him by the notorious "body-snatchers" Burke and Hare—a princely sum to that odious pair who existed in a state of near destitution. Herbert Ballinger, however, was not one of the degraded poor. On the contrary, he was an inordinately successful businessman whose clientele included members of Boston's "Brahmin" class. Assuming that Ballinger *was* MacKenzie's confederate, there must, I felt sure, be another inducement for his actions besides mere monetary considerations.

What troubled me chiefly at the moment, however, was not the question of the daguerreotypist's motives. Rather, it was the startling idea that *he* was the owner of the mysterious watch key found by little May Alcott. Assuming that I was correct, how could that object conceivably have ended up beneath the bathtub where the murder took place? It was true—as I had just learned from Mr. May—that Ballinger had spent time inside the bedroom while making his portrait of Elsie Bolton's body. But that had occurred *after* the departure of the Alcott girls. If the key did in fact belong to the daguerreotypist, there appeared to be only one logical explanation—shocking as it seemed.

It was *Ballinger* who murdered Elsie Bolton! The key had become dislodged from his watch chain during the drowning, perhaps while the victim violently kicked her feet in an effort to free herself from her killer's lethal grasp. Later, after discovering that the key was missing, Ballinger contrived to return to the May home to retrieve it, under the pretext of taking the memorial picture of Miss Bolton. By then, however, the tell-tale item was gone—taken by the little Alcott girl.

I was already convinced that Ballinger helped Dr. MacKenzie procure dead bodies for dissection. To think that he might also *create* some of those corpses required no very great leap of imagination. After all, Burke and Hare themselves had done precisely that, dispatching more than a dozen victims, whose bodies were then sold to the unquestioning Dr. Knox. If the daguerreotypist occupied a very different social position from that of Burke and Hare, perhaps he shared another characteristic with that infamous pair—a willingness to commit murder in order to supply his medical associate with fresh anatomical specimens.

All this, I realized, was pure speculation. Many questions remained unresolved. Among other things, I wondered how—if my theory was correct—Ballinger had come to select Elsie Bolton as a victim. Mr. May had implied that the daguerreotypist knew nothing about the girl until after her death. But, of course, there may have been a prior connection between them of which the old man was unaware.

In any event, I felt infused with a heightened resolve. What had appeared to be a simple case of larceny involving Dr. Farragut's precious ingredients had now taken on the aspect of something infinitely more sinister—a dark conspiracy involving the plundering of graves, the desecration of corpses, and the commission of cold-blooded murder!

My sense of urgency was made even more acute by my lingering guilt over the death of young Jesse McMahon—who, it now appeared, might have been culpable of nothing more serious than the pilfering of a piece of silverware. If—as the boy's grief-stricken mother insisted—her son was truly innocent of the murder, it was my obligation to help establish that fact.

These were the thoughts I revolved in my mind as I directed my steps toward Pinckney Street.

Upon my previous entrance into Mrs. Randall's home, I had been surprised by the unwonted sound of laughter. Now, as I opened the front door and stepped inside the spacious foyer, I was struck by a very different acoustic phenomenon—a complete and all-pervasive *stillness* that, for reasons I could not explain, immediately impressed me with a deep sense of foreboding. For a moment, I remained absolutely motionless, straining my auditory faculties to the utmost. In spite of my efforts, however, I could not detect the slightest noise.

In itself, there was nothing alarming about this fact. Mrs. Randall after all might have stepped out on an errand or retired to her bedchamber for a midafternoon nap. The same was true of her disemployed servant, Sally. Nevertheless, I could not shake off the sensation of premonitory dread that oppressed me as soon as I entered the house.

Skeptics will argue that my recollections of that moment have been retrospectively colored by my knowledge of succeeding events. There is, of course, no way to disprove this theory. I can merely assert that a feeling of extreme, of *inordinate,* trepidation pervaded my spirit—even before I first grew aware of the horror that had occurred in my absence.

Leaving the vestibule, I looked into the library, thinking that, perhaps, Mrs. Randall had fallen into a doze while perusing the soporific contents of Dr. Marston's egregious volume. The room, however, was devoid of human presence. I then proceeded to the stairway, intending to ascend to my bed-chamber. As I began to mount the first steps, I glanced toward the dining room, the entrance to which was visible from my vantage point.

Instantly, I beheld a sight that froze the current of my blood. One of the dining chairs had been overturned and was lying backward on the wooden floor. Beside it, staining the boards, was a quantity of dark crimson fluid that I saw at once was blood.

An irrepressible tremor pervaded my frame as I hastened toward the dining room. No sooner had I stepped inside than I froze at the ghastly— the appalling—spectacle that confronted me.

The room itself was in a state of the wildest disorder. The furniture was broken and thrown about in every direction. Shattered pieces of chinaware were scattered all around. Several of the lace curtains had been torn from their supporting rods and lay in a tangled heap at the foot of the windows.

Blood was everywhere. The small quantity I had initially discerned was the merest fraction of the amount that bespattered the walls and floor. It was as though someone had taken an entire bucket of sanguinary fluid and flung it, in great sweeping arcs, about the dining room.

Struggling to subdue the intense sentiment of horror that threatened to unman me, I cautiously made my way farther into the room. It was only then that I perceived the source of so much gore.

The bodies lay beside each other at the opposite end of the room. Had I not taken note of Mrs. Randall's garb earlier in the day when she and I had conversed in the library, I would not have been able to recognize her. Both her torso and head were fearfully mutilated—the latter so much so as to scarcely retain any semblance of humanity.

Her maidservant, Sally, who lay sprawled several feet away with a large butcher knife clutched in her right hand, had suffered only a single, albeit exceedingly gruesome, wound. Her throat had been cut, producing a gaping incision from which thick clots of blood continued to ooze.

The intensity of my reaction to this hideous spectacle may be readily imagined. My brain reeled and I grew deadly sick. It was obvious at a glance that both women were beyond any aid I could offer.

Spinning on my heels, I dashed from the house—burst into the street—and began shrieking for help.

CHAPTER NINETEEN

⟨⁓⟩

H ERE, DRINK THIS. It'll do you good."
Huddled miserably on the armchair in which—only several
hours earlier—Mrs. Randall had been so comfortably ensconced, I looked
up in surprise at the source of this remark. So absorbed had I been in my
grim contemplations that I had not noticed anyone enter the library.

It was Constable Lynch who stood before me. In one extended hand he
held a crystal goblet, filled nearly to the brim with a dark-colored liquid
that—from both its fragrance and hue—I judged to be Madeira.

"Found a bottle in the sideboard," the constable continued. "Just about
the only thing in that whole damn room still in one piece."

For a moment, I hesitated to accept his offer. I recalled the solemn
pledge I had made to Muddy prior to my departure—i.e., that I would not,
under any circumstances, permit so much as a drop of alcohol to pass my
lips during my sojourn in Boston. As I fixed my gaze on the enticing beverage, however, I felt my resolution waver.

Surely, I thought, my darling aunt would not wish to see me suffer, when
my anguished state might be alleviated by a few medicinal sips of wine.
After all, in securing my pledge, she could not possibly have envisaged the
fearful—the *harrowing*—circumstances that had so thoroughly unstrung
my nerves.

My reasoning seemed unassailable to myself. Reaching out with both
trembling hands, I took the goblet and quickly brought it to my lips. The ef-

fect was nearly instantaneous. A delicious warmth suffused my frame. The quaking of my limbs grew less severe. My heart resumed something of its normal rhythm. For the first time since I had run screaming into the street, I was able to ponder the events of the preceding hour with a measure of calm.

The sidewalk in front of Mrs. Randall's home had been deserted when I burst from the front door, calling for help. My cries, however, had quickly alerted her neighbors, several of whom had gone dashing off in different directions in search of the police.

The first officer to appear was a young man named Higginbottom, who had been patrolling nearby on foot. Grabbing him by the arm, I had hurried him into the house and pointed to the bodies sprawled at the far end of the dining room. His initial reaction was scarcely less violent than my own had been. At his first glimpse of the hideously mangled pair, his complexion grew cadaverously pale and he appeared about to swoon, reaching out to clutch the wall in order to keep himself upright.

His response was perfectly understandable, in view of the sheer ghastliness of the scene. Though the gaping (and apparently self-inflicted) wound to Sally's throat presented an exceedingly shocking sight, it was Mrs. Randall's fearfully butchered corpse that induced the greatest horror—nausea—and revulsion.

The upper part of her torso had been savaged to such an extent that her dress was virtually shredded, leaving large areas of hacked and bloody flesh exposed. Even more ghastly were the injuries that had been inflicted on her head and face. I shall spare the reader a full description of these awful mutilations, which had rendered her features so unrecognizable. I will merely state that of the countless outrages she had suffered, the most appalling was the one to her eyes. These had been gouged from their sockets and flung to the floor. Not content with this atrocity, her maddened attacker had then used her blade to chop away at the orbs, until there was nothing left of Mrs. Randall's once-beautiful eyes but a gelatinous mass that floated in a puddle of gore.

Sickened to the core of my being by the awful spectacle, I had staggered into the library and collapsed in the armchair. When other officials began to arrive—including the pair I knew from the Bolton tragedy, Constable Lynch and Coroner Tilden—I did my best to answer their questions concerning my discovery of the bodies. I had then been left alone in the library, where I remained in a state of extreme mental agitation while Lynch, Tilden, and their colleagues examined the crime scene.

Only once in the course of the succeeding hour did I arise from my place, to draw the curtains in the library in order to prevent the growing mob of morbid curiosity-seekers from peering in through the windows. Otherwise, I had kept to my seat, seized with a convulsive trembling which did not begin to subside until I had quaffed the nerve-soothing beverage that had just been offered me by Lynch, who—I inferred—was now done with his investigation.

Carefully setting the half-empty goblet down on the side table—where Dr. Marston's slender volume still lay, just as Mrs. Randall had left it—I thanked the police officer for his thoughtfulness. The wine, I assured him, had proven to be a welcome tonic for my overwrought nerves.

"Good," he said. Then, pointing his chin in the direction of the dining room, he added: "Tilden wants to see you. In there."

Having no wish to subject myself to another glimpse of the two horrifically butchered women, I received this news with a little gasp of dismay. I could see from the determined expression on Lynch's countenance, however, that there was no point in protesting. A spasm of dread coursed through my frame, as though Lynch's pronouncement had instantly undone the palliative effects of the Madeira.

Reaching over to the side table, I grabbed the goblet by its stem and quickly drained the remainder of its contents. Thus fortified, I rose from my seat and followed the constable out of the parlor.

Upon entering the dining room, I immediately noticed Officer Higginbottom, the young policeman who had been the first to arrive on the scene. He was standing in a corner, making notes in a small writing tablet. At first, I could not discern Coroner Tilden. It was not until Lynch and I stepped around the table that I saw the elderly gentleman seated on his haunches beside the bodies, stroking his chin in a contemplative manner.

As I came up beside him, he gazed at me through the thick lenses of his octagonal spectacles, then slowly rose to a standing position. I was struck, as I had been on first meeting him, by both the inordinate boniness of his frame and his decidedly unkempt appearance—particularly his long, straggly gray hair, which had evidently not received the benefit of a washing in many weeks.

Keeping my eyes averted as much as possible from the carnage on the floor, I asked if he had arrived at a verdict concerning the tragedy.

"It would appear that the servant killed her mistress, then took her own life," he said. There was a thick reek of salted herring on his breath, which—

in combination with the redolence of blood that suffused the room—induced an immediate sensation of queasiness within me that I struggled to suppress.

"Officer Higginbottom has been outside talking to the neighbors," he continued. "Several of them confirmed what you've already told us about the trouble between the two women. Let's assume that while you were gone this afternoon, they became embroiled in an argument that got out of hand. That would seem to be the obvious explanation, at any rate."

There was something in the way in which he emphasized the word "seem" that suggested an element of doubt. Peering at him curiously, I said:

"That, indeed, was my own initial assumption. While seated in the library, however, I have had occasion to ponder the matter more thoroughly. I confess to feeling puzzled by one aspect of the case."

"Yes?" said Tilden, staring at me with eyes that—seen through the thick glass of his spectacles—appeared grotesquely enlarged.

"It is true that Sally, Mrs. Randall's maidservant, has been exceedingly distressed by her dismissal. Just this morning, I overheard her bemoaning her situation in the most pitiable way. Even assuming, however, that her sense of bitterness and betrayal led her into a quarrel with Mrs. Randall, it seems scarcely credible that such a confrontation could have resulted in *this.*"

"Hard words can lead to bloodshed, Poe," said Lynch. "I've seen it plenty of times."

"Of that I have no doubt," I said. "Permit me, however, to pose a question, Constable Lynch: Have you ever seen violence of this extraordinarily savage nature perpetrated by a *woman?*"

"Well, no," he replied after a momentary pause. "Can't say as I have."

"There *was* Mary Cole," interjected Coroner Tilden, referring to the infamous Cambridge matricide who had slain her mother during a trifling dispute that somehow escalated into murderous rage.

"I am very familiar with that case, having read daily, minutely detailed accounts in the penny papers," I said. "As you will recall, the perpetrator of that outrage killed her aged mother with a single hatchet-blow to the skull—an act that, however appalling, proves rather than refutes my point. The same holds true of the crimes of another notorious murderess, the hopelessly demented schoolteacher, Abigail Barnes of Burlington, Vermont, who, several years ago, viciously slew three of her young charges. Here, too, the victims were cleanly dispatched, each dying of a single stab-wound to the heart. Compare that with the sheer—the *overwhelming*—number of injuries inflicted on Mrs. Randall by her attacker."

I paused for a moment to permit my auditors to absorb this information before continuing thusly:

"It would be folly to deny that—despite their designation as the 'gentler sex'—women are capable of homicidal passions. The annals of crime are filled with females of the most bloodthirsty nature, from Lucretia Borgia to the multi-murderess Hortensia Williams, who rid herself of no fewer than seven husbands. In the great majority of such cases, however, these assassins commit their crimes by insidious, often surreptitious, means—poison being the preferred weapon of the female killer. Even when other, more brutal methods are employed—a hatchet or dagger, as in the two cases previously adduced—the fury of the female murderer tends to be spent once the atrocity is accomplished. Rarely, if ever, do we find the sort of frenzied, gratuitous savagery characteristic of the present crime, in which the victim's body is subjected to an inhuman assault long after life has fled. Such postmortem enormities are almost exclusively perpetrated by the *male* of the species, who possesses a capacity for sheer unbridled barbarity lacking in the heart of even the most degenerate female."

"Just what are you getting at, Poe?" asked Constable Lynch.

"I shall be happy to elucidate my meaning," I said. "Before doing so, however, I would like to ask Coroner Tilden why he has asked to speak to me."

"There's something I'd like you to see," said Tilden, gazing down at the maidservant's corpse. "Take a look at her wrists."

Filled with curiosity, I squatted beside the body and peered closely at the exposed flesh above each of Sally's hands, while Constable Lynch crouched beside me. Almost at once, I noticed two faint but unmistakable contusions encircling her wrists like bracelets of bruised skin.

"She was tied up," I said with a gasp.

"What?" exclaimed Constable Lynch.

"Her wrists were tightly bound prior to her death," I elaborated.

"Yes," said Tilden, "that's what I think, too."

"Well, I'll be damned," muttered Constable Lynch.

"I now understand, Coroner Tilden, why there was a note of uncertainty in your voice when you offered your conclusion," I said. "Permit me to congratulate you on having observed this exceedingly important clue."

"Well, I didn't want to make the same mistake twice," said Tilden. "Not after overlooking those marks on the Bolton girl's ankles you were clever enough to spot, Mr. Poe."

"But what the devil does it *mean*?" asked Lynch, standing erect.

Ignoring this query, I drew a deep breath and turned my gaze upon the ghastly wound that transected Sally's throat. After studying this for a moment, I then reached down and—suppressing my instinctive aversion to such a disagreeable task—gently inserted the index finger of my right hand into her gaping mouth, running the tip over the back of her tongue and the interior wall of her cheek. It took but a moment to verify my suspicion. Rising to my feet, I addressed the policeman thusly:

"What it means, Constable Lynch, is that this is not—as it has been made to appear—a case of murder-suicide. Rather it is a singularly grisly and cold-blooded act of double homicide."

"What in blazes makes you say *that*?" exclaimed the constable.

"Why else would the woman's wrists have been tied up?" said Tilden.

"Well, I don't know," said Lynch. "But that don't prove she was murdered."

"Perhaps not in itself," I observed. "There are other indications that her death was not self-inflicted, however. For one thing she was not merely bound, but *gagged*."

At this pronouncement, both men uttered ejaculations of surprise.

Here I extended my right hand for their inspection. Pinched between thumb and finger were several long gray threads. "I found these fibres on the back of her tongue and the interior wall of her cheek. They are almost certainly the remnants of a piece of fabric—perhaps a rag—stuffed into her mouth to stifle her cries."

Taking the slender strands from my fingers, Lynch examined them narrowly before passing them over to Tilden, who subjected them to a similar scrutiny.

"But there is even more persuasive evidence that Sally, like her mistress, was the victim of homicide," I continued. "Permit me to draw your attention to the weapon employed in the atrocity. It is clutched in Sally's right hand. Now, as may readily be supposed, a desperate resolve is required to commit suicide in this grisly fashion. A tentative stroke of the blade will not suffice. The sharpened edge must be *dug* into the flesh, then swiftly drawn across the throat."

Extending my right forefinger, I slid it across my own throat, miming the act of suicide.

"As you see, a right-handed person taking his own life in this manner will draw the knife from left to right. Since considerable pressure must be applied at the beginning of the cut, the incision will be deepest on the *left* side of the neck, and shallowest on the right, where the blade emerges.

"In Sally's case, however, the opposite is true. The deepest part of the incision appears on the *right* side of the neck, the shallowest on the left. Adding this fact to the others, we are left with only one conclusion. Sally did not take her own life. Rather, she was bound, gagged, and slain by the same bloodthirsty fiend who slaughtered Mrs. Randall. Afterward, the bodies were arranged to make it appear as if a murder-suicide had taken place."

"Remarkable," said Tilden. "Once again, Mr. Poe, you have managed to observe a critical detail that completely escaped my notice. How in the world do you *do* it?"

"From childhood's hour, I have not been as others were," I replied. "I have not seen as others saw."

"Let me get this straight," said Constable Lynch. "You're saying we got us another madman on the loose?"

"Perhaps not *another*," I pregnantly replied.

"What the hell is *that* supposed to mean?" said Lynch.

"I will explain in a moment," I replied. "First, however, I must put a question to you both. Tell me, Officer Lynch and Coroner Tilden—have either of you recently lost a watch key?"

This seemingly irrelevant query induced a startled response from the two men, both of whom—after a momentary pause—replied in the negative.

"I thought as much," I replied. "Your answer adds weight to a suspicion of mine that has been growing stronger by the moment: namely, that this horrendous crime was committed by the same individual responsible for the death of Elsie Bolton."

"What the devil are you talking about, Poe?" snorted Lynch. "You think the McMahon boy came back from the grave? Sounds to me like you been reading one too many ghost stories."

"I do not refer to that ill-fated lad," I replied, ignoring Lynch's crude sarcasm. "For reasons I shall expound upon in a moment, I have come to believe that while Jesse McMahon was certainly present in the Mays' home at the time Miss Bolton was drowned, he himself was innocent of that terrible crime. No, the culprit I mean is someone else entirely."

"Go ahead," said Lynch, regarding me with a look of intense skepticism. "I'm all ears."

"Have you heard of a daguerreotypist named Herbert Ballinger?" I asked.

This question elicited a very surprising reaction from the two men. They started visibly, as if jolted by an electrical current, then exchanged an exceedingly pointed look.

"I perceive that his name is indeed familiar to you," I said.

"I'm sorry to say, Mr. Poe," Coroner Tilden remarked with a sigh, "that, for once, you are mistaken. There's no possible way that Mr. Ballinger could have committed these murders."

It was now my turn to evince intense surprise. "Why, whatever do you mean?"

"Herbert Ballinger is dead," said Tilden. "His body was found early this morning in his studio. It's lying in the morgue right now. Constable Lynch and I saw it with our own eyes—hours before Mrs. Randall and her servant were killed."

Chapter Twenty

S O THUNDERSTRUCK WAS I by Tilden's words that I could do nothing but gape at the coroner in mute astonishment. Several moments passed before I found my voice—and even then, I could only speak in a stammering manner:

"Dead! But how?—where?—when?"

"To take your questions in order, Mr. Poe," said Tilden, "he was killed by an explosion in his studio at a very early hour of the morning—approximately nine o'clock."

"An explosion?" I echoed, still struggling to make sense of this extraordinary development.

"I know little about the process of daguerreotypy," said Tilden. "Evidently, it requires the use of highly combustible fluids. Sometimes—as I'm sure you know, Mr. Poe—people accustomed to working with dangerous materials become somewhat lax in their handling of them. It seems that Mr. Ballinger was smoking a cigar while engaged in his business and carelessly placed it too close to one of his open chemical bottles. Neighbors say they heard a loud *bang*, followed by the shattering of glass. A fire immediately broke out in the studio. Several of the neighbors very courageously rushed into the burning building and managed to drag out Mr. Ballinger's body. But they were too late to save him, I'm afraid. He died instantly."

"Just as well," interposed Constable Lynch, who—upon perceiving my startled response to his seemingly callous observation—added: "Don't mean to sound harsh, but that bottle blew up smack in his face. Awful damn sight. Can't imagine wanting to live with a phiz like that."

"And the studio?" I asked.

"Ashes mostly," said Lynch. "Firemen tried to save it, but . . ." The shrug with which he concluded this statement eloquently conveyed the futility of the firefighters' efforts.

"Any other suspects come to mind, Mr. Poe?" asked Coroner Tilden after a brief pause, during which I desperately sought to put my confused thoughts into order.

"I confess that your news about Mr. Ballinger has left me somewhat stymied," I said at length. "I continue to believe, however, that the murder of Mrs. Randall and her maidservant was committed by the same individual who drowned Elsie Bolton. This conviction, it is true, cannot be logically proven. It is based largely on intuition. Still—while hesitant to employ a concept so hopelessly tainted by its association with the muddle-headed mysticism of Mr. Emerson and his acolytes—it can scarcely be denied that there exists, deep within the human soul, an innate faculty that supplies us with knowledge by instinctive rather than intellectual means."

"You mean a *hunch*?" said Tilden.

"Call it what you wish," I said. "But there is another, more tangible reason to suspect that the same bloody hand was involved in both the Bolton murder and the present atrocity."

"Yes?" inquired Coroner Tilden.

"The fact that, in both of these instances, the deaths were made to appear other than what they proved to be," I said. "A drowning in the former case, a murder-suicide here."

"I suppose there's something to that," said the coroner, meditatively tugging at his lower lip.

"Furthermore," I continued, "I cannot rid myself of the feeling—or *hunch*, to use Constable Lynch's colloquialism—that Mr. Ballinger, though perhaps not the perpetrator after all, was somehow connected to these horrors. Therefore, while I do not at present have another suspect in mind, I believe I know where a possible clue to the killer's identity might be found."

"Where that?" Lynch eagerly inquired.

"The morgue," I replied.

As it happened, my suggestion coincided with the design of Coroner Tilden and Constable Lynch, who were already planning to make the morgue their next destination. Arrangements had to be made to transport the two corpses to that grim repository, where they would remain until claimed by relations.

Before taking our leave, Lynch instructed Officer Higginbottom to go upstairs—bring down a bedsheet—and use it to cover the bodies. He also gave commands to the other policemen, who—by that point—had arrived at the scene, instructing them to make sure that no unauthorized persons entered the house—an order necessitated by the very real possibility that some morbidly minded curiosity-seeker or unscrupulous reporter might attempt to sneak into the residence and make off with a grisly memento of the crime.

Lynch's precautions in this regard seemed fully warranted the moment we emerged from the house. Despite the inordinately cold weather and gathering twilight, the street was mobbed with people, including a dozen newspapermen, who set up an instant clamor for information. Lynch took a moment to address the reporters, telling them that the mistress of the household, a widow named Mrs. Randall, had been stabbed to death by her disgruntled maidservant, who had then committed suicide. As he afterward explained to me, he offered this version of events for two reasons: first, because he did not wish to incite a panic by suggesting that an unknown maniac was on the loose; and second, because he felt that it would benefit our investigation if the killer believed he had gotten away with his ruse and did not suspect that we were on his trail.

Pushing our way through the crowd, we mounted Coroner Tilden's carriage. As the vehicle made its way through the narrow, rapidly darkening streets, the three of us maintained an absolute silence, each deeply absorbed in his thoughts.

As the reader is aware, my suspicions had lighted on Herbert Ballinger for a number of reasons, among them my conviction that—as a creator of mortuary images—he was in an ideal position to identify well-preserved corpses that would make prime subjects for dissection. I had also concluded that—somewhat in the manner of Burke and Hare—he had progressed to actual homicide, perhaps beginning with the murder of Elsie Bolton, who had been killed in such a way as to preserve her excellent physical condition. Knowing that Ballinger, through his daguerreotype business, had a direct association not only with Miss Bolton but with Mrs. Randall as well, I had further deduced that he was responsible for the death of the latter, along with her servant, Sally.

Now, as the carriage rattled and jounced over the cobblestoned streets, I became aware that there was a glaring flaw in my reasoning. If Ballinger's motive for murder was to create well-preserved cadavers that could be used for anatomical study by Dr. MacKenzie, how could I account for the condition in which Mrs. Randall's corpse had been left by her killer? A body so grievously butchered was utterly useless as a medical specimen. And if Ballinger was not Dr. MacKenzie's accomplice in the procuring of illegal bodies, then he could not possibly be the person who had stolen Dr. Farragut's case. In short, I appeared to be no further along in my own quest than I had been yesterday, when I first returned to Boston!

That I had not recognized the defect in my thinking sooner could be attributed, I felt, to the lingering effects of the Madeira, which—while fortifying my nerves—had somewhat fuddled my mind. Still, I could not wholly regret having imbibed that inspiriting beverage. For as our vehicle grew closer to the morgue with each passing minute, I was keenly aware of the task that awaited me—one that would require every particle of self-possession I could muster.

By the time we arrived at our destination, darkness had fallen. The street in front of the deadhouse lay silent and deserted. Stepping down from the carriage, I strode to the entrance and gazed up at the façade.

Instantly, I felt stricken with an utter depression of soul—an iciness, a sinking of the heart which I can compare to no earthly sensation more properly than to the afterdream of the reveler upon opium. What was it, I wondered, that so unnerved me in the contemplation of the building? I was forced to conclude that my reaction had less to do with its particular architectural features (which were barely distinguishable in the pervading gloom) than with my awareness of its grim—its *doleful*—function. The mere thought of the ghastly objects contained within those massive stone walls was more than sufficient to inspire me with a sentiment of intense—of overpowering—dread.

Passing through the main doorway, my companions and I proceeded down a narrow, dimly lit corridor whose rough gray walls were utterly devoid of ornamentation. In another moment we found ourselves in the chamber of the dead.

The room measured approximately twenty feet square. Its floor was tiled in brick. Its walls were of a singularly unwholesome shade of green.

The lurid glow of several gas jets—the only source of illumination at that late hour—contributed greatly to the overall atmosphere of sheer—of *insufferable*—ghastliness.

Occupying the center of the room were five stone tables on iron frames, each bearing a human corpse. Except for one of these—that of a tiny male babe whose still-attached umbilical cord made it sufficiently plain that the poor creature had been heartlessly disposed of immediately upon birth— each body was discreetly covered with a sheet, only the head, neck, and shoulders being left exposed.

One was a young woman whose purple, swollen features plainly evinced that she had been found in the river, evidently a suicide. Another was an exceedingly corpulent fellow with a heavy mustache whose lifeless body (so Tilden informed me) had been found in an alley in an unsavory neighborhood of the city. The reason for his death had not yet been established, though he appeared to have perished of natural causes, perhaps—Tilden speculated—from the strain placed on his heart by his excessive weight. The third was an inordinately coarse-looking man with a badly scarred countenance who had been stabbed to death during a brawl in one of the low dives near the harbor.

The last was Herbert Ballinger.

Viewed from several yards away, the daguerreotypist's visage appeared to be entirely daubed in tar. Only upon my nearer approach did I perceive that the black substance covering his face was his horribly charred skin.

For a moment, dizziness overwhelmed me. Closing my eyes, I clutched at the edge of the marble slab. At length—the vertiginous sensation having in large measure subsided—I took a deep breath and looked down again upon the hideously blackened countenance of the figure stretched out before me.

Though the epidermal tissue of the face had been burned to a near crisp by the explosion and ensuing fire, the features themselves had retained their general contour. I had, of course, seen the daguerreotypist on only one prior occasion, when Sissy and I had visited his studio to inquire about the cost of a portrait. Based upon that single, exceedingly brief encounter, the body on the table certainly appeared to be that of Ballinger. Even so, I could not help but wonder how—in view of the corpse's severely damaged countenance—a definitive identification had been made. I therefore put the question to Coroner Tilden.

The elderly gentleman said nothing in reply. Instead—to my great surprise—he stepped closer to the table and, reaching out his gloved right hand, inserted the thumb and first two fingers into the gaping mouth of the corpse! A moment later, he withdrew his digits, which were clutching a small object that he held out for my inspection. It was, I saw, a small, curved strip of metal holding several molars.

"Here's your answer," said Tilden. "Mr. Ballinger was missing a few of his back teeth. He was wearing this dental plate. The fellow who made it was able to identify the corpse."

In an instant, I could feel my heart begin to race with excitement.

"And who, may I ask, was the dentist in question?" I inquired, though I already knew what the answer would be.

"Why, it was Ludlow Marston," came the expected response.

There can be little doubt that, in the vast majority of cases, the solution to a mystery involves a slow and painstaking process of logical analysis that leads—only after many false ideas, misguided theories, and mistaken conceptions—to the correct explanation. On rare occasions, however, the answer will come in a flash. To be sure, such revelations only *appear* to be the product of sudden unbidden insight. In reality, they require a long foreground of intense, ratiocinative labor. Only to a mind already prepared to receive them by endless hours of the most arduous mental exertion are such seeming *epiphanies* likely to arrive.

The thought that smote me at that instant brought with it a sense of absolute certainty. Still, I could confirm my belief in only one way. The mere contemplation of what I must do filled me with a sense of the deepest revulsion. I knew that I must act at once, before my resolution faltered.

Squeezing my eyes tight, I quickly bent over the corpse and applied my open mouth to its gaping, horribly cracked lips.

Behind me I could hear my companions emit loud exclamations of shock and confusion. A powerful hand—clearly that of Constable Lynch—clutched me by the shoulder, as though to yank me away from the cadaver, to which I must have appeared to be delivering an impassioned kiss.

Shaking off Lynch's grasp, I reached up with one hand and—placing it squarely upon the center of Ballinger's unmoving chest—pressed down firmly, forcing the contents from his lungs, while I myself inhaled as deeply as possible. Then—holding my breath—I pulled myself erect and turned to face my companions, whose faces wore looks in which outrage and stunned disbelief seemed equally commingled.

"What the hell?" cried Lynch.

"Have you gone mad, Mr. Poe?" exclaimed Tilden.

For another moment, I merely stared at them mutely, my cheeks ballooned outward to their fullest extent. All at once, I exploded into an un-controllable bout of giggling.

Lynch and Tilden exchanged a flabbergasted look, then regarded me again with amazement.

So convulsed was I with hilarity that it took a full minute before I could speak.

"I was right, ha!-ha!-ha!" I said. "Ballinger was—ha!-ha!—murdered, just like the three women! Ha!-ha!"

"Get hold of yourself, man," said Coroner Tilden, clutching me by the shoulders and administering a little shake. "What on earth has gotten you?"

"Laughing gas," I replied, reaching up to wipe away the tears of merri-ment that had leaked from my eyes. "Ballinger's lungs are filled with it."

CHAPTER TWENTY-ONE

⌒

T HE INTENSITY OF my reaction to the nitrous oxide is not to be wondered at. My sensitive temperament has at all times rendered me inordinately susceptible to intoxicating substances. Even before inhaling the
gas, I was already feeling light-headed from the Madeira urged on me by
Constable Lynch. The small quantity of nitrous oxide transferred from the
corpse's lungs into my own was more than sufficient to induce in me an extreme state of giddiness.

Still seized with spasmodic fits of chuckling, I spun on my heels and
hurried from the deadhouse, followed closely by my two companions. My
hasty departure was motivated by two considerations. Even to myself, my
laughter seemed shamefully out of place—if not positively indecent—
within that hushed and somber realm. I hoped, too, that the cold night air
would help restore my sobriety.

Standing on the sidewalk, I opened my mouth—tilted back my head—
and drew in deep, thirsty breaths of the bracing atmosphere. Almost instantly, my head began to clear. Lynch and Tilden, who had positioned
themselves in front of me, now began to barrage me with questions, de-
manding to know exactly what had just transpired.

"I can well understand your shared sense of confusion," I said, addressing them both. "The grotesque, if not ghoulish, action you just witnessed
must have seemed like the behavior of a madman. I can assure you, however, that it was performed with the greatest deliberation. By no other

means could I corroborate the suspicion that had suddenly taken hold of me."

"Keep talking, Poe," said Tilden, eyeing me warily, as though not entirely convinced of my sanity.

"As you know," I said, "I am firmly persuaded that the deaths of Miss Bolton, Mrs. Randall, and Sally are the work of one person. For reasons that I have not yet fully disclosed, I had come to believe that the killer was Herbert Ballinger. Upon hearing of Ballinger's death, I was, of course, forced to revise my deductions.

"It occurred to me at once that Ballinger might also have fallen victim to the unknown murderer. As we have established, the latter operates according to a very particular *modus operandi,* disguising the manner of his victims' deaths so as to divert attention from himself. Was it possible, I wondered, that the same was true in Ballinger's case? Could he, too, have been murdered by someone who then staged the death to look like an accident?"

As I spoke, my breath issued in ghostly wisps of vapor that mingled in the frosty night air with those emanating from the partly open lips of my silent auditors.

"Had Ballinger's studio not been reduced to ashes," I continued, "it might have been possible to examine the room in which his body was found, and determine if arson had been committed. Since that option was foreclosed, there was only one way to proceed—i.e., by examining the corpse itself.

"At a glimpse of the horribly charred cadaver, there was, of course, no reason to believe that the daguerreotypist had died of any other cause than the explosion and ensuing fire. It was not until I heard the name of Dr. Ludlow Marston that an idea struck me with almost palpable force.

"It need hardly be said that if Elsie Bolton, Mrs. Randall, and Herbert Ballinger *had,* in fact, been killed by the same madman, the latter must be an individual connected in some way to all three of these individuals. (I do not include Sally in this calculation, as her death, I believe, was merely an adjunct to that of Mrs. Randall.) Dr. Marston—as you yourselves are well aware—was associated with Elsie Bolton, who had been one of his volunteers on the day prior to her death. Mrs. Randall, too—as I knew from several of her comments—had attended at least one of his performances at the Boston Museum and may possibly have spoken to him afterward to convey her admiration. As for Ballinger, he was not only a patient of Marston's, he also made the daguerreotype portrait which appears as the frontispiece of the latter's execrable book of so-called poetry, *The Dentalogia.*

"When, in explaining how Ballinger was identified, you invoked Marston's name, my mind very naturally connected the dentist with his famous laughing gas demonstrations. Indeed, it is virtually impossible to think of one without the other. The realization immediately followed that nitrous oxide offers an ideal way to render a person unconscious—or, indeed, if a sufficient quantity is administered, even to commit murder. From there, it was a very short leap to the hypothesis that Ballinger was already dead when the blaze was started—i.e., that he had first been asphyxiated with laughing gas before being set on fire.

"There was, of course, only one way to test my theory: by attempting to draw some of the suspected contents of the victim's lungs into my own. The unnaturally euphoric sensation I immediately experienced has utterly confirmed my belief."

All during my discourse, my companions had listened with rapt attention. Indeed, so deeply engrossed was Constable Lynch that he seemed wholly unaware of the large drop of moisture that had leaked from his nose and now depended from the very tip of his prominent olfactory organ. All at once, he began to sniffle loudly—then, after rubbing at his nostrils with the back of one gloved hand, said:

"Let me see if I got this right. You're saying that all these people were killed by Marston?"

"My deductions," I replied, "are indeed sufficient to engender that suspicion."

"But what in God's name would be his motive?" asked Coroner Tilden.

"That portion of the mystery remains unriddled," I said. "The answer is known only to the perpetrator himself. I suggest, therefore, that we seek out Dr. Marston without delay, even if we must interrupt his nightly performance at Mr. Kimball's museum."

"He ain't there, not tonight," said Lynch. "Museum's closed on Thursdays."

"Then the course of our investigation is clear," I said. "We must proceed at once to Dr. Marston's residence and pray that we find him at home."

From my conversation with Moses Kimball, I knew that Dr. Marston saw his private patients on Tremont Street, close to King's Chapel. Assuming that—as was true of most dentists—Marston's practice was conducted at home, I directed the driver of the carriage to that neighborhood.

Upon arriving at our destination, Tilden, Lynch, and I disembarked from the conveyance and began searching for Marston's abode. Our task was greatly facilitated by the brightness of the moonlight. Within minutes, we had located the house—a handsome brick edifice with a brass plate beside the door engraved with the dentist's name and occupation.

Viewed from the front, the house appeared to be unoccupied, all the windows being pitch black. As we moved around the side, however, we perceived the warm glow of lamplight filtering through the drawn curtains of a tall window on the ground floor.

We returned to the front doorway, where Coroner Tilden immediately began rapping on the brass knocker. When no one responded, he tried again, this time even more insistently. In the ensuing silence, he cast a questioning look at Lynch, who—after a momentary pause—reached into his pocket and extracted a set of keys. After sorting through these, he inserted one of them into the lock-hole and, in another moment, succeeded in undoing the latch and opening the door.

"Skeleton key," Tilden whispered in my ear—a wholly unnecessary comment, as I had, of course, instantly surmised the nature of the implement.

Stepping inside, we paused in the lightless vestibule and listened intently. No sound was to be heard.

"Anyone here?" called Lynch.

This interrogative brought no reply.

A warm glow being visible in the hallway, we proceeded in the direction of the light and soon found ourselves in a small, handsomely appointed parlor that evidently served as the dentist's waiting area. The mild beams of an astral lamp diffused a pleasing illumination throughout the room, whose *decora* was entirely given over to objects relating to Marston's profession.

An exquisitely wrought sculpture of a human molar—evidently fashioned of the finest Limoges porcelain—occupied the center of the mantel, which also held a small marble bust of Pierre Fauchard—the so-called "Father of Oral Surgery"—as well as a bronze plaque adorned with a bas-relief image of Hippocrates setting the broken jaw of a Greek warrior. The walls were hung with elaborately framed engravings portraying milestones in dental history, from a medieval barber-surgeon wielding an enormous pair of pincers to John Greenwood's invention of the mechanical tooth-drill from parts taken from his mother's spinning-wheel. The bookcase shelves were filled with volumes on dentistry, including a facsimile copy of the ancient Chinese text *The Art of the Tooth-Healer*—a splendidly bound edition of Fauchard's *Le Chirugien Dentiste*—and a three-volume set of Josiah Flagg's *Essentials of Oral Anatomy.*

It was immediately clear that—in addition to serving as an antechamber for his patients—the room was put to more domestic uses by the dentist himself. Lying inverted on the cushion of a chair was an open volume bound in red morocco. This proved, upon closer inspection, to be a copy of Theodore S. Fay's laughably inept, unaccountably popular novel *Norman Leslie: A Tale of the Present Times,* whose enormous commercial success was yet another disheartening sign of the hopelessly debased sensibility of the American reading public. On a small table beside the chair stood a half-empty glass of milk, alongside a small plate containing a partially eaten cheese sandwich.

At the sight of these simple, perfectly mundane objects, I was instantly seized with a sense of the deepest apprehension. Clearly, Dr. Marston had recently been present in the room. Where was he now? To be sure, there was no *necessary* reason to assume the worst. He might, for example, have merely stepped outside to make use of the privy. Still—in light of the profoundly disconcerting events of the day—I could not help but feel that there was something distinctly ominous about the abandoned book and half-consumed snack.

My fears received almost instantaneous confirmation; for at that very moment, Constable Lynch, who had moved to the far end of the parlor, threw open a connecting door leading to the adjacent room—stepped inside—and emitted a startled cry.

Tilden and I hurried to his side. Though the room was in darkness, its most prominent features were visible in the light spilling from the parlor. From its various accoutrements—glass-fronted medicine cabinet, table arrayed with surgical implements, treadle-operated drill, basin, pitcher, and spittoon—I perceived that we were standing inside Marston's office. An adjustable chair, controlled by a side-mounted wooden level, stood in a far corner. Occupying the seat was an inert male figure, his head thrown back, his right hand clutching an object that was held to his gaping lips.

My heart quailed—and quavered—and sickened—with a spasm of dread; for I knew, even before Lynch struck a match and put it to the nearest lamp, precisely what its beams would reveal.

"Oh Lord," gasped Tilden as light suffused the room.

The motionless person in the chair was Ludlow Marston. He was holding a pistol whose muzzle was inserted in his mouth. The back of his head had been blown out by the force of the blast, the wall directly behind the chair being spattered with blood, bone, and brain tissue.

Emitting an imprecation of unusual profanity, Lynch started toward the apparent suicide. He had taken no more than a step, however, when I reached out and grabbed him by the arm, halting him in his tracks. As he shot me a baffled look, I pointed to the floor, where a trail of small, crimson marks—half-moon in shape, as though produced by bloody boot-heels—led from the rear of the dental chair to the window.

Someone else had clearly been in the room with Marston and had snuck out after the latter's death.

As my companions—carefully avoiding the sanguinary stains—began to examine the room for other clues, I remained frozen in place. My mind was in a state of the wildest disorder, my sense of confusion extreme. My initial belief—that the murders of Elsie Bolton and the two female members of the Randall household could be laid to Herbert Ballinger—had been proven false. Now it appeared that I had been equally mistaken about Ludlow Marston. Some other, still unknown madman was at large in the city. His identity and motivations, however, remained as mysterious as ever.

Pondering the impasse to which my investigation had led, I was suddenly overcome with an utter depression of the soul. This hopeless—even despairing—sensation was accompanied by an acute feeling of pity for the victims of the killer. I thought of Mrs. Randall, who had treated me with such unwavering kindness. Ludlow Marston, too—however ludicrous his literary pretensions—had never conveyed anything but the highest regard for me and my work. That these two estimable people had met such appalling ends was a horror almost too painful to contemplate. What sort of monster would commit such atrocities? And *why*?

At that moment, as though divining my thoughts, Constable Lynch—who had opened a small storage closet and was peering inside—declared: "It wasn't robbery, that's for damn sure."

"What did you say?" I asked, shaking myself from my grim reverie.

"It wasn't no thief that did this," came the reply.

"What makes you say that?"

Reaching both hands into the closet, Lynch removed something from an upper shelf, then turned and held it out for my inspection.

"No thief would've left without taking *this*," he said.

At the sight of the object, I was rendered dumbstruck with amazement. I could feel my mouth drop open and my eyes bulge from their sockets. The thing in Lynch's hands was indeed an article of such singular beauty and obvious value that no mere burglar would have neglected to take it. Indeed, I knew for a certainty that it had already been stolen once from its rightful owner.

It was a magnificently crafted box of burled walnut, inlaid with ivory in elaborate floral designs and equipped with exquisite bronze fittings.

I was staring at Dr. Farragut's missing medicine chest!

CHAPTER TWENTY-TWO

MY EMOTIONS AT that instant it is folly to attempt describing. Foremost among them was the sheer—the overwhelming—astonishment to which I have already alluded. Here in the most unexpected of places we had stumbled upon the treasure I had so desperately been seeking. How in heaven's name had it come to be in the dentist's possession? I could not begin to say. At the moment, however, that question seemed of relatively minor importance. The mere fact that Dr. Farragut's stolen case had been found was all that mattered.

Perceiving the look of wonder upon my visage, Lynch said: "What's going on, Poe? You recognize this thing?"

"I do indeed," I replied in a voice that trembled audibly with excitement. "It belongs to Dr. Erasmus Farragut of Concord, from whose home it was stolen several days ago. It contains the precious and largely irreplaceable ingredients from which he produces the all-natural elixirs that have effected such miraculous cures in his patients. My purpose in returning to Boston was to search for this very treasure, upon whose recovery the health of my dear wife, Virginia, now depends."

"Well, I'll be damned," said Lynch, giving the box a gentle shake. This action produced a peculiar clatter, as of the rattling of wooden beads.

"Perhaps, Constable Lynch," I said, "it would be better not to agitate the box in that manner. The contents might be exceedingly delicate, though I cannot say for certain precisely what they are."

"Well, there's one way to find out," Lynch replied, stepping over to the washstand upon which the basin and pitcher stood.

Hurrying to his side, I quickly removed these two objects and set them on the floor while Lynch placed the box upon the top of the stand.

Upon trying the latch, I found that the case was tightly secured. Lynch's *passe-partout* proving too large for the little lock-hole, he stepped to the dental chair, where Tilden was peering at poor Dr. Marston's head-wound, and asked the coroner to move aside. Lynch then rummaged through the pockets of the corpse for several moments before returning to the washstand with a small key clutched between his right thumb and forefinger. An instant later, the case stood open.

Occupying the bottom half of the interior was a pair of intricately carved wooden doors, outfitted with filigreed hinges and knobs of the purest silver. The upper portion consisted of a single drawer with a finely wrought handle of the same precious material.

As I held my breath expectantly, Lynch reached both hands to the bottom of the case—took hold of the little silver knobs—and pulled open the doors.

Instantly my olfactory sense was assaulted by an intensely disagreeable odor, as of tainted meat. Wrinkling my nose, I bent over and peered into the compartment. What was my surprise to see that it was completely empty!

"Phew. What the hell's in there?" said Lynch. "Skunkweed?"

Reaching a hand into the compartment, I groped all around. "Whether or not Dr. Farragut employs the leaves of the *Symplocarpus foetidus* plant in concocting his cures, I cannot say," I grimly remarked. "At present, however, there is nothing at all in here."

"What about the drawer?" asked Lynch. Even as he spoke he grabbed the silver pull. Owing to his excessive eagerness, which caused him to give the little handle an inordinately forceful *yank*, the drawer came flying completely out of the box—and from it there spilled a multitude of small, ivory objects which bounced and rolled across the floor!

"What the—?" cried Lynch.

Though I had no difficulty, of course, in identifying these objects as adult human teeth, the sight of so many of them scattered to and fro upon the floorboards was sufficiently jarring to cause me to gape at them in bewilderment for several moments, while my mind raced furiously to account for their presence in Dr. Farragut's case.

Coroner Tilden, who had been drawn by the clatter of the falling teeth, now stood at my side. Lynch, in the meantime, had bent to one knee and was now examining an unusually large lateral incisor that was cupped in the palm of his hand.

"Good Lord!" exclaimed Tilden. "Why, there must be a hundred of them at the very least. Where in the world did they all come from?"

Turning to face the elderly coroner, I looked directly into his watery eyes, which widened noticeably as I answered.

"From the mouths," I said, "of corpses exhumed from the grave."

Twenty minutes later—having left Coroner Tilden to tend to Ludlow Marston's remains—Constable Lynch and I stood before the front door of Alexander MacKenzie's residence. Cradled in my arms was Dr. Farragut's now-empty medicine chest, which I had carefully wrapped for protection in the woolen lap-robe from the carriage.

No light was visible from any of the windows of MacKenzie's elegant brownstone, though—in view of the lateness of the hour—this fact was hardly surprising. Indeed—despite the urgency of the situation—my companion, assuming that the anatomist was already asleep, seemed reluctant to disturb him.

"You sure about this, Poe?" he asked, his right hand poised on the knocker.

In truth, I could not claim to be positive about virtually any aspect of the increasingly bewildering case. Of one thing, however, I felt confident: There was an almost certain link between Dr. MacKenzie and the murdered dentist.

It was the teeth that had led me to this conclusion. Seeing them strewn by the dozen across Marston's floor, I suddenly remembered a peculiar exchange I had overheard while concealed inside the skeleton-cabinet in Dr. MacKenzie's anatomy school. The young man named Jack had asked if Elsie Bolton's teeth should be "taken care of" right then and there. In reply, his companion, William, had suggested that the task be deferred until the next morning, as there was "no point in ruining the face" of the still-comely cadaver.

At the time, I had attached little importance to this bit of conversation. It was not until I saw the drawerful of teeth spill from Dr. Farragut's stolen case that I understood its significance.

Elsie Bolton's teeth were to be extracted and sold as dental replacements.

Throughout the ages, false teeth have been fashioned from various substances: wood, metal, ivory. The finest dentures, however, have always been those made from actual human teeth. That Marston himself manufactured such appliances I knew from Moses Kimball, who had so proudly displayed his handsome new set to me during my recent visit to his museum. Dentures made in this way (as Kimball himself had discovered) were exceedingly costly, bringing substantial profits to those practitioners who could supply them to their clientele.

The exorbitant price charged for these items was attributable only partly to the time and skill required to produce them. Largely, it resulted from the difficulty in procuring the raw material. Dentists were willing to pay a handsome premium to anyone who could provide them with a steady inventory of human teeth. And the people who were in the best position to fill this need were those with access to corpses.

For centuries, the teeth from dead bodies had formed a frequent article of sale to dentists. Indeed, certain grave-robbers had limited themselves to the removal of teeth from disinterred corpses. These small and easily concealed articles could be sold for sizable sums without the risk entailed in exhuming entire cadavers. In one notorious instance, an eighteenth-century "resurrectionist" named Cooper, under the pretense of seeking out a burial place for his recently deceased wife, obtained access to the vault of a meetinghouse in Kent and proceeded to remove the teeth of the entire buried congregation, which he pocketed and sold to a London dentist for no less than fifty pounds. Another infamous figure, a licensed sutler named Merriwether, who followed the British army during the Peninsular War, would scavenge the fields of battle, plundering teeth from the fallen soldiers. Within a year, he had collected so many of these ghoulish artifacts that he was able to open a small hotel at Margate from the proceeds of their sale!

Upon seeing the teeth pour forth from the drawer of Dr. Farragut's medicine chest—and recalling the conversation between the two medical students—I instantly surmised that Marston obtained the raw material for his dentures from the specimens dissected in MacKenzie's anatomy school. Indeed, it seemed entirely possible that, among the hundreds of incisors, canines, and molars scattered across the dentist's floor, were the ones plucked from the mouth of poor Elsie Bolton!

Now—as Constable Lynch appeared to hesitate in announcing our presence—I assured him once more that it was absolutely imperative that we interview the anatomist without delay.

"Hope you know what you're doing," he answered with a shrug, then rapped several times on the door.

For a moment, all was silence within the house—a circumstance that could not fail to infuse me with a sense of foreboding in view of the surfeit of horrors I had already experienced that day. Lynch had just knocked a second time, however, when we heard a tremulous voice cry out: "Hold on, hold on. I'm coming as fast as I can."

A moment later, the door opened inward, revealing a stooped, exceedingly ancient fellow garbed in nightdress and sleeping cap and clutching a candlestick in one bony hand.

"Who the deuce are you?" he demanded in a cracked voice.

"Constable Edmund Lynch. And this is Mr. Edgar Poe. You MacKenzie?"

"Heavens no," said the old man. "I am his servant, Prescott. The doctor is asleep, as all respectable people should be at this hour."

"Well, best wake him up," said Lynch. "We need to have a word with him."

For a moment, the old man merely continued to study us from the doorway, a wary look upon his pinched, inordinately wrinkled visage.

"Go on, go on," Lynch said impatiently. "We're here on urgent police business."

Emitting a sigh of resignation, the old man turned and, shuffling ahead of us, led us to the library, where he enkindled an Argand lamp before disappearing again into the darkness of the hallway. An instant later, we could hear the sound of his labored breathing as he mounted the stairs.

Seating myself on a claw-footed sofa, I placed the still-shrouded case on the cushion beside me, while Lynch made a circuit of the room, examining its embellishments. In short order, he came to a halt before a large engraved portrait displayed in a heavy gilt frame above the mantel.

"Now, *there's* a nasty-looking customer," he remarked.

Rising from my seat, I came up beside him and studied the picture for a moment. Its subject was a fierce-looking fellow with a carbuncular nose, bristling eyebrows, and an excessively pointed goatee of the sort often seen in popular depictions of Lucifer. He was garbed in the manner of a Renaissance scholar and, in one hand, clutched an implement that appeared to be a scalpel.

"Unless I am mistaken," I said, "this formidable fellow is the sixteenth-century anatomist Dr. Pietro Baglioni. One of the most enlightened scientists of his age, Baglioni was renowned for his public dissections, which he performed several times a year in the Archiginnasio amphitheater at Bologna."

"Public dissections? You mean to tell me that people came to watch him carve up dead bodies?" marveled Lynch.

"By droves," I replied. "Indeed, Baglioni's anatomical demonstrations were among the most popular spectacles of the age. Every seat in his amphitheater was invariably filled, despite an admission fee equivalent to five of our own dollars."

Lynch shook his head and made a clucking noise with his tongue. "Eye-talians," he muttered in a tone that seemed to say: *What else would you expect of those degenerate foreigners?*

"The fascination with the grim—the ghastly—the ghoulish—is not restricted to any single nationality, Constable Lynch," I remarked. "Rather, it is a universal human trait. You observed it yourself earlier today in the morbidly curious crowd gathered outside the home of poor Mrs. Randall. For better or worse, there is something in our common nature that is powerless to resist the dark allure of Death—perhaps because, in looking so directly into its loathsome visage, we are hoping to divest it of its awful mystery."

"Well put, Mr. Poe," came a resonant voice from behind me. "But then, you are something of an expert on the subject, are you not?"

Turning, I found myself looking at a tall, middle-aged gentleman so handsomely garbed and immaculately groomed that it was difficult to believe he had just been roused from bed. His face was a notable one. The features were as cleanly cut as those on a Greek medallion—all except the chin, whose strange protuberant broadness detracted greatly from his otherwise attractive appearance. His forehead was of the sort phrenologically associated with the highest intelligence. The silken jet curls clustering over his brow made a striking foil to the scholarly pallor of his complexion.

"You *are* Poe the writer?" continued this gentleman.

Bowing my head in acknowledgment, I said: "And I presume that you are Dr. MacKenzie?"

"The same," replied the gentleman. "Well, I must say this is quite a surprise. I've enjoyed many of your tales, Mr. Poe. Particularly the one about the fellow who is placed in a mesmeric trance *in articulo mortis.*"

" 'The Facts in the Case of M. Valdemar,' " I replied. "It is one of my own favorites as well."

"Pure poppycock, of course," said MacKenzie with a chuckle. "But deliciously entertaining."

The patronizing tone of this remark could hardly fail to rankle. "It was not intended as a scientific essay," I said in a somewhat frosty tone, "but rather as a work of fiction designed to elicit an intense emotional response in the reader."

"As it most certainly does," replied MacKenzie, who then turned to my companion and said: "And you are Constable . . . ?"

"Lynch," answered my companion, who was regarding the physician with an openly appraising look. "Edmund Lynch."

"Ah yes," said MacKenzie, who, I could not help but notice, did not invite us to be seated. "So, gentlemen—what, pray tell, is so urgent that it could not wait until morning?"

"Ever hear of a dentist named Marston?" asked Lynch.

"The nitrous oxide man?" said MacKenzie. "Of course. I attended one of his performances several months ago. What about him?"

"He's dead," said Lynch. "Murdered."

"How dreadful," said Lynch, who appeared sincerely surprised by the news. "But I still don't understand what you're doing here."

By way of reply, I stepped to the sofa—took hold of the lap-robe covering Dr. Farragut's case—and pulled it away with a flourish.

"Have you ever seen this?" I asked.

MacKenzie's mouth fell open, and I could hear his sharp intake of breath. It was not, however, a gasp of recognition, but rather the opposite: the sound of a man setting eyes for the first time on an object of such inordinate beauty that it could not fail to startle.

"Magnificent," he said. "What exactly is it?"

I explained that it was a unique handcrafted chest belonging to Dr. Erasmus Farragut of Concord.

"Farragut?" said MacKenzie. "You mean that charlatan who claims that all diseases can be cured by hot pepper?"

Having been informed by Dr. Farragut that MacKenzie maintained a public pose of utter disdain for the Thomsonian method, I ignored the contemptuous tenor of this remark and merely replied: "That is indeed the gentleman of whom I speak."

"But what's this got to do with Marston?"

"On Monday," I replied, "this case, in which Dr. Farragut stored his most precious natural substances, was stolen from his home. Not more than one hour ago, it was found among Dr. Marston's possessions. Dr. Farragut's ingredients, however, were gone."

As I spoke, I carefully scrutinized Dr. MacKenzie's countenance for any visible sign—a tell-tale twitching of the lips, clenching of the jaw-muscles, or rapid blinking of the eye—that might indicate a guilty awareness of the theft of Dr. Farragut's secrets. His face betrayed nothing, however, beyond increasing perplexity.

"In place of its original contents," I continued, "the chest was found to be full of human teeth. These were evidently used by Dr. Marston to produce dentures for his patients."

"Poe here figures they came from dead bodies," interposed Lynch.

"Ah, now I begin to see," MacKenzie said. Stroking his prognathous chin, he gazed down at the floor and said, as if musing aloud to himself: "So *that's* who he's been selling them to."

"He?" I said. "To whom, may I inquire, are you referring?"

"My associate, Mr. Ballinger," answered MacKenzie. Then—observing the pointed look that passed between Lynch and myself—he regarded us with a frown and said: "What is it?"

"Ain't you heard?" asked Lynch.

"Heard what?" said MacKenzie in an apprehensive tone. "Please, gentlemen, I wish you'd simply tell me everything at once instead of in this piecemeal fashion."

"Very well," I said. "Herbert Ballinger was found dead early this morning, evidently killed by the same madman who murdered Dr. Marston, along with two other victims—an exceedingly estimable woman named Mrs. Randall and her maidservant. In each of these cases, the killer made it appear as if some other cause—accident, suicide, or domestic dispute—had led to the person's death."

Upon receiving this intelligence, MacKenzie seemed positively stricken, his pallid complexion turning a ghastly shade of gray. Staggering backward several steps, he dropped heavily onto the cushion of an armchair that stood beside the hearth, and stared up at us with an expression of incredulous horror.

"There is reason to suspect," I continued, "that the man who committed these atrocities was also responsible for the death of Miss Elsie Bolton, who was drowned in her employer's bathtub last week."

"Miss *who*?" said MacKenzie, who appeared to have been rendered half-stupefied by these revelations.

"Elsie Bolton," I repeated. "I confess to being somewhat surprised that you do not recognize her name. After all, it was her corpse that you and your helpers removed from the grave last evening and transported back to your anatomy school for dissection."

As might be expected, this pronouncement elicited an intense reaction from both MacKenzie and Constable Lynch. The latter emitted a shout of amazement, while the anatomist half-leapt from his seat with a wild cry of: "What did you say?"

For a moment, I made no reply, while I inwardly debated the advisability of revealing my full knowledge of MacKenzie's illicit activities. At length, resolving to speak the truth at any cost—even at the risk of exposing myself to charges of criminal trespass—I addressed him thusly:

"The time for subterfuge has passed, Dr. MacKenzie. Too much is at stake—including, very possibly, other human lives that may well be lost unless the perpetrator of these horrors is found without delay. I shall therefore withhold no relevant facts from you, even those of a self-incriminating nature. I do so in the expectation that you will respond with an equal degree of candor.

"Even as we speak, my darling wife, Virginia, lies gravely ill in the Alcott home in Concord, where she is under the care of Dr. Farragut. However much you may profess to scorn that gentleman, his methods have proven highly efficacious in numerous cases. It was a terrible blow, therefore, when this chest, containing his most vital ingredients, was stolen from his home before he could prepare the medication for my wife.

"Determined to do all in my power to recover his *medica materia,* I came to Boston and, last night, snuck into your anatomy school to search for the missing case. I did so under the belief that the theft was committed at your behest. Though you and your two student helpers were unaware of my presence, I was hidden inside your skeleton-cabinet when you brought in Miss Bolton's corpse.

"The ensuing conversation—in which you referred to a precious item from Concord whose delivery was imminent—persuaded me that I was correct. I subsequently concluded that your confederate was Herbert Ballinger, to whom you had been introduced by your disgraced student Horace Rice. Owing to his work as a maker of postmortem pictures, Ballinger could assess the corpses of newly deceased Bostonians and inform you of those that would make desirable specimens for dissection. Indeed, he could even have supplied you with daguerreotype images of the bodies so that you could gauge their suitability for yourself.

"For reasons that it is not necessary to explain, I soon became convinced that Ballinger did not merely appraise the condition of his deceased subjects but, in certain cases, actually caused their deaths. It was only when he himself was killed that I was forced to revise my belief. Someone else is at large who has been murdering people associated with the daguerreotypist. It is a matter of the utmost urgency that we identify this madman before he strikes again. I therefore appeal to you to share any information that might lead to his capture—and, not incidentally, to the recovery of Dr. Farragut's still-missing secrets, upon which all my hopes for my dear wife's recovery remain pinned."

During this confession, Dr. MacKenzie's not-unhandsome visage registered a range of emotions, from amazement to outrage to something resembling sympathetic understanding. It was not he, however, but rather Constable Lynch who broke the brief silence that followed the conclusion of my speech. His face wrought into a look of extreme indignation, he angrily exclaimed:

"Dammit, Poe, what the devil were you thinking, breaking into his place like that? Why, I could arrest you right now, should MacKenzie here choose to press charges!"

Turning to look directly into the police officer's blazing eyes, I calmly replied: "I am fully cognizant of that fact, Constable Lynch. It is a matter of interest to me, however, that—while threatening me with arrest—you have said nothing to Dr. MacKenzie, who has routinely engaged in the highly illicit, not to say repugnant, act of grave-robbing."

This rejoinder rendered Lynch momentarily speechless. As he continued to glare at me in silence, MacKenzie slowly rose from his seat and—speaking in a voice not untinged with sadness—addressed me thusly:

"There would be no point in arresting me, Mr. Poe, as the good constable well knows. His superiors wouldn't stand for it."

"Ah, then it is true," I replied. "You are guilty not merely of grave-robbing but of the bribery of public officials."

This scathing accusation elicited an unexpected response from the anatomist. Far from denying it, he merely shrugged and said:

"It's the way of the world. But you mustn't think the worse of our police chief and his subordinates for turning a blind eye to my nocturnal activities. They understand its necessity. The still-benighted laws of our land impose impossible restrictions on the practice of anatomy. Without human bodies to study, American medicine will remain hopelessly mired in ignorance—a breeding ground for humbugs like your friend, Farragut. The men I pay off may possess their fair share of avarice, but they are wise enough to see that medical progress depends on what I do. Herbert Ballinger understood the same thing. But of course, he once studied medicine himself."

"What?" I exclaimed.

"That's right. In Baltimore. I don't know the whole story, only that he abandoned his dream of becoming a physician some years ago. But he maintained a lively interest in the subject. It's one of the reasons he was eager to assist me. Your deductions regarding poor Herbert are remarkably acute, Mr. Poe—up to a point, at any rate. He did indeed use his situation as a maker of memorial pictures to find subjects for me. And he asked very little in return. I gave him the teeth, which he apparently sold to Dr. Marston. And occasionally he asked to take pictures of the bodies before and after dissection. He was fascinated with the process of death. But it's ludicrous to suppose that he had anything to do with murd—"

All at once, MacKenzie gave a start, as though struck with a sudden realization.

"What is it?" Lynch inquired.

"Bowden," said MacKenzie with a frown. "Have you spoken to him?"

"Who?" asked Lynch.

"Benjamin Bowden," said MacKenzie. "Herbert Ballinger's assistant."

Owing, no doubt, to the unprecedented events of the day—which had thrown my mental processes into a state of excessive agitation—I had entirely forgotten about the existence of Ballinger's helper. Now there arose in my mind a vivid image of that gentleman, whom Sissy and I had met during our sole visit to the daguerreotypist's studio. I recalled his limping walk—his somewhat brusque manner—and his almost fraternal resemblance to his employer.

"He ain't around anymore," said Lynch in response to MacKenzie's query. "Seems him and Ballinger had a falling-out a few days ago, and Bowden left town. Least that's what the neighbors told us."

"There's something *wrong* about that fellow," said MacKenzie. "My impression—though I may be wrong—is that he once spent time in prison. Exactly why Herbert hired him, I can't say. But *he's* the man I'd be searching for, if I were you."

Lynch, who had extracted a small pad from his pocket, rapidly jotted some notes before glancing up at MacKenzie. "And what about Mr. Poe here? You intend to bring charges?"

Regarding me with a look devoid of resentment or ill-will, MacKenzie said: "No, I suppose not. I, too, have a dearly beloved wife. If, heaven forbid, she should ever fall ill, I would do everything in my power to save her, the law be damned. Which is why, Mr. Poe, I encourage you to forget about Farragut's botanical nonsense."

"But I myself heard you speak of an item of incalculable worth whose arrival from Concord you were eagerly expecting," I said. "Do you mean to say that you were not referring to Dr. Farragut's stolen case and its secret ingredients?"

"Heavens no," said MacKenzie. "It's true that Herbert brought me something very precious from Concord. But it had nothing to do with Farragut's quackery. And it wasn't stolen, but properly bought and paid for."

"And what, if I may inquire, *was* this object?" I asked.

"See for yourself," said MacKenzie after a brief pause. Crossing the room to his desk, he slid out the center drawer and removed a sheet of paper, which he then carried back and handed to me.

As Lynch peered over my shoulder, I studied the page. It contained a technical drawing of the sort that might be submitted as part of a patent application. The object depicted was a sarcophagous-shaped box, equipped with various curious features, including several hinged panels and an interior platform of narrow wooden slats.

"You can imagine what a boon this will be to my work," said MacKenzie in a tone of the deepest satisfaction. "No longer will I have to race against time while dissecting my subjects. I will be able to preserve them for days—even weeks! Can you tell what it is, gentlemen?"

Indeed, I could—though I was filled with a sense of utter confusion as to how it had come into the anatomist's possession.

It was a picture of Peter Vatty's Corpse Cooler.

PART FOUR

Behind a Mask

CHAPTER TWENTY-THREE

MacKenzie had never heard the name Peter Vatty. He knew only that the unique refrigerated casket had been invented by a local craftsman from Concord whom Herbert Ballinger had met during a recent visit to that village. Ballinger had reported back to MacKenzie that the design for this remarkable contrivance could be obtained for a certain sum of money, which the anatomist was only too happy to provide. Ballinger had then returned to Concord—completed the transaction—and brought back the plan, which he had delivered to MacKenzie just a few hours prior to his own murder.

The anatomist having concluded his tale, Lynch declared that—in light of this new information—Ballinger's helper, Benjamin Bowden, must now be viewed as the likely assassin. The Boston police, he avowed, would spare no effort to track down the fellow, whose sudden flight from the city appeared suspicious in the extreme. A few moments later—after thanking MacKenzie for his help—Lynch and I took our leave and climbed aboard the waiting carriage.

Seated in back—Dr. Farragut's empty medicine chest resting on my lap—I was overcome with both physical and mental exhaustion. I could scarcely form a coherent thought, and felt in desperate need of the sweet nepenthe of sleep. But where was I to obtain such refreshment? Clearly, I could not return to poor Mrs. Randall's abode. Even if the two dreadfully mutilated corpses had been removed to the morgue—as I assumed was the case—I could not possibly enjoy a single moment's rest in a place fraught with such horrid associations. In view of my pitifully straitened circumstances, a hostelry was also out of the question.

Only one solution suggested itself. Twenty minutes later—having provided the driver with the appropriate address—I bid farewell to Lynch and disembarked in front of the house of the Alcott girls' uncle, Mr. Samuel May. The old gentleman—whom, of course, I was forced to rouse from his slumber—was much surprised to see me at that unseasonable hour. But after hearing a (much condensed) account of the dismaying events of the day, he very kindly led me to a guest room, where—after stripping down to my undergarments—I threw myself onto the bed and immediately sank into oblivion.

By the following morning—after a lengthy, if not wholly untroubled, sleep—I felt sufficiently clearheaded to plan my next step. Thus far, my mission could hardly be accounted a success. Though I had located Dr. Farragut's stolen case, the whereabouts of its precious contents remained as mysterious as ever. To be sure, if—as MacKenzie insisted—Farragut's botanical method was nothing but quackery, there was no point in continuing my search. But MacKenzie's word on the subject was not to be trusted. Like all members of the medical establishment, he was a sworn enemy of the Thomsonian approach to healing. In any case, all conventional methods for treating my dear wife's disease having proved futile, I had no other choice but to place my hopes in Dr. Farragut's all-natural cure.

But where to look next? The answer seemed clear. A chain of evidence led from Dr. Farragut's stolen case to Ludlow Marston to Herbert Ballinger to Peter Vatty. While the Boston police pursued their hunt for Benjamin Bowden, my own course pointed in another direction.

I must return, without delay, to Concord.

Among the countless oracular pronouncements to be found in the writings of Ralph Waldo Emerson—Concord's most celebrated citizen—is the observation "Nature always wears the colors of the spirit." While not entirely lacking in a certain gnomic eloquence, this statement—like virtually all of Mr. Emerson's aphorisms—is so utterly at variance with plain common sense as to amount to little more than pseudo-mystical *hogwash*.

The sheer inanity of this statement was brought home to me upon my arrival at Concord. It was an afternoon of singular beauty and serenity. Far from corresponding to the tranquil loveliness of the landscape, however, my soul was in a state of excessive turmoil. Had Nature truly been wearing the colors of my soul, the sky—instead of being of a brilliant autumnal blue—would have been dark with the swirling forms of violently agitated storm-clouds.

My troubled emotional state is not to be wondered at. The awful events of the preceding days had cast a deep pall over my spirit. This somber frame of mind was exacerbated by my failure to recover Dr. Farragut's ingredients.

At the same time, my spirit was not *wholly* enshrouded by gloom. How could it be? For within moments, I was to see my darling Sissy. Though I dreaded the thought of imparting my news—which could not fail to shock and disappoint her—the prospect of our imminent reunion filled me with joy.

Approaching the Alcott's charming abode, I could hear, through a partially open window, the sound of a girlish voice, which—though pitched below its normal key—was clearly that of Louy.

"Foiled again!" she was declaiming in a crude approximation of villainous manhood. "Some demon works against me! A little longer and I should have won a rich bride. But I will have her yet—and wring her proud heart till she shall bend her haughty head and beg for mercy!"

Surmising that I had arrived during a rehearsal of the little girl's melodrama *The Witch's Curse*, I hesitated before announcing my presence, not wishing to interrupt the proceedings. By and by, Louy having reached the end of her speech, I rapped on the door.

A moment later, the door flew open. There stood Louy herself. I saw at once that my supposition had been correct, for she was gaudily costumed in a plumed cap—scarlet cape—flowing shirt—and baggy pantaloons stuffed into tall yellow boots. Her narrow waist was girded with a wide leather belt through which was thrust a wooden sword fashioned from the slat which she had salvaged from Peter Vatty's yard.

At her first glimpse of me, her sparkling gray eyes crinkled with delight. Then, arranging her countenance into a look of mock-solemnity, she turned on her heels and led me toward the parlor.

Peering through the arched doorway, I perceived that all three of Louy's siblings, along with my own beloved wife, were cozily ensconced in the room, each busily engaged in a task related to the production of the play. Anna, the oldest, sat in a rocker, stitching a long train to a white linen gown evidently meant to be worn by a princess. Little May, crayons in hand, was seated cross-legged on the floor before a large sheet of paper, drawing a picture of a distant hill dominated by a medieval castle. Lizzie (with one of her damaged dolls on her lap) was snuggled on the sofa, fashioning what appeared to be a grizzled wig from a bunch of horsehair. Beside her sat Sissy, a woolen shawl about her shoulders and a pair of scissors in one surpassingly elegant hand. She was cutting a piece of cardboard into the shape of a guitar. Completing the charming picture was the family cat, who was hunched before the blazing fireplace, his favorite rubber ball clutched between his paws. Of the entire household, only Mrs. Alcott was not to be seen.

Pausing at the threshold, Louy plucked off her cap, bowed with a flourish, and—speaking in the same low-pitched voice she had been using a few moments earlier—announced:

"Joyful tidings! A great ambassador has arrived who doth crave an audience with miladies. Pray bid him welcome, for he hath traveled a mighty distance to be with us here today!"

She then stepped to one side and—with a sweeping motion of her cap—beckoned me to enter.

As I crossed into the parlor, I was greeted with a chorus of gasps, the loudest and most excited of which issued from the throat of my darling wife. Quickly setting aside her scissors and cardboard, she made as if to rise. Not wishing to cause her any unnecessary exertion, I hastily set down my luggage (which, in addition to my own grip and Dr. Farragut's case, consisted of the carpetbag holding the items I had selected for P. T. Barnum)—hurried to the sofa—and, bending over, rained a torrent of kisses upon her alabaster brow. Gazing up at me—a blush rising to her cheeks from my unwonted outburst of passion—Sissy exclaimed: "Oh, Eddie, what a wonderful surprise!"

At that instant, I heard a warm, motherly voice behind me. "What is all the commotion, my dearies? Oh, Mr. Poe! How nice to see you!"

Turning, I perceived that Mrs. Alcott had just emerged from the kitchen. She was wearing an apron heavily dusted with flour. This—along with the heat-induced flush suffusing her plain yet pleasing countenance—made it clear that she had been engaged in the preparation of bake-goods.

"The mere language of mortality cannot possibly convey the joy I feel in being here," I earnestly replied.

Louy, who had once again donned her chevalier's cap (the plume of which appeared to have come from an old feather duster), suddenly let out an astonished cry. Looking in her direction, I saw that her gaze was riveted upon the wooden case.

"Is—is that it, Mr. Poe?" she stammered. "Dr. Farragut's stolen medicine chest?"

I confirmed that it was.

All eyes now turned to look upon the exquisite receptacle.

"How perfectly splendid," exclaimed Anna. "Why, it must be worth heaps and heaps of money."

"I've never seen anything so beautiful," marveled Lizzie. "Not even the grand piano in old Mr. Laurence's house."

"It *is* a handsome thing, no doubt about it," said Mrs. Alcott, "though rather too showy for my taste."

"I agree with Marmee. In fact, I think it's rather ostensible," sniffed little May, who evidently meant to say "ostentatious."

"I knew you'd find it, Eddie," said Sissy, giving my right hand a fervent squeeze. "I never had a single moment's doubt."

The reader will have no trouble understanding the anguish I felt at these words. I had not merely failed in my mission but, in doing so, had betrayed Sissy's faith in my abilities. The thought was so painful that I could hardly bring myself to confess the truth. And yet I knew that I must do so at once. Every moment of delay only made the situation more agonizing.

Lowering myself onto the sofa beside my wife, I tenderly enfolded one of her hands in both my own. "I fear, Sissy dearest," I said, "that your confidence has been sadly misplaced."

"Why, what do you mean, Eddie?" she said, peering intently into my eyes.

Such was my sense of utter and abject failure that I could barely return her gaze. "It is true that I have succeeded in recovering Dr. Farragut's case," I said. "The precious ingredients it contained, however, are still missing."

This revelation brought startled ejaculations from several of the Alcott sisters. Sissy, by contrast, merely looked at me in silence, while her countenance registered a variety of emotions: confusion, disappointment, anxiety. Very quickly, however, these were superseded by a look of concern—not for herself, but for *me*.

"Don't be so upset, Eddie dear," she said, patting my hand in a reassuring manner. "Tell me what happened."

"When discovered," I said, "Dr. Farragut's case had been emptied of its contents. Whether these have been destroyed or preserved by the thief, I cannot say, though there is reason to think that the latter is the case."

"Then there's still hope?" interposed Louy.

"There is always cause for hope, dear," said Mrs. Alcott, "so long as we trust in the strength and goodness of our Heavenly Father. I feel in my heart that He won't let anything bad happen to Virginia."

While desperately wishing to share in the good woman's faith, I could not help but be aware that a number of inordinately bad things had been allowed to happen to other human beings in recent days. Indeed—though I was loath to be the cause of any further distress—there was no point in withholding the truth from Sissy and the Alcott females, who would hear it sooner rather than later, as the news quickly spread from Boston.

Accordingly, I said: "I fear that I have other, even more dismaying, tidings to report. During my sojourn in the city, a series of singularly brutal murders occurred. The victims, I regret to say, were people known to us all."

The effect of these words upon my auditors may be readily imagined. Sissy gasped and intensified her grip on my hand. Lizzie let out a whimper and clutched her injured dolly tightly to her bosom. Little May leapt to her feet and ran to the side of her mother, who placed a protective arm around the child's narrow shoulders. Anna set down her stitchery and looked at me with a deeply apprehensive expression.

Only Louy betrayed a certain quality of eager expectation. Eyes wide and shining, lips slightly agape, she stared at me as though anticipating a thrilling tale of Gothic terror.

"The victims," I continued, "were Dr. Ludlow Marston, Mr. Herbert Ballinger, and"—here I turned to address Sissy directly—"our hostess Mrs. Randall and her maidservant, Sally."

This announcement provoked an outburst of incredulous gasps, stricken cries, and horrified exclamations from all six females.

"Christopher Columbus!" said Louy. "That *is* awful news—just about the most shocking I've ever heard!"

"I can't believe Dr. Marston is dead," said May. "I had such a jolly time at his show, and now I'll never get to see it again!"

"Poor Mrs. Randall," said Sissy, her eyes filling with tears. "Who would want to harm that dear sweet woman?"

"Mr. Ballinger—murdered!" said Anna, whose complexion had turned as white as the garment on her lap. "Why, it's too dreadful for words."

"Wasn't he the man who made that lovely daguerreotype of you girls?" asked Mrs. Alcott, gesturing toward the portrait of the four Alcott sisters that now occupied a prominent place on the mantel.

"He's the one, all right, Mother," said Louy. "And a capital fellow he was, too. Very kind and polite and ever so cultivated. It breaks my heart to think of him dead."

"But who was responsible, Eddie?" asked Sissy. "Have the police made an arrest?"

"Not yet," I replied, "though they are of the opinion that the perpetrator is a man named Bowden, who worked as Mr. Ballinger's assistant."

"Do you mean the fellow who hobbled when he walked?" asked Anna.

"He's the one, yes," I said.

"I remember him!" cried May. "And to think—I felt sorry for him because of his handicraft!"

"You mean 'handicap,' May," said Louy. "And it wasn't as severe as all that. Just a slight limp."

"He seemed like such a nice gentleman," said Lizzie in a tremulous voice. "Very quiet, like me. I thought he and Mr. Ballinger were brothers."

"They *did* bear a resemblance to each other," said Anna.

"But *why*, Eddie?" said Sissy. "Why would he commit such horrible crimes?"

"His motives are unknown," I said. "At present, all that can be said is that there appears to be a connection between Mr. Ballinger and the other victims, two of whom—Dr. Marston and Mrs. Randall—had employed his service as a daguerreotypist." Not wishing to upset the Alcott sisters any more than was absolutely necessary, I made no mention of their friend Elsie Bolton, whose death I also suspected was linked to Ballinger.

My effort to avoid alarming them was to no avail, however; for, no sooner had I spoken, than Anna exclaimed:

"But *we* did, too. Employ his services, I mean."

"Mercy on us!" cried May. "What if he should come after *us*?"

"That is exceedingly unlikely," I declared. "Mr. Ballinger, after all, had many, many clients, the vast majority of whom are in no apparent danger. Moreover, all of Bowden's crimes have thus far been confined to the city."

"Still," said Lizzie, "I *do* wish Poppa were here to protect us."

"Fear not, fair damsel," said Louy, withdrawing her wooden sword from her belt and raising it high in the air. "No harm shall befall thee while this stout arm and shining blade are here to shield thee from peril!"

"Really, Louy," chided Anna. "This is no time for levity."

"I don't mean to make light of such a dreadful situation," said Louy, resheathing her mock weapon. "But I hate to see you girls worry yourselves sick when there's nothing to be frightened about."

"Louy is right," I said. "The Boston police are making every effort to track down the suspect. They are sure to apprehend him in short order—if, indeed, they have not already done so.

"In the meantime," I continued, turning again to face Sissy, "I believe that there is someone here in Concord who knows more about the missing contents of Dr. Farragut's case than he has heretofore admitted."

"Who is that, Eddie?" asked Sissy.

"Peter Vatty," I said, producing yet another burst of astonished cries from the Alcotts.

"I just *knew* he was fibbing when we went to see him," said Louy. "Didn't I say so, Mr. Poe?"

"Indeed, your observations in that regard corresponded precisely to my own," I said.

"But what makes you think that he has information about Dr. Farragut's ingredients, Eddie?" asked Sissy.

During my ride back to Concord that morning, I had resolved that— when recounting my adventures to Sissy and the Alcotts—I would withhold all references to grave-robbing, corpse-dissection, and other such macabre matters. Accordingly, I now replied to my wife in the following manner:

"There is little need for you to know every detail of the case, Sissy dearest, certain aspects of which are of an excessively unsettling nature. Suffice it to say that the missing medicine chest was found in the home of Dr. Marston. Based on the evidence, it would appear that the dentist received this article from Herbert Ballinger as part of a transaction between the two men. But how did Mr. Ballinger obtain it? Clearly from someone in Concord. For a number of reasons, I believe that person to be Peter Vatty, whom Ballinger recently visited for business reasons. Whether the chest was stolen by Vatty himself or by an accomplice, I cannot say. In any case, I am determined to confront him about the matter."

Though this remark was addressed to Sissy, it was Mrs. Alcott who replied. "I don't mean to question your authority on this matter, Mr. Poe, but everyone knows that Mr. Vatty keeps completely to himself. Why, he is even more of a hermit than Henry Thoreau, who often leaves his cabin on Walden Pond to come to town. Do you really think he might have an accomplice?"

"I believe that is a distinct possibility," I replied with an emphatic nod.

"But who?" asked Mrs. Alcott.

For a moment, I hesitated to respond, knowing that my answer could not fail to be a source of further anxiety. At length—seeing no way to evade such a direct question—I said: "Do you recall the red-bearded beggar who appeared at your kitchen door last week?"

"You mean that frightful-looking man who gave me such a scare?" said May.

"The same," I said. "Shortly after that incident, I observed the same unsavory-looking fellow lurking on your property. He was also seen by Mr. Thoreau marching through the woods in the direction of Peter Vatty's farm. Though Mr. Vatty denied all knowledge of the man, he did so in a decidedly unconvincing way. As a result, it is my firm opinion that he and Mr. Vatty are, if not confederates, at least acquaintances."

"I saw him, too!" interposed Anna, causing the rest of us to turn in surprise toward the seated young woman.

"What did you say, dear?" asked Mrs. Alcott.

"The other day, as I was walking to Clara Moffat's house, I saw that fellow by the edge of the woods," said Anna. "He didn't speak a word, just looked at me in the queerest way. I didn't tell you about it, Marmee, for I didn't want to worry you, and after all, nothing bad happened. But the look in his eyes! Mercy—I shan't ever forget it, not as long as I live!"

This revelation had a palpably unsettling effect on the younger of the two Alcott sisters. May emitted a little noise of distress and threw her arms around her mother's waist. At the same time, Lizzie—still hugging her injured doll to her chest—snuggled closer to Sissy, as though for protection.

"Well, dearies," said Mrs. Alcott after a moment. "We have heard much distressing news this day, there can be no doubt about it. But after all, while there are many joys in life, there are also times of great trouble, and we must learn to face them with strength and courage and faith in our Heavenly Father, whose love and care for us never tires or changes. And now, my girls, I propose that we celebrate Mr. Poe's safe return with a little treat—for unless my nose deceives me, my pie is ready to come out of the oven."

"Three cheers for Marmee!" cried Louy, extracting her sword once again and raising it high in the air. "A little treat will do us heaps of good! Come, miladies, let us to table, where we shall feast away our worries with the help of Mother's splendid apple pie!"

CHAPTER TWENTY-FOUR

⌒

B Y THE FOLLOWING morning, the weather had changed. The sky—so pellucid the previous afternoon—was now ashen and sober. The leaves that had shone with such autumnal brilliance now appeared withered and sere. A harsh wind tore them from the gnarled branches and whipped them through the air like swarms of startled bats. The mere sight of the inordinately damp and dreary day caused an icy shiver to course through my frame. Turning from the window, I quickly performed my ablutions and threw on my clothing, while Sissy slumbered in the bed across the room.

Stepping from the chamber, I closed the door softly behind me and tip-toed downstairs. The hour being excessively early, I assumed that, like Sissy, the rest of the household was still asleep. I was greatly surprised, therefore, when I heard the sounds of culinary activity issuing from the kitchen. Proceeding in that direction, I found Mrs. Alcott standing by her workbench, engaged in the preparation of some species of batter.

"Why, good morning, Mr. Poe," the stout, motherly woman said in a cheery voice. "You are up early."

"And you even earlier, Mrs. Alcott," I cordially replied.

"Well, I have never been one to linger in bed," she remarked. " 'Make hay while the sun shines,' I say. Not that it is shining today. Come, sit down and have a nice plate of buckwheats. You will need something hearty to keep you warm if you are venturing out in this dreadful weather."

Thanking her for her offer, I took a place at the small table that stood near the hearth, while my hostess proceeded with her cooking. Ten minutes later, she placed a heaping plate of the intensely savory cakes before me, along with a pitcher of cream and a steaming mug of coffee.

As I tucked my napkin into my collar and snatched up my utensils, she seated herself across from me and said: "So you are off to speak to Mr. Vatty?"

Having just inserted a large forkful of pancake into my mouth, I merely nodded in confirmation.

"I do hope that you will succeed in your quest," said Mrs. Alcott, a look of concern coming over her visage. "Dr. Farragut has been perfectly splendid—a 'trump,' as Louy would say. He has visited each afternoon, just as he promised, and supplied Virginia with various herbal medicines that have done her much good. Still, he has confided in me that, without the missing ingredients, he cannot hope to achieve a permanent cure."

These remarks merely confirmed what I already knew. Upon my arrival the previous afternoon, I had rejoiced to see Sissy so far recovered as to be out of her sickbed and happily assisting the Alcott girls in their amateur theatricals. Even so, I could not fail to notice the unmistakable signs of her lingering affliction, clearly visible in the febrile glow of her cheeks—the too, *too* glorious effulgence of her eyes—the transparent waxy hue of her lofty forehead.

"Well," continued Mrs. Alcott with a sigh, "we must all bear our burdens and deal as best we can with whatever care and sorrow God sees fit to send. I shall pray every day for Virginia's recovery. I have grown terribly fond of her, you know. I have almost begun to think of her as one of my own little women."

"For her part," I answered, deeply touched by the good woman's heartfelt words, "my wife tells me that she has come to feel as though she were a sister to your own lovely daughters."

"And we feel the same!" interposed a familiar voice from behind me.

Turning, I saw Louy standing in the doorway, dressed, as she normally was, in a simple blue gown and calico apron. Her thick chestnut hair was pinned up and tucked under a net.

"Good morning, dear," said Mrs. Alcott, rising from her chair. "And are your sisters awake?"

"Anna and Lizzie have just gotten up and are washing their faces," said Louy, striding to the table and seating herself in the chair beside mine. "May is still abed, that sleepy-head."

Bidding her good-morning, I asked the high-spirited child what inspired her to rise so early, in contrast to her siblings.

"That dozy way don't suit me," said Louy, rubbing her hands eagerly as her mother set a plate of buckwheat cakes before her. "Not being a pussycat, I don't like to spend my time snoozing by the fire."

"From what I have observed," I said, "your own cat appears to be an unusually active member of the species *Felis domestica*. Indeed, only moments ago, I saw him rush through the door flap in his eagerness to get outside."

"Oh, Barnaby does his share of napping," said Louy. "But not all day. He likes to go out and have adventures. So do I. Which is why I thought I'd come with you to Mr. Vatty's."

So surprising was this statement that I nearly expectorated the mouthful of coffee I had just sipped from my cup. Swallowing the beverage with a gulp, I looked at Louy and said:

"While your company is always welcome, Louy, I do not, in the present instance, feel that it will serve a particularly useful purpose."

"But I helped last time, didn't I?" she protested. "I could tell when Mr. Vatty was lying. I daresay I might do some good again."

"There can be no doubt that your impressions of Mr. Vatty were exceedingly valuable," I said in a kindly tone. "Now that I am familiar with that singularly eccentric gentleman, however, I feel strongly that it is best to approach him on my own. My interrogation of him will require the greatest delicacy and concentration on my part. Your presence at our interview would be—at the very least—a distraction, both to him and to myself."

"Well, I certainly don't wish to poke myself where I ain't wanted," said the little girl.

"Besides, dear," interposed Mrs. Alcott, "I need all of you girls at home this morning. You know how eager I am to finish that quilt to give to poor Mrs. Hummel before winter sets in. If that is to happen, we must all help with the sewing."

"Very well, Marmee," said Louy. "I shall do my duty here without grumbling."

For this sweetly submissive declaration, the little girl was rewarded with a kiss on the brow by her mother.

"Besides," continued the little girl, "I still have heaps to do before my play premieres tonight. The scenery must be set up in the barn and the seats arranged for the audience. I've invited every child in the neighborhood, you know, so I expect there will be quite a crowd. You'll be there, too, won't you, Mr. Poe?"

"Most certainly," I replied. "Please make sure to reserve a box seat."

"You might have to bring your own box, in that case," answered Louy with a smile, "for I can't promise anything more luxurious than some benches made of old planks."

"That will be perfectly adequate," I said. Then consulting my pocket watch, I added: "And now I must be off."

"That reminds me, Mr. Poe," said Louy, observing me closely as I re-placed the timepiece in my pocket. "Was Uncle May happy to get his watch key back?"

"I imagine he was, dear," said Mrs. Alcott, who obviously knew of the letter I had received from her daughter while in Boston. "Knowing my brother as I do, he must have been quite vexed to discover it missing."

During the past several days, so much had happened of a profoundly disconcerting nature that I had temporarily forgotten about the small golden key. Now—still intent on shielding the Alcott females from my sus-picions about Elsie Bolton's murder—I answered Louy thusly:

"Upon the receipt of your letter, I immediately proceeded to your uncle's abode. As it happened, however, the key did not belong to him. In-deed," I continued, extracting the little object from my vest pocket and ex-tending it toward the girl, "I have it right here. As its owner is unknown, it belongs—by the law of possession—to its finder, who in this case is your younger sister May."

"Well, that's awfully queer," said Louy, taking the proffered key and ex-amining it with a puzzled look. "Where in the world could it have come from?"

"I am not sure," I truthfully replied.

Moments later, after bidding farewell to Mrs. Alcott and her daughter, I went to the hallway, removed my heavy cloak and beaver hat from their wall-pegs, and took my leave.

Outside, the clouds hung oppressively low in the heavens and the wind blew so fiercely that I was forced to retain a firm grip on my hat brim as I walked. As I made my way along the wooded path that led toward Vatty's farmstead, I revolved in my mind the perplexing matter of the unidentified watch key.

As the reader will recall, my initial assumption was that the key be-longed to Herbert Ballinger. Indeed, its discovery at the site of Elsie Bolton's murder was the clue which had led to my conclusion that the daguerreotyp-ist was not merely a scoundrel but a homicidal maniac.

It now appeared that the madman was not Ballinger himself but his assistant, Benjamin Bowden. I continued to believe, however, that the little object belonged to Ballinger, who had clearly been missing his watch key at the time I first met him. How, then, had the daguerreotypist's watch key come to be present at the crime scene? Only one answer seemed plausible. Somehow, Bowden had managed to remove the key from his employer's watch chain and leave it at the murder scene to incriminate his employer.

While not *fully* satisfied with this explanation, I could not, at the moment, conceive of another. My failure to do so must be attributed to various factors. So physically and emotionally debilitating had been the awful events of the past several days, my mental faculties were not operating at their usual, extraordinary level of acuity. In addition, my thoughts, for the most part, were not focused on the apprehension of the killer—a task that now rested in the hands of the Boston police—but on the retrieval of Dr. Farragut's missing medications and on my impending interview with the man who, I believed, could lead me to them: the death-haunted eccentric Peter Vatty.

In the somber light of that gray, dreary morn, Vatty's farmhouse appeared, if possible, even more decrepit than it had on my earlier visit. Shaking off the incubus of dread that settled on my heart at my first glimpse of the weatherworn edifice, I mounted the rickety front steps and crossed the porch, whose sagging boards groaned loudly beneath my feet. Several windows looked onto the porch, but my efforts to peer through them proved futile, as the glass was so thickly coated with grime as to be nearly opaque.

As I approached the front door, I saw that it was standing slightly ajar. Putting my mouth close to the opening, I called inside, but received no response. I then rapped several times on the door. The force of my blows caused it to swing inward on its leather hinges, thus affording me a partial view of the excessively gloomy interior.

"Hello!" I called. "Mr. Vatty?"

No one replied.

Thinking that the recluse might be in his workshed, I left the porch—crossed the rank and rubbish-strewn yard—and pounded on the door of the little building, but again with no results.

It was clear that Vatty was nowhere on the premises. As I stood before the shed, wondering how best to proceed, I heard the distant report of a fowling-piece. Knowing that Vatty (who rarely ventured into town for supplies) must subsist on rabbits, squirrels, waterbirds, and other small game, I surmised that he was off on a daily hunting expedition. How long he might be gone I could not say, but—judging from the sound of the discharge—the shooter appeared to be at a considerable distance.

From my present vantage point, I could clearly see the front of the house. As I gazed at the door—still standing halfway open—I was possessed of a sudden, admittedly reckless, but nonetheless *irresistible* impulse.

Vatty, I was convinced, knew more than he had acknowledged about Dr. Farragut's missing ingredients. I could not, however, count on his revealing their whereabouts to me. Here was a chance to look for them myself. Perhaps I would turn up the stolen items inside his home; perhaps not. In any event, in my present desperate frame of mind, the opportunity seemed too precious to waste.

Hurrying back to the house, I made my way across the creaking porch (half-expecting it to collapse beneath my weight), and slipped through the door, closing it behind me.

For several moments, I remained motionless, while I waited for my eyes to adjust themselves to the pervading gloom. A stale, intensely unpleasant aroma—only slightly less repellent than the sickening stench of Dr. MacKenzie's anatomy school—suffused my nostrils, causing me to grimace in disgust. At length, my vision having adapted to the murky atmosphere, I began to step slowly down the narrow hallway.

My cautious pace was necessitated by the excessively chaotic condition of the house. Piles of refuse lay everywhere: mouldering feed sacks, mildewed horse blankets, rusted farm implements, battered metal tubs, stacks of decaying newspapers, broken china, shattered pieces of furniture, and countless other excessively corroded objects impossible to identify. I had, of course, known people who were reluctant to dispose of their outworn possessions. Vatty, by contrast, seemed to be someone who not merely saved but jealousy *hoarded* his trash. His home appeared to be little more than an enclosed rubbish heap.

Carefully making my way through the unholy clutter, I turned a corner and came to a startled halt. At the end of the corridor, the dull orange glow of candlelight emanated from an open doorway. Was Vatty at home after all? With racing heart, I called out his name, my voice sounding unsteady in my ears. No one replied. Subduing the qualm of dread that had taken hold of me, I continued along the rubbish-strewn passageway until, reaching the open door, I peered inside.

The sight that greeted me brought an involuntary gasp of amazement from my lips. From my present vantage point, only a small portion of the room was visible to me. I could see enough, however, to tell that it was a bedchamber. There was a mahogany armoire—an ornate washstand—a Sheraton easy-chair beside a marble-topped side table. The walls were covered with floral paper and hung with framed prints depicting biblical scenes.

What made the sight so surprising was the impeccable condition of the room. No contrast could have been greater than that between its extreme— its *inordinate*—tidiness and the wild disorder I had thus far encountered. It was as though Vatty had limited his housekeeping to this single room, while allowing the rest of his abode to descend into utter squalor.

Only in one regard did the chamber resemble the rest of the house—i.e., in the rank, repulsive smell that was perceptible even from the threshold.

Reaching out a hand, I rapped on the open door. When no one responded, I stepped inside and gazed about.

My eyes immediately lit upon the bed—a mahogany four-poster. Something was stretched out on one side of the mattress.

For a moment, I could not grasp what I was seeing. Or rather—though I recognized the object on the bed—I refused to accept the evidence of my senses. My brain reeled. My vision swam.

Staggering backward, I clutched the top of a nearby bureau for support. As I did, I became aware of a peculiar sensation, as though I had grasped the tail of a dray horse. Gazing down, I saw that I had placed my hand atop a thatch of exceedingly coarse hair of an unnatural flame-colored hue. Two wires bent into hooks were attached to the orange-dyed horsehair, allowing it to be looped to the ears and worn as a false beard.

A quivering moan issued from my throat. Spinning on my heels, I bolted from the room. Heedless of the obstacles, I ran headlong down the hallway, knocking over the precarious heaps of rubbish in my path, banging my shins painfully against all manner of wooden and metal debris. Reaching the front door, I threw it open.

Peter Vatty stood framed in the doorway, a rifle clutched in his hands, his visage wrought into a look of insane fury.

A terrified shriek burst from my lips. Vatty raised his rifle, aiming its butt at my head. My hands flew up in a protective gesture—but too late.

An explosion of brilliant white light flared within my skull, accompanied by a paroxysm of intense—searing—pain. Then the blinding light vanished—the pain was cut short—and all was darkness—and silence— and utter oblivion.

CHAPTER TWENTY-FIVE

⌒

How long I remained in my unconscious state I cannot say with precision. I can only recall a period of utter insensibility, followed by an uncannily vivid—profoundly *unsettling*—nightmare, in which a ghastly female figure, clad in the habiliments of the grave, emerged from the subterranean vault in which she had been prematurely interred. Gliding into the chamber where I slept, she tore strips of rotting cloth from her blood-mottled shroud and used them to bind me by the wrists to the bedposts. Then, stretching out beside me on the mattress, she placed her clammy lips close to my ear.

Though wild to escape the touch of the unspeakably vile creature, I was unable to move my body, my arms being securely tethered to the bed. As her foetid mouth drew nearer, I turned my head as far away from her as possible. The violence of my effort caused my forehead to throb painfully.

"One kiss," she whispered in a lilting voice. "That is all I crave."

A scream of the purest anguish arose in my throat. Perspiration burst from every pore. All at once—before I could summon my agonized yell—I came awake.

My first sensation was one of intense relief that the appalling phantasm had been nothing more than a horrid dream. A minute passed before I grew fully aware of my surroundings and realized with a shudder that my true situation was even more appalling than the nightmare from which I had just emerged.

I was back inside the immaculately neat, candlelit bedroom. I was seated in the Sheraton chair, to which I was securely fastened by a long, excessively frayed leather strap resembling a badly worn surcingle. It passed in several convolutions around my arms and upper torso, binding me to the chair-back.

Directly facing me was the mahogany bed. Peter Vatty was standing beside it, bending over the thing that occupied the left side of the mattress.

It was a corpse, recognizable as that of a woman, from its mouldering gown and the long strands of wiry hair that sprouted from its skull. The countenance was so hideously desiccated as to resemble that of an Egyptian mummy. Its fleshless mouth was drawn back into a hideous rictus, revealing a set of gruesome yellow teeth. A pair of small wooden orbs, painted to resemble eyeballs, had been placed into the hollow sockets. Its feet were shod in dainty boots, and on its hands it wore cream-colored kidskin gloves embroidered with a delicate floral design.

The rotted thing—as I had realized upon first seeing it—was very evidently the decomposed body of Vatty's adored bride, Priscilla Robinson. She was garbed in the dress in which she had been buried prior to her exhumation.

The gloves, however, were clearly of a more recent vintage. Indeed, I could not fail to notice that they were the missing pair belonging to Anna Alcott.

In his right palm, Vatty cradled a jar of cobalt-blue glass, from which he was removing small dollops of a glistening ointment with the first two fingers of his opposite hand. Then, reaching down, he applied the substance to the loathsome visage of the cadaver, gently massaging it into the cracked and leathery skin, while—in a high-pitched, singsong voice—he crooned over and over again a stanza from the ancient ballad "The Unquiet Grave":

> " 'Tis I, my love, stands by your bed,
>   And will not let you sleep;
>   For I crave one kiss of your clay-cold lips,
>   And that is all I seek."

As I gaped in frozen horror at this grotesque—this *stupefying*—scene, a low, terrified whimper reached my ears. It was not until Vatty abruptly ceased his ministrations and turned in my direction that I realized the sound was issuing from my own throat.

Seeing me awake, Vatty set the octagonal blue bottle down on the side table and came to stand before me. Reaching to his waist with his left hand, he extracted a large-bladed hunting knife from an old leather sheath attached to his belt. He then waved this formidable implement before my face and—his repulsive visage twisted into a look of sheer, *unutterable* hatred—snarled:

"You damned filthy sneak. I ought to gut you right now."

Even in my excessively overwrought state, I was cognizant of a sharp, strangely familiar odor emanating from the hand that held the weapon. My mind was in too great a tumult, however, to immediately identify the aroma.

So intense was the emotion induced in me by the madman's threat that I endeavored in vain to reply. My powers of speech totally failed, fear having caused every bit of moisture to vanish from my mouth. At length—with great effort—I managed to say, in a hoarse, constricted voice:

"But surely you would not commit such an atrocity in full view of your wife. For I take it that the figure occupying your bed is none other than your own beloved Priscilla, whom you have saved from the horrors of the grave and brought back home to be with you."

Vatty's eyes flickered in confusion. He quickly peered over his shoulder at the bed before turning his maddened gaze back at me.

"She can't see nothing. She ain't alive. Not just yet."

I perceived that *my* only hope for remaining alive lay in keeping the maniac talking for as long as possible while I frantically sought some means of escape. Struggling to maintain a tone of amiable interest, I therefore addressed him thusly:

"I assume, however, from your statement that you expect her resurrection to be accomplished at any moment."

"Should be," Vatty replied, though in a somewhat uncertain manner.

"It was wise of you, then, to supply her with such lovely eyes in preparation for her imminent revival," I said. "And I cannot help but admire her gloves, which—if I am not not mistaken—bear a remarkable resemblance to a pair owned by Miss Anna Alcott."

Regarding me narrowly, Vatty said: "You got a keen eye, I'll say that for you, you son of a bitch. Them's the Alcott gal's gloves, all right. I seen her wearin' them one Sunday morning a while back. I always did enjoy lookin' at that Anna. She's real pretty. Just like Priscilla. But Mr. Alcott, he threatened to have me arrested if I kept lingering around his property. So I made me up a disguise, so I could come up to the house from time to time and get a peek at her. Then one night, I just snuck in whilst everyone was asleep and stole her gloves for Priscilla."

"That was exceedingly clever of you," I said. "Particularly as the windows and doors are kept tightly locked at night."

"There's more'n one way to skin a cat," said Vatty with a peculiar, self-satisfied smirk, as he scratched his crooked nose with the knobby index finger of his right hand.

I have commented before on the unusual, if not *grotesque,* appearance of Vatty's arms, which were so inordinately long as to seem positively simian. Now, as I gazed up at him, a realization struck me.

"Of course," I said. "There is another means of access to the house—the little cat-flap built into the kitchen door. For someone with your impressively elongated limbs, it would have been a simple matter to thrust your arm inside—reach up—and undo the latch."

"You got that figured right," Vatty acknowledged. "That's a good head you got on your shoulders, Poe. Too bad you won't have it there long."

And so saying, he raised his weapon to my throat and pressed the sharpened edge against that protuberant mass of thyroid cartilage commonly denominated as the "Adam's apple."

At the touch of his knife, the very marrow in my bones turned to ice and an irrepressible tremor coursed through every fibre of my being. Struggling mightily to subdue my trembling (for I feared that the merest movement of my head might cause his blade to slice into my flesh), I gazed up at him with imploring eyes and said:

"Your sense of indignation is fully justified, Mr. Vatty. There can be no doubt that, by violating the sanctity of your home, I have been guilty of a grievous wrongdoing. I urge you, however, to consider the consequences of the bloody act of vengeance that you are contemplating. While my violent death might afford you a momentary sense of satisfaction, it will almost certainly lead to your prompt arrest and probable execution. Your wife, Priscilla, will be left unprotected and—in view of her present, unfortunate condition—inevitably be returned to the grave."

My words appeared to have the desired effect. The look of furious resolve evaporated from Vatty's face and was replaced by a vacillating expression. Lowering his blade, he glanced behind him toward the bed, then, pulling at his slack lower lip, muttered: "Maybe you're right. Can't let nothin' happen to Priscilla. Not till the medicine takes hold."

"Am I correct in assuming," I asked, "that the medicine to which you refer is the substance I saw you rubbing into her skin?"

"That's right," said Vatty. "He promised it would bring her alive again."

"By *he,*" I ventured, "do you mean Mr. Herbert Ballinger?"

Vatty looked at me with narrowed eyes. "How the hell do you know *that?*"

"I am somewhat familiar with that gentleman," I answered, "having visited his daguerreotype studio in Boston. Is that where *you* met him?"

Vatty shook his head. "Naw. It was in Osborne's tavern, maybe three, four months back. We got to talkin'. I found out he took pictures of dead folks. When I mentioned my invention, he got real interested. Said it might be worth a lot of money. I told him money don't interest me, just bringing my Priscilla back. So we worked out a deal. I'd trade him my plans for the cooler in exchange for the medicine."

That Vatty had fallen victim to a cruel—an *unconscionable*—deception was painfully clear. Despite his many egregious traits—from his repulsive appearance to his ghoulish obsession—my heart swelled with pity for him; for his actions, however insane, were driven by an emotion with which I could fully empathize: the boundless love of an adored young wife.

"I just can't figure it," Vatty continued. "He swore it'd take no more than a week. But"—here, a distinct note of desperation entered his voice—"it's been near a fortnight already and she still ain't come round!"

"Mr. Vatty," I said gently, "permit me to ask you a question. Besides the ointment, did Mr. Ballinger supply you with any other medications?"

"Just that damn cream," he said, turning to indicate the cobalt-blue jar.

For the past several minutes, my view of the bed had been obstructed by my captor. Now, as Vatty shifted his stance, I once again caught a glimpse of the ghastly, disinterred cadaver.

Dizziness overcame me and I quickly shut my eyes. It was not merely the hideous appearance of the mummified body that caused my heart to quail; it was my awareness that—without Dr. Farragut's medications to forestall, if not reverse, the progress of her disease—my own darling wife would, before long, be transformed into precisely such a monstrosity.

Several moments passed before I was able to speak in a relatively normal voice.

"Like you, Mr. Vatty, I have a wife who means more to me than life itself," I declared. "Like your own Priscilla, my Virginia has been afflicted with a dreadful illness. It was in the desperate, and clearly misguided, hope of finding certain missing medical ingredients that I made my unauthorized entry into your home—an act which no one can deplore more than I. As one husband to another, I beg you to accept my apology and to release me from my bonds so that I may continue my search for the items that may yet restore my wife to health."

For several moments, Vatty said nothing, though it was clear from the wildly fluctuating expressions on his face that two radically different impulses—toward punitive violence on the one hand and forgiveness on the other—were warring within him. All at once, he extended his knife and—emitting a maddened cry—came at me.

I shut my eyes, expecting to feel the fatal thrust of the blade at any second. Instead, I felt it slip beneath the strap that held me to the chair. In another instant, I was free.

I sprang from my seat and—without bothering to retrieve my hat (which had been knocked to the floor)—made for the doorway. As I did, Vatty stepped to the bed, lowered himself onto the mattress, and turned to embrace the skeletal remains of his long-dead wife.

Staggering to the end of the cramped, chaotic hallway, I threw open the front door and fled.

CHAPTER TWENTY-SIX

THE HORRORS I had experienced within Vatty's abode—combined with the debilitating effects of the head injury I had suffered at his hands—rendered me unfit for sustained physical exertion. Making my way to the edge of the tangled and gloomy woods that bordered his property, I found a fallen maple tree and seated myself on the stump.

My thoughts were in a state of the greatest indistinctness and confusion. Propping my elbows on my thighs, I buried my face in my hands and sat motionless for several minutes while I waited for my thinking faculties to return. At length—feeling somewhat restored by the fresh, if excessively chilly, air—I raised my head and took stock of the situation.

Had I emerged from Vatty's home to find that darkness had fallen, I would not have been surprised. I had lost all track of time while imprisoned within his chamber of horrors. In point of fact, the sky—though still deeply overcast—appeared slightly *brighter* than it had been when I first set out that morning. Consulting my watch, I saw that the hour was still quite early—several minutes shy of noon.

All at once, a gust of wind brought the redolence of balsam pine to my nostrils—and with it, a sudden realization. Even in my terrified state, while watching Vatty massage his mysterious ointment into his dead wife's loathsome visage, I had been aware that the substance smelled strangely familiar. Now, I realized *why*.

I myself had been treated with the same unguent. It had been applied to my injured hand by P. T. Barnum following my unfortunate *contretemps* in Hoffman's saloon several weeks earlier.

In short, it was nothing more than a bottle of Dr. Farragut's All-Natural Botanical Healing Balm. In exchange for a single bottle of this beneficial, though hardly miraculous, substance, Peter Vatty had been tricked into trading away the plans for his potentially lucrative invention to the conniving Herbert Ballinger, who had evidently promised the grief-crazed recluse that the ointment had the power to restore the dead to life!

But how, I wondered, had Ballinger acquired Dr. Farragut's medication?

My head throbbed painfully, and the raw wind made me shiver. Had the hour been later, I might have returned at once to the Alcott residence, so that Sissy would not grow worried over my prolonged absence. As the day was still young, however, I knew that she would not be overly anxious.

Rising somewhat unsteadily to my feet, I pulled my cloak close to my body and made for the path that led to Dr. Farragut's home.

Under ordinary circumstances, the journey from Vatty's property to Dr. Farragut's house would have been nothing more than an easy stroll, the distance being less than a mile. In my present weakened condition, however, the walk proved excessively arduous—so much so that, by the time I neared my destination, the mere act of placing one foot before the other required a nearly superhuman effort.

Just a short distance more, I silently reassured myself, *and you will be able to rest in the comfort of Dr. Farragut's parlor. Very possibly, he will be able to treat your head injury with one of his all-natural elixirs. If nothing else, he will certainly offer you a fortifying cup of tea. Thus refreshed, you will be able to make your way back to the Alcott home with little, if any, difficulty.*

These encouraging thoughts filled me with the strength to complete my journey. The reader may imagine my disappointment, therefore, when—upon entering the clearing around the physician's abode and trudging toward his veranda—I noticed that his carriage was gone from its place in the barn. My loud rapping on his front door—which went unanswered—confirmed the fact that Dr. Farragut was not at home.

The prospect of hiking onward to the Alcott residence—even by means of the shortcut Louy had shown me—was too disheartening to contemplate. I desperately needed to rest indoors for a brief period before continuing home. Muttering a silent prayer, I reached for the knob. To my great relief, the door was unlocked. Pushing it open, I stepped into the darkened hallway—made my way to the parlor—and, after lighting a table lamp, sank down upon the horsehair sofa with a moan.

There were unmistakable indications that Dr. Farragut had recently been enjoying the comforts of the handsome parlor. Several logs glowed in the fireplace, suffusing the room with a delicious warmth. Standing on a small table beside the armchair was a tall glass containing the dregs of a viscous, greenish-brown beverage. A slender book, bound in green morocco, lay on the cushion of the chair.

From these signs, it appeared that, prior to his departure, Dr. Farragut had been reading the volume while imbibing one of his own botanical concoctions. Peering at the book, I saw that it was the very work that had so absorbed my interest while I waited for Sissy to be examined during our first visit to Dr. Farragut's office: i.e., Mr. Richard Palmer's fascinating survey of bizarre ancient beliefs, *Medical Delusions of Olden Times.*

Had I not felt so fatigued, both physically and mentally, I might have beguiled the time by perusing more of Palmer's book while I waited for Dr. Farragut to return. As it was, I merely reclined my head on the back of the sofa and stared at the fire in a kind of stupid lethargy.

I must have dozed off at once; for the next thing I knew, I was being shaken gently by the shoulders. Opening my eyes, I stared about in confusion. It was not until my vision focused on the kindly—deeply concerned—visage looming over me that I remembered where I was.

"Dr. Farragut," I said with a sob of relief.

"Poe, my good fellow, are you all right? Good Lord, what a goose-egg! Here," he said taking me by the arm and helping me to my feet. "Come with me. I have just the thing for you."

Rising somewhat unsteadily from the sofa, I was startled to see the physician's priceless medicine chest just inside the parlor entrance, where it had been set down on the floor.

"Your case!" I exclaimed. "How . . . ?"

"I've just come from the Alcotts'," he replied. "My daily visit to your wife. They told me you'd returned yesterday with the chest. I don't have to tell you how happy I am to get it back."

"You will be less pleased to learn," I said, "that, while I have succeeded in procuring the chest itself, my efforts to recover the contents have thus far been futile."

"Yes, yes, I heard all about it from Virginia," said Dr. Farragut. "Don't trouble yourself about that now, my friend. Just come along with me. I'll have you patched up in no time."

Ushering me down the hallway, he stepped into a darkened room, ignited a lamp, then beckoned me inside and pointed to a bow-back chair that stood beside a handsome walnut desk. Seating myself, I gazed about the room while the elderly physician crossed the carpeted floor to a glass-fronted cabinet.

From its various accoutrements, it was clear that the cozy, comfortably appointed chamber served as both Dr. Farragut's office and examination room. In addition to the desk, several chairs, bookshelves, and cabinet, it contained a long, narrow table equipped with cushion and pillow—another, smaller table holding a variety of shining implements—and a screened-off corner where patients could divest themselves of their outer garments.

The walls were hung with antique prints of assorted herbs and other medicinal plants, along with a painted portrait of a scholarly-looking gentleman clutching a caduceus in one hand and, in the other, a sprig of *lobelia inflata*. From these allegorical emblems, I took him to be none other than Mr. Samuel Thomson himself, the founder of the botanical school of healing.

"Ah, here we are," said Dr. Farragut, who had been searching through the myriad vials, bottles, and other small receptacles that filled his cabinet. He then came to stand beside me, a cylindrical stoneware jar clutched in one hand.

Removing the cork, he dipped two fingers into the mouth of the jar and extracted a generous portion of a thick, yellowish substance, which he proceeded to smear on my injury. So tender was the area that I could not keep from emitting a whimper of pain at his touch.

"Forgive me," he said. "Didn't mean to rub you the wrong way, so to speak. Quite an impressive lump. Did I say goose-egg? More like an *ostrich* egg. Hope that excellent brain of yours didn't get scrambled, ha-ha. Here, let's put a bandage over that."

Opening a drawer in his desk, he removed a roll of linen, from which he proceed to tear a long, narrow strip. He then bound the fabric loosely around my head and knotted it in back.

"There!" he said, seating himself in his desk chair. "Now, tell me, Poe—what on earth happened? Mrs. Alcott said you'd gone to see Peter Vatty again."

"So I did," I replied. Already the pain in my brow had begun to abate, soothed by the delightful, if somewhat ill-smelling, emollient. "This excessively large edema was the result of that visit. It was produced by the butt of Mr. Vatty's fowling-piece."

"Do you mean to say that he assaulted you with his rifle?" exclaimed Dr. Farragut. "Why, you must go see Sheriff Driscoll at once!"

"That would not, I fear, be an appropriate course of action," I said.

"But the man's a menace," cried Dr. Farragut. "Always traipsing through the woods with that gun of his, taking potshots at woodchucks and any other creature that crosses his path. Thinks nothing of trespassing on his neighbors' land. Had to warn him off my own property a time or two."

"I am afraid," I said, "that, on this occasion, it was *I*, not Mr. Vatty, who was guilty of trespassing."

"How do you mean?" asked Dr. Farragut.

"I snuck into his home during his absence in search of your stolen ingredients."

For a moment, the kindly physician merely stared at me in silence. "Do I understand you to say that *Vatty's* the thief?" he inquired at length.

"So I believed at the time I intruded so ill-advisedly into his home," I said, refraining from mentioning the hideous discovery I had made there. "I am now persuaded that—while Mr. Vatty is almost certainly insane—the true culprit was someone else."

"And who might *that* be?"

"Are you familiar with a gentleman named Ballinger? Herbert Ballinger?"

Even before he answered, I saw that he recognized the cognomen, for his eyebrows shot up in surprise.

"Ballinger," he said. "Now, there's someone I haven't thought about in many years. Yes, I knew a fellow by that name. Hardly call him a gentleman, though. But why on earth do you bring up Herbert Ballinger? Surely you don't think that *he* had anything to do with the theft of my secret ingredients?"

"I do indeed. Before explaining *why*, however, I must ask you to divulge everything you know about that individual."

Farragut's cheeks ballooned outward as he exhaled a long sigh. Then, leaning back in his chair, he rested his interlaced hands upon his stomach— crossed one leg over the other—and addressed me thusly:

"I knew him in Baltimore, twenty, twenty-five years ago. I was attending anatomy school there. I studied traditional medicine, you know, before discovering the wonders of the Thomsonian method. During my last year there, Ballinger enrolled in the school. He was hardly more than a boy, but very sharp, very quick-witted. Very amusing, too. As deft with a joke as with a scalpel. A real cut-up, you might say.

"It took me a while," he added, "to recognize just what sort of creature he really was."

"And precisely what sort would that be?" I inquired, struck by the exceedingly grim tone that had entered the voice of the normally genial physician.

My query was answered with another. "Are you familiar with the term 'moral imbecility'?" asked Farragut.

"Of course," I replied. "It is a concept formulated by the eminent German psychologist Metzengerstein, to describe a mental condition that affects the moral sphere alone. A person suffering from this disease shows no impairment of his *intellectual* faculties. On the contrary, he typically displays a very high degree of rationality. The *moral* sentiment, however, is completely lacking from his makeup. He possesses no conscience—no capacity for empathy or remorse. To such a man, other human beings are merely objects to be exploited for his own profit and pleasure."

"You have described Herbert Ballinger to a tee," said Farragut. "With one small modification. It was not only the living he exploited. He also preyed upon the dead."

Far from being shocked, I felt a thrill of vindication at this statement.

"I cannot pretend to be surprised by your remark," I said, "for it corresponds to certain deductions I myself have made. Before I share these with you, however, I must ask you to tell me everything you know about Ballinger's illicit activities."

"Very well," said Dr. Farragut, uncrossing his legs and sitting erect in his chair. "Herbert's interest in medicine had nothing to do with helping others. As you say, such men care only about themselves. For Herbert, as for others of his ilk, nothing mattered but his own needs. And he used cadavers to satisfy them."

"To what sort of need do you refer?" I inquired.

"Some of it was purely monetary," said Farragut. "Oh, he was a cunning one, our Herbert. To give you an example: He cooked up a devilishly clever life-insurance scheme. Persuaded another young student to take out a policy, naming Herbert as beneficiary. He then studied the newspaper obituaries each day. Every time some poor young fellow passed away, Herbert would head out to the cemetery at night and dig up the grave. Must've unearthed a half-dozen bodies before he found one that bore a rough resemblance to his accomplice. Then the two of them faked the latter's accidental death, substituting the corpse for the real person. When the insurance company paid up, they split the ill-gotten gains—though, knowing Herbert, I'm sure he ended up with the lion's share."

"I assume that the other disinterred bodies were returned to their resting places," I said.

"Heavens no," said Farragut. "Why let perfectly good corpses go to waste? Herbert snuck them back to the lab, stripped them of their flesh, then had a taxidermist friend mount the skeletons as anatomical specimens. From what I understand, he made several hundred dollars selling them to local physicians."

"From your account," I said, "it appears as if Ballinger realized a significant sum from these vile practices."

"I'm sure he did," said Farragut. "But it wasn't all business with Herbert. Some of it, I'm afraid, was pleasure."

"Why, what do you mean?" I exclaimed.

Dr. Farragut's features arranged themselves into a look of extreme distaste. For a moment, he merely regarded me in silence, as though reluctant to pursue so unsavory a subject.

"You must be aware, Mr. Poe," he said at length, "that there exists a certain sort of man—if you wish to dignify such creatures with that name—who prefers the dead to the living. No sight is more thrilling to them than the corpse of a lovely young woman. To gaze upon her unclothed form—upon the marble complexion, the shapely white limbs, the snowy, blue-threaded bosom—provides them with unimaginable ecstasy. Needless to say, an anatomy school offers these degenerates ample opportunities to gratify these horrible interests."

"I have no doubt that what you say is true," I observed, recalling with a shudder the disgusting banter I had overheard in Dr. MacKenzie's dissection lab, as his two students conversed over the disinterred corpse of Elsie Bolton.

"But there is even worse," said Farragut. "Some of these monsters aren't content with merely ogling the dead. They are prey to abominable urges, and are not satisfied until they have vented their lusts upon their inanimate victims. I shall say no more about the matter—it's too awful to speak of. Only that Herbert Ballinger was such a one."

"B-but how do you know?" I stammered, feeling my head spin at the mere thought of such appalling—such unspeakable—depravity. To be sure, I had read of cases in which the living continued to cohabit with the dead.

King Herod was said to have slept beside the body of his adored wife Marianne for several years following her demise; while the Mad Queen Juana of Castile reputedly did the same with the corpse of her deceased husband, Philip the Handsome. Indeed, I myself had just witnessed Peter Vatty lovingly embrace the hideously desiccated remains of his long-dead wife.

However dreadful to think of, these instances—in which desperately bereft individuals refused to relinquish the bodies of their loved ones to the grave—were at least within the realm of the comprehensible. To think, however, that there were men who actually engaged in the carnal act with female cadavers strained credulity.

"I witnessed it myself," said Farragut. "I was walking home one night, quite late—or rather, quite early, for it must have been nearly two in the morning. I'd been out carousing with some chums. Used to be a bit of a tippler, I blush to say. As I strolled past the anatomy school, I saw a light burning in a window. That seemed very odd. So I decided to investigate. By then, I had risen to the rank of assistant, so I had a key to the place. Once inside, I saw that the light was coming from the dissection room. I could think of no earthly reason why anyone would be in there at that time. So I tiptoed to the doorway and peeked inside. I will spare you a complete description of what I saw. Suffice it to say that Herbert was diverting himself with the corpse of a comely sixteen-year-old girl that had been brought in just that afternoon."

Though Dr. Farragut's office was unheated, I found that I was sweating profusely beneath the bandage he had wrapped around my head. Extracting my handkerchief, I wiped away a drop of perspiration that had trickled into my eye, then asked: "And what did you do?"

"Reported it at once to the physician who ran the school, of course," said Dr. Farragut. "Herbert was expelled the next day. He blamed me entirely for his disgrace. Swore he'd get revenge." Dr. Farragut shrugged. "That was the last I heard of him. As far as I was concerned, he just vanished from the earth. Like the bald man's lost toupee—hair today, gone tomorrow."

While this pun was even more labored than most of Dr. Farragut's efforts at *paronomasia*, I obliged him by arranging my mouth into what I hoped was a convincing simulation of a smile.

"But come, Poe—it's your turn now," he continued, apparently satisfied with my reaction. "What leads you to think that Herbert Ballinger, of all people, is behind this affair?"

Returning my handkerchief to my pocket, I addressed him thusly: "Far from having disappeared, Herbert Ballinger has, until recently, been residing nearby—in Boston, where he operated a successful daguerreotype establishment. In addition to his studio portraits, he did a thriving business in memorial pictures made of newly deceased persons in their homes."

"That sounds like Herbert's kind of business, all right," said Farragut.

"This part of his profession," I went on, "allowed Ballinger to judge which cadavers would make the most suitable specimens for anatomical study. He then passed this information on to Dr. Alexander MacKenzie, who, with the help of his students, stole the choicest of the bodies as soon as they were buried."

"So I was right about that scoundrel MacKenzie," exclaimed Dr. Farragut.

"You were correct about his illicit mode of acquiring subjects for dissection," I said. "I do not believe, however, that he was involved in the theft of your secrets. It was Ballinger alone, I feel certain, who was responsible for that crime."

Dr. Farragut looked somewhat dubious. "Are you quite certain of that?"

"Reasonably so," I said. "That Ballinger—by your own admission—had a motive for doing you harm only strengthens my conviction."

"Well, there's no doubt that he was a vindictive rascal," said Farragut. "But go on with your story, Poe."

"In exchange for Ballinger's services," I said, "Dr. MacKenzie gave him the teeth of the dissected cadavers. Ballinger supplied these to a dentist named Ludlow Marston, who augmented his income by making them into dentures for his well-to-do patients."

"Well, you know what they say—'Be true to your teeth or they will be false to you,' " said Farragut. "Ludlow Marston, eh? Now, why is that name so familiar?"

"In addition to his private practice, Dr. Marston was one of the leading attractions at Mr. Kimball's Boston Museum, where he was known for his highly entertaining nitrous oxide demonstrations."

"Ah yes," said Dr. Farragut. "I never attended one of his shows myself, but I've heard about them, of course. He was a poet, too, I believe?"

"In a manner of speaking," I said, moderating my true opinion of the dentist's egregious writings out of respect for the dead.

"In any event," I continued, "it was in Dr. Marston's office that your stolen case was found. In view of his dealings with Ballinger, it seems likely that the dentist received that priceless object from your old nemesis. This theory is strengthened by a discovery I made only a short time ago, while trapped in Peter Vatty's abode."

"And what discovery was that?" asked Farragut.

"That Ballinger was recently in Concord," I replied. "Moreover, it appears that he was inside this very house."

This statement so surprised Dr. Farragut that he started, as though from the shock of a galvanic battery.

"Peter Vatty was given a bottle of your All-Natural Botanical Healing Balm by Herbert Ballinger, who persuaded the recluse that it possessed supernatural powers," I explained. "This behavior is, of course, thoroughly consistent with your description of Ballinger as a practiced confidence man. As he clearly did not receive the medication directly from you, only one explanation seems plausible: He stole it from your office at the same time he purloined your medicine chest."

"Well, bless my soul," said Farragut, shaking his head. "It *does* seem to point to Herbert, all right. I suppose I'm lucky he settled for knocking me unconscious."

"Indeed you are," I said. "During the last few days, a number of people associated with this affair have met horrible deaths. Initially, I deduced that most of these murders were perpetrated by Ballinger himself. It now appears, however, that they were committed by his criminal associate, an individual named Bowden."

"Never heard of the man," said Farragut, "though he must be a bad one, if he's working with Herbert."

"I am afraid that they are no longer confederates," I said.

"Do you mean they've had a falling-out?" asked Farragut.

"I mean," I said grimly, "that one of the murder victims was Herbert Ballinger himself."

This intelligence seemed to render Dr. Farragut speechless. For a moment, he merely gaped at me in openmouthed wonder.

"Herbert Ballinger . . . *murdered*?" he said at length. Then, drawing in a deep breath and exhaling it slowly, he added: "Well, I suppose it's for the best. One less madman in the world."

"I fear," I said with a catch in my voice, "that I cannot share your feelings of relief. On the contrary, with Ballinger gone, the chances of recovering the rare ingredients required for Virginia's medication seem almost negligible." And here, I was so overcome with a sense of hopelessness that I covered my eyes with a hand and emitted an involuntary sob.

In response to this despairing outburst, Dr. Farragut did something wholly unexpected. He moved his chair several inches closer to mine— placed a hand upon my knee—and, in an inordinately cheerful voice, exclaimed: "But Poe, there's no need to worry about that anymore. That's what I was trying to tell you before."

Lowering my hand from my eyes, I gazed at him in bewilderment.

"I don't need the stolen ingredients anymore," he continued. "I've gotten hold of another batch."

"What!?" I cried, hardly daring to believe what I was hearing.

"That's right," he exclaimed, giving my knee an exuberant slap. "It's in my laboratory right now. Everything I need to make up the pills for Virginia."

"B-but where?" I asked, so astonished by the news that I could barely formulate a coherent sentence. "How?"

"Came across a little package of the stuff," Dr. Farragut replied. "I'd stuck it on a shelf a few weeks ago and completely forgot about it. That's what happens when you reach my age, I'm afraid. Your brain starts to become youthless, ha-ha."

"But this is wonderful news!" I cried, so overcome with emotion that I had to restrain myself from leaping to my feet and embracing the good-natured physician. "How long will it take you to prepare the medication?"

"Why, I can have it ready in a few hours. I'll bring it by tonight. I've been invited to attend young Miss Alcott's play, you know."

"Then I shall take my leave at once and leave you to your work," I said, rising quickly from the chair.

"Shall I drive you back to the Alcotts'?" asked Dr. Farragut, getting to his feet.

"No, no," I said. "You must begin your preparations without delay. I am perfectly capable of walking home. Between your marvelous salve—which has quite eliminated the pain from my head—and this remarkable, wholly unlooked-for development, I feel thoroughly reinvigorated."

Proceeding to the front door, I paused at the threshold to shake hands with Dr. Farragut. "I shall see you again very shortly," I warmly declared.

"Yes, indeed," he answered. "I'm very much looking forward to tonight's production. I understand Miss Alcott is quite the playwright."

"She is apparently an unusually talented young woman who aspires to achieve fame and fortune from her writings," I replied. "I have not had the heart to inform her that, in financial terms at least, the lot of the professional author is exceedingly bleak in America—a nation infinitely more devoted to commerce than to art."

"Writers are born, not paid—eh, Poe?" said Farragut with a twinkle in his eye.

At that moment, my heart was so full of gratitude toward the elderly physician that—despite the tiresome nature of his relentless punning (to say nothing of the bitter grain of truth contained in his latest quip)—I burst into a prolonged peal of laughter.

Then, still chuckling, I turned and—with a lighter step than I had taken in many a day—headed for the pathway leading to the Alcott home.

CHAPTER TWENTY-SEVEN

B UOYED BY Dr. Farragut's surprising news, I quickly traversed the distance between his home and the Alcott residence. As I approached the *terminus* of the path, I could see, in the gaps between the thinning branches of the trees, the gambrel roof and massive stone chimney of Hillside. A glance at my pocket watch informed me that the time was half-past four o'clock.

Since departing from home that morning, I had experienced a series of the most startling, even shocking, events. I now looked forward to passing the remainder of the day in the congenial surroundings of the Alcott abode, enjoying the amateur theatricals of Louy and her sisters with my darling wife snuggled beside me.

I had, of course, not the slightest inkling that yet another surprise awaited me at home.

Upon emerging from the woods, I saw a handsome bay horse tethered to the post in front of the house. Evidently, the Alcotts had a visitor. My immediate reaction to this discovery was one of mild disappointment. I had been eager to return home and recount my adventures (excluding, of course, those details unsuitable for female sensibilities), while Sissy and the others listened raptly to my tale. Now, with another party present, I could no longer expect to be the sole focus of their attention.

That the women of the household were happily engrossed with the unknown caller was confirmed the moment I stepped through the door, for I could hear them exclaiming in wonder at some observation he had evidently just made. As I proceeded in the direction of the parlor—whence these convivial sounds emanated—he spoke again, causing me to come to a sudden startled halt; for his rich booming voice was one with which I was exceedingly familiar.

"Remarkable creature, perfectly remarkable. I've been offered—well, I wouldn't expect you to believe what I've been offered for it. Why, just yesterday Moses Kimball said to me, 'Come now, Phineas, name your price—I *must* have that six-legged antelope.' But my goodness, I'd as soon think of selling my wife. Why, there isn't another living curiosity like it in all of Christendom!"

As the reader will doubtless perceive from this remark, the voice belonged to my old friend P. T. Barnum, whose presence in the Alcotts' home was so utterly inexplicable as to render me dumbstruck with amazement. Continuing toward the parlor, I paused at the threshold to stare in silent wonder at the charming, if wholly bewildering, scene.

Mrs. Alcott was seated in her favorite chair, surrounded by her daughters. Louy and Lizzie were perched on either arm of the chair, while Anna leaned against the back and May rested on her mother's lap. All four of the girls, along with their beloved "Marmee," were gazing fixedly at the showman, who sat on the sofa beside my own darling Sissy.

So spellbound were all six of the females by their celebrated caller that they remained completely oblivious of my presence. All at once—as though sensing my proximity—Sissy glanced over her shoulder and exclaimed: "Oh, Eddie, you're back!"

Instantly all eyes turned toward me.

"Poe, m'boy!" cried Barnum, springing to his feet. "There you are! By Jove, just look at that headband you're sporting! Why, I'll be blessed if you don't look positively piratical! All you need is a cutlass, an eye patch, and a parrot perched on your shoulder and you'll be ready to go buccaneering!"

"Are you all right, Eddie?" asked Sissy, who had come to stand before me and was now gazing up at my bandage with a look of extreme concern.

"Come, have a seat, Mr. Poe," said Mrs. Alcott, who had also risen from her place and hurried to my side, while her daughters flocked around her like a brood of chicks.

"There is no cause for concern," I said, stepping into the parlor and allowing Sissy to lead me by the hand to the sofa, where I lowered myself onto the cushion while my dear wife sat beside me. "It is an exceedingly minor injury."

"Still and all, you *do* look a little peaked, Mr. Poe," said Louy. "You can't be too careful with head injuries, you know. Do you remember, Marmee, that time I was climbing the big oak tree behind Dove Cottage and fell from the high branch and saw double for a week before I started to feel better?"

"Yes, dear, we were all terribly worried about you at the time," said Mrs. Alcott, "but we prayed very hard for your recovery and our prayers were answered."

"Tell us what happened, Eddie," said Sissy, gently stroking my right hand.

Having resolved to shield my female auditors from the horrors I had witnessed inside Peter Vatty's ghastly abode, I now concocted a harmless "white lie" to explain my injury:

"As I hastened through the woods this morning," I said, "I caught my toe upon a tree root and fell to the ground, striking my brow against a small rock. I sustained a small, though painful, contusion. Dr. Farragut—to whose home I repaired following my interview with Mr. Vatty—has treated it with one of his remarkable salves, and I have already achieved a nearly complete recovery."

"Then you've heard the good news about Dr. Farragut's ingredients?" said Sissy, giving my hand a squeeze.

"I have indeed," I said, returning her smile. "Even as we speak, he is preparing his special medication, which he intends to deliver several hours from now when he arrives for Louy's production.

"But, tell me," I continued, turning to Barnum, who had seated himself beside me on the sofa. "What on earth are you doing here, Phineas? I do not hesitate to say that I am excessively surprised by your presence."

"Well, of course, dear boy, that's understandable—perfectly understandable," he replied. "Still, there's no mystery about it. Tragedy has brought me here—the murder of poor Emma Randall, Fordyce Hitchcock's sister-in-law. Horrid crime, absolutely appalling—one of the most abominable acts of butchery in the annals of human depravity! Terrible blow to poor old Fordyce. Never seen him so broken up in all the years he's worked for me. First the loss of his brother, now this. He's the nearest kin, you know, so it fell to him to to make the burial arrangements. He planned to travel to Boston by himself but I wouldn't hear of it. Of course, it meant closing down the museum for several days—no one there to manage the operation with both of us gone, you see."

"Closing the museum?" I said. "That must represent a significant loss of income for you, Phineas."

"Significant?" exclaimed the showman. "Why, the word doesn't cover the magnitude of the situation. *Staggering* is more like it. Lord bless me, you wouldn't believe the business I've been doing ever since I unveiled my latest attraction—my genuine six-legged Springbok antelope from the plains of equatorial Africa! Just telling these dear ladies about it when you showed up. Still, I didn't hesitate for a moment. 'Fordyce,' I said, 'I shall not let you travel to Boston alone, even if it means sacrificing a fortune! When it's a choice between friendship and money, money be damned!' Excuse the language, ladies, but those are my exact sentiments. Can't help myself. Just the sort of fellow I am."

While I knew from personal experience that the showman was, in fact, capable of acts of great generosity, I could not help but suspect that his motives for traveling to Boston were not purely altruistic. At the moment, however, I was too weary to inquire further into the matter.

"But Phineas," I said, "how do you come to be here in Concord?"

"Why, I'm here to see how you and your dear wife are getting along, m'boy," he replied, as though surprised that I would pose a question with so obvious an answer. "I learned that you were lodging at the home of Mr. Alcott. Brilliant thinker, your husband," said Barnum, turning to address Mrs. Alcott. "One of the greatest minds of the age. Admired his writings for many years. Never really *understood* them, of course. No mistaking their genius, though."

"Why, that is very kind of you to say, Mr. Barnum," said Mrs. Alcott. "We are all quite proud of him."

"Anyways, Poe," the showman went on, "I couldn't wait to see how Virginia was making out under the care of Dr. Farragut, so I thought I'd take a day trip and come see for myself. Imagine my delight when I walked in the door and found the great man himself! What an honor to meet him! Well, you know what I think of him, Poe. Absolute miracle-worker! Greatest healer since Hippocrates! And quite the humorist, too."

"Oh yes," interposed little May, gazing at me with a delighted expression. "He told the funniest joke you ever heard, about the time Shakespeare decided to earn some extra money by selling Swiss cheese, but people refused to buy any of it from him, so he asked what was wrong with it, and they said: 'No holes, bard.' "

This ostensible witticism sent the little teller into a paroxysm of such violent laughter that she seemed in danger of choking.

"Well, it's not as funny as all *that*," said Anna, gazing down at her sibling with a disapproving look.

"Speaking of cheese," said Sissy in a solicitous tone, "have you eaten anything since breakfast, Eddie?"

I confessed that I had not.

"Heavens," said Mrs. Alcott. "You must be famished. Can I get you something, Mr. Poe? Mr. Barnum has given us the nicest basket of goodies."

"Oh yes, you should see the splendid treats he's brought," said Louy. "Such riches! There are cakes and fruits and English toffees and all sorts of delicacies!"

"A mere trifle," said Barnum with a dismissive wave of one hand. "Don't like to drop in unannounced without a little gift for my hosts. Something I learned from the Marquis de Bellegarde. Lord, but that man knows a thing or two about etiquette—true Frenchman, you know, Frenchman to the backbone. Never comes to my house without a case of the finest Burgundy wine. I always say to my wife, 'If you want to see fine manners, give me a French marquis every time.' There's just something about those fellows that—"

"At the moment," I said, interrupting the showman's peroration, "I am far more tired than hungry. Perhaps I shall retire to my room and take a short nap, so that I will be fully alert for tonight's performance."

"Splendid idea, m'boy," said Barnum. "We'll wake you up for the show. Can't tell you how much I'm looking forward to it. Reminds me of my own boyhood in Bethel. Used to put on all sorts of productions—magic acts, comical plays, that sort of thing. Charged a nickel for admission. Found a living albino tree-frog once and displayed it in a jar. Made almost five dollars—quite a tidy sum for a ten-year-old boy back in those days. What do *you* girls charge?"

"Why—nothing," said Louy. "We invite everyone for free."

Barnum gave a start, then regarded the little girl closely, as though to see if she was jesting.

"Free?" he said at length. "Mighty queer way of doing things."

"It is not queer at all, Mr. Barnum," Mrs. Alcott chided gently. "Money is a needful and precious thing—and, when well used, a noble thing—but I never want my girls to think it is the only prize to strive for. I would rather see them grow up to be poor men's wives if they were happy and beloved than queens on thrones without contentment or peace."

As a person whose life was one of both material privation and marital bliss, I could not fail to be touched by Mrs. Alcott's simple, heartfelt sentiment. Reaching over to place a fond osculation upon Sissy's alabaster brow, I rose to my feet and excused myself to the assemblage. I then proceeded upstairs to the bedchamber used by Sissy and myself.

CHAPTER TWENTY-EIGHT

C LOSING THE DOOR, I stepped to the washstand—removed my bandage—and examined myself in the mirror that hung above the basin. A large, unsightly protrusion was visible just above my right eye. I palpated it gently with my fingertips. Though exceedingly tender to the touch, the lump was by no means intolerably painful—thanks, no doubt, to the efficacy of Dr. Farragut's ointment.

Leaving the bandage on the stand, I turned toward my bed. As I crossed the room, I inadvertently stepped upon a round object that would have caused me to lose my footing and go crashing to the floor had I not reflexively reached out and grabbed hold of the bureau. Regaining my balance, I looked down and saw a bright red rubber ball—the favorite toy of the Alcott's pet feline, Barnaby. Evidently—in response to Anna's insistence that the object be removed from downstairs—Lizzie had placed it up here in her room.

Fearing that Sissy might accidentally slip on it and hurt herself—as I myself had nearly done—I picked it up and placed it atop the bureau, where it rolled several inches before coming to a rest against a child's hairbrush.

Stripping off my jacket, I folded it neatly and laid it across the back of a chair. I then perched on the edge of the mattress and removed my shoes. Having completed these preparations, I lay back on the bed, emitting a deep sigh of pleasure as my head settled onto the pillow.

Directly across from the bed was the shelf containing Lizzie's collection of maimed and damaged rag dolls. I was gazing at these pathetic playthings when, very abruptly, I dropped into a profound slumber.

My dreams were of a singularly unsettling nature. I saw my darling wife seated in Dr. Farragut's parlor, a mournful expression on her haggard countenance. "Oh, Dr. Farragut," she said to the kindly physician, who stood before her, his priceless medicine case clutched in one hand, "I am so frightened of dying."

"Take heart, dear lady," he replied, reaching into the receptacle and extracting a large, crimson-hued tablet. Removing it from his hand, she swallowed it with some difficulty.

The effect of the medication was nothing less than miraculous. Almost at once, Sissy underwent an apparent alteration for the better. A rosy flush suffused her sickly complexion—her pallid lips grew pink with health—her dull eyes sparkled with renewed vivacity. This astonishing transformation made my heart leap with joy.

This feeling, however, was exceedingly short-lived; for—as I gazed upon my wife's incomparably lovely visage—her features continued to change, acquiring a coarsely voluptuous quality that was utterly at variance with the angelic purity of her nature. Her mouth—now the color of ruby—curled into a lascivious smile, revealing a set of brilliantly white, peculiarly pointed teeth; while her sapphire eyes blazed with an unholy light.

Turning toward me, she reached out and whispered in a tone of diabolical sweetness: "Come to me, my husband. My arms are hungry for you. Come, and we can rest together."

An unwonted emotion—compounded equally of revulsion and desire—arose in my bosom. All at once, I saw that the female creature beckoning so seductively to me was not Sissy at all, but rather the Mays' murdered servant, Elsie Bolton, restored to life and wholeness.

But no! Very abruptly, her features underwent still another transformation, seeming to melt like heated wax before resolving themselves into the countenance of the flayed and eviscerated shop-girl, Lydia Bickford, whose daguerreotype portrait I had discovered in the battered grip belonging to her lover, the homicidal anatomy student Horace Rice.

"Come, my husband, come," she repeated as she rose from her seat and began to shuffle toward me, her plump, naked arms held out before her.

A strangled cry issued from my mouth, and—in an effort to elude her embrace—I staggered backward several feet, bumping into someone to my rear.

"Clumsy fool!" came a voice that I took to be that of Dr. Farragut. When

I turned to look behind me, however, I was startled to see not the elderly physician, but Herbert Ballinger!

"You!" I gasped. "What have you given to my wife to cause this odious transformation?"

"Oh, just a little heart medicine," he said with a chuckle. "I am very pleased with the results. Look!"

Turning around again, I cried out in wonder at the sight that met my eyes. The female being now coming toward me with a lubricious leer and extended arms was no longer Lydia Bickford, but little Louy Alcott! She was garbed in nothing but a flimsy white shift.

All at once, she paused—lowered her arms—crossed them over her body—and gripped the cotton fabric with both hands. Then—to my unspeakable horror—she began to raise the garment slowly, exposing her bare, slender limbs, beginning with the ankles.

I stood there paralyzed by the shocking sight, not wishing to look but unable to close my eyes or turn away as more of her pale young flesh came into view.

A helpless whimper arose in my throat. Perspiration burst from every pore. I was shaken with a violent trembling.

At that moment, I mercifully came awake.

For a moment, I lay there in a state of the utmost confusion, not knowing where I was. By slow degrees, I grew cognizant of my surroundings. From the atmosphere of the room—which had grown considerably darker since I entered—it was evident that I must have been asleep for at least an hour. The afternoon had given way to evening. Leaping from the bed, I replaced those items of apparel I had doffed prior to my nap, then stepped out to the landing and descended the stairs.

In contrast to the sociable sounds that had filled the house earlier, a total silence now prevailed. Entering the warmly illuminated parlor, I was surprised to see that no one was there besides Barnum, who was standing by the mantel, studying the daguerreotype portrait which the Alcott girls had brought back from Boston for their mother.

"Ah, there you are, Poe," he exclaimed in response to my greeting. "Back from the land of Nod at last. That was quite a snooze. Just about to head upstairs and rouse you."

"Where is everyone?" I inquired.

"Out in the barn. Show's about to begin. Just waiting for a few stragglers to arrive."

"Is Virginia there, too?" I inquired in a somewhat anxious tone, picturing Sissy shivering in the damp, unheated structure while waiting for the play to commence.

"Why, of course she is—why wouldn't she be?" said Barnum. Then, perceiving my concern, he added: "No need to worry, m'boy. She's bundled up as warmly as the Amazing Ooglik, my authentic Alaskan Esquimo. Mrs. Alcott made sure of that. Lord bless me, but your Virginia seems happy as a cricket. Perky as I've ever seen her."

"She is very much heartened, I am sure, by Dr. Farragut's discovery of the special ingredients needed for his potion."

"Of course, of course," said Barnum, taking me by the arm and conducting me to the foyer. "I've heard the whole story. Thank the Lord he turned up that spare jar of rare herbs and whatnot. Now it's just a matter of whipping up his magic pills and your wife will be back to normal in a flash."

"I ardently hope that you are right," I said.

"Why, there's no question of it, m'boy, none in the world," said the showman, donning his overcoat and beaver hat, while I threw on my heavy cloak. "The man's a marvel—you've seen it yourself." Opening the door, he then stepped out onto the front porch, while I followed directly behind.

Though the night air was exceedingly chilly, the heavy clouds which had hung so low throughout the day had entirely dissipated. Overhead, innumerable stars sparkled in the heavens, while a radiant three-quarter moon cast a spectral glow upon the landscape.

Descending from the porch, Barnum and I made our way to the rear of the house. As we rounded the corner, the hulking shape of the barn came into view. A warm yellow light streamed from the partially open doorway, while a happy childish din could be heard emanating from the cavernous interior.

"I do not see Dr. Farragut's buggy," I said as we strode across the yard.

"Just taking his time preparing his miracle cure," said Barnum. "Doesn't want to rush things—wants to get it all just right. That's the way it is with your scientific geniuses. Take Professor Eschol Sellers, my Amazing Mental Prodigy. Needed almost six months to perfect the perpetual-motion machine displayed in my Hall of Technical Marvels. Well worth the wait, though. One of the biggest attractions in my museum—draws like a dogfight!"

"Perhaps you are right," I said, my breath emerging into the cold night air in small wisps of vapor. "I hope, however, that the good doctor arrives before the start of Louy's show."

"Yes, I was hoping he'd get here early myself," said Barnum. "Oh well, just have to postpone our discussion until afterward."

"Discussion?" I said.

"An idea that came to me earlier," said the showman. "A little business proposition."

"Aha," I exclaimed, coming to a halt just outside the half-open barn door. "I thought as much."

"Why, what do you mean?" said Barnum.

"Though in no way doubting the sincerity of your desire to see how Sissy and I have been faring here in Concord," I said, "I suspected that there might be an ulterior motive to your visit."

"Why, Poe," said Barnum, "you wound me, m'boy—cut me to the quick!" In the light issuing from the doorway, I could see that his visage had assumed an exceptionally *shocked* expression. "I was thinking only of you and your dear wife when I decided to travel here! Doing business with Dr. Farragut was the furthest thing from my mind! It wasn't until I met the man himself that the notion occurred to me!"

Though intensely curious as to the nature of the business he hoped to conduct with the elderly physician, I was unable to ask the showman for a more detailed explanation; for at that moment, I heard my wife hailing me from inside the barn. Entering, with Barnum beside me, I paused inside the threshold and surveyed the scene.

Though the entire rear half of the barn was hidden in shadow, the anterior portion was warmly illuminated by a half-dozen lanterns, some placed on overturned wooden crates, others depending from hooks screwed into the massive beams. Wrapped in a plaid woolen coat with a brown leghorn bonnet on her head, Sissy was perched upon a makeshift bench fashioned from a rough-hewn plank resting on several heavy pieces of wood. Beside her sat Mrs. Alcott and her daughter Lizzie, whose inveterate shyness prevented her from assuming any *rôle* in the proceedings other than that of spectator.

The remainder of the audience consisted of a dozen or more children of both sexes, some of whom were seated on the floor, others on bundles of hay. All were chattering in eager, excited tones as they watched the last-minute preparations being carried out atop a small platform at the front of the barn.

Dressed in their picturesque costumes, Louy, May, and Anna were putting the finishing touches on what appeared to be a make-believe grotto contrived from fallen tree branches, piles of old cloth, a discarded clotheshorse, a few potted shrubs, and assorted odds and ends. In this undertaking they were being assisted by a squat, shaggy fellow whom I recognized at once as their old family friend Henry Thoreau. Standing upon an upright wooden keg, several tenpenny nails clamped between his lips and a hammer in hand, he was affixing a large sheet of canvas cloth—upon which little May had painted a fanciful woodland scene—to a low rafter.

Walking over to the bench, with Barnum at my side, I greeted Sissy and her two companions warmly. Reaching up with one hand, my wife gave my own right hand an affectionate squeeze, then spoke several words I was unable to discern, their sense being drowned out by the din issuing from the increasingly clamorous juvenile audience.

Bending closer to Sissy, I asked her to repeat her statement.

"I said that you look very refreshed from your nap," she said, smiling up at me.

I acknowledged that my rest had done much to reinvigorate me. "And you, dearest Sissy—how are you feeling? Are you dressed warmly enough? Your fingers feel somewhat cool to my touch."

"I'm fine, Eddie," she replied. "Very excited about the show. I've been looking forward to it for days."

At that moment, Barnum tapped me on the shoulder and—pointing his heavy chin toward the front of the barn—asked: "Who's that fellow with the nails in his mouth?"

I explained that it was Henry Thoreau, a friend of the Alcott family who, like Mr. Alcott himself, was a member of Mr. Emerson's so-called "Transcendental" circle.

"Don't say?" said Barnum. "Well, I suppose I'll mosey over and introduce myself. Always like to get to know the natives."

As Barnum made his way toward the stage area, I glanced toward the doorway and said: "I wonder what is keeping Dr. Farragut?"

"Yes, I do hope he arrives soon," said Mrs. Alcott. "I'd hate to start the show without him, but we can't wait forever. The little ones are getting somewhat antsy, I'm afraid."

Indeed, the hubbub produced by the increasingly restive audience was growing louder by the minute.

"Perhaps I shall go stand by the door and await his arrival," I said.

"That won't make him get here any sooner, Eddie dear," Sissy gently chided.

"Very true," I replied with a smile. "I am too anxious, however, to sit still at present."

Navigating around the raucous children disposed about the floor, I walked to the end of the barn and positioned myself by the doorway, where I peered into the darkness. I could see nothing besides the rear of the Alcotts' house, framed by the dark shape of the surrounding woods. Assuming that Dr. Farragut would arrive in his carriage, I listened intently for the sound of his conveyance but could hear nothing.

A few moments later, Barnum came to stand beside me.

"Queer sort of fellow," said the showman when I asked what he thought of Mr. Thoreau. "You know me, Poe—straight talker. Say what I mean and mean what I say. This Thoreau chap, though, seems to speak in riddles."

"Yes, I am all too familiar with the rhetorical obscurities of Mr. Emerson and his disciples," I replied, "who seem incapable of communicating the simplest thought without resorting to the sort of philosophical *mumbo-jumbo* that, for sheer mystification, outdoes even the wild Pantheism of Fichte."

"Er ... yes, yes, I see what you mean," said Barnum. "But as I was saying, this Thoreau evidently spent a few months in New York back in forty-three. Lived on Staten Island. I take it he didn't think very highly of our city ways. Visited my museum on one occasion to view my genuine African cheetah. You've seen the critter, Poe—marvelous beast, absolutely astounding! Fastest thing on four legs! Acquired at incalculable expense! Only living specimen of its kind in the entire Western Hemisphere! So I ask him what he thought about the beast, and he says: 'It's not worth the while to go hunting cats in Zanzibar. Is not our own interior white on the chart?' Now, what the devil do you make of *that*?"

I was about to explicate Thoreau's typically gnomic remark by reference to the Transcendental belief in the existence of an innate Divinity that can be known solely by introspective means. Before I could speak, however, Louy Alcott came hurrying up beside me. She was dressed in the same gaudy costume she had been wearing the previous day—plumed cap, scarlet cape, flowing shirt, and baggy pantaloons stuffed into tall yellow boots—and her countenance wore a look of mild irritation.

"What is the matter, Louy?" I inquired.

"I've forgotten my sword," she said, glancing down at her belt, which—I now saw—was lacking the make-believe weapon she had fashioned from the discarded wooden slat.

"Mercy me, what a rattlebrain I am," the little girl continued. "It is just as Marmee says. I'd lose my own head if it wasn't screwed to my shoulders!"

"I shall be happy to fetch your trusty blade for you, Louy," I said.

"That's very nice of you, Mr. Poe, but it will be quicker if I do it myself. I shan't be gone long." And so saying, she stepped from the barn and dashed off across the moonlit backyard toward her house.

"Ha! Just look at her go!" exclaimed Barnum. "Swift as my African cheetah. Quite a sprinter, that girl. Why, I'd wager she could outrun any boy in Christendom!"

"Knowing Louy as I do," I replied, "I can think of no compliment that would please her more."

At that moment, there was an eruption of hilarity from the little spectators behind us. Gazing over my shoulder, I saw that this outburst had been occasioned by a mishap involving Mr. Thoreau, who had accidentally tumbled from atop the keg, landing heavily upon his posterior. Whether he had simply lost his footing or been stricken with a sudden episode of his bizarre soporific ailment, I could not say. In any event, he was quickly helped to his feet by Anna Alcott, who—garbed as a fairy-tale princess—came rushing to his aid.

"The natives are growing restless," said Barnum. "Better get this show on the road or there'll be trouble, mark my words. Believe me, Poe, there's nothing worse than an audience of children. Make 'em wait too long and they'll turn into a mob of howling savages. Had a theaterful of tykes who nearly tore my auditorium to pieces one time just because Signor Giovanni's Astounding Magical Act was delayed for twenty minutes while we tried to get the damn fool sobered up. I tell you, m'boy, Doc Farragut better show up soon or we'll have a riot on our hands."

"You have yet to explain, Phineas," I said, "what sort of business proposition you intend to make to Dr. Farragut."

"Why, it's the greatest idea in the world!" exclaimed the showman. "Amazed I didn't think of it before! And here's the beauty part—it will require virtually no effort at all on the part of Dr. Farragut! True, he'll have to give up his practice, sell his house, and move to New York City. But that's a small price to pay in return for what he'll be getting!"

"And what, precisely, will that be?" I inquired.

"Why, stupendous fame and fortune, of course!" said the showman. "I intend to make him a star! Just picture it, Poe! The great Erasmus Farragut lecturing three times a day at Barnum's American Museum on the marvels of botanical medicine! Bottles of his All-Natural Botanical Healing Balm on sale following the performance! The greatest boon to mankind since the discovery of fire! Small bottles, fifty cents; large ones, a dollar! Just thinking about the incalculable service we'll be performing for humanity makes my heart swell with pride! Not to mention the money! Why, there's whole Atlantic Oceans of cash in it, gulfs and bays thrown in!"

"Do you really think," I inquired, "that audiences will flock in such numbers to attend a medical lecture?"

"Why not? Just look at that dentist fellow, Marston. Pulled in enormous crowds for Moses Kimball. Poor Moses! Dropped in to say hello as soon as I arrived in Boston. He's dreadfully broken up over Marston's murder—absolutely shattered. Well, who wouldn't be? Moses was a tad tetchy on the subject, but I gather that Marston's death means the loss of several hundred dollars a *week* for the Boston Museum!"

"Yes," I said, "I understand that his popularity had grown even greater in past weeks."

"Incidentally, Poe," said Barnum, "Moses told me that you'd dropped by the museum to sort through the belongings of that young fiend, Horace Rice. Turn up anything interesting?"

"In point of fact, I *did*," I replied. I then went on to describe the daguerreotype portraits of Rice and his doomed mistress, Lydia Bickford, which I had found in the former's battered grip.

"It was my discovery of these pictures," I explained, "which led me to conclude that their maker, a daguerreotypist named Herbert Ballinger, was centrally involved in the recent series of ghastly murders that claimed the life of poor Mrs. Randall, among others."

"Wonderful job, m'boy—absolutely superb!" cried Barnum. "You've acquitted yourself magnificently! And that's not just my opinion—everyone says so! Bless my soul, Constable Lynch thinks the world of you—praises you to the skies! Why, you'd blush to hear him!"

"Constable Lynch?" I exclaimed with unconcealed amazement. "How can you possibly be aware of his feelings toward me?"

"Why, he and I had a brief chat when I paid a visit to police headquarters," said Barnum. "Thinks you're nothing less than a genius! Greatest investigative mind of all time! Make Vidocq look like a bumbling schoolboy! Heavens, if it weren't for you, the police would still be groping around in the darkness. They'd never have guessed Ballinger's part in these horrors—not in a thousand years!"

"Then you've already heard about Ballinger?" I said, still marveling at the showman's knowledge of the shocking events in which I had been involved during the preceding week.

"Heavens yes," said Barnum. "Lynch told me all about him. Sounds like the very devil. Well, I must say, he got his just deserts. 'He who lives by the sword' and all that. Not that any man really deserves such a gruesome end. Saw his body at the morgue. Hideous sight! Barely looked human."

As the showman talked on, a realization began to dawn upon me. Why such an obvious thought had not occurred to me before can only be attributed to the vitiating effects which that day's unprecedented events had wrought upon my intellect. Undoubtedly the blow to the head that I had received from Peter Vatty's rifle-butt also contributed to the uncharacteristic *sluggishness* of my mental processes.

"Am I correct in inferring," I said to the showman, "that—beyond your very commendable wish to provide comfort to your grieving friend, 'Parson' Hitchcock—you traveled to Boston with a view to obtaining artifacts related to the recent spate of grisly crimes?"

"Well, yes, I suppose you might look at it that way," said Barnum. "That wasn't my *main* reason for coming, of course. Standing by Fordyce in his hour of need was uppermost in my mind. But as long as I was here, anyway—well, you know me, Poe, always looking for ways to kill two birds with a single stone. One of the keys to my stupendous success!"

"And may I further assume," I said, "that—in visiting the city morgue— you were hoping to acquire some macabre relic connected to Herbert Ballinger? Perhaps even a portion of his actual corpse for display in your museum?"

"Well, you needn't seem so shocked, m'boy. Nothing wrong with exhibiting the preserved remains of a fiendish criminal for educational purposes! Has to be done tastefully, of course. Why, you've seen that lovely display case I had constructed for the amputated left arm of Anton Probst, removed from his body right after he was hanged for slaughtering the entire Deering family. Beautiful piece of work—absolutely first-rate craftsmanship! Cost me a small fortune. Worth every penny, though. Why, you can hardly get near it on a Sunday, the crowds are so thick!"

"And were you successful in obtaining one of these coveted items?" I inquired in a somewhat dry tone of voice.

"Not so much as a pinky finger," said Barnum, emitting a sigh loud enough to be heard over the laughter and squeals of the children. "Devlin seemed positively scandalized by the idea!"

"Devlin?" I said.

"The morgue superintendent," said Barnum. "Bless me, you should have seen the look on his face—you'd think I was suggesting something improper! Pity. Would've loved to get my hands on his left foot—Ballinger's, I mean, not Devlin's."

"His left foot?" I said. "And why were you so interested in that particular extremity?"

"Didn't you see it?" asked the showman.

I replied in the negative. During my visit to the morgue—as the reader will recall—all of my attention had been focused on the contents of Ballinger's lungs. At no point had I examined the lower portion of his body, which was entirely hidden by a sheet.

"Devlin pointed it out to me," said Barnum. "Remarkable appendage, absolutely one-of-a-kind. Never seen anything like it—and that's saying a good deal. Dreadfully deformed. Toes all melted together, you might say, as if the flesh were made of wax. Apparently some sort of birth defect. Must've walked with a terrible limp."

"Limp?" I said. "Why, Mr. Ballinger walked in a perfectly natural fashion. It was his assistant, Benjamin Bowden, who was afflicted with a pronounced li—"

"Great Scot, are you all right, Poe?" said Barnum. "Why, you've gone white as a sheet."

Indeed, I could feel the blood drain from my face as my heart ceased to beat. Terror clutched at my throat, making speech an impossibility.

"What is it, m'boy?" Barnum asked, his brow deeply furrowed as he studied me narrowly.

Gazing wildly about me, I saw that Sissy was happily engrossed in a conversation with Mrs. Alcott. For the moment, at least, my absence would go unnoticed.

Without a word, I bolted from the barn and hurried through the darkness toward the house. I had just turned the corner when Barnum, one hand clutching the brim of his hat so as to keep it from flying off his head, came running up beside me and, grabbing me by the arm, brought me to a halt.

"What in blazes is going on, Poe?" he demanded. Despite the short distance we had traversed in our headlong rush from the barn, the exertion had left the portly showman short-winded.

"Herbert Ballinger is alive!" I cried.

"Alive?" he exclaimed. "Why, what are you saying, m'boy? You saw his body laid out in the morgue just as I did!"

"That was not Ballinger," I declared. "It was his assistant, Benjamin Bowden. Ballinger murdered him, then made it appear as if he himself had died in an accidental blaze. The two men bore a striking resemblance to each other. The variations in their appearance were obliterated by the disfiguring effects of the fire. Why I did not suspect the truth before I am at a loss to say."

In the moonlight, Barnum looked perfectly flabbergasted. For the first time in the years since I had met him, he seemed at a loss for words.

"I must borrow your horse," I declared in an urgent tone.

"My horse?" he managed to say. "But why?"

"Dr. Farragut is in grave danger," I replied. "I must warn him without delay. I only pray that I am not already too late. You must return to the barn at once. Do not say anything that will alarm the women and children. When Sissy inquires as to my whereabouts, tell her that I was stricken with a sudden bout of dyspepsia and will return as soon as I am able."

Nodding, Barnum turned and hurried back to the barn, while I continued to the front of the house, where his horse remained tethered to the post.

A warm yellow glow, emanating from the open doorway, illuminated the patch of lawn upon which the animal stood. Evidently, the door had been left open by Louy, who had yet to emerge with the object she had gone to fetch.

As I began to free the horse's reins from the post, my gaze fell upon something strange lying just inside the doorway.

It was Louy's wooden sword. And it appeared to be broken.

An indescribable uneasiness took hold of my spirit. Dropping the reins, I hastened up the porch—hurried into the house—and knelt to examine the make-believe weapon.

I had not been deceived in my observation. The sword *was* broken. Its blade was split in half, the edges bristling with splinters, as though it had shattered from the force of a savage blow.

Seized with a spasm of alarm, I stood upright and looked toward the parlor. The sight that met my eye froze the currents of my blood.

The room was in a state of violent disarray. I could see overturned chairs—a little spindle-legged table lying on its side—books, sewing baskets, and other objects strewn across the floor.

Cupping both hands around my mouth, I desperately shouted out the little girl's name. No one replied.

Perhaps, I thought, *she is up in her garret and out of hearing.*

I made my way down the hallway toward the staircase. All at once, a cry of dismay burst from my lips.

Lying halfway up the stairs was Louy's plumed cap.

I dashed up the steps, taking them two at a time. No sooner had I reached the second-floor landing than I saw—to my inexpressible horror— that the door of the bedroom used by Sissy and myself was hanging halfway off its hinges, as though it had been locked from within, then battered down by force.

I rushed inside the room. Like the parlor, it showed signs of a terrible struggle. The washstand had been knocked over, the bedclothes torn from the mattresses, the curtains ripped from the rods.

It was not these indications of violence, however, that caused my brain to reel—my heart to quail—and my spirit to be possessed with a sense of intolerable anguish. These reactions were caused by something so small and seemingly innocuous that at first I failed to notice it.

Placed in a seated position on the windowsill was one of Lizzie Alcott's damaged dolls. In its lap rested the red rubber ball—the plaything of the little girl's pet feline.

Terror caused the marrow to congeal in my bones. There could be no doubt as to what had transpired.

Ballinger had been in the house. And he had taken Louy!

Chapter Twenty-nine

T HAT LOUY WAS in the most dire imaginable peril was beyond question. A sequence of frightful images flashed through my mind with bewildering rapidity: the livid corpse of Elsie Bolton—the horribly butchered remains of Mrs. Randall and Sally—the body of Ludlow Marston slumped in his dental chair, brain matter defiling the wall behind his shattered head. So appalling were these thoughts of Ballinger's previous victims, that, for a moment, I was paralyzed beyond the possibility of making any exertion.

At length, I recovered some degree of presence of mind. Not another minute must be wasted if Louy's life was to be saved. Haste was of the essence. I must seek help at once.

Before I could put this resolution into effect, I was startled by an unexpected noise—the sound of someone moving stealthily through the lower portion of the house. My heart beating wildly, I crept to the bedroom door, stuck my head into the hallway, and strained my auditory faculties to the utmost.

At that instant, the intruder called out: "Hello! Anyone here?" My amazement was extreme—for I recognized at once that the voice belonged to Dr. Farragut!

Rushing down the stairs, I found the elderly physician standing at the entrance to the parlor, a small, black leather satchel clutched in one hand and a look of confusion on his visage as he surveyed the wild disorder of the room.

As he turned in my direction and observed the anguished expression wrought upon my own countenance, the color left his ruddy cheeks and he gasped: "My God, what's happened?"

Grabbing him by the shoulders, I replied in a tremulous voice: "Louy Alcott has been abducted by Herbert Ballinger!"

"What?" he cried. "How is that possible?"

"While we waited in the barn," I said, "Louy returned by herself to the house to fetch a prop needed for her performance, at which point she was evidently set upon by Ballinger. The disorder you see around you is the result of her courageous attempts to fight off the madman. Unhappily, the sounds of her struggle could not be detected in the barn, owing to the inordinate degree of noise created by the young audience members."

"But Ballinger is dead!" cried Farragut. "You told me so yourself."

"I was mistaken," I answered. "The corpse identified as Ballinger's was, in reality, that of his assistant. Ballinger evidently staged his own death as part of a diabolical scheme, the precise nature of which can only be surmised. What *is* certain is that he is still alive and at large here in Concord. At first, I feared that you yourself were his intended victim. It is now all too apparent that his depraved sights were set on Louy Alcott."

"But why would he come after the child?" asked Farragut, who seemed utterly aghast at these horrid revelations. "How did he even know of her existence?"

"She and her sisters had their portrait made by him during their recent visit to Boston," I said, indicating with a motion of my chin the daguerreotype case standing undisturbed on the mantel. "According to all accounts, he was particularly taken with Louy's sharp wit and effervescent personality."

Here, I experienced a sudden, overpowering sense of self-reproach. "Just yesterday," I continued with a moan, "Lizzie and May expressed their anxiety that they might be in danger, and I blithely reassured them that their fears were baseless. Perhaps if I had only taken their concerns more seriously—"

"Get hold of yourself, man," said Farragut, "you aren't to blame. We must act, and act fast, if we are to save the girl from that fiend. Who knows what horrors he has in mind for her."

"You have echoed my own thoughts precisely," I said, recalling with a shudder the train of hideous images that had rushed through my mind just prior to Farragut's arrival.

"The first thing to do is notify Sheriff Driscoll," said Farragut. "His house is in town. Come—we'll take my carriage."

Grabbing my arm, Farragut hurried me outside to his conveyance. As he climbed into his seat, I swiftly took the place beside him. He then removed his carriage-whip from its side-mounted brass holder and cracked it above the haunches of his horse, which immediately started at a trot toward the Lexington Road.

As we sped along the rutted thoroughfare, Dr. Farragut—his voice wobbling with the jouncing of the carriage—said:

"Tell me something, Poe. What made you so sure that Herbert was dead in the first place?"

"His corpse was identified by Dr. Marston by means of a dental plate fashioned by the latter," I said, raising my voice so as to be heard above the rumble of the vehicle. "I can only assume that the two men were working as fellow conspirators. Perhaps they were attempting to perpetrate an insurance fraud of the sort you yourself described to me earlier today."

"Clever, very clever," said Farragut.

"Yes," I replied. "There can be little doubt that Ballinger possesses a mind of singular—of *diabolical*—cunning."

"No, no," said Farragut. "I meant *you*, my dear Poe. That brain of yours is really quite amazing."

There was something exceedingly peculiar about the tone of this comment—a note of cheerful satisfaction that seemed bizarrely inappropriate, given the extreme gravity of the situation. Glancing over at the elderly physician, I peered at his face. Even in the luminous moonlight, however, I was unable to read his expression.

At that instant, Farragut yanked on the reins, causing the carriage to come to such an abrupt halt that I was nearly ejected from my seat.

"Blast!" cried Farragut.

"Why, what has happened?" I exclaimed after recovering my balance.

"Didn't you feel it?" said Farragut. "The horse began to hobble. Must have gotten a pebble wedged under one shoe."

"I felt nothing of the kind," I said.

"Quickly, Poe," said Farragut, ignoring my remark. "There's no time to waste. Hop down and take a look, will you?"

Leaping to the ground, I hurried forward and, squatting on my haunches, peered closely at each of the animal's hooves. I could see nothing amiss. The animal was standing in a perfectly normal fashion, showing no signs of discomfort.

At that instant, I became aware that Dr. Farragut had dismounted from the vehicle and was now standing directly behind me.

"I can see nothing wrong," I said. Swiveling my head to peer at him over my shoulder, I was surprised to see that he was clutching his carriage-whip in a peculiar, inverted fashion, the wooden handle protruding from his right fist like a truncheon.

"Sorry, Poe," he said. "I know it's been a difficult day for you. But—as I've always said about that fool Marston's ridiculous poetry—it's about to go from bad to verse."

"What?" I exclaimed, beginning to rise from my squatting posture.

I never succeeded in doing so—for at that instant, Farragut raised the whip-handle and brought it down on my forehead with savage force.

Landing directly on the injury I had suffered earlier in the day, the blow produced an explosion of blinding white pain and caused me to drop to my hands and knees.

Though filled with the most intense agony and nausea, I was still conscious. I did not, however, remain in that condition for long. In another instant, my assailant struck again, this time delivering a vicious blow to the back of my skull.

With a fluttering moan, I pitched forward onto the road. Darkness supervened. All sensations appeared swallowed up in a mad rushing descent, as of the soul into Hades.

Then silence, and stillness, and the night were the Universe.

CHAPTER THIRTY

M Y RETURN TO full awareness occurred in distinct stages. At first, I grew cognizant of motion and sound—the tumultuous motion of my own heart and, in my ears, the sound of its beating. This was followed by a tingling sensation pervading my frame. Then the mere consciousness of existence, without thought—a condition which lasted long. Then, very suddenly, *thought,* and shuddering terror, and an earnest desire to comprehend my true state. Then a rushing revival of soul and a full memory of the events culminating in Dr. Farragut's vicious—cowardly—and utterly inexplicable assault.

So far I had not opened my eyes. I was aware that I was seated upright on an inordinately uncomfortable high-backed chair. A dank, mouldy aroma suffused my nostrils, suggestive of the unwholesome atmosphere of a basement or cellar. I could discern the nearby sound of several male voices engaged in conversation, though their words were too indistinct for me to apprehend.

For the first time since regaining consciousness, I attempted to move my arms—but in vain. They were tightly fastened by the wrists to the arms of the chair. My ankles, I quickly discovered, were similarly tethered to its legs.

Parting my eyelids, I gazed around me. By this point, I had already formed a general idea of the true nature of my situation. The sight that greeted me confirmed my deduction in every significant respect.

I was indeed inside a cavernous cellar, illuminated by the glow of several flambeaux protruding from iron sconces affixed to one wall. Apart from a crude table made of roughly hewn planks, there were no furnishings to be seen. A pair of large, glass-stoppered, amber-hued bottles stood on the table, along with a shallow tin pan and several bundles of varying shapes and sizes, each wrapped in dirty white cloth and secured with a coarse piece of twine. A butcher's knife and cleaver jutted from the center of the table, their blades thrust into the deeply scored surface.

The surrounding walls were covered with rough plaster. At the most remote end of the cellar was a projection, caused by a false chimney or fireplace. A sizable number of bricks had been removed from this structure, exposing an interior recess, in width about four feet, in height and depth about three. The dislodged bricks lay in a mound at the foot of the projection, along with a quantity of mortar and sand. A trowel was also visible on the earthen floor.

The muffled conversation that had reached my ears was emanating from two men who were conferring a few yards away from where I sat. One of these was Dr. Farragut. The second had his back toward me. There could be no mistaking his identity, however, particularly in view of the distinctive object standing nearby: a daguerreotype camera supported by a wooden tripod.

There was one other person in the cellar. She sat beside me, bound to her chair in an identical fashion, with lengths of stout rope encircling her ankles and wrists.

The little girl had evidently been watching me closely for any signs of revival. Now, seeing me awake, she cried out in a tremulous voice: "Oh, Mr. Poe, thank goodness you're all right! I was mortally afraid that you would never wake up! Your poor head! Are you badly hurt?"

In point of fact—though the twice-battered place on my forehead throbbed painfully—I did not appear to be suffering any very severe effects from the cudgeling I had received at Dr. Farragut's hands. My vision was clear and my mental processes operating at their normal level of acuity.

Before I could reply to Louy's query and inquire as to her own well-being, Farragut and his confederate—alerted by the sound of the little girl's voice—ceased their conspiratorial whispering, turned in our direction, and, stepping forward, positioned themselves in front of our chairs.

This was the first time that I had set eyes on Herbert Ballinger since the morning, approximately one week earlier, when Sissy and I had gone to his studio to see about having our daguerreotype portraits made. His features were, of course, unchanged, though—in place of the friendly smile with which he had greeted us upon the former occasion—his mouth was now curled into a sneer of cold contempt.

As for Farragut, his expression bore no trace of its usual benevolence. In the lurid glow of the torchlight, his visage looked positively *diabolical,* and his eyes blazed with an unnatural lustre.

"There, there, child," said Farragut, addressing Louy even while keeping his fierce gaze fixed upon me. "Your friend, Mr. Poe, is just fine. A bit sore, no doubt, but otherwise unharmed. Dear me, do you think I would do anything to put that splendid brain of his at risk? No, no—a damaged organ is of little use to me."

Precisely what the elderly physician meant by this latter remark I was at a loss to say, though its ominous import could hardly be ignored.

"Well, I think you are perfectly hateful to treat us this way," exclaimed Louy. "If I were a boy, I'd tear off these ropes and give you both a sound thrashing. Just see if I wouldn't!"

"Ha-ha," chortled Farragut, turning to his younger confederate. "What a fiery little pepper-pot! I told you she had spunk, didn't I, Herbert?"

"Perhaps a bit too much for her own good," growled the latter.

Glaring at the daguerreotypist—whose right hand, I now noticed, was loosely bandaged with a strip of white cotton cloth—Louy exclaimed: "It's a pity my sword was only a wooden toy and not a real one made of metal, or I would have struck off your hand instead of just scratching it!"

His face turning bright red, Ballinger lunged toward Louy's chair, while raising his left arm crossways over his chest, as though preparing to deliver a vicious backhanded slap to the helpless child.

"No!" I shouted, struggling violently against my bonds.

"Stop!" cried Farragut, interposing himself between the little girl and the enraged daguerreotypist.

"Come, Herbert," Farragut continued in a pacifying tone. "You don't want to spoil the child's face, do you? Not yet."

For a moment, Ballinger said nothing. He merely glowered at the little girl, his nostrils flared, his lips squeezed tight in fury, his bosom heaving. At length, the angry flush subsided from his face and his breathing resumed its normal rhythm.

"No, I suppose you're right," he muttered. "But she'd better keep that damned yap of hers shut if she knows what's good for her."

"I'll see to that," said Farragut. Digging into his trouser pocket, he removed his handkerchief—crumpled it into a ball—and, bending over Louy, forced open her mouth and thrust the cloth inside.

To witness the child treated in such a cruel manner was nearly unbearable. In my own helpless condition, however, there was nothing I could do to assist her, beyond offering a few words of commiseration and encouragement.

By this point, there could be no doubt that Louy and I were in the gravest conceivable peril. Escape seemed impossible. Our only hope lay in forestalling whatever fiendish plan Farragut and his murderous accomplice had in mind, until our rescue could be effected. I had told Barnum that I was on my way to the physician's abode to warn him about Ballinger. If Louy's disappearance had been discovered by her family and friends, it was possible that a search party might already be on the way.

Accordingly, I turned my head toward Farragut and addressed him thusly: "Though flattered, of course, by your description of my ratiocinative organ as 'splendid,' I fear that you may have overestimated my mental powers. In view of my present circumstances, it would appear that I have utterly failed to unravel the mystery in which I have been embroiled."

"Why, Poe," said the doctor with a look of mock surprise, "you do yourself an injustice. All things considered, you acquitted yourself quite brilliantly, just as I knew you would. You discovered a very great deal about my old friend here. You even managed to retrieve the case he stole from me."

Turning toward the daguerreotypist, who was regarding me through narrowed eyes, Farragut added: "Mr. Poe was right about many things, wasn't he, Herbert?"

"Dead right," said Ballinger, arranging his mouth into a sinister smile.

"Nevertheless," I said to the elderly physician, "I remain deeply puzzled by many aspects of the case. Not the least of these, of course, is the *rôle* you yourself have played in it."

"*Rôle?* Why, I have played no *rôle*," said Farragut. "I merely wanted my special ingredients returned. Now that Herbert has given them back to me, all is well."

"I see," I said. "Then the story you told of finding other, small quantities of these miraculous substances among your shelves was . . . ?"

"A little white lie," said Farragut. "There are no others. Only the ones over there on the table. Would you care to see them?"

"Very much so," I remarked.

While Dr. Farragut made for the table, the daguerreotypist walked over to his apparatus and—lifting it by the wooden legs so that the camera itself rested upon his right shoulder—carried it across the room and repositioned it close to the flaming torches.

"Have courage, Louy," I whispered to the little girl, leaning my head as close to her chair as my bonds would allow. "Help is even now on its way. I am certain of it."

Gagged with Dr. Farragut's handkerchief, the courageous child could do nothing more than nod vigorously in response. Despite our dire situation, the look in her eyes was not one of fear, but rather of fierce determination. I could not fail to notice, however, that her arms—lashed by the wrists to the chair—were wriggling in a peculiarly agitated way.

At that moment, I redirected my attention to Dr. Farragut, who had re-turned from across the room and was now standing directly before my chair. He carried in his hands the smallest of the cloth-wrapped bundles I had seen on the table. Undoing the twine, he proceeded to unwrap it. As he did so, my nostrils were suffused with a singularly unpleasant—though oddly familiar—odor, which I quickly identified as the same foul smell that had wafted from his medicine case when it had first been opened after its discovery in Dr. Marston's office.

"There," said Dr. Farragut in a satisfied tone as he exposed the contents.

So sheerly grotesque was the object held out for my inspection that, for a moment, I could only gape at it in bewilderment. It was a shriveled, reddish-brown object, somewhat larger than the fist of an adult male. At length, I could no longer fend off the dreadful truth.

"It is a heart," I gasped. "A human heart!"

Beside me, I could hear a terrified whimper issue from the throat of Louy Alcott.

"That's right," Dr. Farragut said pleasantly. "The lungs and skin are in the other packages."

A feeling of delirious horror filled my soul, accompanied by a sensation of intense nausea.

"These," I said in a choked voice, "are the missing body parts of the hideously butchered shop-girl, Lydia Bickford!"

"Why, yes," said Dr. Farragut, as though I had just made the most self-evident observation imaginable. "Herbert sold them to me after he killed the girl."

So, I thought, the murdered girl's lover—the doomed medical student Horace Rice—was guiltless all along, just as he claimed. He went to the gallows an innocent man—framed by his depraved acquaintance, Herbert Ballinger!

"B-but surely," I stammered, "you cannot mean that this loathsome organ is one of the ingredients you employ in concocting your medications!"

"You needn't be so shocked," said Farragut. "You've had a look at

Palmer's book. Surely you recall what he writes about the use of human body parts for healing purposes."

Even as he spoke these words, something flashed upon my mind—an image of Dr. Farragut giving my ailing wife a strange, blood red tablet while saying: "Take heart, dear lady." This vision, I now recalled, had come to me several hours before, as I lay napping in the Alcott girls' bedroom after returning from Farragut's home. Evidently, I had intuited the truth in my sleep—perhaps as a result of having observed Palmer's volume lying open on Dr. Farragut's chair earlier that day. That I had arrived at this insight while dreaming should come as no surprise; for there can be little doubt that there exists, deep within our souls, a hidden faculty whose wisdom surpasses that of our waking intellects and which supplies us with invaluable insights while our conscious mind slumbers.

Now, staring at the elderly physician with a look of horrified disbelief, I gasped: "Do you mean to say that you have been experimenting with the ancient, barbaric practice of cadaveric medicine?"

"Heavens no," said Farragut with a chuckle. "At least, not in the old-fashioned sense. After all, we're living in the nineteenth century, not the Dark Ages! No potions made from a woman's periodic flux to relieve the pangs of menses or anything as nonsensical as that. No, no. My method is based on the most up-to-date principles of modern, all-natural medicine. After all, what do our bodies consist of but pure, organic substances? Combining small amounts of human tissue with the appropriate botanical ingredients can produce miraculous results. Do you know that I myself used to suffer from such severe cardiac weakness that I could barely leave my bed? Now look at me! And it's all because of my All-Natural Miracle Heart Elixir!"

"But in dispensing your medications," I said, "you are turning your patients into unwitting cannibals!"

Farragut shrugged. "Human beings have indulged in cannibalism for eons, Mr. Poe. And to no ill effect. Indeed, as you well know, there are many places on earth where the consumption of human flesh is practiced as a sacred ritual."

For a moment, I made no reply. It could no longer be doubted that, behind his façade of enlightened benevolence, the elderly physician was an utter—an *irredeemable*—madman. I knew, however, that if I hoped to keep him engaged in conversation—thereby delaying the doom that awaited Louy and myself—I must act as though he were a perfectly reasonable being.

Accordingly, I arranged my features into a look of sincere interest and said: "Am I correct to assume, then, that the secret ingredient needed to prepare my wife's medication was a portion of Lydia Bickford's excised lungs?"

"That's right," Farragut said cheerfully. "Though, sad to say, I'm afraid it might be too late for your darling Virginia. Pity—she's a dear, dear girl. But I doubt she'll survive much longer. Another coughin' fit and she'll be fit for a coffin, ha-ha."

"You and those damned puns of yours," snorted Ballinger, who—having finished setting up his apparatus beside the torches—had now rejoined us.

In fixing their attention on me, the two men had temporarily turned their backs to Louy. Peering around Farragut's body, I saw that the little girl was seated with her eyes squeezed tight, evidently to avoid the sight of the ghastly organ so proudly displayed by the hopelessly deranged physician. Both of her arms, I observed, were still quivering noticeably—an apparent indication of her intense agitation.

Though Farragut's inordinately callous remarks concerning Sissy's health had filled me with a mixture of anguish and rage, I could not permit myself to lose control over my emotions. Struggling to keep my voice as steady as possible, I addressed the two men thusly:

"Perhaps you gentlemen will satisfy my curiosity about one matter."

"And what might that be?" said Farragut, rewrapping the ghastly, desiccated organ in its cloth.

"If Mr. Ballinger supplied you with the anatomical parts taken from the Bickford girl," I asked, "why did he then steal them back from you?"

"Oh, just a little misunderstanding," said Farragut, extending his free hand and delivering a companionable slap to Ballinger's shoulder. "Herbert and I have been doing business for many years—ever since we knew each other back in Baltimore. But even the best of friends have their occasional falling-out. Herbert felt, very justifiably, that the material he'd harvested from the Bickford girl was of an unusually high quality. He wanted more than our agreed-upon fee. We had a little disagreement that got out of hand. Naturally, I couldn't turn to the police. But who needs the police when *fate* brings the great Edgar Allan Poe to the door? I knew you'd locate my stolen property. All I had to do was point you in the right direction."

"In the end, however, I did *not* succeed in recovering the purloined items," I said.

"Oh, I'm certain you would have, given a little more time," said Farragut. "But by then, I'd figured out a way to convince Herbert to return them voluntarily. During my daily visits to the Alcott home, you see, I discovered that there was something he had taken a keen interest in. Knowing my old friend Herbert as I do, I knew how much pleasure he would get from possessing it. So I sent him a letter offering to help him get his hands on it."

There was no need for me to inquire as to the nature of the "thing" to which the elderly madman was referring. From the moment I had discovered that Louy had been taken by Ballinger, I knew what horrors lay in store for her. Farragut's words merely confirmed my deepest fear—that the little child had been abducted to gratify the daguerreotypist's unholy lust.

"You musn't think," said Farragut, "that Herbert only cares about money. Pleasure means as much to him as profit."

I directed my gaze toward Ballinger. "Like the pleasure of killing Elsie Bolton," I said with more than a trace of bitterness in my voice. "And poor Mrs. Randall, who, I assume, first attracted your malign attentions when you came to make the memorial picture of her deceased husband."

"That's right," sneered Ballinger. "Only it's not just the killing. It's what comes *afterward*."

Gazing quickly toward Louy, I attempted, without success, to read the expression on her face. I could only hope that the monstrously depraved implications of Ballinger's remark would make no impression on her virginal ears.

"Too bad I never really got to enjoy that Bolton wench," Ballinger continued. "Had to sneak out of there fast when that damned delivery boy showed up."

Poor Jesse McMahon, I thought. *My nagging sense that he had committed no crime more serious than the pilfering of a silver spoon was correct after all.*

"You learned about Elsie from Ludlow Marston, didn't you?" I asked.

Ballinger nodded. "We had dinner the night she volunteered for his show. He couldn't stop blabbing about her."

"But surely," I said, "your murder of Dr. Marston, as well as of your assistant, Benjamin Bowden, could not have been motivated by the same perverse desires that led you to slay the women. In the case of the dentist, it appears that the two of you had a mutually advantageous relationship. You were a reliable source of precious human teeth, obtained from the exhumed cadavers used by Dr. MacKenzie. In exchange, Marston evidently supplied you with a quantity of nitrous oxide, a substance which—in view of its anesthetizing effects upon susceptible females—would be exceedingly useful to a man of your anomalous predilections. That Marston knowingly misidentified the badly charred corpse suggests that he conspired with you in some manner of fraud. My guess is that you persuaded him to cooperate in what he believed to be an infallible insurance swindle. You would provide a badly disfigured corpse, presumably one obtained from the dissection lab of Dr. MacKenzie. Marston would then identify the body as yours, based on false dental evidence. A large insurance policy would be settled on your behalf, and the proceeds split between yourself and Marston.

"In fact," I continued, "you never intended to use an exhumed body. Instead, you murdered your assistant, Bowden, perhaps because he knew too much about your nefarious doings. Marston himself was subsequently killed for the same reason. With the world now believing that you yourself were dead, you could easily vanish from Boston—where your increasingly brazen crimes would have undoubtedly brought you under the unwanted scrutiny of the police—and commence a new existence elsewhere."

"Ha!" cried Farragut. "Didn't I tell you he was a wonder! What a brain! I can hardly wait to get my hands on it."

"Wh-why, what are you suggesting?" I exclaimed, though—in light of what I now knew about the medical lunatic—his meaning was all too clear.

"I have been very eager to experiment with a new recipe for the treatment of brain disease," said Farragut. "Unfortunately, I lacked a single vital ingredient—until now."

This answer induced in me a state of such extreme—such violent—dizziness that it was only with the greatest effort that I kept myself from falling into a swoon.

"Let's get on with it, Erasmus," said Ballinger. "We're just wasting time. Here, give me a hand."

As I struggled to subdue the feelings of terror that threatened to unman me, the two men stepped behind me and, grabbing the rear of the chair, tilted it backward and began to drag me toward the cellar wall, where the daguerreotype camera had been positioned close to the light of the torches.

"What are you doing?" I cried.

"I'm going to take your picture, Mr. Poe," said Ballinger. "That's what you wanted, isn't it? You've seen my other memorial portraits. Yours will be the pride of my collection."

Here, then, was the dreadful fate that awaited me at the hands of the two maniacs. I was to be killed by Ballinger, who would make a daguerreotype image of my corpse. Farragut would then remove my brain for use in his ghastly concoctions.

As for Louy, my death would leave her utterly alone with the two fiends. The horrors that lay in store for her were too appalling to contemplate.

"You are both mad!" I cried. "You cannot conceivably get away with your hideous designs. When my remains are discovered, suspicion will immediately fall upon you, Dr. Farragut, and the subsequent police investigation will inevitably lead not only to your own arrest but to that of Mr. Ballinger."

"Oh, I doubt very much that your body will be found," said Farragut. "It will be very efficiently disposed of. I was going to tell you *how*, but—knowing how much you enjoy puzzles—I'll offer you a riddle instead. What is Henry Thoreau's favorite watering hole? See if you can figure it out in the moments that remain to you."

"Do me a favor, Erasmus," said Ballinger. "See those two chemical bottles? Mix about a cupful from each in that pan, so I can soak the picture in the solution as soon as I'm finished here."

"Happy to oblige," said Farragut, who then strode to the table, unstoppered the bottles, and began to pour the prescribed quantities into the tin pan.

"And now, Mr. Poe," said Ballinger, grinning malevolently as he took a step closer to my chair with both hands held out before him.

Desperately, I threw myself from side to side in the chair, while leaning my head as far back as possible. But my attempts to break free of my restraints were, of course, futile. As Ballinger's hands closed around my neck, I could hear a muffled, low-throated scream issue from the direction of the little girl's chair.

All at once, another sound reached my ears: the muted thud of footsteps directly overhead. Someone was moving through the house! The dying ember of hope harbored within my bosom now flared into brilliant life. My delaying tactic had succeeded. Help had arrived in the very nick of time!

Releasing his grip on my throat, Ballinger turned quickly to Farragut, who frowned deeply and said: "Keep on with your business, Herbert. I'll take care of our visitor."

Setting down the chemical bottles, the mad physician then hurried upstairs, shutting the basement door behind him.

Our only chance for survival now lay in alerting the unknown party to our predicament. With that end in view, I opened my mouth to produce the loudest scream possible. Before I could make a sound, however, Ballinger clamped my throat in a powerful grip, digging his thumbs deep into my Adam's apple.

I gasped convulsively for breath—a shudder resembling a fit of the ague shook every nerve and muscle of my frame—I felt my eyes starting from their sockets—a horrible nausea overwhelmed me—my vision began to dim.

In that instant, several things occurred in swift and bewildering succession. Emitting a startled grunt, Ballinger loosened his death-hold and turned to look behind him. I heard a *sloshing* sound, as of agitated liquid, followed by a loud *splash*. Ballinger—his back toward me—let out an agonized roar as his hands flew up to his face. Staggering several steps, he fell to his knees, revealing—to my utter astonishment—the person of Louy Alcott!

She stood there, free of her gag and bonds, holding the tin pan used to prepare the daguerreotypist's chemical solution. It was this exceedingly caustic fluid which she had evidently just flung directly into Ballinger's eyes.

Rubbing the heels of his hands into the sockets of his orbs, Ballinger screamed: "You damned little bitch! I'll skin you alive!"

"You horrid, horrid man!" cried Louy.

I could see that, though momentarily incapacitated, Ballinger would be sufficiently recovered in another few moments to make good on his threat. A sickening sense of impotence suffused my bosom; for, with my limbs still fastened to the chair, I was powerless to assist her.

I cast my gaze wildly about the cellar. All at once, I saw something that caused my heart to leap.

"Louy!" I cried. "The camera!"

Taking my meaning at once, the intrepid little girl sprang to the apparatus and—lifting the heavy wooden box from its support—carried it back in both hands to where Ballinger knelt, shaking his head from side to side while rapidly blinking his eyes. Evidently, his vision was beginning to clear. He had just placed his hands on the floor and was starting to push himself into an upright position when Louy, with a grunt of effort, raised the heavy camera as high as her strength would allow and brought it crashing down on the top of Ballinger's skull. He collapsed onto his face without so much as a groan.

Rushing to my side, the little girl attempted to undo the knots of the ropes that bound my arms to the chair—but to no avail.

"Over there!" I cried, pointing my chin at the table. "The knife!"

Leaping over the daguerreotypist's inert body, Louy dashed across the cellar and grabbed hold of the knife by its handle. The point was so deeply embedded in the wood of the table that it required the use of both of her hands and several moments of intense exertion to pull the implement free.

She had just managed to do so when we were startled by the unmistakable *bang* of a firearm being discharged overhead.

"Quickly, Louy!" I called to the child.

In another instant, she had leapt to my side and sliced away the ropes encircling my arms. Taking the knife from her hand, I reached down—freed my legs—and sprang to my feet.

Thus far, Ballinger had not stirred. Selecting two of the longest pieces of the severed rope, I knelt beside him—pulled his limp arms behind his back—and bound them tightly by the wrists. I then secured his ankles.

"Please hurry, Mr. Poe," urged Louy. "I won't breathe easy until we are well away from this dreadful place!"

Slipping the knife into my belt, I grabbed Louy by the hand and made for the steps.

Just then, we heard the basement door fly open. Footsteps came pounding down the stairs. A moment later, a wild-looking figure stood before us, clutching a rifle from whose muzzle there drifted a thin plume of smoke.

It was Peter Vatty.

Chapter Thirty-one

Y OU!" HE GASPED, his red-veined eyes widening as he looked back
and forth between Louy and myself. "I thought I had seen the last
of you."

All at once, his gaze fell upon the bound, prostrate figure behind us.

"Move aside," he growled, raising his gun and starting forward.

"Wait!" I cried, interposing myself between Vatty and the fallen daguerreotypist. "What do you intend to do?"

"What do you think?" Vatty said harshly, his visage wrought into a look
of sheer—of *diabolical*—hatred. "Lying to me the way he done. Pretending
that worthless shit of his would bring my Priscilla back."

Beside me, I could hear Louy's shocked intake of breath at the man's
profanity.

"But how did you know Ballinger was here?" I asked, hoping that his
murderous rage would dissipate the longer I kept him talking.

"Saw him ride up to the place," said Vatty. "I was cutting through Doc
Farragut's property after a day's fishing in Sandy Pond. Hightailed it back
home and fetched my gun."

"And where *is* Dr. Farragut?"

"That old fool. Swearing that Ballinger wasn't here, when I seen him
with my own two eyes. I warned him I'd put a hole in his middle if he didn't
get out of my way. Now," he added, leveling the gun at my breast, "I'm
telling you the same."

I could see that there was no reasoning with the madman. While deploring his apparent determination to exact vengeance from the daguerreotypist, I had no intention of putting myself and my little companion at risk for the sake of a creature like Herbert Ballinger.

Without another word, I grabbed Louy by the hand and hastened her up the staircase. We then bent our steps toward the front of the house. As we passed the examination room, a low, tremulous groan reached my ears. Pausing, I saw the body of Dr. Farragut, sprawled face-up on the floor, a large crimson stain discoloring the bosom of his shirt.

"Wait for me outside, Louy," I said to the little girl, who—with a rapid nod of agreement—hurried toward the doorway.

Stepping into the examination room, I knelt beside Farragut. I could see at a glance that the gunshot wound in his chest was mortal.

All at once, Farragut's frame was agitated by a very slight quivering. His eyelids unclosed themselves, and he gazed about dully. His lips began to move, as though he was struggling to speak. Bending my ear to his mouth, I heard him say, in a barely audible whisper: "Am . . . am I dying?"

Only moments before, as I sat bound and helpless in the cellar, Farragut had viciously taunted me by referring to the "coughin' fit" that would make my darling wife "fit for a coffin." Now I was seized with a terrible impulse to give the dying physician a taste of his own noxious medicine. Spiteful puns sprang to my lips: *I fear, Dr. Farragut, that, like the inhabitants of the Concord cemetery, your situation is exceedingly* grave. *Indeed, it appears that you have taken a turn for the* hearse. *Seeing you in such a condition, my heart* bleeds—*though not nearly as copiously as your own.*

I did not actually speak these words. Even as I gazed down into his visage, the last vestiges of color drained from his complexion, his eyes rolled upward in their sockets, his jaw fell open, and he exhaled his last, stertorous breath.

Leaping to my feet, I dashed from the house and emerged onto the front porch, where my little companion stood waiting.

"Is Dr. Farragut dead?" she asked.

Nodding, I quickly glanced around for the elderly physician's buggy, which I hoped to commandeer so that Louy and I could return to her abode at the greatest possible speed. Much to my disappointment, I saw that the vehicle had been unhitched and stowed inside its little shed.

"Well, Louy," I said to the little girl. "It appears that we must proceed on foot."

"I wish I were a horse," she replied. "I'd put you on my back and run all the way home and we would be there in no time. But as I'm just a girl, we must do the best we can. Thank goodness the moon is so bright. We shan't have any difficulty finding our way."

"Not so long as we keep to the main road," I said. "Even on a night as luminous as this, the shortcut through the woods would be difficult to negotiate."

Descending the front steps, we set off across the yard toward the Lexington Road. We had gone only a short distance when the stillness of the night was broken by the muffled crack of a discharged rifle, emanating from the bowels of Dr. Farragut's house.

To be faced with the prospect of a horrible death only to enjoy an unlooked-for reprieve is an experience productive of the most intense emotions. Foremost among these is a sense of sheer—of overpowering—exhilaration.

Having emerged from the ghastly confines of Farragut's cellar, I felt like one reborn—as though, having suffered a cataleptic seizure and been entombed while still alive, I had been miraculously delivered from the grave. Each inhalation of the cold night air tasted more delicious to me than a draught of the finest Amontillado wine.

Louy evidently felt a similar emotion. Striding rapidly at my side, she was even more voluble than normal, as though her sudden liberation had unleashed a torrent of words. She marveled at the perfidy of Dr. Farragut—conveyed her incredulous horror at the abominations he had revealed—denounced the daguerreotypist as a heartless villain—and made it clear that, while deploring Peter Vatty's reliance on vigilante justice, she could not, under the circumstances, muster any sympathy for his two victims, especially Ballinger.

"I think he's the most horrid man that ever lived and deserves no mercy whatsoever!" she exclaimed, referring to the daguerreotypist. "Still, I don't quite see why Mr. Vatty hates him so much. Mr. Vatty said something about 'bringing her back,' and how Mr. Ballinger had lied to him. What did he mean by that, Mr. Poe?"

Though I did not wish to lie to my little companion, I had no intention of describing the horrors I had discovered in Vatty's home, such ghoulish matters being wholly unsuitable for the innocent girl. Accordingly, I replied thusly:

"As you yourself are perfectly aware, Mr. Vatty has never recovered from the untimely death of his beloved wife, Priscilla. He still harbors the mad belief that one day she may yet return to him. Mr. Ballinger, preying on the poor man's desperation, sold him, at considerable expense, a spurious potion that would ostensibly resurrect his bride."

"Christopher Columbus!" exclaimed the little girl.

"But tell me, Louy," I said, wishing to change the subject as quickly as possible. "How did you manage to free yourself from your bonds? My own limbs were so tightly fastened to my chair that I could scarcely move them."

"I have you to thank for that, Mr. Poe," she replied. "Do you remember the time we were all at the show at Mr. Kimball's museum? You and Virginia were seated right behind us, and when Professor Powell performed his coffin trick, you told her how he escaped by tensing his arms and legs when he was being tied up and then relaxing his muscles and wriggling free. I confess that I was dreadfully cross with you at the time for spoiling the magic—which only goes to show that you can never tell when something that vexes us no end will turn out to be all for the good, just as Marmee says."

"Indeed," I replied, "it is one of the paradoxes of human existence that unfortunate, at times even tragic, occurrences may prove, in the long run, to have unexpectedly beneficial results."

Under ordinary circumstances, a brisk hike along the Lexington Road from Dr. Farragut's abode to the Alcott residence would have taken no more than minutes. Owing to the condition of my legs, however—which felt excessively stiff and sore after having been so tightly bound to the chair—I was able to proceed at only a moderate pace. After twenty minutes, we still had not reached our destination.

By then Louy had at last fallen into silence. All at once, as we approached a bend in the road, the sound of hoofbeats reached our ears. In another moment, three horsemen, moving at a trot, came into view.

At our first sight of this trio, we halted in the center of the road and called out a loud "Halloo."

"By Jove, it's them," cried one of the riders, whose booming voice I instantly recognized to be that of my old friend Barnum.

Spurring their steeds, the three men galloped up to us and quickly dismounted. As I had already perceived, one was the showman. The second was Henry Thoreau. The last was a tall, broad-shouldered fellow with an enormous paunch, a profusion of side-whiskers, and a large pistol thrust into his belt. From the evidence of this firearm, I deduced that he was Sheriff Driscoll.

"Mr. Thoreau!" cried Louy, leaping forward and throwing her arms around his waist—a gesture that appeared to cause the inordinately re-served Transcendentalist a considerable measure of discomfort. He recoiled slightly, raising both of his hands as if uncertain as to where to place them. At length, he reached down and gingerly patted her back. When he ad-dressed her, however, his voice was full of an unabashed warmth.

"I am delighted to find you unharmed, Louisa," he said. "The sight of a marsh-hawk gliding over Concord meadow at dusk could not give me more pleasure."

"Lord bless me, I'm glad to see you, m'boy—perfectly delighted to see you!" cried Barnum, enveloping my right hand in both of his own and shak-ing it fervently. "I've been worried sick about you and the girl—everyone has! Why, the whole village is in an uproar! Search parties out everywhere." He then quickly explained what had occurred after he and I parted.

When Louy had failed to return from the house, her mother had gone in search of her. The wild disorder of the rooms left little doubt that something untoward had occurred. When Barnum revealed that Herbert Ballinger was evidently alive and at large in the vicinity, a scene of the great-est consternation ensued. Thoreau had immediately set off for town to alert Sheriff Driscoll. The latter, however, was not to be found either at home or at the jailhouse. Eventually he was located at the home of a neighbor—a bachelor (like himself) named Stackpole with whom he often shared an evening meal, followed by a cigar, a glass of cider, and a companionable game of checkers. Though Driscoll immediately sprang into action, nearly another half-hour elapsed before a sufficiently large number of searchers could be assembled.

"Well, of course, every able-bodied man in town is scouring the country-side right about now. Some womenfolk, too. The three of us were just on our way out to Doc Farragut's place," Barnum said in concluding his story.

"You will find it to be a scene of the most dreadful carnage," I grimly replied.

"What's that you say?" exclaimed Sheriff Driscoll. "Carnage?"

While the three men listened raptly—uttering occasional ejaculations of shock and amazement—I proceeded to recount what had happened to Louy and myself. I revealed the appalling truth about Dr. Farragut—explained his insane medical beliefs—summarized his long, criminal asso-ciation with the death-besotted madman Herbert Ballinger—and described the ghastly fates that had been planned for Louy and myself. I then re-lated the unexpected arrival of Peter Vatty and the violent acts he had com-mitted in his vengeful rage against the daguerreotypist, who—I said—had deceived him in an unforgivable manner. I said nothing, of course, about the disinterred corpse with which Vatty continued to share his nuptial bed—an omission designed to spare the sensibilities, not only of Louy Alcott, but also of Henry Thoreau, who—as the reader knows—had been hopelessly in love with Priscilla Robinson.

It was Thoreau who broke the stunned, protracted silence that followed my recitation. "The wisdom of the great poets is unceasingly true and all-illuminating, like the daily dawning of the sun," he observed. "I've never known a more affable soul than Erasmus Farragut. But as Shakespeare says: A man may smile and smile and still be a villain."

"Yes," said Louy, "smile and tell silly jokes, too."

"So *that's* what happened to the Bickford girl's missing skin and organs," said Barnum, in a peculiarly speculative tone, as if musing aloud to himself.

"And you say that Peter Vatty has killed both of them?" interposed Sheriff Driscoll.

"Dr. Farragut was shot in the chest," I confirmed. "We saw his lifeless body as we fled the house. As for Ballinger, we did not stay to witness his execution. Still, there can be little doubt that he, too, has been violently dispatched, however circumstantial the evidence upon which this conclusion is based."

"Some circumstantial evidence is very strong, as when you find a trout in the milk," said Thoreau.

"Never figured Peter Vatty for a killer, crazy as he is," said Sheriff Driscoll, puffing out his cheeks, then deflating them with a protracted exhalation through his tightly puckered lips. "Well, I'd best go see if he's still holed up at Doc Farragut's place. Perhaps you gentlemen ought to head back home with the girl. There's likely to be some trouble, and I don't want anyone else getting hurt."

"Nonsense, my good man," said Barnum. "Wouldn't think of abandoning you—wouldn't consider it for an instant! Lord bless me, do you imagine that P. T. Barnum would turn tail and run at the first whiff of danger? Why, I've faced down whole mobs of cutthroats in my day without so much as blinking an eye!"

"I, too, shall accompany you back to Dr. Farragut's residence," I said. "My familiarity with the motives behind Mr. Vatty's murderous rampage may prove useful to you in your attempts to apprehend him."

"Come, Louisa," said Thoreau, "I will take you home." Then, turning to me, he added: "You can use my horse, Poe. We'll go afoot. It's a short walk from here to Hillside, if you know your way through the woods."

"Mr. Thoreau can see in the dark like an owl," said Louisa.

Bidding us good-bye, the little girl turned and ran to catch up with Thoreau, who was already striding toward the trees. In another moment, the two of them had vanished.

Driscoll, Barnum, and I quickly mounted our steeds and set off at a canter toward Dr. Farragut's residence, arriving there less than ten minutes later. Securing the reins of our horses to the hitching post, we then mounted the porch steps and paused by the open front door.

"You two wait here," said Sheriff Driscoll. Then, drawing his pistol from his belt, he slipped inside the house.

Hardly daring to breathe, Barnum and I stood with ears cocked toward the doorway, listening intently. We could hear the lawman cautiously make his way through the interior. Very suddenly, he halted, as though he had come upon something and paused to examine it.

"He has found Dr. Farragut's body," I whispered to the showman.

Presently, Driscoll's footsteps started up again. A moment later, he reached the head of the staircase leading down to the basement, for we could hear him call: "Peter Vatty? You down there? It's Sheriff Driscoll."

These words were followed by absolute silence.

"If you're down there, Peter, you'd best come on up!" called the sheriff. Again—silence.

"All right—then I'm coming down!" shouted Driscoll.

By straining my auditory faculties to the utmost, I could just manage to discern the faint sound of his descent. Several inordinately tense moments ensued, during which I could feel my heart hammering against my breastbone.

My anxiety had reached a nearly unendurable pitch when the thump of rapid footsteps reached my ears. In another instant, Driscoll emerged from the house.

"He's not there," he said, thrusting his firearm back into his belt.

"That is not entirely surprising," I remarked, "for—having fulfilled his bloody mission by slaying Herbert Ballinger—there would have been no reason for him to remain on the premises."

"Ballinger's not there, either," said Driscoll.

"What!" I exclaimed.

"I saw Doc Farragut," said the sheriff. "He's dead, all right, just like you said. But there's no sign of this Ballinger fellow."

"But that is impossible," I said. "When Louy and I left the cellar, he was lying unconscious with his hands tightly bound behind him. Moments later, we heard the discharge of a rifle—audible proof that Vatty had accomplished his murderous design."

"Oh, I've no doubt that Vatty shot the man," said Driscoll. "I could see where he was lying on the dirt floor, and there's a pool of blood right there. But there's no body."

"Well, that's odd," said Barnum. "That's mighty peculiar. Dead bodies don't just get up and go walking around. Not as a general rule, anyway. Of course, it happens from time to time in *your* stories, Poe m'boy, but— Great Scot! Look there!"

Raising a hand, the showman pointed to a spot behind me. Turning, I saw, in the distance, a bright orange glow above the treetops.

"A fire!" I cried. "Where—?"

"Peter Vatty's place!" exclaimed Driscoll.

In another instant, the three of us were back on our horses. We rode at a rapid clip for nearly a mile before turning onto the weed-choked bypath leading to Vatty's property.

As we came in sight of the farmstead, we saw that both the main house and the little workshed were ablaze. A crowd of people had already gathered. Several of the men held wooden buckets, having apparently attempted to fight the fire with water drawn from Vatty's well. But their efforts were in vain. By the time we arrived, there was nothing to do but watch the two structures burn.

The little shed was entirely consumed within an hour. A short time later, the blazing roof of the farmhouse fell inward with a roar. The walls collapsed soon afterward. When the first faint rays of sunrise began to lighten the skies, only the massive stone chimney remained standing amidst the smouldering ruins.

It was Sheriff Driscoll, exploring the wreckage, who discovered the grisly remains: a pair of corpses—so hideously charred as to scarcely retain any semblance of humanity—lying side by side in the ashes of what had evidently been Peter Vatty's bedroom.

The natural assumption—shared by everyone present (except myself)— was that the second body was that of Herbert Ballinger. Only I knew the ghastly truth: that Vatty had chosen to immolate himself beside the corpse of his beloved.

But what, then, had befallen the vanished daguerreotypist?

CHAPTER THIRTY-TWO

~

"THERE'S SOMETHING I don't understand, Poe m'boy. How did you know that Louy had been snatched by Herbert Ballinger?"

This query came from P. T. Barnum, who was seated to my right at the Alcotts' dining room table. It was early Monday evening, slightly more than twelve hours after the events recounted at the conclusion of the previous chapter.

I had spent much of the intervening time in a profound and unbroken slumber. After the discovery of the two incinerated skeletons in the ashes of Vatty's farmhouse, Barnum and I had returned directly to Hillside, where I had received a joyful greeting from Sissy. I had also been given an exceedingly warm welcome by Mrs. Alcott, who—in a voice laden with emotion—thanked me profusely for having rescued her daughter from the clutches of the two madmen. Strict honesty compelled me to point out that, in actuality, it was Louy who had freed *me* from my bonds. But this protestation was taken as a sign of my exceptional modesty and only added to the lustre of my presumed heroism.

By then, I had reached a point of such exhaustion that I was barely able to form a coherent sentence. Dragging myself upstairs, I collapsed into bed and slept uninterruptedly throughout the remainder of the day. When I awoke, evening had already fallen. Upon descending, I found the other members of the household seated at the table, which was absolutely laden with delicacies. Some of these, I learned, had been purchased by Barnum, who had made a special trip into town for that purpose. Others had been supplied by various neighbors, who had been coming by the house all day to express their pleasure at the happy resolution of the affair.

Feeling perfectly famished, I had immediately tucked into the food. In between bites, I had answered questions about the previous night's adventure, omitting only those facets of the case unsuitable for my female auditors. Louy also contributed to the narrative, though she, too, was careful to avoid any details that might prove distressing to her siblings, especially the inordinately sensitive Lizzie.

Now, before responding to Barnum's query, I looked across the table at Louy, who had just inserted a large spoonful of blancmange into her mouth. "Would you care to explain, Louy?" I asked.

"It was a rebus," she mumbled through her food, drawing a somewhat disapproving look from her older sister, Anna, who seemed about to chide the younger girl for talking with her mouth full, before thinking better of it.

"A rebus?" said Barnum. "Bless me, what's that? Sounds like one of the rare, exotic creatures in my world-famous menagerie!"

"It is a species of pictorial riddle," I answered, then provided a succinct definition of the term.

"Your own name might be made by adding the letters 'um' to a picture of a barn," interposed Louy, who had swallowed the last of her pudding.

"Ha—ingenious, very ingenious indeed," said Barnum. "But surely, Louy, you don't mean to say that you left an elaborate picture-puzzle for Poe!"

"Mercy, no," said the little girl, "though as my idea *was* rather clever, I'll tell you all about it. I came to the house to fetch my wooden sword and I was just on the point of returning to the barn when the front door burst open and there stood Mr. Ballinger with the strangest look in his eyes. Heavens, what a fright he gave me! Before I could so much as let out a scream, he came rushing toward me with his hands outstretched, looking for all the world like the Big Bad Wolf in the story of Little Red Cap. So I struck out at him with the sword and hit him so hard that the blade snapped and cut his hand. He let out a yelp and I dropped the sword and went tearing upstairs, meaning to shut myself in the bedroom. I had just turned the lock when he began to pound on the door like a maddened bull. I saw that he would batter it down in no time. I was frantic to leave a message telling what happened, but there was nothing to write with. And then my eyes fell on Barnaby's cat toy, which, for some odd reason, was resting on the bureau. So I put it together with one of Lizzie's injured dolls and set them in a place where I knew Mr. Poe would see them."

"Upon perceiving these items," I said, "I immediately deduced—from both their peculiar arrangement and conspicuous location—that Louy had deliberately left them as a clue. It took but a moment for me to realize that the combination of the words 'ball' and 'injure' formed the name 'Ballinger.' "

"Astounding—perfectly astounding!" cried Barnum. "Why, you're a natural-born wonder, Louy! I've never heard of such quick thinking! Oh, I foresee a grand future for you, my child! Who knows—perhaps one day you'll be a featured attraction at P. T. Barnum's museum! Louy Alcott—The Girl with the Lightning Brain!"

"Oh, I shall get famous before I die, see if I don't," said Louy, "though I mean to do it by writing splendid books that will earn heaps of money and astonish everyone."

"I haven't the least doubt that you'll do it, Louy," said Lizzie, gazing at her elder sister with a worshipful expression.

"You can write a book about us!" exclaimed little May. "I'm sure people would love to read all about our family, and the capital times we have, and how clever and talented we all are, especially me! Why, it's bound to be a smacking success!"

"I think you mean 'smashing,' dear," said Mrs. Alcott with an indulgent smile.

"Oh, no," cried Louy, "I don't intend to write sentimental stuff about young women going to parties and falling in love and other such rubbish. I'm going to write the kind of books I like best—all about murderers and cannibals and corpses that come back from the dead. Just like Mr. Poe's stories!"

"Well, Eddie," said Sissy in a somewhat sardonic tone of voice, "I see you've had a wonderful influence on the child."

Turning to my left, I gazed at my darling wife, who was regarding me with a look of fond amusement. As I studied her surpassingly beautiful—if markedly drawn and pallid—visage, my heart was so sorely charged with both love and sorrow that it felt ready to burst.

Her first emotions, upon seeing me that morning, had been a mixture of the greatest happiness and relief. When I subsequently revealed to her the truth about Dr. Farragut's monstrously charlatanical practices, she had expressed, along with the inevitable shock, a grateful sense of having been saved from the horror of ingesting his cannibalistic concoction.

Nevertheless, she could hardly fail to be depressed at the outcome of our quest. The hope which had brought us to Concord had turned out to be yet another will-o'-the-wisp. Though she struggled bravely to conceal her disappointment, I could see in her eyes that she had resigned herself to the inevitable. The awareness that there was nothing more to be done to stave off her approaching dissolution was almost more than I could bear.

"By the bye, dearies," said Mrs. Alcott, addressing her four daughters, "I've got a treat for you after we have finished supper."

"Is it a letter from Father?" exclaimed May.

"As a matter of fact, it is," said Mrs. Alcott to the joyous whoops of her brood. "A nice long letter. He is well and thinks he shall be home by the day after tomorrow."

"Three cheers for Father!" cried Louy, tossing her napkin up in the air.

"Are you sure you and Virginia can't stay with us a few days longer, Mr. Poe?" asked Mrs. Alcott, turning her gentle gaze upon me. "I'm sure that Mr. Alcott would be very happy to meet you."

"Thank you for your offer, Mrs. Alcott, but we have already imposed upon your hospitality far longer than we intended," I graciously replied. "Moreover—though we could not have asked for more loving, maternal attention than that which you have lavished upon us—we are exceedingly eager to be reunited with our own dearest Muddy, from whom we have rarely endured such a prolonged separation. I regret that we must depart prior to your husband's arrival, for I would have greatly enjoyed meeting him." This last statement was, of course, mere courtesy. In truth, I could think of nothing more dreary than the prospect of spending time in the company of so insufferably pompous a personage as Bronson Alcott.

"Bless my soul," said Barnum, leaning back in his chair and patting his ample belly with both hands, "but that was a remarkable feast, perfectly remarkable. Can't recall when I've enjoyed a better meal. Why, it beats the one I had at Buckingham Palace, beats it all hollow! Prince Albert fancies himself a gourmet, but the fellow knows as little about fine eating as I do about running the British Empire! 'You must try the soused tripe, Phineas,' he kept saying. Well, I couldn't very well refuse him. Lord, I could barely get it down my gullet! Excellent brandy and cigars, though, I'll say that for him. Speaking of which—I believe I'll step outside for a moment and have a smoke. Care to join me, Poe?"

My finely wrought constitution being unusually susceptible to the intoxicating effects of tobacco, I rarely indulged in cigars. I could see by Barnum's expression, however, that he wished to speak to me in private. I therefore excused myself from the table and followed him outside.

The evening was unseasonably warm and, like the previous night, brightly illuminated by the moon. Seating myself on one of the old slat-back chairs arranged on the porch, I watched as the showman removed an enormous Havana from the inner pocket of his frock coat—bit off one end—lit the other with a phosphorous match—then lowered himself into the chair beside mine.

"Well, m'boy," he said with a sigh, "things haven't turned out quite the way we hoped. Thank heavens we discovered the truth about Farragut before I started peddling his poison at my museum. You know, I always *sensed* there was something wrong with that man—felt it the moment I first laid eyes on him! Ah well, what's done is done. No sense dwelling on the past. Tomorrow's another day. You mustn't despair about Virginia. We'll find the right doctor for her yet. 'Where there's life, there's hope'—that's P. T. Barnum's motto. Why, just look at me! Do you think I'm about to sink into the Slough of Despond just because I've suffered such a bitter disappointment? Ha!"

"Disappointment?" I said. "What precisely do you mean?"

"Why, those pieces of the Bickford girl—her heart and skin and so on," said Barnum. "Thought they'd disappeared forever—then they turn up in Farragut's cellar! Well, you know how eager I've been to get my hands on 'em. Driscoll turned me down flat, though."

"Do you mean to say," I asked in amazement, "that you offered to acquire them from Sheriff Driscoll?"

"Why, yes, of course. Why not? Terrible thing to let such treasures go to waste—breaks my own heart just thinking about it! Offered him—well, you wouldn't believe the price I was willing to pay. Wouldn't hear of it, though. Had some high-minded notion about shipping the pieces back to Boston to be buried with the rest of the girl's body. Got all huffy about it. Acted the same way when I proposed buying Ballinger's skeleton—or what was left of it after the fire."

For a moment, I merely stared at the showman, whose sheer—whose *shameless*—audacity never ceased to astonish me. "If it will make you feel less aggrieved," I said at length, "the skeleton found alongside Peter Vatty's was not, as widely presumed, that of Herbert Ballinger."

This remark so startled Barnum—who had just taken a long draw on his cigar—that his mouth fell open, releasing a large puff of smoke into the night air.

"What!" he exclaimed. "Then whose *was* it?"

Leaning closer to his chair and lowering my voice (for—though Sissy and the Alcott females were well out of earshot—I did not wish to take even the smallest risk of being overheard), I proceeded to describe the appalling truth about Peter Vatty and his unspeakable connubial practices. Naturally, this revelation came as an utter shock to the showman, who—like everyone else present at the conflagration—had assumed that the second set of bones found in Vatty's incinerated farmhouse had been that of the daguerreo-typist.

"Extraordinary—perfectly extraordinary!" Barnum exclaimed. "Just think of it—sharing your bed with a corpse! Why, it's the most horrid thing I've ever heard—worse than anything in your own stories, m'boy, and that's saying a good deal! Still, it clears up one mystery, at least. I couldn't under-stand why Vatty would drag Ballinger's carcass all the way back home and lie down next to it before taking his own life."

"Yes," I said, "though, at the same time, it only gives rise to another, equally mystifying question—i.e., the actual whereabouts of Ballinger's re-mains."

"But why didn't you tell Driscoll about all this?" asked Barnum.

"I knew that if I shared the information with Sheriff Driscoll, it would, in the way of such things, soon become general knowledge," I replied. "There is one man in particular who, I feared, would be utterly devastated by the truth. I refer to Henry Thoreau. Years ago, Mr. Thoreau was an im-passioned suitor of Vatty's bride, Priscilla Robinson. He has apparently con-tinued to harbor the strongest feelings for her. Indeed, his lingering grief over her death was almost certainly a factor in his decision to abandon so-ciety and retreat to his hermitage on the shores of Walden P—"

I did not complete my statement, for at that instant, a realization struck me with such palpable force that I was propelled from my chair and onto my feet.

"Great Scot, Poe!" cried Barnum. "What on earth's the matter?"

"I must borrow your horse," I exclaimed, descending the porch and hur-rying toward the hitching post.

"My horse?" echoed Barnum, who had sprung to his feet and come bustling after me. "But why? Where the deuce are you going at this time of night?"

"I will explain everything to you upon my return," I said, mounting the steed. "In the meantime, please inform Sissy and the others that I have been called away on a matter of extreme urgency. I will be back shortly." And so saying, I pulled at the reins and rode away.

———

A quarter-hour later, I arrived at Dr. Farragut's residence. The house was entirely shrouded in darkness. Tying up the horse, I mounted the porch—pushed open the unlatched front door—and stepped inside.

Though every light had long been extinguished, I had been inside the house often enough to find my way in the gloom. Bending my steps toward the parlor, I found and lit an oil lamp. In its dull glow, I saw that nothing had changed since my previous visit. Lying open on the cushion of the easy-chair was Palmer's *Medical Delusions of Olden Times*—the book that had inspired the crazed physician to undertake his ghastly experiments with medications compounded of herbal ingredients and human remains.

With lamp in hand, I proceeded down the central hallway. As I passed the examination room, I glanced inside. Farragut's body had, of course, been removed, though I could discern, even in the shadows, the dark discoloration on the floorboards where his bleeding corpse had lain.

In another moment, I reached the stairway leading down to the cellar.

Cautiously I made my way down the rickety steps. At the foot of the descent, I stood for a moment and gazed about me. Little had changed since Louy and I had been held captive in that dismal place. In the dim light of the oil lamp, I saw the chairs to which we had been bound—the boxlike daguerreotype camera lying on the floor—the rough wooden table with its amber bottles and butcher's cleaver. Ballinger's body was, of course, gone—as I knew it would be. I now believed, however, that I could locate its whereabouts.

I raised my lamp and peered across the cellar. The rays, however, were not sufficiently strong to illuminate the remoter corners. With racing heart, I made my way across the floor.

All at once, I came to a halt and let out a little cry. As the reader will recall, I had earlier noticed a projection in the wall from which several rows of bricks had been removed. Now I saw that the hole thus created had been re-sealed!

I was right! I had solved Dr. Farragut's final conundrum.

When I had warned Farragut that he would fall under immediate suspicion when my corpse was discovered, he had responded with a riddle: "What is Henry Thoreau's favorite watering hole?" At the time, the answer struck me as absurdly simple. He intended, so I assumed, to weigh down my body with rocks and sink it in the depths of Walden Pond.

It was only while sitting on the porch with Barnum that the truth came to me. Once again, the incorrigible physician had been indulging his penchant for labored wordplay. The real answer, I had suddenly realized, was a pun: not "Walden," but "*walled-in!*" The recess in the false chimney had been prepared as a sepulchre for my remains. That explained the mound of bricks, sand, mortar, and trowel I had noticed at the foot of the projection.

In figuring out Farragut's puzzle, I had also solved the mystery of Ballinger's missing corpse. There could be only one explanation for the sealing-up of the recess in the wall. After shooting the daguerreotypist, Peter Vatty had carried the corpse across the cellar, stuffed it into the hole, then hurriedly replaced the bricks. The fate that Farragut had planned for me had been visited upon his loathsome accomplice!

Why Vatty had gone to such trouble was, of course, a great puzzle. Since he obviously intended to return home and end his own life, it could not possibly have mattered to him whether his victims' bodies were discovered or not. Certainly, he had not bothered to conceal Farragut's corpse.

Truly, I thought, *there is no way to fathom the motives of a madman. In view of the virulent hatred he bore for Ballinger, perhaps Vatty felt that he could inflict one final injury upon the daguerreotypist by disposing of his corpse in this ignominious manner.*

Even as these thoughts crossed my mind, I was hit by an idea so horrible that it caused every separate hair on the nape of my neck to stand erect.

Seized with an irrepressible trembling, I stepped closer to the wall—drew back one foot—and delivered a sharp kick with the toe of my boot to the bricked-up area.

Almost at once, there came an answering sound from behind the wall—a low, tremulous, agonized groan.

My breast heaved—my knees tottered—my whole spirit became possessed by an abjectless yet intolerable horror. Evidently the gunshot that Louy and I had heard while fleeing the house had not proved fatal. Either deliberately or inadvertently, Vatty had merely wounded his enemy before interring him within the wall.

Herbert Ballinger had been entombed while still alive!

My instinctive reaction was to look for an implement with which to free him: a pick, an axe, or a hammer—anything with which I could break down the wall. Even as I cast my gaze about the cellar, however, another, very different feeling began to steal over me.

The impulse to rescue the daguerreotypist from his anguish was born from a sense of our common humanity. But did a creature like Herbert Ballinger—whose enormities surpassed those even of an Elah-Gabalus—

truly deserve the designation of *human being*? The mere enumeration of his victims—Lydia Bickford and Elsie Bolton, Mrs. Randall and Sally, Ludlow Marston and Horace Rice (whose death he had so diabolically orchestrated), and heaven knew how many others—suggested that he was more demon than man.

His atrocities, moreover, were not limited to murder. He had horribly and repeatedly violated the dead. He had tried to strangle me, after which he evidently intended to perform his unspeakable perversions upon little Louy Alcott. Perhaps most unforgivably, he had conspired with Dr. Farragut to produce a ghastly medication that—had their hideous plan succeeded—would have turned my angelic wife into a cannibal!

As I revolved these thoughts in my mind, a cruel—an *implacable*—sentiment took hold of me. All trace of sympathy for the daguerreotypist vanished. In its place there was only a savage desire to see him suffer the torments of the damned. Though such vengeful urges are shameful to confess, they exist, to a greater or lesser degree, within every human breast. To pretend otherwise is mere hypocrisy.

At that moment, a faint, muted sound issued from within the wall. Stooping, I placed an ear to the bricks.

"For the love of God!" came the tremulous voice.

"Yes," I answered, "for the love of God."

Standing erect, I strode from the cellar and returned to the Alcott abode. At no point, then or in the future, did I breathe a word of my discovery to a living soul. Even now, as I pen these words, the monster's bones remain undisturbed in their ghastly crypt.

In pace requiescat!

AUTHOR'S NOTE

⌒

THIS IS A work of imaginative fiction in which—following the lead of my protagonist—I have permitted my fantasies to run free, if not rampant. The following, however, are historical facts:

During the early decades of the nineteenth century, New England was swept up in a wave of enthusiasm for the "botanic" cures of Dr. Samuel Thomson, who preached that all diseases were caused by cold and could therefore be treated with heat-generating herbs, such as red pepper.

Moses Kimball, proprietor of the Boston Museum, was P. T. Barnum's close friend and confidant. For years, the two men corresponded regularly, sharing both personal and professional secrets and trading performers and attractions. (It was through Kimball that Barnum acquired the first of his legendary "humbugs," the infamous "Feejee Mermaid.") Another of Barnum's most trusted associates was his lifelong friend "Parson" Fordyce Hitchcock, who—before entering into the showman's employ—had been a Universalist minister.

Nitrous oxide demonstrations were a popular form of stage entertainment in the 1830s and '40s. (Among those who made their living as an itinerant laughing-gas showman was Samuel Colt, future inventor of the famous six-shooter.)

The Dentologia: A Poem on the Diseases of the Teeth is an actual work of literature.

By 1845, photographers were already in the business of creating postmortem daguerreotypes, advertising their availability to take "likenesses of deceased persons."

In the United States, the modern method of "arterial embalming"—in which a liquid preservative is injected through the veins—didn't come into widespread use until the Civil War. Before that time, undertakers relied on various devices to slow decomposition. Among the most popular were patented coffins with built-in ice chambers. These refrigerator caskets were commonly known as "corpse-coolers."

Henry David Thoreau really did suffer from narcolepsy.

Louisa May Alcott, nineteenth-century America's most beloved creator of children's literature, began her career as the author of popular "sensation" stories—lurid tales of murder and mystery, violence and revenge. One of these early potboilers—a story called "V. V.; or Plots and Counterplots"—was an homage to the detective fiction of Edgar Allan Poe.

ABOUT THE AUTHOR

HAROLD SCHECHTER is a professor of American literature and culture at Queens College, the City University of New York. Renowned for his true-crime writing, he is the author of the nonfiction books *Fatal, Fiend, Bestial, Deviant, Deranged, Depraved,* and *The Serial Killer Files.* He previously featured Edgar Allan Poe in his acclaimed novels *Nevermore, The Hum Bug,* and *The Mask of Red Death.* He lives in New York State.

ABOUT THE TYPE

This book was set in Minion, a 1990 Adobe Originals typeface by Robert Slimbach. Minion is inspired by classical, old style typefaces of the late Renaissance, a period of elegant, beautiful, and highly readable type designs. Created primarily for text setting, Minion combines the aesthetic and functional qualities that make text type highly readable with the versatility of digital technology.